FOR WHAT
ABOUT T

For What You Are About to Receive

MICHAEL ANTHONY

Africa House Publishing Ltd
The Lower Tithe Barn
Church Square
Melbourne
Derbyshire DE73 8JH
Email: Africahouse@btinternet.com
Web: www.africahousepublishing.com

ISBN 9780995549104

British Library Cataloguing in Publication Data.
A catalogue record for this book is available from the British Library.

Cover design: MECOB

Cover artwork: Jane Leedham

Typeset by Born Group

Printed and bound in the UK by Clays Ltd, St Ives plc

For Matthew and James
And their wives, Laura and Efe

'If you want to go fast, go alone
If you want to go far, go together.'

From an old African proverb

Chapter One

The girl staggered out of the Green Door nightclub. A street lamp illuminated her gaunt face. She hesitated, trying to steady herself against the wall. The cold air touched her thin cotton dress and she pulled the raincoat tight around her body.

'I'm sorry, Mr Rudinsky,' she cried, looking pleadingly at her client, 'Not tonight.'

'*Seru vy kurva*,' Rudinsky shouted, reaching out for the girl in a drunken stupor. 'You take my money!'

She managed to fend off his rough hands but slipped on the wet pavement, and collapsed into the gutter.

'Get up, bitch!' he shouted, gripping her arm.

'Stop, you're hurting me!'

'You like play games, hey?' Rudinsky dragged the girl to her feet. 'I show you,' he said, striking her across the face.

The light drizzle on the deserted side street had turned to a steady rain. For two hours Mallory had been sitting alone in a quiet corner of a Spitalfields pub, staring at a glass of Scotch whisky. Now he was weary and on his way home.

The girl's panic-stricken cry caught his attention. She was silhouetted in the tunnel of light cast by the street lamps. Before the assailant was aware of his presence, Mallory was beside him. He gripped the

1

man's shoulder, swung him round and raked the palm of his hand across his face. The force of the blow sent the man sprawling to the ground. He instinctively raised his hands to protect himself.

'No more, no more!' he cried, breathing hard.

Mallory stepped back from his victim, and saw that blood was dripping from his broken nose. Satisfied the man was no longer a threat, he turned his attention to the girl.

'You all right?'

The girl had managed to stagger away and was clinging to a lamp post. Her eyes darted around in search of Rudinsky but he had already disappeared.

Mallory repeated the question but still the girl said nothing. God, this was all he needed – a hooker in deep shit with her client. Was the price not right? Unlikely; the girls weren't known to be selective in this part of town. He removed a packet of Camel from his jacket and offered her one. In the sliver of light from the match he noticed her bright red lipstick, smeared down one side of her pale face. The heavily made-up eyes were blank. It was as though she did not even see him. She leaned against the wall and drew deeply on the strong tobacco. Her matted, shoulder-length hair hanging beneath the iconic French beret smelled of cheap booze and cigarettes. Long legs, barely covered by her skirt, were accentuated by stiletto heels, the tools of her trade.

'You look like you could use a drink,' he said, gesturing towards the nightclub. He handed her a handkerchief to wipe her face and gently took her arm. Her body was rigid with fear.

'No! *No*!' she screamed.

'I'll come with you.'

'You don't understand!'

'I'm trying to help.'

'It's not you,' her shoulders slumped, 'my client.'

Suddenly he realised the implications of what he had done. 'Look, you can't just stay here, standing in the rain.' His eyes narrowed. 'Let me call you a cab; I won't be–'

'I cannot go home!' She shivered and wrapped her arms around her frail body.

The desperation in her voice stopped Mallory in his tracks. He knew he should've ignored the cry for help. But for some unknown reason he felt an urge to protect the girl.

'Look, I know of a little bar that stays open late.'

The girl stood rigid on the spot, hands clenched firmly in her raincoat pocket.

'Are you coming or not? You'll be safer away from here.'

The girl bit her lip and shifted uneasily.

Mallory had had enough of this nonsense. He turned to walk away. Before he had chance to think of what he would do next, the girl stepped off the pavement and obligingly followed.

They crossed the main road and entered a narrow alley. Halfway down the cobblestone street a sign above a bar flashed OPEN TILL LATE. Six scrubbed-pine tables were squeezed into the tiny room. The bar stretched along one wall, a long row of optics and a tarnished mirror behind it. Two men were sitting at the counter drinking shorts. Mallory guided the girl to a corner table.

'What can I get you?'

Her eyes were fixed on the late-night drinkers. It was as if she hadn't even heard his question.

'Whisky…?'

She shrugged.

'Whisky it is then,' he said, striding across the terracotta-tiled floor.

The barman was wiping down the wooden counter and clearing away the slop trays beneath the beer pumps. 'Last orders,' he announced, somewhat impatiently, rubbing his podgy hands down his beer-stained apron.

'Two single malts, water and ice. Make them doubles, please.'

'This ain't the West End, mate; we don't have any of your fancy whiskies here.' He stroked the few grey hairs he had left on his bald head. Then he scratched his bottom.

3

'Fine, whatever you've got.'

The barman reached for a bottle of Bell's and poured a double shot over the ice into each glass. He slid the tumblers across the counter with a jug of water and held out his hand.

'Two pound fifty.'

It appeared that neither single malt or civility were on offer at this establishment. Mallory paid the bill and carried the drinks back to the table. The girl was staring into space. The dull light cast shadows across her wide, slanted eyes and high cheekbones. She'd removed her raincoat and hung it over the back of her chair, and he saw how painfully thin she was.

'*Santé*,' he whispered, raising his glass in a feeble attempt to lighten the mood.

She looked him full in the face. Then, unable to hold his gaze any longer, she picked up the glass and sipped the whisky. She shuddered at the taste but still she said nothing.

Mallory glanced around the shabby room. It had a reputation as a low-key local; a place for taxi drivers looking for a late-night drink away from the rowdier clubs and bars further up the road. The mournful music had been switched off and now all that could be heard were the men's drunken voices as they dissected the previous night's football match. He turned back to the girl. She was still in a world of her own.

The barman finally brought the situation to a head. 'Drink up! We close in five,' he shouted, setting about sweeping the floor.

The men at the bar nodded to him. 'Night, Pete,' the elder of the two said, before staggering up the steps. 'Same time tomorrow.'

Mallory downed the last of his whisky. 'We should go.'

The girl said nothing, just looked at him with an expression akin to that of a dog waiting for its master's next command.

Out in the deserted alley it had started to drizzle again. The rain seemed to compound the girl's anxiety. Mallory recognised her fear. He knew all too well what it was like to be adrift in an alien country. After twenty years, little had changed.

The loneliness was still there, a companion that followed him everywhere.

He glanced at the girl. She cast a pathetic figure. What would she do? Where would she go? Her options were limited: it was either home to face a terrible beating, or wander the streets in the rain. She blinked her eyes to dispel the tears, a hopeless look of resignation on her face. And in that moment he knew that even the smallest spark of life must not be extinguished.

'Come, you can stay with me for the night,' he said, walking off down the street. The girl fell into step behind him. When he turned around to check on her, she gave him a barely perceptible nod. And he wondered for a moment just what the hell he was doing.

Chapter Two

A faded hardwood door led to the studio flat above the newsagents. Mallory heard the girl's steps behind him on the shabby staircase. He opened the door and switched on the overhead light. The naked sixty-watt lamp illuminated an austere room with a double bed, settee and an easy chair. A pine dining table and a couple of wooden chairs stood near the window. On the wall, someone had erected a simple laminate shelf, which housed an assortment of well-thumbed books, mainly novels. A cheap print of Modigliani's *Nude Sitting on a Divan* hung above the shelf. Next to this, and half hidden by an old wooden box, was a portrait of Jeanne Hebuterne, his mistress.

'I bought it to go with the nude,' Mallory said, noticing the girl's eyes on the Hebuterne portrait. He shifted uneasily and wondered why he felt the need to explain.

The girl slumped into the settee, clearly at her wits' end. 'I'm sorry to have been so much trouble,' she said, starting to cry.

This was not an emotion Mallory handled easily. 'Look, it's really no trouble at all,' he said, shuffling about in embarrassment. 'I'll make up the bed for you.'

'Please don't go to any trouble. If I can just sit here.'

'You'll get a better night's sleep on–'

'I don't think I could sleep – I'm past the point of tiredness.'

Mallory was too exhausted to argue. He removed a duvet, pillow and blanket from the laundry cupboard, and placed them beside the girl. 'Will you need anything else?'

She shook her head.

'Good, then let's get some sleep.' He glanced at his watch. 'I have a meeting in the morning.' Suddenly he realised he didn't even know the girl's name. 'I must apologise; I haven't introduced myself.' He held out his hand. 'Mallory.'

'I'm Madeleine.' She pronounced the name with a foreign accent. Her hand was soft and her long fingers free of jewellery. A broken nail scratched his palm. 'Thank you. For everything.'

Mallory smiled and felt his cheeks redden. 'Here, let me take your coat – it's soaked through. Do you need the bathroom?'

She shook her head and kicked off her heels.

'There's a blanket in the cupboard if you feel cold.'

'I'm fine. Please, don't worry about me.'

Mallory nodded and walked to the bathroom. Sallow eyes, set in a face framed with bedraggled hair, stared back at him from the mirror. He grabbed his toothbrush and smothered it in tooth-paste. When he was done removing the traces of another late-night boozing session, he rinsed out his mouth and rubbed his hand down the side of his chin. The two-day stubble could wait till the morning. Then he opened the door. The girl was sitting up on the settee and staring out of the window. 'Try and get some sleep,' he said, removing his shirt. 'You'll feel better in the morning.' He reached over to turn off the bedside lamp.

The girl's voice stopped him. 'Please, can you leave the light on?'

'Sorry, I didn't…' He pulled the blanket up to his chin and closed his eyes. Sometime later he thought he heard a toilet flushing, but he was too jaded to take much notice.

At the first sign of dawn Mallory was instantly awake. It was a habit formed many years before, during his days fighting in the Rhodesian Bush War. Then he remembered the girl. He lifted his head cautiously off the pillow. The early morning light was reaching out across the room and he could just make out her shape beneath the duvet cover. Suddenly a police siren shattered the silence, but the girl did not stir. Conscious of the time, he slipped out of bed and crept to the bathroom. Although Mallory was only in his mid-forties, the steel-blue eyes hinted at a life of hardship. Tight lips, devoid of laughter, did nothing to enhance the overall look of resignation to a life on the run. This bloody late-night drinking would have to stop or God knows where it would all end, he thought, splashing his face with cold water. But he knew it would never happen. The booze helped him to forget the atrocities.

He pushed his long brown hair off his forehead and thought again of the girl. He'd made it a rule never to bring anyone back to his flat and now, for the first time, he'd changed the game. Never mind, with any luck she would be gone before he returned from his meeting. What was her name … Marilyn? No, that wasn't it. Michelle? Marianne? He was sure it began with an M but for the life of him he couldn't remember. Moving quietly through the kitchenette, he half filled the kettle and flicked on the switch. His back was to the room, but intuition told him he was being watched. He turned round. The girl was sitting up, the duvet wrapped around her body, staring at him.

'Good morning,' he murmured softly. 'Sorry if I woke you.'

'I was already awake.'

'Can I get you anything? Tea? Coffee?'

'Please, just coffee – weak, with a little milk.'

He handed her the cup. 'Sugar?'

She shook her head.

'Look, there's no rush to go. Please, use the bed.'

The girl simply sipped at the coffee. Rest had at least removed some of the anxiety from her eyes. Finally she spoke.

'Where do you work?'

'I'm a lawyer. I have a meeting with my boss, over in Shoreditch.' He thought briefly of Andrei Vadislav. 'Friend' would be a more apt description for the charismatic barrister who had taken him under his wing almost twenty years ago. They'd met by chance in a dingy late-night haunt and Mallory had been intrigued by the Russian's story. His grandfather had been a supporter of Tsar Nicholas and the Romanovs. It had been 1917, the start of the Russian Revolution. The lives of the Vadislav family had been in danger so they fled their homeland for the safety of England. Theirs was a fortunate tale, of aristocrats rich enough in gold and jewels to begin a new life, away from the clutches of the Soviets. Andrei had been sent to Eton and then on to Oxford, where he'd studied law. After graduating to Chambers the world had been his oyster – ahead lay an illustrious career as a barrister in the City. But instead he had taken the path of the devil, representing some of the more dubious characters in the underbelly of the East End. Why he had opted for this less salubrious route, Mallory did not know. Nor did he care.

After a long drinking session, Mallory had revealed that he, too, was a lawyer. This was just the person the Russian was looking for and he immediately offered him a job. Lost in the East End of London, Mallory was now beyond the clutches of the Zimbabwean courts.

'A meeting?' The girl was hesitant.

He shrugged nonchalantly. 'I take notes for a barrister.'

'Is it necessary? I mean, it's just that,' anxiety clouded her face, 'I'm frightened … of being on my own.'

'Look, you're quite safe here.'

Madeleine's eyebrows furrowed and she bit her lip.

Mallory hesitated. Did he really want to get into this? But the sight of the girl, sitting there helpless and neglected, struck a chord on his conscience. 'Look, sit tight until I come back. Then we'll think of something.' He looked at his watch; he was already late and he'd had enough of this nonsense. He picked up a stack of papers from the pine table and placed them in an old leather briefcase.

'Please don't be long, *se il vous plait*.'

He hesitated for a moment longer than he'd intended. 'Where are you from?'

The girl's eyes rested on the floorboards. She appeared reluctant to talk. Eventually she looked up. 'Paris,' she said, 'we lived in Neuilly-sur-Seine. Near the university.'

Paris, Mallory repeated to himself. The City of Romance. It was somewhere he'd only read about. He glanced at the girl. 'Lock the door and get some sleep. I'll be back shortly after midday.' He was halfway down the stairs when the thought suddenly struck him: what if the girl was a thief? She'd only told him her first name and for all he knew that was false. Then he laughed. What was he so worried about? Apart from his beaten-up laptop and a half-written manuscript, there was really nothing of any value in the flat.

Outside on the street a newspaper boy yelled the headline: 'Left-wing students occupy the Sorbonne. Get the news – read all about it!' Mallory dug around his pocket for a few coins. He paused for a moment, skimming the headlines. The report on the front page highlighted clashes between police and students on the streets of the Latin Quarter after they had seized the university. It reminded him briefly of the French call girl, alone in his flat.

Chapter Three

Sunday morning and the streets of Shoreditch were deserted. Plastic pint cups, remnants of the previous night's drinking, lay discarded in the gutters like fallen leaves. The Blue Angel advertised happy hour from 7 to 9 p.m. and a late-night show with eight different girls. Pasted to the pavement billboard was a life-size poster of a young woman posing suggestively in her lingerie. In the cold light of day the club looked exactly what it was – a decadent den of inequity. Mallory knocked on the heavy wooden door. He had the feeling of being watched through the small spyglass before a heavy-set man opened the door. 'Yes?'

'Mallory. Mr Vadislav is expecting me.'

Satisfying himself that Mallory was not armed, the doorman indicated the corridor. 'You follow me, please.'

A flight of steps led down to a circular dance floor that dominated a darkened room. At its centre was an ubiquitous stainless steel pole, glinting in the blue neon light. Empty champagne bottles, unwashed glasses and ashtrays overflowing with cigarette butts were scattered across the surrounding tables. A stale smell lingered in the room. To one side of the seating area was a mirrored bar, with an impressive array of spirits. A girl's voice reached out from the PA system, singing a simple gypsy folk ballad that somehow seemed out of place in the squalid nightclub. Mallory followed the doorman past the bar. Through an open door he could hear conversation and immediately recognised the Russian's voice.

'Mr Mallory, sir.'

'Show him in, Antun.'

Mallory shuffled past the big man into the office. He acknowledged the barrister with a nod and a smile.

The thin, poker-faced Bulgarian rose to his feet and offered his hand. His head was no higher than Mallory's shoulders. 'Good to see you again, Mr Mallory – can we get you something to drink?' He raised his thin eyebrows. It was an affliction that accompanied his voice each time he spoke. The hand was cold and clammy, and Mallory held it only as long as it was polite to do so. He looked down at Andrei's cup.

'Black coffee, one sugar, thank you, Georgi.'

'Please – sit down,' Georgi said, indicating an empty chair.

'Do you have your notes from the last meeting?' Andrei asked.

Mallory opened his briefcase and withdrew a bundle of papers. After checking they were in the correct order, he handed them to the barrister.

No one spoke while Andrei read the summarisation. Then a loud knock broke the silence and Antun reappeared with the coffee. When the door had once again closed, Andrei looked up from the brief. 'Georgi, the prostitution charge against you appears to hang on a thread.' He rubbed the stubble on his chin and slowly nodded as he reread the paperwork. 'But I feel confident we can overturn the drugs charge.'

The Bulgarian ran his hand over his dark, neatly cut hair. It was plastered to his head with a thick gel and his deep tan was suggestive of sunnier climes. A gold medallion hung around his neck and there was a nervous twitch in his eyes. He waited patiently.

'The evidence is weak at best and the witness for the prosecution unreliable. However,' Andrei paused to allow the words the effect they deserved, 'the allegation that you are importing girls from Ukraine is far more serious.'

12

Georgi shifted in his chair. The nervous twitch in his eye had returned. 'Mr Andrei, always they make this nonsense for me. Why?'

Andrei glanced at the defendant over the top of his glasses. 'You have told me the girl,' he looked at his notes, 'Yana, no longer works for you. However, she claims you brought her to England from Ukraine as a striptease dancer – against her will, I should add. Then you forced her to work as a whore. Olek is willing to testify on the girl's behalf.'

'How they say this? Olek is pimp! Yana comes looking for work.'

Andrei knew the Bulgarian was lying. 'Then perhaps we should go with the lesser charge of prostitution and fight the abduction accusation on the basis that the girl is trying to blackmail you?'

'And if they say I guilty?'

'This would be your first conviction,' Andrei said, placing his glasses on the table and flexing his fingertips. 'You'll get a heavy fine and perhaps a suspended prison sentence.'

'I frightened for jail, Mr Andrei.'

The Russian glanced at his notes again. 'You say the girl in question now works for one of your competitors.' He looked up at Georgi. 'And is on the game?'

The Bulgarian nodded, his eyes on the cigar smouldering in a bronze ashtray. 'It's true, Mr Andrei.'

'If we can prove this, I believe we'll get an acquittal.' Andrei flexed his fingertips. 'We'll use the argument that she was taking liberties with clients as your reason for her dismissal.'

The worry on the Bulgarian's face disappeared for a moment. 'Is perfect!'

Mallory said nothing; he'd taken an instant dislike to the night-club owner at their previous meeting. He was a small-time racketeer and an out-and-out liar. But he couldn't let this cloud his judgement. He was here to take notes and, as such, he left the talking to the barrister.

Andrei placed the court papers on the table and opened his diary. 'We have three weeks until your first court hearing. I suggest

13

we meet here again in ten days' time to go through the tribunal procedure.' He glanced across at his assistant. 'Okay with you, Mallory?'

Mallory nodded and made a note on his pad.

'Good. Then let's call it a day, Mr Borisov.' The Russian stood up, collected his papers and shook hands with his defendant.

'I thank you,' Georgi said, ringing a bell below his desk. 'I see you in ten days.'

Back on the street, Mallory breathed deeply. Although the air reeked of diesel fumes from an old lorry labouring along the cobblestones, it was preferable to the oppressive stench of the nightclub.

Andrei noticed and laughed. Then his eyes switched to the traffic warden making her way towards his car. 'I'm going back to Soho; can I drop you off somewhere?'

'I'll walk. I could do with the exercise.' He reached into his pocket for the packet of Camel. 'Actually, before you go there's something I wanted to ask you. Have you got a minute?'

Andrei raised an eyebrow.

'I've got myself into a bit of a … situation.' Mallory paused, unsure of how to continue.

'Yes…?'

'She's a working girl.'

A half-smile crept across the barrister's lips.

'It's not what you're thinking!'

The Russian couldn't help but shake his head. 'Go on…'

'She was being knocked about. I came to her rescue.'

The traffic warden had reached Andrei's car and was looking at her watch. There were seven minutes still left on the meter. She waited, trying her best to appear nonchalant. The Bentley Continental was obviously too good an opportunity to miss.

'Look, I have a meeting this afternoon; can your problem wait until tomorrow? Say, nine o'clock … at the office?' He turned his attention to the warden. 'Oh, and bring your notes on the Blue

14

Angel. I have a suspicion that one of the prosecution witnesses has something to hide.'

'Thanks, Andrei.' One more day would hardly make a difference. With any luck, the girl would've made her peace with the club by then and there'd be no need for the appointment.

'Good! That's settled then. Now, I'd better disappear before I make that warden's day.'

Chapter Four

Mallory loved the walk through central London when the sun was out. Parts of Camden reminded him of Salisbury, in the days before it became Harare. Pigeons, as fat as spotted guinea fowl, flocked to the square off Brunswick Place, attracted by the children scattering bread. It was almost two in the afternoon and he was hungry. The little café advertising quiches with a complimentary glass of wine caught his attention. Then he thought again of the girl. Had she come to her senses and made a decision about her future? She did say Paris. It was a big city where one could easily lose oneself. Or maybe she still had family and friends elsewhere in France. Either way, it was too dangerous for her to remain in London.

In the distance, a busker's voice reached out to him. The young girl was standing alone on the pavement, strumming a Spanish guitar and singing a song he remembered from long ago. Her voice was soft and husky and the words captivated him.

Our steps rang tunes on cobblestone,
through the hollow night we walked alone.
Into a coloured room of fantasy,
far from all reality.

Oh God! How long had it been? Surely almost twenty years. Rhodesia.

With Anna.

And in that tiny room I found the truth,
the ecstasy of our youth.
Now the only belief I hold as true
is the way that I once knew you.

The only belief I hold as true! He knew what the words meant to him – it was how he'd once seen Anna. That part of his life was so deeply embedded in the past he sometimes wondered if it had ever really happened at all. Now this voice was taking him back there, to a pool fed by a small river outside Salisbury, a grassy bank, jacarandas touching the water.

Those endless days.

At the time, he'd thought they would never end. How gullible he'd been. Because when the war came, nothing was ever the same again. His job as a circuit lawyer often meant long months away from Salisbury and it had taken a toll on both their lives; there was barely a chance to think of Anna as he stood in one courtroom after another, fighting for the Africans' freedom. The court cases had consumed him. He likened them to how a surgeon must feel when he loses a patient in theatre, the only difference being that the guerrillas, or freedom fighters as they called themselves, died at the end of the rope rather than the scalpel. It was difficult now, to remember the names of the men he'd represented. Their faces continued to haunt him. When the death sentence was passed, he'd been unable to meet the eyes of the condemned men. The cries of the distraught families howling in the public galleries were his nightmares. And after everyone had left the courtroom and the madness had died down, he'd often sit on the hard wooden bench and relive the case in his mind. Where had it all gone wrong? He knew the answer, of course. The guerrillas

17

were dead before they ever faced a judge. They were black, so they would hang.

And in that tiny room he found the truth.

In the evenings he would drink himself into oblivion in the hope that it would help him forget what he had been a part of. But the torment stayed with him. Not so Anna. He had finally lost her when white racists had daubed his house with the words KAFFIR LOVER – GET OUT OF OUR COUNTRY.

The song came to an end. The young busker looked around at the small crowd, her slender hand resting lightly on the strings of her guitar.

Mallory's eyes were wet. He walked up to the musician and dropped a handful of coins into her battered guitar case. She smiled at him and mouthed her appreciation. Then he turned away, shaking his head to release the memories that had haunted him for so very long.

Chapter Five

After buying a French stick, ham and a slab of Brie at Paula's Patisserie, Mallory let himself into the building with his spare key. He was met by loud voices coming from the upstairs landing. The Spanish couple. They'd only recently moved in next-door, but already it was clear from the constant quarrelling that their relationship was on the rocks. He hoped they'd settle their differences. But he wasn't about to get involved – steer clear of trouble and remain inconspicuous. If only he'd thought of that the night before. Avoiding eye contact with the couple, he opened the door to his flat, envisaging an empty room, possibly left in disarray after the girl's departure.

The sight that greeted him could not have been more different. The bed had been made, the duvet folded on the settee and the dishes washed up. One of the old chipped tumblers, which should have been discarded years ago, stood on the dining table, only now it was filled with bright yellow daffodils. Their presence alone seemed to breathe new life into the previously dank space. His eyes continued to take in the room, noticing a change here and there … a book replaced on a shelf … a tea towel hung neatly on a rail … the kitchen worktop cleared of crockery and glasses.

The door to the bathroom was slightly ajar and he heard the toilet flush. Then the girl appeared, wearing his old grey sweater and little else. Having returned, from God knows where, she was unrecognisable from the pitiful creature he'd brought home.

'I borrowed this,' she whispered, pulling the hem of the jumper down. Her smile was hesitant. 'It's rather big, isn't it?'

Mallory was captivated by her presence. Suddenly he realised what a woeful spectacle he must look, standing with his mouth agape, holding a plastic shopping bag. He closed the door and stepped into the room. 'Big? God no! It fits you perfectly.' He smiled uneasily. 'But you didn't have to clean the flat, Madeleine.'

She moved across to the settee and sat down, putting her feet beneath her bottom. 'It was the least I could do after all your kindness,' she said. 'And you remembered my name!'

He struggled to contain a nervous laugh. If she could have read his mind she'd have known that her name was not amongst those he'd searched for the previous night. In fact, he'd no idea where it had just come from. Suddenly he was glad of the flash of inspiration. He looked down at the shopping bags he was holding. 'Have you eaten?' he asked, placing the bags on the kitchen worktop. 'It's just ham and Brie, and there's a bottle of Pouilly in the fridge.'

'It sounds wonderful,' she said, standing up. 'Please, let me prepare the food – you pour the wine and set the table.'

Mallory pulled the cork on the Pouilly. 'Did you manage to get some sleep after I left?'

'Not really – the traffic, the trains.'

'That's one of the problems with this flat,' he replied, sheepishly, 'but it's pretty well all I can afford at the moment.'

Madeleine put down the bread knife and turned to face him. 'If only you knew,' she said, 'being here is,' she paused to gather her thoughts, 'how do you say … like living again.'

'Well, you certainly seem to have made it that way – I don't think this room has ever seen a duster, never mind a vase of flowers! But then it has never seen a woman either.'

Madeleine smiled and turned back to the kitchen sink. 'I'm glad you like the daffodils. They're the cheapest of blooms yet they

–20–

bring such warmth into our lives, don't you agree? The stallholder convinced me that they were the right choice. He is such a nice man; it was lovely to talk to someone who does not see me as … well, you know what I mean.' She wiped her eyes.

Mallory ignored the nonchalant remark and half filled two large glasses with Pouilly. He handed one to the girl. 'To vineyards washed by sunshine! To you, Madeleine, back from despair.'

'Please don't say that. I mean the last sentence.' There was still the remnant of a tear on her cheek. 'Let's forget about yesterday. Here's to now,' she said, raising her glass.

'I'm sorry. Sometimes I can be–'

She sat down and put her finger to her lips. 'And no apologising.'

The rain had stopped and temporary market stalls had been set up along the pavement. A child was crying in the street. She had let go of her balloon, which floated up past the window. A butcher's voice bellowed out from the far end of the row of stalls: 'Chickens, two for the price of one – last chance today!' The hustle and bustle was a world away from the little room where they shared their simple lunch. Mallory thought of the folk singer and the words of the song: *'Our steps rang tunes on cobblestone – through the hollow night we walked alone'*. The nostalgic verse seemed to reflect the events of the previous night. It was all a part of yesterday, a part of a life that Madeleine wanted to forget. He touched her glass and looked into her eyes. They revealed little of the secrets of her past. It was some moments before she spoke again.

'When I was at the nightclub, I would dare to dream that something like this was possible. But as time went by it became just that; a dream.' She had moved her chair back from the table and crossed her legs, her bare foot almost touching his jeans. A lock of hair fell across her forehead as she leaned forward. 'Mallory? Is that your Christian name?'

He shook his head. 'My only name.'

'I have never known anyone with just one name.'

21

How much did he tell her? Although the wine drew words from forbidden places, almost as if one was opening a Pandora's box, he remained cautious. 'The name reminded my mother of the English mountaineer,' he replied, deciding to fabricate the truth.

The girl sat back in her chair. Her eyes were focused on the glass. The Sauvignon appeared pale in the artificial light. 'The *English* mountaineer, how strange!'

'Strange? Why?'

'Because you are not English, of course! That much even I can tell.'

Mallory studied the girl's face. It was innocent and as open as a book. He held up his hands in mock surrender. 'You got me!' He laughed. 'I'm from Zimbabwe.'

'Oh, how exotic!' There was excitement in her voice. 'Zimbabwe! I've always wanted to go to Africa.'

'Exotic!' He laughed. 'Perhaps at one time. Now it's pretty well gone to the dogs.'

'Is that why you are here, in London?'

He nodded.

'And you were also a lawyer in Zimbabwe?'

'It was known as Rhodesia back then.' He picked over his lunch, trying to think of a way to divert the conversation. But before he could do so, the girl was speaking again.

'It is an exciting life – being a lawyer?'

Mallory shook his head. 'No, not always. We represent some pretty despicable characters.'

'Like the scum at the Green Door?'

Mallory was suddenly cautious. 'I don't know the people you work for.'

'So why do you do it?'

'I'm sorry?'

'Represent the dregs of *société*?'

He threw up his arms in mock defence. 'It's a job.' He thought briefly of the Green Door. 'I guess it's not easy for either of us.'

22

'Your life is nothing like mine!' She slammed her glass on to the table. Her face was pale and her hands were clutched tightly together. And yet there was a melancholy beauty that he had seen briefly before, although he could not remember where. 'You could not even begin to understand.'

'Then why the Green Door?'

The question took her by surprise. 'I don't want to talk about it.' She was looking straight ahead now, almost as if she were alone.

'It's just that you don't look like a girl who works the night-clubs.'

It was some moments before Madeleine answered and she chose her words more carefully than he had done. 'What does "a girl who works the nightclubs" look like exactly? I know of women who are housewives during the day and whores at night. *And* they enjoy it.'

'Do you?' Mallory was again unsure of his words.

'What do you think?' She laughed cynically and rubbed her thigh. 'That I enjoy entertaining men? You must be crazy!'

'Then why–'

She flared up again. 'What business is it of yours?'

Mallory was taken aback by the harsh response. 'I would like to help you.'

Madeleine's eyes were downcast, almost as if she was busy studying the knots on the wooden floorboards. Her face gave very little away when she finally looked up. '*Help me*. I wish you could. I wish anybody could!' She took a deep breath before speaking. 'I came to England from France three years ago. I was never meant to be … I'm actually a singer and a dancer.'

Suddenly a loud scream in a foreign language interrupted the conversation. Heavy footsteps on the stairs were followed by the crash of the street door and then silence.

'Sorry about that. My neighbours – sometimes I wonder if the Spanish Civil War ever ended!' The girl screwed up her fore-head in confusion. Mallory waved his hand as if to say don't worry about it. 'So you sing at the club?'

For just a minute she wore that look of yesterday. 'I don't want to go back there.'

'But what will you do? You can't just walk the streets.'

'Lucille does.'

'Who is Lucille?'

'A friend of mine. She was only eighteen years old when she caught a disease from a client. The club threw her out.' There was an awkward moment of silence.

Mallory thought of her predicament. Girls that worked these haunts had few assets beyond their bodies and their youth. And time would eventually destroy both. He screwed up his face and tried to think of something to say to raise her hopes. 'We need to sort out a room for you. Where they can't find you.'

'They will always find me,' she whispered.

'London's a big place.'

'Not big enough...' She lowered her eyes and appeared to be grappling with a problem. 'Perhaps I can stay here with you?'

Mallory stifled an incredulous laugh. God, what would his land-lady, the righteous Mrs Johnson, have to say about that! But the girl was desperate and he couldn't find it within himself to throw her out. He briefly nodded. 'There is one proviso: if I am to help you, I need to know everything.' Someone was shouting in the street. Mallory stood up and closed the window. Then he moved his chair closer to the girl's. She still had not spoken and he wondered for a moment if she'd even heard the question. Then he took her hand. There was no response. 'I'm sorry to pry into your life but you—'

She removed her hand and flicked a strand of hair from her face. 'You are always saying you are sorry! You have nothing to apologise for. You realise I could lie to you? Tell you ... anything?'

Mallory tensed. 'Why would you do that?'

'Because I am ashamed of my life. Don't you see?' she shouted. 'This is not the way I want it to be.' She wiped her hand across her face and crossed both legs on the wooden chair. 'I

24

lived with a man in Paris. He was mixed up with the wrong crowd. It all started out as harmless fun – the parties, the marijuana and the good times.'

Mallory nodded. He knew of the marijuana, but never the good times. He and his fellow comrades used *dagga*, a similar drug, simply as a means to escape the despair of war.

'*Maman* only ever wanted the best for me, but really it was the best for her. She is so, what you would call, bourgeois … you know, white collar, capitalist.' A lock of hair fell across her forehead again and she pushed it away. 'She enrolled me with a strict English-speaking convent school when I was four years old. Why would anyone do that to a child, *pour l'amour de dieu*?'

From convent to call girl: it was difficult to believe. 'So that's why your English is so good.'

'I hated it. And I hated the people – the snobs with their frou-frou homes on the Left Bank. It was all so false. I had to get out.'

'So where did you go?'

She frowned. 'I left the convent when I was eighteen and I never returned. That was when I met Philippe. Before long we were snorting coke in bars and toilets, then in his flat. We were young – what could possibly go wrong?' Her fingers subconsciously tightened their grip on Mallory's hand and her nails dug into his skin, but he ignored the pain. 'It was a Saturday – I remember the day as if it was yesterday. Some "friends" brought Philippe home. He'd been snorting heroin.' She glanced down at the table and realised she was hurting him. 'I'm sorry,' she said, releasing her grip. He smiled to cover her embarrassment and nodded for her to go on. 'It was the start of a downward spiral. In a matter of weeks, he went from snorting to injecting. And I didn't want anything to do with it. He called me such names and hated the fact that I refused to join in; said I was a coward – I can still hear his voice now.' Then she held her hair back from her neck, exposing a thin scar that had been neatly stitched. 'When I flushed his heroin down the toilet he took a knife to me.'

25

'He could have killed you!'

Madeleine sighed. 'I should have left him then but he needed me. We only had bar work and the drugs were taking all our money. I pleaded with him to go to the *clinique* – he kept on promising…' She gripped her glass and screwed up her eyes to stop herself crying, but it was to no avail.

Mallory moved closer. He wanted to hold her but he wasn't sure if it was the right thing to do, or even if it would have the desired effect. Her body tensed and then relaxed and for a moment he said nothing. He was out of his depth. The easy option was to open another bottle of wine. He looked at the girl.

'I'm sorry,' she said, wiping the tears with the back of her hand. 'Thank you, no more to drink.' Then as an afterthought, 'Perhaps just water.' He handed her a tissue. She wiped her face. The anxious look had disappeared from her eyes. But her chin was still quivering. 'Do you wish you had never walked past the Green Door?'

'No,' he said, not quite able to believe his response when only this morning he'd hoped she would be gone. He let the tap run cold before filling a tumbler. 'Look, if it's difficult…'

She shook her head vigorously. 'No; it's been such a long time since I've been able to talk to anyone like this. It's a relief to share my problems.'

Share her problems! The girl had found the courage to confront her fears. The least he could do was to hear her out.

'So what happened when you couldn't pay them?'

A cold wind blew down the narrow alley and rattled the old casement. The girl did not even appear to notice. 'I tried my father. He wouldn't give me a cent – "*argent de la drogue*", drug money, is what he called it.'

'What did you do?'

'The dealers gave us credit. Then Philippe lost his job and we could no longer pay them. The threats terrified me. They said they would get what we owed them. One way or another.'

26

Mallory removed the packet of Camel from his pocket. He offered one to the girl. His hands were shaking from anger as he struck the match. 'And you didn't go to the police?'

'*The police*? They're not interested in people like us – another dead addict makes their job that much easier.' Her lips trembled. She drew heavily on the cigarette, gazing silently out of the window. Some of the stallholders were starting to pack their wares away for the evening. 'The people, they fascinate me,' she eventually said.

'In the market?'

'The way they dismantle their booths. They remind me of the gypsies that used to camp in the field opposite our house in Neuilly-sur-Seine. I was only a young girl then, perhaps nine or ten; I would sneak out, cross the road to the field and play with the gypsy children. Sometimes they would let me feed their horses. Then the police came to evict them. And that was the end of that fairy tale.'

Mallory rubbed his nose and waited for a suitable moment to resume the conversation. The opportunity finally came when the girl turned away from the window. 'You were telling me about Philippe?'

Without looking at him, she started to speak. But a kind of sadness had crept into her voice. 'He tried so hard to kick the habit. He would wake up at night crying, and apologise for dragging me into his murky world. He told me to leave. But I couldn't. I loved him – I wanted to look after him.' Her voice faltered. 'Then the next day I came home from work and found the front door open. Philippe was dead in the bath. It was an overdose.' She was staring out of the window again. 'They killed him!'

Mallory said nothing, just reached across and took her hand. But she did not seem to notice.

'For two days I did not leave the flat. I sat with him and talked to him. On the third night, the drug dealers came to see me. They wanted their money – twenty-two thousand francs.'

'*Twenty-two thousand*?'

She looked down at his hand holding hers. 'I know, *c'est ridicule*; I was a barmaid, a part-time singer – I didn't have anything like that kind of money! My parents had disowned me and I had no one to turn to. Then the dealers gave me a lifeline. They offered me a job in London where the wages were good, especially for a singer with what they called a *sophistiqué* French accent.' She laughed, but there was no mirth.

'It was your only way out?'

She nodded. 'They said they would arrange everything, even a flat. And they would also take care of Philippe. After I'd repaid the money, I would be free to return home.'

Mallory reached for the packet of cigarettes. 'So you took the job?'

'The singing, the dancing – it was all just a front.' Her voice rose in anger. 'They sell girls to men. That is how they make their money.'

'That's illegal,' he said, lighting the Camel for the girl. 'This is England! The police would have intervened and shut down the club.'

'You don't understand, they have my passport! Even so, I refused to do what they wanted. So they kept me locked in the basement. No windows or lights, just a filthy mattress to sleep on. It was after they started to hit me and threatened to disfigure my face with acid that I gave in,' she looked away, 'when they broke my arm, they broke my spirit.'

Mallory rose to his feet and began pacing the room, his every step mirroring his frustration. Was this cowardly intimidation any different to that which he'd witnessed in the interrogation huts, during the war? 'The bastards.'

'Oh, they are much worse than that. You cannot believe the filthy things they made me do: the fat, revolting men I had to sleep with. I feel so dirty … inside.'

Mallory swore under his breath. His jaw was clenched tight and he turned to the girl. 'You are not going back.'

'What will I do? They'll find me wherever I go! Their organisation is like a web that hangs over London. They are the spiders, trapping us girls. There is no escape.'

'I deal with animals like this every day.' He took a final drag on the cigarette and stubbed it out in the ashtray. 'Have you any savings?'

'Not much. They give me a little spending money each week and they take care of everything else. It's all added to Philippe's debt.' She blinked her eyes. 'I'll be paying it off until I am old, ugly or too diseased to attract the clientele.'

Mallory knew what happened to the girls once the clubs were finished with them. It was the streets, the pimps and the curb-crawlers. Then finally the drugs. 'That fat bastard outside the club last night – he was a client?'

'An important customer, from Slovakia. He brings a lot of business to the Green Door. Their money buys them their pleasures. Were he not so drunk I would have gone with him last night.' She shrugged. There was an admission of defeat in her voice, a kind of emptiness. 'It's what I'm paid to do.'

Mallory felt her breath on his face when she spoke, a suggestion of nicotine and wine that intoxicated him with its headiness. She had revealed a classical beauty behind the painted face. The big brown eyes, the small nose and the full cupid lips that were so suggestive when she subconsciously ran her tongue over them – all of this captivated him. Yet he hadn't noticed it yesterday. And he knew the reason. Fear had masked what was now plain to see. 'Okay, you can stay here until we can sort something out. But you will need your clothes.' He paused to consider what to do next. 'Where's your flat?'

'No, you can't go there! They'll be waiting for me!'

'That won't be a problem.'

'Please, if–'

'They don't know me,' he said. 'Now what do you need?'

The girl shrugged again. 'My clothes are in the wardrobe. On top of the chest of drawers there is a box with some cheap jewellery.'

29

Then suddenly she sat bolt upright. '*Maman*'s suitcase is under the bed. It has a few items she gave me before she died. It's all that remains from my life in France.'

'I understand.' He passed a notepad and pen to the girl. 'I'll need the address. And your keys.'

'Please, Mallory, I can buy clothes when I find work!'

He ignored her and held out his hand for the directions.

Reluctantly she handed him the pad.

'You have beautiful handwriting.'

She laughed sarcastically. 'My expensive Parisian boarding school. Sister Bernadette used to say that writing is the mirror to your soul. But what good has it done me?'

There were hidden depths to the girl. But for now he had other things on his mind. 'What's your nearest Tube station?'

'Aldgate East.' She sighed, seemingly resigning herself to the situation. Then she reached for her handbag and pulled out a single key. 'It opens both doors.'

Mallory pulled on his coat. Before fastening the buttons, he tucked the shortened knobkerrie into his belt. He'd always carried the African hardwood stick in the bush, and old habits were difficult to shake. Then he slipped a pair of miniature binoculars and a Maglite torch into the inside pocket. There was nothing on his person that would identify him. 'Don't open the door to anyone,' he said.

'Please be careful!'

Mallory noted the look of concern in the girl's eyes.

But he felt no fear; only the anticipation of what was to come.

Chapter Six

Mallory had little trouble losing himself amongst the crowds at Aldgate East. Dappled sunshine cast shadows across the neglected shop fronts. At the busy intersection irritated drivers blew their horns in frustration. The daylight was a welcome relief from the claustrophobic Underground. Taking a deep breath, he searched for the street signs to get his bearings. This was not an area he was familiar with and, just for a moment, he wondered what the hell he was doing here. A newspaper kiosk across the road caught his attention. He waited patiently while the vendor served a customer. When it was his turn, he pulled Madeleine's instructions from his pocket.

'Don't suppose you know where Fournier Street is, do you, mate?'

The vendor spread his arms wide apart in a gesture that told Mallory he hadn't got a clue or perhaps, more to the point, couldn't be bothered. But the woman buying flowers from the pavement buckets had overheard the conversation.

'Go up Commercial Street,' she said, pointing at the intersection. 'You'll pass Wentworth and Fashion Street. Then it's the next on your right. Opposite Brushfield Street. It's a bit of a walk, or you can take the number 27 bus.'

Mallory mouthed his appreciation. There was a long queue at the bus stop on Commercial Street. Looking over his shoulder, he saw the number 27 approaching and was about to join the waiting crowd. Then he decided against it; the walk would give him time to plan his strategy. He was in unfamiliar territory, on a London street as far removed from the bush as it was possible to be and yet … yet in other ways perhaps it wasn't so different. Houses replaced trees, but the enemy was the same.

Ten minutes later, he'd reached Fournier Street. It was built up on both sides with late 17th-century Huguenot town houses and linked to bustling Brick Lane. The street itself was deserted. Mallory noted the house numbers – 34 was halfway down on the opposite side. He sauntered past it with his hands in his pocket, before crossing over to a small café. There were two tables on the pavement. The café door was open and he signalled the waitress. While he waited to be served, he studied the layout of the street.

Madeleine's first-floor flat, with its weathered windows, was conspicuous against the restored white casements of the neighbouring property. Access to the building itself was fairly straightforward. But he knew someone would be looking for the girl; they wanted her and this was the logical place to wait for her.

'Can I help?' From the tone of the waitress' voice, helping him was the last thing she wanted to do. She wore a dirty apron over a long skirt and appeared more interested in the flirty waiter behind the coffee machine than her sole customer. She reached over to wipe the table, and Mallory turned his head away to avoid the stale odour of cigarette smoke that clung to her body.

'Coffee – black, one sugar, please. And a packet of Camels?'

The girl nodded and jotted down the request. Then, picking up a used cup from the adjacent table, she returned to the counter to process the order.

Mallory went back to studying the street. Most of the properties had been restored to how they would have looked in the days of the wealthy silk merchants. Number 34 was the exception. The windows and the front door were dilapidated and the brickwork was daubed with anti-Semitic slogans.

32

He was about to remove the binoculars from his pocket when he heard the waitress' footsteps on the stone tiles. She placed the coffee, cigarettes and an ashtray on the table.

'Let me know if you want more milk.'

He nodded and looked away. When the waitress had disappeared, Mallory focused the Zeiss glasses on the flat. A flimsy net curtain hung at the window. Suddenly the curtain moved and he saw a shadow on the edge of the frame. A man's face appeared in the gap. Mallory immediately dropped the glasses. For perhaps thirty seconds the bandit scoured the street. Then the curtain closed and the room was once again hidden from view. So he was right; they were waiting for the girl. He looked at his watch. In twenty minutes it would be dark. It was time to make his move.

The waitress' voice broke his concentration. 'We close in ten – is there anything else?'

The light was rapidly fading and shadows crept between the terraces. Mallory finished his coffee and dropped three coins into the saucer. 'Keep the change,' he shouted, setting off towards Brick Lane.

The street lamps had dispelled the dusk when Mallory returned to Fournier Street. Number 34 was still in darkness. Three stone steps led up to a faded grey front door. He waited a minute before inserting Madeleine's key. The door was swollen but it reluctantly opened when he put his shoulder to the leading edge. He stepped into the darkened hall and closed the door. Junk mail littered the black and white marble floor titles. Immediately in front of him, a steep, curved wooden staircase wound its way to the first floor. When he reached the galleried landing, he flicked on the small Maglite torch. It exposed a single door and a second staircase that led to the upper floor. Timber shuttering barred the access.

He put his ear to the door and listened for any sounds.

Nothing stirred.

There was at least one man inside the flat. But would he have an accomplice? Mallory continued to wait. Eventually the shuffling of footsteps on floorboards broke the silence and a noisy extractor fan rumbled into life. Whoever was in the room was now in the bathroom. Removing the knobkerrie from his belt, Mallory inserted the key in the lock and eased the door slightly open. A street lamp below the lounge window threw a flicker of light across the floor. He pushed the door another couple of inches until he could see the rest of the room. The bathroom door was slightly ajar but the lounge was empty. It took a moment for his eyes to adjust to the gloom. Moving silently across the floor, he positioned himself next to the bathroom and waited.

The flushing toilet was abnormally loud in the quiet, confined space. The click of the pull switch cut the fan and a hefty man limped into the room. Both his hands were occupied, trying to fasten his fly in the dark.

Mallory swung the knobkerrie in a short arc. The heavy stick caught his unsuspecting victim on the side of his shaved head and the man dropped to the floor. He wouldn't wake for at least twenty minutes. It was sufficient time to search the flat. The Maglite highlighted what he was looking for underneath the bed. The large canvas case was old and frayed at the corners. All it contained was a photograph album and a bundle of letters. He placed the small wooden jewellery box in the case and then randomly bundled clothes on top of the mementoes. A quick rummage around the room revealed little else of value.

Before leaving, he checked the bandit's pulse. The body was still limp, but he wasn't about to take any chances. After tying the man's hands behind his back, he stuffed a worn tea towel into his mouth and secured it in place with a pair of Madeleine's stockings.

It was time to go. He picked up the suitcase and took one last look at the darkened room, which appeared to have known little else but sadness. Then, softly closing the front door, he disappeared into the night.

Chapter Seven

The girl was still huddled on the settee. It was how Mallory had left her two hours ago. On seeing him, her face was suddenly transformed. She jumped up, ran across the room and flung herself at him.

'Oh my God, I was so scared.'

Mallory held her for a moment, surprised by the welcome. The bunch of flowers he'd bought from the street vendor was clutched in his hand. He brought them out from behind her back.

'Daffodils? How sweet of you!' she said. 'It's so long since anyone has bought me flowers.'

'It was the last bunch – I couldn't let him take them home. They're a bit dishevelled, so he threw in the tulips.'

'It's very kind of you.' She smiled shyly. 'I think you are something of a romantic, no?'

He watched her arrange the flowers. The simple act reminded him of Anna. She loved flowers. They would always be scattered everywhere. It was all so long ago. God, he needed a drink – anything to dispel the past. 'Can I fix you a vodka?'

'That would be lovely,' she said, placing the tumbler on the table. Then suddenly she noticed the suitcase on the floor. 'Oh wonderful, you found it! And there was nobody at the flat?'

He didn't want to scare the girl; she was just starting to find her feet again. So he lied. 'The place was empty.'

She smiled and something passed between them. 'Thank you,' she said, opening the suitcase, 'now I can give you your clothes back.'

How she had changed from the previous night. Perhaps she finally felt safe here, away from the club. Or maybe it was something else? Having grown all too comfortable with paying for a woman's company, Mallory was now unsure of how to act, especially as there was such an obvious age difference between them. But then maybe he was reading too much into the situation.

'Tonic? Sorry, I don't have any lemons.'

She nodded and picked up her drink. 'It's fine.'

A gentle drizzle tapped lightly on the windowpane, the droplets running haphazardly down the glass. Mallory felt the girl's closeness. The scent of his Aramis clung to her neck. He gulped the neat vodka down in one, aware he was moving down an unfamiliar road.

'Are you hungry?'

'Starved.'

'I know of a little Italian.'

The girl's lips started to tremble. 'I'm not sure…'

'Nobody will find us at Vettriano's.' In spite of his reassurance the girl still appeared reticent. It was the look on her face that brought home the harsh reality of the situation. The Green Door would be scouring the streets for her and they needed to be careful, at least for now. But the thought of being confined to the flat, as though it were a prison, filled him with dread. Nevertheless, the girl's safety was paramount. 'Perhaps we should leave going out until after my meeting with Andrei.'

'Meeting?'

'I'm seeing him tomorrow – to try and come to an arrangement with the Green Door.'

Madeleine's eyes sparkled. She took a step towards him and kissed him gently on the cheek. 'Nobody has ever gone to this much trouble for me before.'

'It's really nothing,' he stuttered.

'How can you say that?' She looked back over at the suitcase. 'Let's throw caution to the wind! Come, I'll change and you can take me to your Italian restaurant.' When she returned from the bathroom she was wearing a delicate white blouse and a short red skirt over black stockings. The rain now hammered at the window, like an intruder desperate to enter the room.

'You'll catch your death of cold dressed like that – don't you have anything warmer?'

She laughed. 'Just my old raincoat.'

'Here, take this,' he said, handing her his fisherman's jumper.

She pulled it over her head and giggled. It swamped her body. 'How do I look?' she said, rolling up the sleeves.

He eyed her closely. Then he smiled. 'Like a flower whose petals are about to open. An African protea. They hug the mountains above Stellenbosch. I used to stop and look at them whenever I drove north to the Wild Coast. They remind me of you.'

'Why?'

'They are resilient to all adversaries; to the cold winds that blow off the Atlantic and the hot summer sun. Yet when they bloom, they bring the mountains to life.'

She smiled sadly. 'Nobody has said anything like that to me for a long time.'

He picked up the old blue raincoat and hung it over her shoulders. It was shabby but on Madeleine the coat looked anything but cheap. She wore it with confidence, as though it had been created by one of the finest fashion houses.

When Mallory opened the front door, the raw chill greeted him like an unwelcome stranger. A shiver ran down his back, and it wasn't because of the cold corridor. Despite his assurances to the girl, he couldn't avoid the fact that someone – out there, in the concrete jungle – was looking for them. Someone he would have to face sooner or later.

Chapter Eight

It was late and the little Italian restaurant was about to close. However, the proprietor decided to make an exception for the couple. The L-shaped dining area culminated with a well-stocked wine bar, above which hung smoke-stained prints of Italian lakes and old Alfa Romeo racing cars, conveniently placed to hide the cracks on the walls. The simple wooden tables had all been reset and decorated with single plastic roses.

The waiter directed them to a corner table before handing them menus. Madeleine sat facing the room. The few diners in the restaurant were finishing off their desserts and coffees. She removed the scarf that covered her hair. 'An hour ago this seemed like a good idea.' She scratched the top of her hand with her fingernail. 'Now I'm not so sure.'

'Don't worry,' Mallory said, trying his best to put the girl at ease. 'This place is well away from the Green Door.'

'You're probably right,' she said with a resigned shrug.

He looked down at the wine list. 'Okay with a Sauvignon? It should go well with the pasta.'

'Is it French?' A half-smile appeared in her eyes. 'The bottle we had at the flat was lovely.'

'They have a Pouilly Fume,' he said, summoning the waiter and pointing to the menu.

'An excellent choice, sir!'

Mallory looked at the girl. She appeared to finally relax. The night out would surely do them both good. He moved the vase with the plastic flower to the edge of the table. The action was unnecessary but it seemed to break the invisible barrier between them. 'This is perhaps a stupid question,' he ventured, 'but when were you last truly happy?' It was the first thought that came to mind and he wasn't quite sure why he'd asked it. But the girl didn't hesitate in her response.

'I've never been happy since Philippe died.'

'Never?'

'Every part of my being was unhappy: my body, my mind – even the clothes I wore.' She clutched her hands again and glanced over his shoulder. 'The club had total control of me. They wound me up like a toy and then set me in motion. And I did whatever they said.'

'And now that you have escaped?'

'I am happy here with you, on this night, in this restaurant. It is all I ask for … being able to take one day at a time.' They were words spoken with sadness. 'Can you understand that?'

With any other woman, Mallory would have questioned the motive. But with Madeleine, living day to day seemed the most natural thing in the world. They had met by chance; should he not leave it as such? He was about to respond to her question when the waiter returned to the table with the wine and withdrew the cork. The pale liquid splashed the bottom of his glass. He inhaled the delicate bouquet. It spoke of grapes languishing on vines, somewhere on the hills of the Loire. Then the wine touched his lips and he closed his eyes. For what could only have been a moment, he was transported back to the little valley of Franschhoek – famous for its Sauvignon – and his three days' leave before the Bush War. It was the last of the good times. Shaking his head, he opened his eyes and fixed them on the girl.

39

'It's perfect – you'll love it. In a strange way, it reminds me of South Africa.'

The waiter nodded his approval and continued to pour.

'To summers gone and summers to come,' Mallory said, holding up his glass.

'I would rather forget summers gone,' she replied.

'You're right; to live in the past is to never embrace the future. Let's toast tomorrow.'

'No, let's think only of the present – anything more frightens me.'

He put his glass down. 'We have to talk about the future sometime, Madeleine, preferably before I see Andrei tomorrow. Do you have any idea what you will do?'

She looked away, seemingly studying the pictures on the walls. He knew they could have been anything from cheap prints to priceless masters because she was not really seeing them. A modern rendition of a Puccini opera played softly to the last few diners.

'It is kind of you to let me sleep on the settee.'

Mallory smiled gently. 'I'm afraid it will have to be temporary.'

The girl's eyes widened. 'Please let me stay … please.' The worried look on her face was a warning.

Mallory twisted the stem of the glass between his fingertips. He could feel the glow of the wine in his head. Why was he hesitating? Why did he ignore her plea? Shouldn't he be welcoming her with open arms instead of questioning her every move? He reached across the table for her hand. 'I'm rather set in my ways. But look, let's take one step at a time. First, we have to appease the Green Door. Then perhaps a job – you're a singer, right?'

'A jazz singer. But I don't know whether I can work in London.'

The waiter approached the table to take their order. Mallory gestured to Madeleine.

'The *penne all'arrabbiata, s'il vous plaît.*'

'And the carbonara,' he said, replenishing the girl's glass.

A coquettish grin crossed her face. 'You wouldn't be trying to take advantage of me, would you, Mallory?' The fear of just a moment ago seemed to have disappeared. Like a chameleon, she changed her colours to suit the situation, and there was something of the hunter about her.

'I hardly think you're helpless!' He laughed out loud. 'Now, where were we?'

Madeleine sighed and ran her fingers through her hair, playing with the strands. It was a habit that captivated him. The candlelight was reflected in her eyes and they seemed to look right through him. He shifted uneasily. Then the table of diners across the room broke the awkward silence. They were toasting each shot of brandy and complimentary Limoncello with raucous singing and laughter. The girl giggled at their antics. Then she turned her attention back to Mallory and placed her hand over his.

'So, I told you how I came to be in England. Now it's your turn. You are Zimbabwean, no?'

For some moments he said nothing. The conversation from the noisy table centred on bonuses. It must have been a good year for the bankers judging by the amount of alcohol they were getting through. But then, thinking about it, perhaps not: this wasn't exactly the most salubrious of places for such an occasion. 'I was *Rhodesian*. Now I'm probably more of an Englishman.'

'Of course, I remember now. Rhodesia – it's not somewhere I know. We learned about the French colonies in Africa at school, mainly West Africa. In fact, some years ago I read a book about the Mau Mau in Kenya. It was so violent; I was at a loss trying to understand how they could commit these terrible atrocities – and against their own people!'

'Zimbabwe's much the same. It was another stupid bloody tribal war.'

'Were you involved in the fighting?'

He nodded.

'But if it was a tribal war, why were *you* fighting?'

Her innocence was refreshing. 'I guess you could say that we were also a tribe – a white tribe.' Strange how he had never really

41

looked at it that way before. 'But my heart wasn't in it.' He was about to expound on the thought when the waiter returned with the food.

'Is there anything else, sir?' Mallory looked at the girl.

'Not for me, thank you.'

The waiter smiled and took his leave. Madeleine's eyes followed him to the corner table. Then she turned her attention to Mallory again and spoke softly. 'Tell me about Africa, when you were a lawyer. Was that before the war?'

'I was a defence lawyer,' he said slowly, in an attempt to play it down, 'what the Africans called a "bush lawyer". The whites had a different name for me.' He picked up his fork. 'To them, I was a "wog lover". Or "Kaffir lover", as they put it.'

'I'm not sure I understand?'

'I defended African guerrillas on death row. It wasn't exactly the done thing in those days, a white man trying to save blacks from the hangman's noose.'

'But why were they on death row?'

Why indeed? Too often he'd asked himself the same question. It was a bloody travesty of justice. But that wasn't what the girl wanted to hear. 'Africans inciting violence and caught with weapons such as guns, knives or even knobkerries were for the chop.'

A frown came over Madeleine's face and she wrinkled her nose. '*Knob* what…?'

'Knobkerrie – it's a hardwood stick. For fighting. The poor bastards had little chance of mercy unless we had a fair judge, which in a bloody racist society was hard to come by.' He looked away for a moment. 'They shared cells on death row with the leaders of the banned political parties.'

The girl leaned forward in her chair. 'Banned? Why were they banned?'

'Rhodesia was a white society. That was what the war was all about. They were fighting minority rule. But they went about it all the wrong way.'

42

'What do you mean?'

'They abducted young men from their villages and threatened them and their families with death if they disobeyed orders. They were just farm boys; they had no choice but to join the cause. One day they were planting their mielies, the next they were blowing up installations and killing innocent civilians. When they were hauled up before the courts, we tried to impress their predicament upon the judges, but it only ever fell on deaf ears. I was their last chance at freedom. But rarely did they escape the noose.'

Madeleine shut her eyes. 'But how can you hang someone just for being a member of a political party?'

'In the eyes of the law they were terrorists. Now the world calls them "freedom fighters". I guess in hindsight that's about right. After all, they were fighting for their country.' He laughed but it sounded more like a hollow cry for help.

'But the farm boys … they had no choice? How could they…?'

'It still haunts me. Sometimes I wake in the night in a cold sweat and see them again, standing before the court in their prison uniforms, as the judge reads out the sentence. The poor buggers didn't even understand him – barely any of them spoke English. Then the fucking judge had the audacity to say, "May God have mercy on your soul" as he signed the death warrant. He didn't give a shit about their souls.' Mallory realised he was shouting and grabbed the edge of the table to calm himself down. The waiter looked up at him from behind the bar. 'I'm sorry,' he said, glancing around the room, 'this shit still gets to me.'

'You don't have to apologise,' she said, picking up her water glass. 'I also have nightmares. But yours must be terrible.'

He tried to laugh but it was more like a snarl. 'After the trial I would visit them in their cells. They had no name, just a number. Life was cheap. They'd say, "it's okay, bwana; it's not your fault." They were apologising to *me*, for the inconvenience *they* had caused. Shit, what bloody inconvenience? It should have been me apologising to them for failing to secure their release! We'd sit together in the stinking cells, chain-smoking and talking of the future, when the land would one day be Zimbabwe. Future, what fucking future? They would never see Zimbabwe.'

'I'm sorry.' She smiled sadly. 'Look, now it's me apologising.'

'It's okay; like you, I've kept the past bottled up for too long. I was never able to understand it and I don't think I ever will. They tortured these men for their confessions! I've seen the wounds, where the bastards attached the electric cables. They held their heads under water, almost to the point of drowning. The poor buggers signed the confessions just to stop the pain!' He paused to look at the lights beyond the window. It was late and yet people still walked the streets. When he next spoke, his voice was softer and touched with sorrow. 'At least the noose put an end to their suffering.' He took a deep breath. 'We're the ones who have to live with all the shit now.'

'But what did it achieve?'

'*Achieve*?' His mouth twisted in a smirk. 'Well, they got their democracy, after a decade of us killing each other. They also got their one man, one vote. But then Mugabe managed to turn even that into a farce. In reality it achieved nothing, absolutely bloody nothing.'

The waiter brought the cheese and placed the platter on the table. 'Would you like a port or maybe a brandy – on the house?'

Mallory glanced at the girl and she shook her head.

'Thank you, but I think I've had enough.'

44

Chapter Nine

It was almost midnight when they left the restaurant. They walked on streets that were still bustling with revellers leaving the clubs. Girls in short skirts flirted with young men, and music floated out of the bars. The rain had eased off but a persistent drizzle tapped on the pavement and small puddles filled the hollows in the slabs. A taxi passed slowly by, its yellow sign glowing in the dark. Mallory was about to raise his hand to hail it when Madeleine stopped him.

'Can we walk?'

'Sure,' he said. 'But it's at least half an hour.'

She moved closer. 'It doesn't matter, I'm not tired.'

A group of kids wished them well through drunken laughter. Across the street a policeman walking his beat paused to watch the group, but when he saw they meant no harm, he moved on. In a darkened doorway, a tramp lay huddled beneath a dirty blanket. Before him on a crusty towel stood an old tin can. Madeleine stopped by his side.

'Mallory, do you have a few coins?'

The tramp raised his head, anguish in his eyes. Mallory thrust a note into his hand. He usually wouldn't have bothered, since the money would most likely go towards cheap booze. But then, did it really matter if it brought the vagrant a moment of happiness?

And who was he to judge? Here he was, hoping for time with a girl who was twenty years younger than him, while this down-and-out hoped for a moment of oblivion. Were the two of them really any different?

By the time they reached the flat the soft drizzle had turned again to rain. Mallory put his finger to his lips. 'My landlady lives on the premises; she's pretty old fashioned when it comes to bringing women home at this hour – says they're "loose" if they're out after ten.'

Madeleine laughed. 'Is that how *you* see me?'

Mallory ignored the remark and opened the door. Taking the girl's hand, he then led her up the stairs. The flat was dark and stuffy. He opened the window before turning on the radio. A violinist was playing Mendelssohn on the all-night show and the tune briefly reminded him of the previous summer, a music festival on the banks of the River Cam, his first break from London – indeed his first holiday – since coming to England. At the time, he'd wished he could have stayed there forever, locked away in that world of make-believe. He turned to the girl.

'A night cap, or is it too late?'

She had removed her raincoat and was sitting on the edge of the settee. Her shoes lay abandoned on the floor. '*Merci beaucoup*, but no.'

How young she looks, he thought, pouring a small measure of whisky into a tumbler, and how alive she makes me feel. He watched as she gently caressed her toes. The top of one of her stockings showed below the red skirt, allowing him a glimpse of her suspenders. She looked innocent enough, but he knew there was no such thing. He pulled out a chair and sat down at the table.

'Do you want the bathroom?'

She nodded and stood up. 'I'm sorry; it's been a long day.'

By the time she returned, he'd made up the settee with fresh linen. Her scent lingered in the room and again he thought how winsome she looked. Her face was becoming familiar to him: the pert little nose; the high cheekbones; the melancholy eyes that seemed to cry out for love, all framed by the soft brown hair that fanned itself across the pillow when she lay down on the sofa bed. She was beautiful, like a meadow of flowers touched by the wind. How had she managed to cast this spell over him in so short a time? And would this face forever possess him? Maybe not; after all, it was the bewitching hour, that time of night when everything was transformed, before the dawn destroyed the magic. He shook his head. God, he was getting melodramatic!

'Thank you for tonight – I don't know what I would have done without you,' she said, briefly opening her eyes again.

He shrugged. She lay there like a leopard, eyeing him in the dark. He felt a sense of vulnerability, almost as though he was once again walking the bush in the still of night. But he didn't want to think about that now. Not when the girl was in the room.

'Do you really believe your friend can help?' she asked, in a drowsy voice.

'I'll know tomorrow,' he said, trying desperately to cover his uncertainty.

'But what will I do for money? Even if they let me go, I have no papers, I'm … I'm an illegal.'

He stared into the dregs of the whisky as if the answer lay in the glass. Papers? Illegal? He knew the feeling all too well. But there must be some way. He racked his brain for a solution. Then the thought struck him like a bolt from the blue. *Her passport!* It was a long shot, but it just might work. He was about to tell her the plan when he realised that she was asleep. He kissed her softly on the cheek. She didn't stir. He had no idea where she would take him. But wherever it was, he knew that he would follow her.

Chapter Ten

Mallory smiled at the young Romanian girl outside La Ronda. He'd run the gauntlet of Soho call girls many times on his way to Andrei's office, yet still they would greet him as a punter.

'A little early for you, Mallory?' she said, swishing her long blonde hair to the side and fiddling with the hemline of her mini skirt.

He laughed. 'Work calls, Lillian!'

'That's what they all say.'

Andrei's office was an unusually high-ceilinged room on the first floor of a Victorian terrace house, which overlooked the row of strip clubs. He'd inherited the entire building from his family and had converted the top floor into a flat, which he used when in London, and the ground floor into an Italian restaurant. As Mallory passed the bay window he spotted Luigi, the waiter, who smiled and waved.

To one side of the restaurant was a heavy wood-panelled door and on the wall next to it, a stainless steel intercom panel. He pressed the button and waited.

'Yes?' The voice from the speaker was flat but unmistakably Russian.

'It's me.'

A buzzing was followed by the release of the lock and Mallory entered the modern hall. A steel and glass staircase led to the first floor. The office door was open. How often had he been in this room and yet it never ceased to intrigue him? In the centre was a large wooden refectory table, which dominated the space. On it were four telephones, stacks of files and a mountain of paperwork, which overflowed from the metal filing cabinet set aside for records of past cases. Organised chaos, Andrei called it. Around the table were six worn-leather easy chairs, one of which was filled by the Russian's enormous frame. He had a telephone to his ear and was staring out of the plate-glass window. Briefly acknowledging his assistant with a half-smile, he indicated one of the chairs opposite him.

Mallory sat down. Only tourists walked the streets at this time of day. He watched them sniggering at the girls' posters that hung outside the clubs. It was still too early for the serious clientele and the opportunists wouldn't be stopping for expensive champagne, or girls. A young couple left Antonio's restaurant, holding hands, laughter on their lips. They stopped outside a club and the man removed his scarf and placed it around the girl's neck. Then they shared a tender kiss. Young love, he thought, somewhat cynically. Then he remembered Madeleine. Could there ever be anything approaching that type of affection between the two of them? Or was this thing with her just another chapter in the bloody mess that was his life? He'd been through a war, loved and lost someone he'd dearly cared for and packed a lot of hard living into a short time. Maybe it was time for a change. He closed his eyes for a moment before picking up *The Spectator* that lay next to a half-finished cup of coffee. The front-page headline – MORAL VALUES FALLING IN MODERN SOCIETY – made him laugh. Most appropriate, he thought, picturing Lillian touting for business on the pavement below. Then he heard the click of the receiver being replaced in its cradle.

'Sorry about that – another prostitution case. I'll run through it with you later. Coffee?'

Mallory nodded and held up the paper. 'How's this for a headline?'

'Journalists! They're always banging on about moral values. It's all a load of bullshit. If these *svolochis* had their way I'd be out of business!' He picked up the telephone and placed the order with Antonio. 'So Mallory, you have me intrigued. It's not often we see you this early.'

'Lillian said the very same thing.'

The Russian laughed. 'You will have all the girls talking about you.' His generous lips had stretched into a broad smile, almost touching the underside of his bulbous nose. This was apparently a throwback to his Romanov ancestors. In fact, Andrei was only half Russian. He was also illegitimate. The unkempt, curly blonde hair certainly seemed to lend credibility to the rumour that his mother was Scandinavian and of a lower class than that of his aristocratic father. He leaned forward in the armchair with his head held high, in the attentive role of a barrister.

'So how can I help, my friend?'

Mallory suppressed a smile. 'Shall we start with the case notes on the Blue Angel?' He passed the stack of papers across the desk.

'As you wish,' Andrei said, skimming through the pages for the relevant information. For perhaps ten minutes he said nothing. Then he looked over his spectacles at Mallory. 'Just as I thought. The woman is lying through her teeth; we'll tear her statement to pieces. This is great work.' When he had finished reading the notes, he removed his glasses and placed them atop the pile. 'Now come; tell me about your problem – you mentioned a call girl? Something about an altercation … outside the Green Door?'

Mallory bit his lip and thought briefly of the night. 'I was on my way home the other night–'

'I did not realise that you frequented such reprehensible establishments,' the Russian said, absentmindedly fingering his pen.

'You know me better than that, Andrei. I'd been to a bar in Spitalfields. Hanbury Street is a shortcut. The girl was being knocked about. I couldn't walk away from that.'

Andrei let out a bellowing sigh. 'The first rule, especially for someone in your situation, is never to get involved.'

'I am involved. She's staying with me.'

'Why would you do that...?'

'She had nowhere else to go!'

Andrei studied his pen meditatively. 'By God, you should know better than to mess around with call girls from clubs like the Green Door.' He put on his glasses and clicked the pen open.

Mess around with call girls! That's exactly what Andrei did when he wanted sex! Although he had to admit that he was at least selective. At times like this Mallory felt like a schoolboy being chastised by his teacher. He'd sat in on too many briefs with the barrister not to know what was coming next. Facts! Facts preceded objectives, and they were all the Russian was interested in.

'Is it possible to speak to the club?'

'The Green Door? Yes, it's possible. But why would you want to help a prostitute?'

Mallory was about to elaborate when the intercom buzzed. 'Yes?'

'Good morning, Mr Vadislav – your coffee.'

'Bring it up, Luigi.' Andrei pressed the door release on the wall unit and a moment later the waiter appeared with the drinks. 'What took you so long?'

'I'm sorry, sir. The restaurant – it is getting very busy this morning with breakfast.'

'Ah, that reminds me,' Andrei said, pointing his pen at Mallory, 'we should reserve a table. Perhaps we can discuss the Blue Angel case over lunch.'

Mallory nodded. His eyes were on the street but his thoughts elsewhere.

Andrei signed the restaurant tab and handed it back to the waiter together with a couple of coins. 'My table, one o'clock please, Luigi.'

'I arrange, sir,' the waiter said, before leaving the room.

'Brandy?' Andrei picked up a bottle of Remy Martin from the silver tray on the sideboard.

Mallory absentmindedly held up his cup. 'Please.'

'This is Remy Martin cognac, you peasant!'

Mallory gritted his teeth. He always had brandy in his coffee at home.

'Wherever did you pick up this disgusting habit?'

'From the guys in Mozambique.' Mallory thought for a moment of the Bush War and the African village outside Tatandica. The Rhodesian helicopter gunships had razed it to the ground because its inhabitants were suspected of harbouring guerrillas. He had first come across the village in the aftermath of the attack. The dead were lying everywhere. In the midst of the carnage, a child, blind in one eye and blood dripping from a horrific wound to his head, hobbled across the kraal searching for his parents. Mallory stood beside a burnt-out rondavel and retched his guts out. That night, as they were retreating towards the border, his friend, Jackson, stepped on a landmine.

He'd known Jackson since school. They'd shared everything – their first game of rugby, their first beer, even selection for Special Forces. The two of them had been inseparable.

The platoon's only signal set was damaged in the blast and they were unable to raise a case-vac, so they carried Jackson on a makeshift stretcher to the clinic at Tatandica … three long hours, with Jackson screaming all the way. Then just before they arrived at the clinic, Jackson stopped crying. It was dark and they could not see his face. But once inside the brightly lit hospital room they realised why Jackson had stopped crying. He was dead.

Sitting on the steps outside the clinic, Mallory had been suicidal. Sergeant Whittaker had found him staring into the night sky, a glazed look in his eyes. After taking him to a local bar and plying him with cheap liquor, they'd put him to bed with a lady of the night. Fortunately he'd passed out cold before anything could happen. The next morning the woman had woken him at dawn and made him a strong black coffee out of the local beans, to which she'd added a generous slug of rough brandy. It was a habit he'd never shaken.

But the Russian didn't need to know.

Andrei flinched as he poured the cognac into the coffee cup. 'Mozambique,' he muttered, shaking his head. 'What provincial people.'

'So what did you guys drink in the freezing Russian winters?'

'Local distilled vodka.'

It was Mallory's turn to laugh. 'And you lecture me on refined taste?'

Andrei ignored the jibe and poured himself a shot of the brandy into a crystal balloon glass. 'So, my heathen friend; let me hear more about your problem with the woman. And remember: you are talking to a barrister.'

Mallory laughed. 'How can I forget?' The law work apart, a strong friendship had grown between the two men; they trusted each other. He withdrew a packet of Camels from his pocket and offered one to the Russian. Andrei shook his head, a repugnant look on his face, and opened a box of Cuban cigars. Then, striking a long match, he lit Mallory's cigarette before seeing to his own cigar.

Mallory drew the nicotine deep into his lungs and then flicked the ash off the cigarette. 'Yes, she's on the game. But she was forced into it. I took her home because she was desperate. She's sleeping on the settee, nothing more.'

'And she's still with you?'

Mallory nodded. 'When I got back to the flat after yesterday's meeting I didn't recognise her. She was somehow ... different.'

Andrei burst out laughing. 'Most prostitutes are in the morning.'

Mallory was only dimly aware of what the Russian was insinuating. 'Her boyfriend was a junkie and he ran up a massive debt. Then the bastards topped him.'

53

'Right,' Andrei said, his voice a hushed whisper. 'Now you are making sense. So she had to find a way to pay off his dealers. What did she do in France?'

'She's a singer. The dealers offered her a job in London. When she got here they took away her passport and tried to put her to work, "entertaining" clients. She refused to cooperate so they held her prisoner in a basement. She finally succumbed when they broke her arm.'

'And now they are looking for her.

Mallory nodded.

'Where was she living?'

'Fournier Street, down near Brick Lane. I went there yesterday to fetch her clothes.'

'Presumably no one saw you…?'

Mallory shifted uneasily in his chair. 'One of their operatives was there.'

'And?'

'He would've woken with a sore head, nothing more.'

Andrei shook his head and tutted. 'Not that it really matters,' he said, picking up the pad and reading through his notes, 'they'll know the woman was responsible when they see her clothes are missing.'

Mallory immediately realised his mistake. 'I guess so,' he said, staring despondently out of the window. A glimmer of broken sunshine appeared through the surly clouds, lighting up the shabby street like a spotlight. Out there on the pavements were people who led uncomplicated lives. And here he was trying to hatch a plan that would save a girl from the clutches of the underworld, a girl he knew almost nothing about.

Andrei stood up. The Cohiba lay dying in the ashtray but the air was still impregnated with its smell. He picked up the bottle of brandy and refilled his glass. Then, pouring another into a fresh tumbler, he handed it to Mallory. 'Okay, so where do we go from here?'

'Didn't you once tell me you'd had some dealings with the consortium that owns the Green Door? Someone called Fowler?'

The Russian nodded. 'It's one of Enrico Tommaso's franchises. Fowler and his partner Cavatore run it and pay Tommaso a percentage.'

'How well do you know them?'

'Some years ago we represented the club at the Old Bailey.' There was a cold look in Andrei's eyes and his lips tightened. 'The charge was prostitution, but if I remember rightly they were also into sex trafficking.' He walked over to the filing cabinet, opened the second drawer and removed a file. Then, after laying it out on the table, he started to read the contents. The shrill ring of the telephone made Mallory jump, but there was no reaction from the barrister as he continued to rifle through the documents. A few seconds later the answer-phone clicked in and a woman's voice came through the speakers. It was followed by the soft hum of a fax machine, the only noise in an otherwise still room. Eventually the Russian's deep voice broke the quiet.

'Just as I suspected. The prosecution's case stated that the proprietor, Cavatore, and his partner in crime, David Fowler, were importing girls from Romania. I wouldn't normally take on such work but this was...' he sighed, 'a special favour.'

'Favour?'

'For an important client who passes a lot of work my way.' He rubbed his hands together. 'I could pretty much name my price on this one. But it was more important to me that the girls were compensated and returned home. Furthermore, I wanted an undertaking from Cavatore that this shit had to stop. Alas, it appears our friends are up to their old ways again.' He removed his spectacles and looked at Mallory. 'As you well know, while I like to entertain the odd call girl, I draw the line at them being taken from their homes and forced into prostitution.'

'How is this going to help Madeleine? With all due respect, the Green Door has crapped all over your terms.'

Andrei's eyes glinted with devilment. 'A good barrister never leaves any stone unturned.' He flicked to the back of the file and pulled out an official looking document. It was stamped with the court's seal. 'One of the prosecution's prime witnesses – a small-time criminal, Bodashka – was actually guilty of perjury. He changed his story after Tommaso put the heavies on him. I have here his original statement, the one he withdrew, all neatly substantiated.' He smiled to himself. 'I must admit, I found it rather amusing, the way the police handled the case. They were so confident of a result that they thought all they had to do was turn up at court. It must have come as rather a shock to them when Cavatore and Fowler walked free! Of course, we all knew they were guilty as hell. But the jury thought otherwise.'

None of this came as a surprise to Mallory; he'd witnessed many of Andrei's finest performances in the High Court. The eloquent, gravelly voice, reminiscent of Peter Ustinov, was infamous in the halls of justice and it was at its very best when cross-examining witnesses. Prosecuting barristers feared him and knew he would punish any careless preparation severely. 'So they were entirely vindicated?'

'The prosecution requested long prison sentences and they wanted the club shut down. But Cavatore and Fowler were found not guilty on all charges and walked out of the courtroom with their fists in the air. But with this,' he gestured towards the document lying on the table in front of him, 'I think we have what the English call "a bird in hand".'

Mallory wasn't entirely sure what Andrei was driving at. Blackmail was a dangerous game. Even more so when it involved gangsters. Resurrecting the buried statement could open a can of worms. Why would Andrei risk his life by exposing the underworld? None of it made sense. However, in spite of these questions, for the first time since the girl had walked into his life, he felt a glimmer of hope.

'So you think they will cooperate?'

Andrei nodded. 'If the Met were to have the slightest inkling that the Green Door is back in the game, they wouldn't make the same mistake again.' He stacked the papers together and replaced them in the folder. 'We just have to handle this in a way that does not leave the organisation losing face.' Then the hard look was back in his eyes. 'Neither Cavatore nor Fowler will be happy to lose one of their girls, but that doesn't bother me. My concern is Tommaso.'

Mallory shivered. From what little Andrei had told him, he was well aware of what that meant: Tommaso controlled most of the shit that went on in the East End. The Sicilian was a major thorn in the side of the Met. But he couldn't think about that now. The girl was his affair and he was prepared to do almost anything to save her. But they'd need to be careful. Tommaso was no pushover. But then he suspected that neither was Cavatore. Shit, what had he got himself into? His hands were still trembling when he struck the match and lit the cigarette. 'I'm sorry to drop this on you, Andrei. There was no one else I could think of turning to.'

The Russian shrugged awkwardly. Then he loosened off his tie and unbuttoned his collar. 'Think nothing of it, my friend. Your help over the years has been invaluable. It's the least I can do in return.' He looked up from the folder and fixed Mallory with a long, hard stare. 'What I don't understand is why you are going to all this trouble for a prostitute.'

Mallory contemplated the balloon glass. 'When you meet her you will understand.'

Andrei shook his head grimly at the romantic notion. 'You're playing a dangerous game.' He reached for the bottle of brandy. Mallory shook his head at the offer. 'You're an illegal.'

'You don't need to remind me.'

'Listen, Mallory; you must understand that when one is alone in the way this girl is, one needs someone. From what you have told me, she has never been alone before. Even when she was on the game she was not alone; she had her club and her clients, as obnoxious as they are. But now she has no one. Apart from you.'

'What are you getting at?'

'You are a soldier not a saint. The girl is going to grab any Galahad she can – you just happened to be in the right place at the right time. If you want my advice, you should just forget about her.' He scratched the back of his head. 'Women like this are nothing but trouble.'

Women like this! Mallory picked up the brandy glass and drained the last of it. 'You think I should be indifferent to life because of my time in the war? What you don't realise, Andrei, is that being close to death also gives you a regard for life.'

Andrei rubbed the stubble on his double chin. 'I thought I knew you well but perhaps not. Life is full of surprises.' He walked over to Mallory and put a hand on his shoulder. 'Maybe it was fate, you bumping into the girl in her moment of need. But I'm not one to speculate on such matters.' For a moment there was silence. Then he spoke in a serious tone. 'Look, give me a couple of days. In the meantime, keep her safe.' He picked up the brandy glass. 'Presumably you'll eventually want to find somewhere safe for her to live?'

'It had crossed my mind.'

Andrei continued to stare out of the window as if the answer to the problem lay out there on the street. Then he picked up the phone and dialled the restaurant. After a couple of exchanges he replaced the receiver. 'Just as I thought – Antonio's place is still available.'

'Antonio?' Mallory asked, hardly daring to breathe.

'Stefano goes back to Italy next week. Can you believe, the silly bugger has only been with Antonio for a month and he meets an Italian girl on vacation here? They have what you would call "a one night stand" and the girl is now with child!' He shook his head. 'The honour of the family is at stake and they want the man responsible for this deed to marry the girl. You know what some Italians are like.'

'An expensive liaison,' Mallory said, stubbing his cigarette butt in the ashtray.

58

'An inconvenient one. He was a bloody good waiter.' Andrei removed his glasses again. 'Look, it's not much, just a little studio on the edge of Soho. But it's yours if you want it. Antonio's desperate to get it filled.'

'There's just one other problem.'

'My God, what now?' Andrei glanced up at the radio-controlled clock above the sideboard. 'I have another meeting.'

'Madeleine is broke. I can help her in the short term but she'll eventually need a job.'

'That might be trickier,' Andrei said, pushing the hair off his forehead. 'I take it you mean something other than whoring?'

'That was uncalled for!'

'I apologise. It was a stupid remark.' He scratched his head. 'Didn't you say that she was a singer?'

'A jazz singer. I did think of the French Revolution – you know, what with Christophe being the owner and one of your clients.'

Andrei laughed. 'My God, you certainly do have high aspirations! Have you heard her sing?'

Mallory shook his head.

'I can tell you now that Christophe Mitterrand will only take the best.'

There was nothing more Mallory could say. He remained silent, somewhat downbeat. Andrei noticed the despondent look and flicked over a page on his diary.

'I'll have a word with Christophe. If they're interested she'll have to audition, but I warn you: she needs to be good. Very good.'

'You know, Andrei, I've always thought of you as a soldier of the night; that the streets of London were your battleground and money your only motivation. But I see another side now; a soft spot under the façade. I appreciate what you are doing for Madeleine.'

The Russian shifted in his chair, clearly embarrassed. 'Enough of this talk of women and wisdom – it gets us nowhere. Back to work. Can you spare an hour to look over this case while I'm out?' He opened a green box file. In large letters on the inside of the portfolio was the title THE HANGING BELL. He removed an A4 document with the heading Racial Discrimination and Harassment. 'The waitress is a black girl – she's bringing the action against her manager. But get this: the principal witness is the barmaid.' He laughed. 'According to my client, it's a stitch-up – "The barmaid is a fucking liar". His words, by the way. So, it's our job to discredit them.' Andrei slid the particulars across the table and looked again at the clock. 'I have to go – I'll be an hour or so.' He picked up his coat. 'I've had enough of gangsters and villains for one morning.' It was a facetious remark that did nothing to allay the weariness in his eyes. Neither did it go unnoticed.

Suddenly Mallory realised the enormity of the task to which he had burdened his friend.

Chapter Eleven

The court notes on the waitress' case made for easy reading. Andrei was correct in his assumption that it was a fabricated charge. The Gahanna waitress had been promised the assistant manager's job but when this hadn't materialised, she'd concocted the harassment charge against the manager. Having found an ally in the barmaid, she believed she had a strong case. But the barmaid was all foam and no beer, and she kept changing her story. They were demanding an exorbitant amount of money, but were prepared to settle out of court if the Hanging Bell came up with an appropriate figure. Sometimes they make it easy, Mallory thought, smiling to himself.

He'd already jotted down four pages of notes when the Russian returned. 'You're right,' he said, shuffling the pages into a neat pile, 'it's a shoo-in – the two girls are obviously the best of friends, and the other witness–', he scanned down the page, searching for the name, 'Roger Whitely, is a regular customer at the Hanging Bell. He's also been seen in the girls' company at various night-clubs across the East End – there's photographic evidence.'

'Just as I thought,' Andrei said. 'Can you take the folder home and prepare the case before next Tuesday? Now, lunch is on me.' He patted his stomach. 'We'd better make an appearance or Antonio will think I have abandoned him.' This was said in jest: the Russian had a personal table in the restaurant; even if he wasn't due to take it, Antonio would still call him before offering the cover to anyone else.

Most of the diners had already left the restaurant when the two men were shown to the table.

'A bottle of my red please, Luigi,' the Russian said, taking the seat facing the window.

'*Grazie, signor*. Also, the suckling pig is on special today and the fettuccine,' he paused to blow his fingers in the air, 'is excellent.'

'Are you hungry, Mallory?'

'Starved!'

'Then allow me to order for you – we'll start with the *calama-retti*. Followed by your recommendation, the *porchetta*.'

'*Buon la scelta, signor*,' the waiter said, returning to the kitchen.

'I'm impressed, Andrei.'

'Why? Good food and drink are the reasons for living,' he said, nodding to Antonio, who had come over to personally serve the wine.

'*Buon giorno, signors. Tutto bene*?'

The proprietor slowly withdrew the cork from the bottle. He then poured the wine into a decanter and left it on the table to breathe. 'Something to start, *signor*?'

'Just a bottle of *acqua minerale, per favore*.' Suddenly he remembered the flat. He lowered his voice. 'Oh, and a word about the place you wish to rent?'

'*Si, signor*?'

'It's for a friend of Mallory's. References might be somewhat difficult. Are you happy for me to stand as guarantor?'

'Of course, *signor*! Is no problem.'

When the proprietor had departed with their order, Andrei turned to Mallory and nodded as if to say 'Now, that's settled'.

'So tell me, why the Amarone? I mean, what's the occasion?'

Andrei put his hand on Mallory's arm. It made him slightly uncomfortable. 'Does there have to be one?'

'Perhaps not. But you have that grin on your face.'

The Russian laughed out loud. 'You know me too well!' He removed his hand, picked up the decanter and poured the wine. 'You have saved a girl from a horrendous fate. The conquest intoxicates you, but there is a pay-off. You are now her protector.'

'Nonsense!' Mallory said. 'You have a vivid imagination.'

A girl with long black hair walked by the window. Andrei's eyes followed her as she passed. '"Nonsense" you call it?' he said slowly. His eyes were still on the girl. 'I don't think so. The woman blinds you; she manifests herself in everything you do.'

'She has no one else to turn to.'

Andrei deliberated over the explanation. 'You think that the girl you found outside the nightclub is different from the one you left this morning? It is the *same* woman, Mallory.' The teeth showed white between his broad lips when he smiled. 'A diamond has many faces – beauty, avarice, greed … I could go on but I think you get the picture. It also has a face of vulnerability. This helplessness appeals to you at the moment. But if you are not careful, one day it will dominate you.' He picked up the wine and swirled the liquid around in the glass.

'You sound very sure of this.'

A shadow drifted over the Russian's features but it was fleeting. 'Can I give you one last piece of advice?'

'You don't have to say it–'

'I like you too much not to.' His eyes were still on the street but the girl with the long black hair was nowhere to be seen. 'How many times have we been drunk on vodka and ideology? There have been many words exchanged between us but seldom so concerning women. I am a romantic, Mallory. But I am also a pragmatist. And it is because of this that I give you the advice.' He paused for a moment to search for the right words. 'Don't ever give yourself completely to Madeleine. If you do, you will end up waiting for her. But she will never come.'

It was the first time the Russian had used Madeleine's name.

Chapter Twelve

When Madeleine woke up the first thing she noticed was the solitude. The window was closed and only the faint growl of street traffic reached the room. She pulled on a pair of shorts and Mallory's old grey sweater. After making herself a cup of coffee she vacuumed the flat. It wasn't really necessary, but somehow it helped to occupy her mind. It was when she moved on to dusting the shelves that she came across the manuscript, partially hidden behind a dictionary and a well-thumbed thesaurus. She carefully removed the draft and laid it out on the table. On the cover was written the title, CHASING THE LAST OF THE SUN. She turned to the first page. It was hand-written in pencil and littered with alterations and corrections.

The old man looked over the escarpment towards the distant hills. He already knew which way the leopard had gone. All his life he had tracked the big cats and he was as familiar with their habits as a father knows a child.

Suddenly Madeleine felt like an intruder and was about to close the manuscript when a page, folded down at the corner, caught her attention. She removed the sheet. At the top of the page was the title again, followed by a single word: BLURB.

The story of an old man and a man-eating leopard set in the foothills of the Vumba, on the edge of the Chimanimani Mountains. The leopards were the old man's first love and now his only family. But twenty-two people were dead and the hunter had to find the man-eater before the next person died.

Madeleine flicked over a page. Was the old man someone Mallory knew or a figment of his imagination? She continued to turn the pages. Scrawled across each sheet were two lines and the word Delete. How could anyone write so many words and then discard them? Finally, after turning something like thirty pages, she stopped at a point that was free of corrections and started to read again. The passage described the footpaths climbing towards the Chimanimani. She could almost imagine herself there, walking on the blood-red soil flattened by thousands of African feet.

Sumba's faint spoor was just visible on the side of the dusty path. The old man bent down and studied it. Not too many years ago he would have known instantly which way the leopard had gone. But now his eyesight was poor and he hesitated. When he eventually looked up, the sun was in his eyes and the path ahead, climbing towards the mountains, was a blur. He put his hand up to shade his face from the glare. It was then he noticed the imprint of his worn desert boot, clearly visible between the short turfs of mopani grass that spread across the lower escarpment. I am getting old, he thought – there was a time when his spoor would have been as difficult to find as that of the leopard. Now he was clumsy and careless. When his eyes were once again accustomed to the bright sunlight, he searched the trees for any sign of the cat. Nothing stirred. Then, shouldering the old .375 Holland & Holland, he continued up the mountain pass.

Madeleine shut the manuscript and placed it back on the shelf where she'd found it. Then she covered it with the reference books so that it appeared undisturbed. She was about to walk away when she noticed the photograph, placed face down and partially hidden beside a pile of books. She picked it up. It showed Mallory, standing beside a heavy-set man outside what appeared to be a bar. She turned it over. On the back was written *With Lannigan – Bulawayo.* It must've been taken years ago, somewhere in Africa. Her eyes devoured the picture as though she was seeing him for the first time. He stood tall and slim, his rugged chin covered in stubble. The light brown hair, longer than it was now, appeared unkempt. But it was his intense, deep-set eyes that held her attention. On his lips was that lazy half-smile, which hinted at his amusement at whoever was behind the camera lens. The big man beside him had his free arm wrapped around Mallory's shoulder. In his other hand he held aloft a rifle. They wore khaki army fatigues – not uniforms as such, but they were obviously soldiers. But why was the picture face down? Hidden? Perhaps Mallory didn't wish to be reminded of that time. She slotted it back where she had found it. Like the novel, it was another part of his life she knew nothing about.

Just for a moment Madeleine wondered whether she should be wary. She had, after all, revealed the truth of her past life to this stranger. But then why not? Mallory wasn't like the other men she knew – the pimps, the addicts and the gangsters who controlled and abused her. So preoccupied was she with her thoughts, she had failed to notice the time. Suddenly she realised that she hadn't eaten for hours. The fridge was empty, save for two bottles of wine, a can of tonic and half a carton of milk. She delved into her red handbag, which was slung over the back of the dining chair, in search of her purse and found the wad of notes tucked away in the zip compartment. It was the money Rudinsky had paid her. She'd completely forgotten about it. No doubt he would want it back. But they had to find her first. And for the time being, the cash represented a lifeline.

Covering her head with her scarf, she put on her sunglasses and left for the convenience store. Customers, with their baskets of groceries, queued up waiting their turn to pay. They seemed to have not a care in the world and she envied them that luxury. When she finally reached the till the cigarette rack caught her attention and, thinking of Mallory, she added a packet of Camel to her shopping. There was a sense of security inside the store, with the hustle and bustle of the shoppers distracting her from her worries. However, once she left the building she became nervous again. She knew she was being totally irrational. Nevertheless, the feeling persisted and it was only when she was back in the flat that she was able to relax. After packing away the shopping, she made herself a cup of tea and a sandwich. Then she turned on the radio. The news was followed by the play of the day, a story of adolescent love set to the music of the Beatles. It reminded her of a time in Paris when she had not a care in the world. Although her eyes were on the street below, her mind was elsewhere, back in a bar on the Left Bank with Philippe, dancing to the music of the sixties.

Chapter Thirteen

Mallory saw the look of apprehension on Madeleine's face when he opened the front door. It was as if she had seen a ghost.

'Are you alright?'

She took a deep breath and visibly relaxed. 'God, you frightened me!' Then she put her finger to her lips. 'It's almost finished,' she whispered, pointing to the radio. She had worked her brown hair into a neat bun, which exposed her long neck. Just a few stray wisps touched her skin.

Mallory felt again her vulnerability, the bird with the broken wing, and was reluctant to break the spell. 'The Long and Winding Road' was setting the final scene to the drama. He glanced down at his wristwatch; another five minutes and then he could tell her the good news, about the flat and the possibility of an audition. And of course, not forgetting the Green Door and the silent prayer that was on his mind as he rode the train home: *Please God, give her back her freedom.* He was in the throes of removing the foil from the sparkling wine when he noticed the bottle of Rioja on the work surface. It brought with it an old familiar warmth, and any trepidation he might have had after his conversation with Andrei was blown away.

'Asti, Mallory? What are we celebrating?'

Her voice took him by surprise. Nevertheless, he remained silent and concentrated on opening the wine. There was a secretive smile on his face that revealed he had something on his mind.

'Come on, Mallory, don't keep me in suspense!'

'Patience,' he said, easing the cork from the bottle and letting it fly across the room.

'You're making me feel guilty,' she said. 'Here I am asking you not to interrupt my radio play and you have something to tell me. You must think me shallow.'

'Not at all!' he said, passing her a glass. 'I once knew a man who had just escaped with his life from an ambush in the Zambezi Valley. The first question he asked the patrol when they rescued him was who had won the Test match! It shows that life goes on.' He looked into her eyes. '*Santé*!'

Madeleine's eyebrows furrowed. 'What are we celebrating?'

He touched her glass. 'We've found you a small place – in Soho.'

She said nothing.

'And the possibility of a job.'

'A job? But where?'

'The French Revolution. Mitterrand owes Andrei a favour.' He held the bottle over her glass and she nodded. 'You'll have to audition, of course.'

Her face was a mixture of confusion and excitement. 'Of course,' she said quietly, unable to hide the look of despondency that was beginning to cloud her face.

'Look, you'll be fine, I'm sure they'll love y–'

'It's not that.' She sat down at the table.

'Then what is it?'

She started to cry.

'Madeleine, what's wrong?' This wasn't the reaction he'd expected.

'If I sing at the club they will find me!'

'Madeleine, you don't need t–'

'I knew a girl. From Slovakia. The Green Door made her work as an escort. A *prostitute*. She walked out on them. I didn't hear from her for many weeks, no one did. The police eventually found her in the Thames. They only managed to identify her from her bracelet.' She paused to blow her nose. 'I don't want to disappear the same way.'

'That's what I'm trying to tell you. Andrei once represented the Green Door.' He reached across the table for her hand. 'It was over twenty years ago – a prostitution and abduction case at the Old Bailey. He has evidence that was withheld.'

'I'm not sure I understand; what good is that now?'

'A man was murdered. A small-time gangster involved in trafficking. No one was ever charged. It was his statement that was withdrawn and it appears to implicate the guy who runs the Green Door. Someone called Cavatore. Do you know him?'

For just a moment the fear was back in her eyes. 'He is evil.'

'Well then, even better: there's sufficient evidence for the Crown Prosecution Service to reopen the case. A guilty verdict would shut the club down and put most of the thugs behind bars. As such, Andrei is confident they will cooperate.'

'They will let me go?' There was a note of incredulousness in her voice. 'Oh God, Mallory, I must be dreaming.' Her wine glass lay abandoned on the table. She reached over and took the glass from his hand and placed it next to hers. 'You don't know how long I've waited to hear these words.' Then she put her arms around his neck and kissed him. When he started to respond, she let him go and took a step back. 'Am I really free?'

'We'll know for sure in the next couple of days.'

She kissed him again.

Mallory could not believe all this was happening. Of the millions of women in London, how had this butterfly of the night fluttered into his world? Then he realised that this was the first time he'd had feelings for any woman since Anna. And it scared him. Was he just another job to her? There'd been prostitutes before – many times – in their dingy flats. Was Madeleine any different? They would have taught her how to manipulate men in much the same way as any other working girl. Yet he found the thought of doing whatever she wanted as thrilling as it was dangerous. For a brief moment, he saw only the girl and not the trappings that surrounded her. The bottle stood on the table. He filled the glasses and then, turning off the ceiling pendant, he handed her the wine. The room metamorphosed into pale warmth.

She was looking at him in that strange way of hers. 'This afternoon, when I was naked in the shower I thought of you.' She sipped the sparkling wine and then stepped back to study his reaction. 'Is it wrong to say these things?'

The words reached out to him, washed over him and cleaned away all the empty years since Anna. 'No, Madeleine; it's not wrong if it's what you mean.'

Her hand reached out for his glass. By placing it heavily on the table, she spilled some of the wine. But it was of no concern. Then she kissed him, letting her tongue play with his lips. She clearly sensed the hunger. Her hands were behind his head and her fingers in his hair. He responded clumsily, searching for the buttons on her blouse. She laughed at the effort.

'Let me help you.' Releasing herself from his arms, she unbuttoned her blouse. Her small breasts were conspicuously pale in the muted tones of the table lamp. She took him by the hand and led him to the bed. Her presence was like that of a desert wind sweeping across the evening dunes, bringing coolness to the heat of the day. The room dazzled with expectancy. Then she unfastened her skirt. It fell to her ankles and she stepped out of it.

Suddenly nothing mattered – not the Green Door, the Revolution or the screwed up mess that was his life. Nothing, except this strange girl standing naked in front of him.

Chapter Fourteen

They lay together, their bodies intertwined. Her head was propped on one elbow and the sheet had slipped down, exposing her breasts. He ran his fingers across her shoulders where her brown hair rested gently and remembered thinking how she gave herself to everything she did. It was with this same passion that she had made love.

'Why has it taken so long to find someone I want to be with again, Mallory?' She pushed a strand of hair away from her face. 'I thought it would never happen.'

Words spoken in a strange golden half-light. Did she really mean what she was saying? And did it really matter? For now it was enough just to feel her closeness, her breath on his face and the freshness of her scent. Not really knowing how to answer the question, he closed his eyes. She touched his face gently with her fingers.

'What are you thinking?'

It was a time for truths. He took a deep breath before he spoke. 'That first night, when I found you, I thought of every way I could to get rid of you,' he said, opening his eyes. 'The following morning when I left for work, I'd hoped you'd be gone before I came back.'

'And now?'

He thought about the question carefully before answering it, finding words he knew would please her. 'Now I cannot imagine being without you.' Was this a confession in the dark or would it be different in the harsh reality of daylight? Somehow he knew this was not to be. Something had happened in this simple room beneath the cheap print of Modigliani's mistress. And there was no going back.

She laughed, not at him but with him. 'Is that because we have made love?'

'Not just that,' he said, shaking his head. 'You are a wonderful, wicked and enigmatic woman!'

'So you like me *énigmatique*,' she said, accentuating the word with her French accent. She was laughing again with that delicious, wild laugh. 'Do you also like me wicked?'

This time he did not laugh. The awkwardness of the first encounter was behind them. 'I like you in whatever way you want to be,' was all he said, 'just not like the first night.'

She placed her fingers on his lips. 'No more talk of this,' she said, 'at least not for now.'

He removed her hand from his mouth. 'Whisky? I have a good malt.'

'Not for me – it gave me a terrible headache the other night.'

Mallory suddenly remembered the basement bar, where he had taken Madeleine that first night. 'Anything else?'

'No thanks.' She sat up in bed. 'Can I have the bathroom?'

The night was beautiful. The rain had disappeared and the moon was trying to enter the room. A single star appeared above the Victorian tenement across the street. The bathroom door was open. He lay back on the bed and listened to her softly humming 'Plaisir d'Amour'. Water splashed the glass shower screen and the steam cast a mist over the mirror that hung above the washbasin. He could see the faint outline of her body. Then she stepped out of the shower. Her back was to him and he watched her towel herself dry.

73

'Bathroom's all yours,' she said, walking over to the bed and kissing him lightly on the cheek.

'You are so very beautiful, Madeleine.'

'You make me feel beautiful. But now I am famished.'

How easily she changed her moods. What was so important a minute ago was unimportant now. Love, food – human emotions – primeval existence. The thoughts engrossed him. He turned on the shower and let the hot water scald his skin. Then he switched the tap to cold. The freezing temperature rejuvenated his body. It felt good to be alive. The thought was still on his mind when he walked back into the room.

She was sitting at the window staring pensively at the street below. 'Mallory, what is happening to us? Could I be in love?'

In spite of what he had said some hours ago, the words took him by surprise. How easily they slipped off her tongue. Yet there wasn't the slightest trace of ambiguity in her voice. Love! Just a minute ago we were asleep, each in a world of our own, and now this, Mallory thought. 'Nonsense, we barely know each other!'

'What has time to do with it?'

'But love…?' There was the hint of sadness on his face. Could these romantic notions on empty nights really transport them to places of dreams? He smiled gently at the girl. 'We have slept together and yet we know so little about each other,' he said softly, pulling the T-shirt on over his head. The soft glow of a street lamp, its light refracted through the glass, reached out to touch the room and dispel the shadows. 'Perhaps it is the wine that intoxicates us?'

'You are playing with words. Don't make fun of me! I know how I feel.'

He looked at her from across the room, from the table where he now sat. 'I would never make fun of you. I only questioned your vulnerability.'

She picked up the bottle. 'I want to be with you – all of the time,' she said, ignoring his explanation and pouring the wine. The last of the bubbles rose up from the base of the glass

74

and disappeared at the top. 'Is it wrong to feel this way?'

The Russian's words were on his mind. A warning in the dark. He tried to ignore them, but he was drawn again to the image of the girl with the many faces.

'I know you may not feel this way about me right now,' she said softly, interrupting his thoughts, 'but one day you will.'

How confident she was. And how easy it was to go along with her, to use words she wanted to hear, words that would move the world for her. 'Perhaps, one day.'

'I know you will.'

He smiled. 'Then you have the benefit of foresight, which I do not have.'

'You're making fun of me again! But I don't care for it, because there is something you do not know about me.'

'What's that?'

'I have the intuition of a gypsy.'

He sighed. 'Madeleine, please stop this nonsense. You think I treat your words with contempt? I'm sorry if that's how it appears. I was once a soldier; I have seen too much death and sorrow. So forgive me if I am a little cynical about love and happiness and all the wonderful words you use. I lost most of those things on the side of a hill in Mozambique.'

She walked across the room and knelt on the floor beside him, placing a hand on his thigh. 'I will teach you to forget the past, you vagabond from the bush with your cold heart.'

The words floated through the air like bubbles from a toy pipe, so fragile that were they to touch the lightest of objects, they would shatter. He laughed to cover his discomfort and put his hands on her head. Then he bent forward and kissed her. 'Come on now, enough of this silly talk – let's go to Vettriano's.' Then he saw it, that flash in her eyes. Was it fear or disappointment? It was only there for a second and then it was gone.

'Have you ever truly loved someone, Mallory? I mean loved someone in a way that you could not live without them?'

She was asking him about feelings he did not want to resurrect. 'Only once, many years ago.'

'So now you go into your shell like a tortoise, shutting yourself away and not letting anyone in – am I right?'

God, this woman with the instinct of a leopard. Next she would be telling him she could help him with his past, a past she knew nothing about.

'Am I right?'

What was there left to say? He glanced around the tiny room. It was scattered with meaningless objects that could all be packed into one suitcase should he ever need to move. Now here was this girl with the warm brown eyes, telling him she loved him and could help him, and the last thing he wanted to do was run. The small fibreglass figurine of a girl sitting cross-legged on the floor caught his eye. The sculpture had come from a stall on Portobello Road. He had bought it many years ago, because in a curious kind of way it had reminded him of Anna, the way she used to sit on the grass beside the mountain pool with her long blonde hair flowing down to her shoulders and her eyes squinting into the sun. In the days before the War.

'Mallory, speak to me.'

His hand was on her shoulder and his fingers played with the thin chain that hung around her neck as if the object was something to distract him from his thoughts. 'I don't want to talk about the past. I buried it a long time ago in the Zambezi Valley.'

'So how can I help you?'

'*How*? My God, Madeleine, you couldn't even if you tried; you know nothing of my past.'

The sigh was barely audible. She rose to her feet and strode across the wooden floorboards. The flat was too small to contain her restlessness. Cold air entered the room through the gap in the windowpane, like an unwelcome stranger. It made her shiver. She closed the curtain and then turned back to face him. 'When you love me…'

Not that word again, he thought. Used so easily. How many times had it been spoken in this room and other rooms just like it? How many evenings spent in a world of uncertainty?

'When you love me completely, then you will no longer live in your past.'

My God, if it could only be so. Perhaps she really could see it all by gazing into her crystal ball. He looked at the girl who transformed the ordinary things in life into something extraordinary and for just a moment he no longer saw the past. It slipped away like an old coat he had shed and he felt young again, as though he was going with a girl for the first time. A girl who had asked for nothing but his love.

Chapter Fifteen

The proprietor at the little Italian restaurant on Globe Road recognised them immediately. He gave them the same table by the window. Outside, the pavements glistened from the early evening rain and discarded chip papers littered the streets, but Mallory saw none of this. The waiter hovered over the table with the wine list.

'A bottle of Pouilly Fume, sir?'

'You remembered!'

The waiter smiled. 'When you have worked with the public as long as I have, there are some things that one just knows. Besides, you are a couple one does not forget.'

'You are wasted serving tables, my friend – you should be in management.'

The waiter looked unperturbed. 'I was once, sir. But I am happier here.'

'You are a lucky man: contentment is richness above all other.'

The waiter smiled again. 'The Pouilly?'

Mallory looked across the table at Madeleine.

'How can we possibly drink anything else when this kind man has gone to so much trouble?'

'The lady has exemplary taste, sir.'

Mallory laughed at the conspiracy. The waiter pulled the cork and poured the wine; there was no need to taste it – he knew it would be good. How comfortable it all was, he thought. Like the old patchwork quilt his mother laid over his bed when he was a child. She had died when he was away at boarding school. His junior school master had brought him the news and when he'd started to cry the teacher had slapped him and told him to toughen up. That was how it was in those days. He certainly had toughened up, but he'd kept the quilt for many years. It was all he had left of his mother. But those were memories he'd rather not think about now.

The girl was looking at him. The glow of the candle was reflected in her eyes and the flame danced on her face. Hair, still glistening with moisture from the rain they had just walked through, rested gently on her shoulders. She picked up her glass.

'*Santé,* Mallory.'

The smile on her face was all embracing. How easy it was, sitting here in this ordinary little room, a room that was in need of renovation but, in spite of this, Mallory couldn't think of any other place he'd rather be. And it was the girl who made it so. He touched her glass. '*Santé,* Madeleine.'

Her brows were furrowed in pensive thought. She looked into her wine glass before speaking again. 'Tell me more about your Africa,' she whispered softly.

'What do you want to know?'

There was a guilty look in her eyes and she appeared as a naughty child that had been caught out at some indiscretion or other. 'I have a confession.'

Mallory laughed. '*You*? A confession?'

'I'm being serious!' She took a sip of wine as if the very act of doing this would give her the nerve to blurt out her misdemeanour. 'When you were out this morning, I cleaned the flat. I was dusting the shelf...' She hesitated.

'Go on,' Mallory said, sensing where this was going.

'I found your manuscript.'

He laughed. 'Is that it?'

'I read a part of it.' She said this without looking at him. Her cheeks had turned an enchanting red. 'Please don't be angry.'

For a moment he said nothing. Then, reaching over, he took her hand and kissed the palm. It still carried a faint hint of Aramis. 'How can I be angry with you? You, who make me forget everything that is unbearable in this life?' He frowned. 'Anyway, it's just words on a page, nothing more.'

She sat bolt upright. 'That's not true!'

He looked at her with a seriousness and spoke softly. 'Do you read much?'

'Whenever I get the chance. It is an escape for me.'

'Then you will know that what I have written is mere self-indulgence.'

'Your descriptions are beautiful,' she said forcefully, banging her glass down on the table. 'You bring words to life.'

He blinked his eyes to dispel the wetness. She had drawn him in, like a fisherman and he was unable to resist her mastery. 'It is good of you to say that.'

'So, instead of walking the streets at night and drowning your troubles with drink, you can write,' she said, squeezing his fingers. 'I'll be singing at the club. And then in the morning I will come over and make your breakfast and we can spend time together.'

Mallory smiled. She had it all planned out. But although her intentions were good, he wasn't sure he wanted their relationship turned into a suburban drama. He put his glass down. 'You're starting to sound like a wife.' No sooner had he spoken the words, than he regretted them. He saw again the brief flash of anguish in her eyes. And he recriminated. Why did he say words that hurt her when all she gave him in return was love? Why was he so bloody cynical and frightened of forming a relationship? She still held his hand. He raised her fingers to his face. 'I'm sorry – I shouldn't have said that.'

She was about to respond when the waiter returned to take their order.

'Shall we have the same as before?'

'The *penne all'arrabbiata* and the carbonara?'

'What an incredible memory you have, my friend – I'm really quite worried about you!'

'It is like I said, sir, some tables are easier than others.'

'Then we'll have another bottle of the Pouilly, please.'

'Of course, sir.'

'The waiter has a much better memory than you!' Madeleine said, as he left the table. 'Now, let's start again shall we? Tell me more about Africa and how you came to be in England.' She gave him a wink. 'If you can remember.'

He poured the last of the wine before turning the bottle upside down in the ice bucket. 'You already know about my life as a lawyer?'

'Only briefly.'

'Then I suppose I should go back further.' He put down his glass and wiped the wetness from his lips with the back of his hand. 'Let's see – it was 1965. Ian Smith, our prime minister, was having problems holding down the blacks so he declared UDI.'

'UDI?'

'The Unilateral Declaration of Independence, they called it. Basically he was shutting us off from the outside world. But more than that, it was a declaration of war.'

'So if you were black, you didn't have any say in your country?'

'Smithy blamed it on communism. The TV, newspapers – they all told us we were fighting to stop the spread of Russian and Chinese influence across Africa. Every able-bodied male between the ages of seventeen and fifty-nine was called up to join the army. I'd spent the previous five years defending Africans in court. Now I was expected to shoot them on sight.'

'And you thought you were justified in fighting this war?' Madeleine's eyes were wide open in shock. 'Because of communism?'

'It was the greater evil. At least that's how we saw it. Like many Rhodesians, I was just another soldier brainwashed by a

81

system that had no foundation. But the writing was on the wall; we were never going to win this war – there were too many African fighters willing to die for their rights and, aside from South Africa, we were alone, without a friend in the world.' Mallory's eyes were somewhere beyond the street window, beyond the damp pavements and the matchstick figures walking by in their own little worlds. He was back in the bush, back in an Africa he thought was buried forever. He shook his head, subconsciously trying to dispel the images. Why the hell was he resurrecting all this shit? Was the girl right? If talking about the past was the only way to get rid of it, then should he not go there? Madeleine sat quietly, watching him struggle with his demons. 'There was nothing I could do about the war so I guess I just got on with it.'

'When was this?'

'August '72.'

'1972; I was at the convent then.'

He smiled at the thought. She'd been just a child when he was fighting for his life. 'After six months up at Nyanga on the Mozambique border, I was sent to a vast area in the south of the country, known as the Zambezi Valley. Our task was to capture terrorists crossing the river from Zambia and persuade them to work for us.'

Madeleine sensed the tension. She picked up the packet of Camel from the table and lit up two cigarettes. 'Go on,' she said gently, passing him one.

'We were on patrol along the Mbera River, in the Mana Pools reserve, when we walked into an ambush.' His lips tightened. 'One minute we were strolling in the sunshine as if we were on safari, the next we were getting shot to pieces. When I regained consciousness, I realised I'd taken a bullet in the shoulder and had lost a lot of blood.'

'I was going to ask you about the scar.'

He thought of where they had been just a few hours ago and how she had gently run her hand over the old wound. 'An inch or so to the left and I wouldn't be here now. Fortunately, after

82

the initial hit, the terrorists disappeared back across the river and we managed to get a K-car to do a case-vac.'

'K-car?'

'Killer cars, helicopters. They got me out and I spent the next three months recuperating in a Salisbury hospital. When I was pronounced fit for light duty I was assigned to an interrogation unit called G2, on the Mozambique border – as a guard. Those were the worst days of my life.'

An old couple, sitting in the corner, were arguing about the fish and whether it had bones. Mallory wanted to go over to their table and tell them that all fish had bones but instead he just smiled to himself because their petty argument paled into insignificance against his story.

'I thought my life was bad, but compared with yours…'

When the waiter appeared with the food, Mallory took one last deep draw from his cigarette to ease his nerves and then extinguished it in the ashtray. Picking up the glass that had just been replenished, he drank from it slowly. 'Just a different kind of evil. What they would do to the Africans when they interrogated them … their cries for help are still in my head. The only consolation was that I couldn't see what was happening.'

For the next few minutes they ate in silence. Mallory thought of Umtali and G2 and what his life had become. Then he put his fork down and spoke again without being prompted. His voice carried such sadness. 'One day they brought in what they called a "high-profile prisoner" and I was ordered to stand guard inside the cell. It was the first time I had witnessed an interrogation…' Biting down hard on his lip, he shook his head. 'There were four men torturing an African. He was naked and tied to a wooden board with electric cables attached to his body.' He stopped speaking and looked away.

'Mallory, unless you get this terror out of your head you will never be free.' Her voice was sharp.

He shut his eyes tight. 'The guerrilla shackled to the bench was Julian.'

83

'Who's Julian?'

'Julian Chikembe. I'd represented him six years before on a trumped-up terrorist charge.' He picked up the wine glass and drained it in one mouthful. Above Madeleine's head was a spotlight. The intense white beam reminded him of the naked electric lamps hanging from the ceiling in the interrogation room. They highlighted the blood-splattered, breeze-block walls. He could see again the meat hooks in the ceiling. And the iron shackles. But in a strange kind of way, it was the smell of stale cigarette smoke and the sadistic grin on the officer's face that he found most difficult to wipe from his mind. He gripped the empty glass with bloodless hands.

She reached across the table and took the glass from his hand. 'What did they want?'

'Information … guerrilla camps and troop movements.'

'Did he tell them?'

'Not a word. No matter how much they tortured him, he would never give them anything. Shit, I could have told the bastard that he would rather die than talk.' He laughed bitterly. 'Next thing I know, the guards are dragging a woman into the cell. I recognised her immediately; she'd been on trial with Julian. Her name was Mary Madiba. The last time I'd seen her was at a shebang, in the African compound outside Bulawayo.'

'A shebang?'

'A drinking den. Julian and I were noisy and drunk, celebrating the trial victory and his freedom. Mary never drank. She had sat by our side, as serene as the still waters of the Okavango. But in the cell everything was different. She was terrified for her life. They stripped her naked and tied her to a bench beside Julian, shackling her legs apart. On the floor beside the bench was a brazier with a smouldering poker.' Madeleine's face suddenly contorted. '*Oh Dieu nous aide*,' she said, putting her hand over her mouth to stifle a screech. Mallory closed his eyes. He could see again the officer walking around the bench where the woman was shackled.

And he heard the words directed at Julian. They were always in his head. "Okay, you fucking Kaffir. This is your last chance before we *braai* your woman." His face, cloaked in hatred, was the epitome of evil; a white man feeding on prejudice, treating Africans as though they were sub-human.

Madeleine sat completely still. Her face was white but she was determined to hear him out. 'What happened, Mallory?' she whispered.

Suddenly he realised that she, too, had seen her fair share of violence, which made it easier to share his story. 'I kept willing Julian to tell them what they wanted to know, but he stayed silent. Then the officer shouted, "*Braai* the *fokking* Kaffir." The corporal took the poker out of the brazier and held it between Mary's legs. She was screaming and begging Julian to help her but he refused to talk.' He rubbed his hand across his brow and looked up from the table with eyes that reflected the past. 'Unless I intervened, Mary was going to die.'

Madeleine seemed bewildered. 'Oh my God, what did you do?'

Mallory glanced across the room. The old couple were now arguing about the bill, and he shook his head at the irrelevance of it all. 'I ordered them to drop their weapons and untie the prisoners.'

'Did they?'

He smiled sardonically and nodded. 'They heard me release the safety catch on the SLR. It was only the corporal standing near me who wanted to play the hero. I floored him with my rifle butt when he went for his gun. The others did as they were told. Then we tied them up with their own ropes. Just as I was about to gag the officer, he turned to me and shouted – and I'll never forget his words – "You'll swing for this, you fucking wog-loving traitor!".'

For a moment the girl could not speak. Then she whispered, 'Did you kill him?'

Mallory picked up his glass. The sickness rose in his gut. 'I tried to. Julian held me back after I'd smashed the rifle butt into the bastard's face. His hand was on my shoulder. I can still remember his words: "It's not worth it, *nkozi*. You have already crossed the line. Do not add murder to the charge or you will live with it for the rest of your life".'

'*Nkozi*?'

Mallory let out a sigh of relief. All the horrors of the story and here she was, merely cutting through the conversation with a simple question. He wanted to laugh, but he couldn't. 'It means "important man". But I didn't feel important. Mary was slumped in the corner of the room with her back to me, getting dressed. Even that seemed ironic. Then Julian spoke again. And the words struck fear into my heart – "Come, *nkozi*, you cannot stay here now." He was right; I was well and truly in the shit. A court martial, Chikurubi prison and then the gallows. It wasn't an option. So we ran.'

Mallory was silent for a moment while he recalled the night he had escaped with Julian. It was dark and in the distance he could see the campfire where the infantry soldiers slept. And he knew where the guards were positioned around the perimeter of the camp. After locking the door of the cell, the three fugitives had disappeared into the bush. Nobody would discover what had happened until they changed the guard the following morning. And then all hell would break loose.

Madeleine frowned. She was clearly trying to comprehend his actions. 'When you say you ran, where did you run to?'

'We crossed the border into Mozambique.' He picked up the packet of Camel and offered one to the girl. His hands were shaking. Trying to hold them steady, he cupped the match and watched Madeleine draw on the cigarette. The melancholy sounds of a woman singing to the accompaniment of an accordion carried across the room. The cigarette was bitter on his lips. He ignored the taste and drew deeply, holding the nicotine in his lungs. When he exhaled, his body relaxed and his shoulders slumped. A hazy blue smoke encircled the flickering candle, throwing iridescent shadows across Madeleine's face.

She held his hand. 'But what about your family and friends back home – where are they?'

'There is no one back home.' The waiter cleared the plates and Mallory ordered the coffee. 'My folks died when I was a kid.'

'My mother also died when I was young.' She spoke without emotion. 'So tell me; why did you come to England?'

The scrape of chairs. The old couple got up and moved towards the door. The waiter was quickly by their side to help them out of the restaurant. They mumbled their thanks and then suddenly the room was quiet again.

'Sorry, you were saying?'

'I was asking how you came to be in England.'

'The security forces had set up a manhunt for me in Rhodesia. South Africa was also dangerous. So we escaped across the mountains into Mozambique. Then on to England.'

'But why England?'

'Apart from Swahili, English is the only language I speak. And London was far enough away from Africa.' His mouth was dry from talking. There really was not much more he wanted to tell the girl. He certainly did not want to reveal his escape route from Africa. It was something he had never disclosed to anyone, not even Andrei.

He could still vividly remember the dusty road across Mozambique to Beira, bouncing around in the back of an old *bakkie*, amongst the Africans and the chickens. He'd been accompanied by one of Julian's lieutenants, who'd dropped him at Sofala. The tiny village was once the chief seaport of the Monomotapa kingdom. But now it was all different; the shifting sands of the estuary had allowed the sea to reclaim much of old Sofala, leaving it flanked by a mangrove swamp, replete with stagnant waters and malarial mosquitoes. It was from this obscure village south of Beira that he was picked up by a fishing boat, which took him up the coast to Mombasa. Here, in the dead of night, he was transferred to an Arab dhow that was sailing to the Yemen. He had no passport,

87

only a slip of paper signed by a ZANLA commander, with the names of several contacts in each port. It was difficult to believe he was travelling the well-worn liberation army's escape route to the West with a document signed by a terrorist. But he had no other choice. It was his passport to freedom. The most difficult part of the operation had been getting into England. Three days after leaving the Yemen, a freighter flying the Somalian flag had passed the Cumbrian coast on its way to Scotland to deliver its cargo of dates. Just south of Ayr, in a place known as Culzean Bay, stood a lonely fisherman's cottage. It was from here that a strobe light flashed a Morse code message to the freighter. Then an inflatable dinghy was dropped overboard and Mallory was left on the pebble beach. Two days later, he was driven down the back roads of England to a safe house in London's East End.

Julian's debt had finally been repaid.

The girl's voice interrupted his thoughts. 'You told me earlier that you were here illegally. Now I think I understand.'

Mallory nodded and remained silent while the waiter brought the coffee to the table.

'A complimentary brandy, sir?'

'Thanks,' Mallory said, gesturing to Madeleine, who shook her head. 'You are right, of course,' he said, when the waiter had departed, 'we have lived a similar life.'

'What do you mean?'

'No passports or papers,' he said slowly, relieved at last to have moved the subject away from the War, 'at least not for me.'

'Nor me.'

'But at least you have hope,' he said, watching the waiter clear the last of the empty plates from the tables.

'What do you mean, hope?'

It was what he'd tried to tell her the other night, when she was asleep. 'If the Green Door releases you from your contract we're going to request that they return your passport.'

'*My passport! Mon Dieu*, Mallory, you don't know how much that would mean to me.' She shook with excitement at the prospect. 'I did not even dare to dream I would ever see it again.'

Mallory picked up the glass and poured half the brandy into his coffee. He breathed deeply in an effort to remain calm. The burnt-down candle threw its last shadows across the table and he sipped the remainder of his brandy from the glass. It tasted of apple orchards blessed by the sunshine. Through the glass he could see Madeleine's shoulder-length brown hair. It was tousled where she had run her fingers through the strands. The wildness in her eyes reminded him of the spirit of a fish-eagle. It was a face he thought he knew well, but maybe not. It had the potential to love but also to hurt. He knew that once she had her passport, she would be free to pursue her life however she wanted. There would be nothing to fear, nobody to hide behind.

Oh God, what had he done?

Chapter Sixteen

It was three in the afternoon. A damp mist had descended on Lexington Street and umbrellas concealed the commuters' faces. Mallory glanced at Madeleine. She hid her feelings well. Was she happy that she no longer had to tout for business like the girls outside these establishments or did she feel pity for the ones who had fallen by the wayside? The Black Widow was one of the less salubrious joints on lower Lexington. A young girl plastered with make-up stepped forward and offered them a brochure, advertising specials. Madeleine smiled at her and accepted the single sheet of paper. 'Wouldn't have thought that was your sort of place,' Mallory said, a wisp of a grin on his face.

'I've worked in worse.' There was a hint of sadness in her voice.

Mallory immediately realised his mistake. It was a stupid remark. What must she be going through? The prospect of having to audition at one of London's top clubs must be daunting enough. But what if it all failed? Did she see herself back on the streets with the girl from the Black Widow, luring in the punters with promises of 'specials'? He reached for her hand and squeezed her fingers. 'How are you feeling?'

'A little nervous.'

The white face belied the truth. He squeezed tighter. 'It'll be fine.'

'It's my profession, Mallory,' she said, following him through the impressive stained glass double doors of the French Revolution.

This was upper Lexington. The club was deserted. Even without the clientele it was obviously a world away from the Green Door. Chic and stylish, the interior was decked out in glass and stainless steel reminiscent of the art deco period. A poster in the lobby caught Madeleine's eye: TONIGHT ONLY! CAN-CAN AND JAZZ PIANO. A FREE GLASS OF CHAMPAGNE WITH EVERY COVER. Through the next set of doors, a tasteful bronze statue of a nude lady looked out over a circular dance floor, around which were scattered perhaps forty tables. There were no windows in the room, which gave it a nocturnal ambience. Red floor lighting further imbued the setting with a touch of decadence. They were shown to a table away from the dance floor, but even in the darkened corner, Mallory recognised the Russian.

'Andrei! This is Madeleine.'

The Russian stood up and took the girl's hand, brushing each of her cheeks in turn with a perfunctory kiss. 'A pleasure, Mademoiselle.' He smiled confidently. 'Can I get you something to drink?'

'Just a still water, please.'

'And for you, Mallory?' He pointed to a bottle of Stolichnaya on the table and Mallory nodded. When he had poured the drinks, Andrei turned to the girl. 'So, Mallory tells me you are looking for work?' Madeleine nodded, her eyes taking in the room. Andrei sat down and indicated for the others to do likewise. 'Are you familiar with the club?'

Madeleine was about to respond when they heard footsteps and voices. It was Mitterrand. Fine wines had turned his nose and cheeks red, and lined his face with deep wrinkles. An immaculate Hackett Mayfair cashmere suit, which contrasted sharply with a jazzy tie, contained his portly figure. His long grey hair was swept back neatly from his high forehead and tied in a small

91

ponytail. The aura was that of a successful businessman, a reputation that was well-earned.

A black man in jeans, T-shirt and trilby followed a few paces behind Mitterrand. Short peppercorn hair, tinged with streaks of grey, belied his age. But it was his bright blue suede shoes and sauntering walk that caught Madeleine's attention. She moved her chair back from the table and crossed her legs. When the musician reached the stage, he sat down at the grand piano and began to play, loosening his fingers with a few melancholy jazz chords before moving on to more complicated pieces. He was good, really good. Suddenly Madeleine started to fidget with her hands. For the first time since they had entered the room she appeared nervous. Was it the plush surroundings, the Steinway or the accomplished pianist? Mallory suspected it was more the fact that she was out of her depth in such a prestigious club. As Mitterrand approached the table, she turned to Mallory.

'I'm frightened,' she whispered, pressing a hand to her chest.

He squeezed her free hand. 'You'll be fine.'

Mitterrand acknowledged Andrei and then signalled for the waitress behind the bar to bring him a bottle of mineral water. 'I never drink in the day,' he said, addressing Madeleine with a smile before kissing her on each cheek. 'So, you are the jazz singer? Andrei tells me that you are French.'

'*Oui*. I lived and worked in Paris before coming to England.'

'In clubs?'

She nodded again. 'Antibes, on the Left Bank.' She picked up her water glass. 'Perhaps you have not heard of it – it is very small.'

'Is Marco still there?'

'You know Marco...?'

The Frenchman's face was inscrutable. 'It's my business to know what goes on in Paris, Mademoiselle. If you sang for Marco, you must be good.' He stood up and took the girl's hand. 'Come; let me introduce you to Sam.'

The piano player extended his hand. It dwarfed Madeleine's slender fingers. The surprise registered on her face and Sam laughed. 'Ever'body amazed this nigger can play piano with such big chubby hands.'

She smiled softly, unfazed by the racist remark. 'Ray Charles could.'

'Ah Ma'am, surely you ain't ol' enough to know him?'

'I've only seen old movie clips.'

'I played with da man at Carnegie Hall, back in da late sixties. He had da figure to match da hands but jeez, could he play da piano. Ain't nobody like him?'

'He is,' Mitterrand said, directing his attention to the piano player with a mischievous smile. 'Sam worked with Ronnie Rawlings, the famous jazz club entrepreneur, at his revue club. That is, until I poached him. I'll leave you two to get acquainted.' He patted Sam on the shoulder before returning to his seat.

The musician smiled at the girl and broke into a funky medley. He finished it off by running his fingers rapidly across the keyboard. Then he noticed the girl's apprehension and the way she played with her hands. 'Don't you worry none, Missy,' he said. 'If you run off key I'll cover for you. You got anything special in mind?'

The jovial face immediately put Madeleine at ease. 'Tous Les Garçons Et Les Filles'?

Sam shook his head and reached for a music folder. 'Francoise Hardy – sorry Missy, not familiar with dat stuff. S'pose I coulda kinda improvise though. Anythin' else?'

'"Fever",' she hesitated. 'Or perhaps 'Blue Moon'?'

'I'll do them both.' Sam smiled, showing a wide mouth full of dazzling white teeth. 'What key do you want for "Fever"?'

'E chord?'

The pianist started to play the introduction to the song. He looked across to where Mitterrand was sitting and then back at the girl. 'Just come in whenever you're ready.'

Madeleine adjusted the microphone. Then she started to sing. Her voice was unusual – powerful and sad; a French accent tinged with a New Orleans earthiness.

Sam sat up, seemingly stunned by the unpretentious voice. He played from memory, watching the girl's face as she sung. It was as if they had been together all their lives.

In times of loneliness, Mallory would remember this moment. The melancholy in Madeleine's voice arrested the conversation at the corner table. Removing the packet of Camel from his shirt pocket, he offered them around. Both men declined. Then he turned back to the stage, his eyes again on Madeleine, and lit the cigarette. Her voice reached out across the dark room, mesmerising the tiny audience. Just for a moment he thought of the people walking the streets outside the nightclub who would never hear it. And he wanted to go out and shout to them to come in and listen to the amazing voice. But he didn't. Instead he just sat back and embraced the music, his head swathed in cigarette smoke. When she finished the number, Sam went straight into 'Blue Moon'. Again, the air was touched with sadness, but through it all flowed life. The girl had an uncanny way of making each of the men at the table feel like she was singing to them alone. Sam ran his fingers across the keys to signal the end of the song.

Mitterrand stood up and clapped. '*Charmant*, lovely! Perhaps something a little different?'

The girl spoke briefly to Sam and he started to play 'Santa Aqueda', a Basque gypsy song. It was a favourite of the men who fought in the Spanish Civil War. When Sam nodded, she broke into the song. Her voice was both stirring and rebellious. Then Sam stopped playing and she sang without accompaniment, as they would have done in the Basque hills. Each second she was on stage she seemed to grow in stature and confidence. Mallory realised then that he was seeing yet another face.

Andrei began tapping his feet. 'She's good,' he said to no one in particular, 'very good.'

94

'The best I have heard for some time,' Mitterrand agreed.

When Madeleine finished the number, the proprietor beckoned her over. Placing the microphone down on the Steinway, she thanked the musician.

'Da pleasure's mine, Missy. I'm a lookin' forward to workin' with you.'

'I don't have the job yet!'

Sam smiled that big white-toothed smile that reminded her of his namesake in her favourite movie, *Casablanca*. 'Dat's formality, Missy – I ain't never seen Christophe doin' such raptures.'

Madeleine smiled at the Southern American accent and kissed him on the cheek. Then she strolled across the room in her long strides, like she was walking into an imaginary wind. Even her hair seemed blown. She sat down across the table from Mitterrand, crossing her legs. The praise was not long in coming. It started with a small clap from Mallory, which was picked up by everyone around the table.

'*Magnifique*! Why did Marco ever let you go?' Mitterrand said.

She glanced at Mallory. 'It's a long story. Let's just say, it didn't work out.'

'Well, it's his loss. We can certainly use you on our late spot, between ten and two. Let's see, five days a week, eighty pounds a night? Would that be acceptable?'

Would that be acceptable? She would stand on her head singing for that much money. It was more than she had ever earned in her life. 'That's very generous of you, Mr Mitterrand,' she said, still looking slightly anxious. 'And all I have to do is sing?'

The Frenchman appeared puzzled by the question. 'Please, Mademoiselle, call me Christophe. Yes, that is all you have to do. And perhaps sign the odd programme for the customers.' He turned to the Russian and winked. 'Can I leave you to draw up a contract?'

'I'll have something in writing by the end of the week.'

'It's just so unbelievable! I have to thank you all so much.'

95

Mitterrand took her hand. '*Non, ma petite colombe*, it's us who should be thanking you. Now that the formalities are over, perhaps you could come in for a few hours in the afternoon next week, to practise with Sam – say, every other day?'

'Yes, yes, of course, whatever you want, Mr … Christophe.'

Mitterrand smiled and raised his hand. The waitress came over. 'A bottle of the Dom Perignon, please Claire, and four glasses.' For a man who only drank mineral water during the day, he certainly *was* making an exception, and an expensive one at that. He watched the champagne being poured and then raised his glass. '*Santé,* Mademoiselle Madeleine! To a long and happy relationship.' He had barely drunk half the glass before he was back on his feet, taking the girl's free hand. 'Please excuse us, gentlemen,' he said, leading her back over to the piano.

'Well, my friend,' Andrei said, turning to Mallory once the two were out of earshot. 'You can certainly pick them. I thought you said the girl was about to jump off the bridge?'

Mallory ignored the sarcasm. 'That's what I was trying to tell you yesterday – she isn't the same girl.'

'That I can see for myself; she has more confidence than a ring-master. But I also suspect there is a touch of the actress about her.'

'Her voice was as much a surprise to me as anyone.'

'Be careful, my friend; this is a Machiavellian woman.'

'*Machiavellian*?'

'Devious.'

Mallory frowned. 'You've said something like that before and I still have no idea what you're talking about.'

'Actually I think you do. You are from the bush, no? So you will understand that a lion does not eat grass.'

Mallory laughed at the metaphor. But this time it was forced. 'You're talking in riddles! Perhaps she appears that way to you because you do not know her. Behind the façade, she is vulnerable.'

The Russian was unmoved by the confession. 'She's anything but.' He loosened off his tie and opened the top button of his freshly laundered shirt. 'She has all of you eating out of her hand.'

'I still don't understand what you're saying.'

'Be careful, my friend.' He glanced towards the stage. Madeleine was standing beside the piano and laughing with Sam. 'The girl knows what she wants and she knows how to go about getting it.'

Mallory picked up his glass and finished the last of the champagne. His eyes were back on the stage. Was Andrei right? Madeleine had changed; there was little doubt about that. Her compelling allure was a potent attraction. And in that moment he knew that if he tried to keep her, he would lose her. But was it not already too late? Suddenly he felt the oppressive weight of the situation on his shoulders. 'Look, enough of this nonsense – I have to go. Any joy with the flat?'

'Oh, I almost forgot!' The Russian took a key from his jacket pocket and handed it to Mallory. 'When you've shown her the place, can you call by the office?' He paused for a moment while Madeleine ran through a scale with Sam. Then all of a sudden she burst into Gainsbourg's saucy love song 'Je t'aime … Moi Non Plus', replete with her own sound effects. Andrei's eyes grew wide and he turned to his friend. 'My God, whatever will she surprise us with next?'

Mallory burst out laughing. 'I didn't have you down for a prude, Andrei! Besides, Christophe is obviously impressed.'

'You are right, Christophe is smitten.'

'And yet you're not?'

Andrei put his glass on the table. 'We have women like her in Russia. Life makes them what they are. What they are not good at is playing happy families.'

Mallory laughed again. 'I can assure you, Mr Vadislav, that I have no intention of playing what you so eloquently describe as "happy families".'

'Good,' said the Russian, 'just remember: forewarned is fore-armed.'

Chapter Seventeen

The first-floor flat on Peter Street was in the Greek quarter of Soho, just a short walk from the Revolution. The dormer windows that nestled in the eaves overlooked a narrow lane that led away from the clubs and strip joints. Apart from a launderette and a book shop, the only other business on the street was a run-down Malaysian restaurant. Mallory unlocked the door and held it open for the girl. The hall was clean and the wooden stairs freshly painted. He gestured for her to lead the way. When they entered the flat, Madeleine gasped.

'Wow, it's tiny!'

She was already working her way round the lounge, touching the walls and the shelves, and giggling at the strange paintings left by the Italian waiter. Two steps down from the sitting area was a split-level extension that had been renovated and this now housed an open-plan double bedroom and bathroom. It was at least some compensation for the compact living space. Then he heard Madeleine laugh as she opened a pair of wide floor-to-ceiling cupboard doors to reveal a small gallery kitchenette. But it didn't seem to discourage her.

'Mallory, it's absolutely gorgeous!' she said, throwing her arms around his neck and kissing him. 'I'm going to have such fun remodelling the place.'

He looked around the room. 'Well, you won't exactly get lost in here!'

She threw back her head and laughed. 'It's big enough for me.' Then she took hold of his hand. 'Come – look at the bedroom.'

He followed her in. The bed dominated the space, which was otherwise plain and sparse. Although the flat lacked a woman's touch, to her it was a palace. Suddenly he was surprised by the way she had moved on. Just this very morning she'd been scared at the thought of having to leave his place and now here she was, planning a whole new life. Let her go, he heard himself say. Let her find her way. 'It's wonderful,' he said, with a forced smile.

'And so close to work! What more could I ask?'

'Perhaps a fresh coat of paint?'

'Can we? I can already see the colours: cream walls with blue and yellow fabrics for the curtains and the cushions.' She moved across to him and, standing on one leg, she kissed him. He held her in his arms. Beyond her head was the scruffy room. But already she saw it as her boudoir. He envied her that enthusiasm. There had been a time when he would have shared her excitement. But that was long ago. Then he felt her stir. She looked up.

'*Merci*, Mallory. This will be our *place de l'amour*.'

The words were whispered but he chose not to hear them. 'Look, I'm working on a case for Andrei but I'll have a bit of time in between the paperwork if you want a hand decorating?'

She stiffened at the mention of the Russian's name and pulled herself free from his arms. 'Why doesn't he like me?'

'Who?'

'Andrei.'

'What makes you say that?' he said, trying to shrug off the woman's intuition.

'The way he looks at me,' she said, closing the doors to the kitchenette, 'like I have just crawled out from under a stone.'

'It's your imagination. Andrei is the biggest male chauvinist I know.'

'Maybe he doesn't like that I take his best friend away from him.'

'What nonsense!' Mallory laughed out loud, although he was not altogether convinced. Like a chess player, she had manoeuvred him to where she wanted him on the board. 'You're not "taking me away" from anyone.'

The girl smiled. She had said her piece. It was enough. 'Mitterrand says I can start next week. I have my first rehearsal on Tuesday afternoon.' She pushed a strand of hair away from her face. 'And on Saturday I get my first wage. Can you believe that? My first wage! Real money! I want to take you out to dinner when we have finished the decorating.' She stood facing the window that framed the little lane and he thought she might very well be speaking to someone out there in the street below. 'Let's go back to Vettriano's.' Her high-pitched voice mirrored her anticipation. 'Or would you prefer somewhere different?'

'Vettriano's is good,' he said, speaking softly to her back.

'I'll ask Christophe for an advance on my wages so I can buy the paint. Then we'll start right away. *C'est bon*?'

Mallory followed her eyes. They were everywhere, no doubt conjuring up images of the grand design. He picked up his coat from the back of the chair. 'I have to go now.'

'So soon?'

'I need to drop by the office. Shall I see you back in Stepney Green?'

'Don't worry about me,' she said, her eyes surveying the room once again, 'I'm going to spend the afternoon dreaming of colour schemes and curtains. Can I keep the key?'

'Sure. It's all yours now,' he said, in a deadpan voice.

She hadn't picked up on the reticent response because her excitement knew no bounds. 'I still can't believe it.' Then she walked up to him and kissed his cheek. Cologne from the previous night still lingered on her skin. 'Don't leave me alone too long, Mallory.'

100

What a strange thing to say, he thought. But in spite of her request, he knew that she was already no longer with him. Her mind was elsewhere, in a place where he could not go. Something precious had been lost in the tiny room and for the first time he felt the pain. He turned to go. She was staring out of the window, oblivious to his departure. And it was there he left her, closing the door softly as he walked away. He did not look back.

Chapter Eighteen

All the lights were on in the Russian's office. Andrei put his pen down when Mallory entered the room. 'The flat is all right?'

'Perfect. It has given her a newfound energy.'

'That does not surprise me.'

'I feel I am losing her.'

Andrei stood up. 'We all have to move on in life sometime, my friend,' he said, picking up a glass from the sideboard. 'Better that it happens now. Vodka?' Mallory shook his head, but Andrei filled the glass anyway. 'You'll need this when you hear what I have to say. You might also want to alleviate yourself of the problem.'

'*Problem*? What problem?'

Andrei looked over his glasses at Mallory. 'The girl.' Then he sat back down in his chair and picked up the document he had been studying. 'I had a call when you were out, from David Fowler. At the Green Door.'

The scowl disappeared from Mallory's lips. So that's what Andrei meant when he said he would need a drink. He downed half the vodka and waited for the Russian to continue.

'He's not a happy man. They've been looking everywhere for the girl.' He took a cigar out of a silver box and offered it to Mallory. He shook his head and lit a cigarette instead. 'They have a contract out on her. I'm sorry.'

Mallory's face registered the shock. Everything had been going so well and now this. His mind suddenly flashed back, to the moment he'd fled the interrogation room in Zimbabwe to an uncertain future in a foreign land. After all the years of loneliness, he'd thought there was at last an expectation of something better. Now he was no longer sure. It didn't look that way when he left Peter Street. And it sure as hell wasn't looking any better now. '*A contract*?! Shit, that's a bit desperate.'

'We still have a lifeline.'

'Bodashka's statement?'

Andrei drummed his fingers on the desk and nodded. 'You and I are going to pay Messrs Fowler and Cavatore a visit. I'm thinking sooner rather than later – 4 p.m. tomorrow okay?'

At last. The showdown. The final piece in the jigsaw. Madeleine had a job and a flat. All she wanted now was her freedom. Would it bring them closer together? Somehow he doubted it. Were it not for Andrei, none of this would have happened and for just a moment he wondered whether it was a good thing. But it was too late to turn back. He looked at his mentor across the room and smiled gently. 'Will we need help?'

Andrei's eyes squinted and he paused for a moment. 'I don't normally resort to violence, but it might be prudent to have a couple of the boys along, just in case things get awkward. There's a newsagents across the road from the club – they could wait in there.' He lit his cigar and drew heavily on it. 'But I recommend that you leave your knob stick at home – maybe there's still a chance we can resolve this in a, shall we say, civilised manner.'

For the first time since leaving Peter Street, Mallory relaxed and smiled. 'You Russians are such gentle people.' In spite of his joke, he knew that over the years Andrei had faced many hopeless situations and yet he always seemed to overcome the obstacles. Nothing seemed to unsettle him. The man had an uncanny way of turning rocks into gold.

Andrei didn't return the smile. 'Is there anything else I need to know about the girl before our meeting tomorrow?' He was looking out across Soho. 'Something you have not told me?'

Mallory thought for a moment. If Madeleine was telling the truth, Andrei now knew everything. 'I'm sure we've got it covered.'

'Okay, good. The printer's on. Copy everything on this file? Then take it home and read it thoroughly.' There was a worried look on his face.

'Is that it?'

Andrei rested his cigar in the ashtray. 'Not quite. We have a small problem.'

Mallory raised one eyebrow.

'You have heard me talk of Enrico Tommaso.'

'The Sicilian?'

Andrei nodded solemnly. 'I had a call from Palermo shortly after speaking to the Green Door. Alberto Lagano died three hours ago. Tommaso is now the Don, the boss of the Omertà Syndicate.'

'What the hell is the Omertà?'

'The Code of Silence. The syndicate has tentacles that spread across most of Europe. The Green Door is just another one of their franchises.'

A shiver ran down Mallory's back. 'You seem to have kept the details of Tommaso well hidden. Why do I not know more about him?'

'My relationship with Tommaso does not concern you.' The Russian's tone was brusque.

That hurt. Mallory had always believed there to be no secrets between them and here was his friend, pulling a major player out of the hat. He needed to know more about the Sicilian gangster and where Andrei's loyalties really lay. No doubt he would find out soon enough. 'Jeez, Andrei, what the hell are you mixed up in?'

Andrei straightened up and regarded Mallory with disdain. Then his voice softened. 'We all help each other, my friend.' He paused. 'In Russia we have a saying: *Sud'ya predupredil kusat'ruku, kotoraya tebya kormit.* It means: do not bite the hand that feeds you.'

Chapter Nineteen

The shrill ring of police sirens shattered the silence. Madeleine shivered. She put down her book and peered out of the window. There was nothing happening in the street below that would attract the law, at least not that she could see. Then she looked around the bachelor pad. This room, she had told Mallory, she had come to love like no other. And up until today, it was all she had ever wanted. But now she had a job and a flat of her own. And as such, her aspirations had changed. Would this affect their relationship? She thought not. Although there was an age difference, he was at times so much like a child; almost more dependent on her than she was on him. And so easy to manipulate. The very thought clinched her decision; she would suggest they stay in for the night, rather than eat out.

On her way back from the supermarket she noticed a bright yellow cotton fabric displayed in an Indian haberdashery and she bought two metres. It would make a perfect tablecloth.

When everything was set and prepared, she undressed in the bathroom and turned on the shower. The mirror on the wall caught her figure. Stepping under the hot water, she ran her hands down her body, slowly caressing her skin. She knew how to make a man happy.

*

Enrico Tommaso was still on Mallory's mind when he walked into the room. The first thing he noticed was the new tablecloth and the table set for two. 'What's the occasion?' he said, dropping his briefcase on the floor and closing the door. From the look on her face he immediately realised his mistake. But then thankfully she smiled.

'Do you have to ask?'

He walked over and kissed her. The scent of the shower gel and the freshness of her body was a welcome relief after the dank Underground station. 'Sorry! I should know better. But really, Madeleine, the place looks wonderful.'

Her smile widened. 'I thought it would be nice to stay in – I'd like to cook you dinner.'

'I thought you wanted to go to Vettriano's.'

'I don't want to see anyone tonight. Except you.' Then, taking hold of his hand, she led him across to the settee. 'Now, sit down and let me get you something to drink. We'll save the Asti I bought for dinner – vodka okay?'

What had he been thinking of when he left the flat on Peter Street? It all seemed irrelevant now. He looked at the girl as if he was seeing her for the first time. The wide smile had turned mischievous and seemed out of character. For a moment he wondered if she'd been drinking. Or was it just her infectious exuberance? Dressed in a provocative skirt and a flimsy blouse, she was acutely aware of what she was doing, which made the anticipation all the more tangible. 'Vodka's good. Just a couple of ice cubes.'

'No lemon or tonic?'

'Good Lord, no! I drink my spirits like a Russian – neat.' The vodka reminded him of Andrei and tomorrow's meeting, but he decided not to tell the girl anything until after the outcome. He'd also leave reading the report until the morning.

'*Santé*,' Madeleine said, touching his glass. 'Thank you again. For everything.'

'You make your own luck – the audition was amazing.' He sipped the vodka and shuddered; maybe it was time to think about a mixer.

'Sam made it easy.'

'You're being modest.'

'Do you really think so?'

'You know so; Christophe was bowled over.'

Madeleine smiled and sat down. Then she put an arm around his neck. 'What about you?'

'I couldn't take my eyes off you. The way you sang "Santa Aqueda"; it was hauntingly beautiful.' Someone had once told him that praise to an artist was like water to a plant. But he couldn't remember where he'd heard it. Not that it mattered, because the girl had moved up close to him. She took the glass from his hand and placed it on the little side table. Then she pushed him back onto the settee. He did not resist but neither did he help her. When she had removed his jeans, she leant over him and unbuttoned his shirt. The smell of her body was driving him crazy. He started to get up and she pushed him back down again.

'Stay where you are.'

He did as she asked. She knew what she was doing; this had been her work for God knows how many years. But he didn't want to think of that now. She stood over him, one foot either side of his body. Her red, flimsy blouse was open and he could see that she wasn't wearing a bra. In her right hand, she held the glass of vodka. Slowly she lowered her body until she was sitting on his chest. Instinctively, his hands went to hold her, but she pushed them away and slapped him gently across the face.

'No touching until I tell you.'

'You're driving me crazy.'

'Open your mouth.'

He did as he was told. She watched him laugh and splutter as he tried to swallow the vodka. 'I don't do tonic,' he protested, once he'd got his breath back.

'Don't talk! Just drink.'

Her white pants were just inches from his face and his imagi-nation built the excitement. 'God, Madeleine, I want you.'

'Finish the vodka.'

He opened his mouth again and she poured in more of the spirit, letting it run over his face and onto the floor. When the glass was empty, she stood up and unbuttoned her skirt. The white pants looked almost dark against her pale skin. Then, hooking her fingers into the fabric, she slowly removed them. That was all it took. He reached up and pulled her into his arms. Nothing like this had ever happened to him before. And he knew it would never be the same again.

She lay on him, smiling in that strange way of hers as she looked into his eyes. 'Happy?'

He could smell her, touch her, and yet still she asked the ques-tion. He gave her a look as if to say, 'You know I am'.

'So do you love me now?'

Not that word again. In spite of his misgivings, he whispered the words she wanted to hear. 'I love you, Madeleine.' He was still unsure whether he really meant it and thought for a moment of Andrei; the Russian had very little time for love. He paid for girls. For an hour or so they made him feel like the sheik of a harem. To some degree, this had also been Mallory's life before Madeleine. But now it was all so different. Something had happened in that little room, culminating with those three simple words. They would forever be locked in his mind. And the enigmatic smile on her face told him that this was what she wanted to hear above all else. Then, just when he thought he could lie there forever, looking at her, she stood up and pulled on her pants.

'Can I leave you to put on some music and freshen up the drinks while I cook dinner? It'll be fifteen minutes or so.'

Mallory poured the vodka while Michael Nyman played the piano. The first track was the theme from the film *The Piano* and it carried with it the image of a wild and distant shore. Filling her glass with tonic, he then dropped in a slice of lemon and a couple of ice cubes.

'*Santé,* Madeleine. To dreams and distant homelands.'

'To us!' She looked at his glass and winked. 'No tonic?'

'You poured enough of it over me!'

A tempting smile played around at the corner of her lips. 'You didn't like it?'

He wasn't quite sure what she was referring to and he laughed to cover his embarrassment. 'It was wonderful.'

She stood barefoot in front of the cooker. All she wore was one of his T-shirts that barely covered her white pants. He put his arms around her waist and ran his hand over her stomach.

'Patience! I'll ruin the dinner,' she said, sprinkling grated Parmesan onto the pasta. 'Can you open the Asti? It's in the fridge.'

They sat at the table with the yellow cloth. Nyman's haunting piano music reached out across the room, carrying messages that each of them interpreted in their own way, and it seemed like there was nothing in the world but the two of them. A single candle burning on the pine table penetrated the darkness. Its glow shone in the girl's eyes when she looked at him. And there was a want that at first he did not recognise. Why him? She was years younger; trying to recapture a life lost to crime and prostitution. She could have anyone she wanted, anyone at all. He picked up his glass. The wine tasted of fields of gold touched by a Tuscan sun. And the bouquet of wild gooseberries and passion fruit spoke of places they had only dreamt of.

'Will you take me to Africa one day, Mallory? I want to see the sunsets you describe in your book. I want to walk through the bush and see the animals, especially the elephants. And I want to hear the lions roar. Then in the evenings we can sit by the river and watch fireflies dancing over the water. And I want to see all your old haunts, where you once walked with someone else.' She talked with such urgency, almost as if the words would be lost if not spoken, and it left her breathless. 'One day, when I have made a lot of money, I will pay for everything,' she said. 'You will be my safari guide.'

If only that could be true. Listening to her passion for his country, Mallory wanted to pick her up and put her on a plane straight to Zimbabwe – anything to escape the grime of the East End – but instead he just smiled. It was a sad smile which told of his doubt that it would ever happen.

Chapter Twenty

The Green Door was a converted Victorian hosiery factory. In the daylight, it looked exactly what it was: a run-down shit-hole of a place. The suffering and degradation of Victorian girls, slaving sixteen hours a day at a loom, seemed no different to the humiliation the prostitutes endured behind its closed doors today. In the newsagents across the road an old lady was loading her shopping into a trolley. The Indian shopkeeper had one eye on her and the other on the two men idly flicking through the magazines. Neither of them appeared to be interested in what they were reading. The large electric clock above the counter showed that it was a quarter to four. Mallory walked in and bought *The Times*. There were two chairs and a small metal table on the pavement outside the shop. It was where the Indian sat and drank his tea when business was slow. He took a seat and had just started to read the headlines when a black cab pulled up. Andrei stepped out. He handed the driver a large note and indicated for him to keep the change.

'Good afternoon, Mallory,' he said, 'as punctual as ever I see.'

'Your men are inside,' Mallory said, nodding towards the shop.

The Russian sat down at the table. 'Are they that obvious?'

'Wearing trench coats and flicking through *People's Friend*?' I'd say so!'

111

Andrei laughed. 'It's of no consequence.' He glanced over his shoulder. 'I've been through the notes – I don't think we will need them. Do you have the file?' Mallory handed over the contents of his briefcase, including the large brown Manila envelope. 'Have you read it all?'

'First thing this morning.'

'And?'

'I'd rather eliminate the bastards than negotiate with them.'

'That is not an option.'

'So what do you have in mind?'

'The offer on the table is to buy the girl out of her contract.'

'If that doesn't work?'

'Then I'll hit them with Bodashka's statement!' The Russian fidgeted in his chair; there was clearly something on his mind. 'Remind me, has anyone from this club seen you here before?'

'Only the client I knocked about the night I met Madeleine. But it was dark and I doubt he'd recognise me. There was no one else around.'

'And you have never been in the club?'

'You know me better, Andrei.'

'Good. Just one further point: when we're in there, don't talk unless I ask you a specific question relating to the case.'

Mallory sat back in his chair and folded up the newspaper.

The Russian then stood up and glanced at the open door of the newsagents. Half raising his hand to the men in the shop, he then beckoned Mallory to follow him. They crossed the street to the nightclub. An unlocked iron grill covered the front of a heavy wooden door. Andrei pressed the bell once and waited patiently. The door eventually swung open and they were confronted by an enormous black man. His head was shaved and tattoos, depicting what appeared to be some kind of strange African art, covered his bare muscular arms. Mallory tensed. His heart was racing, his body alert. In spite of this, he forced himself to relax.

'Mr Vadislav?'

A horrific scar ran down the side of the man's face but it was the eyes that held Mallory's attention. Notwithstanding the psycho at G2, they were without doubt the coldest he had ever seen. And this was the bastard that they would have used to intimidate Madeleine. He shivered. Andrei saw none of this and nodded in reply to his name.

'Arms in the air please,' the black man said, frisking them down. Satisfied that neither man was armed, he indicated for them to follow him down the steps. They were shown through to a dark room, lit only by a series of dimmed wall lights. The smell of beer, body odour and cigarettes was disguised with cheap disinfectant. The direction led them past several podiums, each topped with a vertical steel pole and some kind of safety net. Mallory felt sick to his guts when he thought of Madeleine and what she would have had to do in here. Beyond the long bar was a heavy oak door and above it a CCTV camera. The doorman knocked. A light glowing red changed to green and the lock mechanism clicked. Two men were sitting at a makeshift desk. In front of them was a bottle of Jack Daniels and a couple of tumblers. The fat man in an ill-fitting suit looked up.

'Shut the door, Mo, and wait outside.'

The accomplice, poker-faced and dressed in pinstripes, was obviously the heavy. He said nothing but the bulge under his suit spoke of a weapon. One hand held his glass while the other was hidden from view. Mallory glanced at Andrei.

The Russian's face was perfectly composed; he could very well have just arrived at a dinner party. 'Mr Fowler – it's been a long time.' He extended his hand to the fat man. 'Where is Mr Cavatore?'

Fowler's face was expressionless, his forehead covered in perspiration. He stood up to return the handshake. 'He's away,' he said, his pig-like eyes assessing Mallory.

'Ah, this is my assistant, Mr Mallory.'

Fowler merely nodded. A neatly trimmed grey beard covered half of his face, disguising his soft, flabby chin and any warmth that might have existed in his features. 'Please sit down,' he said, indicating the chairs in front of the desk. 'A drink?'

Andrei shook his head. Mallory wanted one desperately but he too declined the offer.

'So, Mr Vadislav,' Fowler said, taking his seat behind the desk, 'you have something we want very badly.' The high-pitched voice was almost feminine, but there was a hard, no-nonsense edge to it. He was obviously not one to indulge in small talk.

The Russian smiled thinly. 'If you're referring to Miss Laurent then yes, I am aware of her whereabouts. But I do not "have" her, as you suggest. I am merely here to *represent* her.'

'The girl owes me money.'

Andrei relaxed into the chair and crossed his legs. 'The last time I defended you, Mr Fowler, I made it quite clear that I would only represent you on the understanding that you cease all involvement in sex trafficking.'

Fowler threw his arms into the air, a look of pure disdain on his face. '*Sex trafficking*? What the fuck are you talking about? That's not our game.'

'The girl tells me otherwise.'

For just a moment Fowler's self-righteous mask dropped and the cruelty was plain to see. It twisted his mouth, his nostrils flared and his face turned white with fury. 'She's a fucking liar and a cheap slut! I try to help her and this is how she repays me?' The Russian remained quiet. 'What the hell has she been telling you?'

'Mr Fowler, let's cut the bullshit.'

Mallory flashed a look at the heavy. His left hand was on his lapel while the right hand was undoing the button on his jacket. Shit, was the bastard going for his shooter? He sized up the desk – it was free standing and would be easy to overturn. Carefully, so as not to attract attention, he eased his chair closer to the target.

Fowler glanced at the heavy. A telepathic message flashed between the pair of them and the bodyguard removed his hand from his lapel. 'That bitch of a woman – she's been nothing but trouble.'

'Then you'll be more than happy to be rid of her.'

Suddenly Fowler's attitude changed and in this controlled state he appeared even more dangerous. 'What is your interest in Miss Laurent, Mr Vadislav?'

Andrei bristled at the change in tone. 'As I mentioned earlier, she is my client.'

'So, now she has money for barristers. Money the whore owes me.'

'You are well aware that she has no money.' He paused. 'And I take it you use the word "whore" figuratively.'

Fowler pushed his chair back from the desk and picked up the whisky glass. 'You seem to be going to a lot of trouble for Miss Laurent. Perhaps you do not know her as we do,' he said, playing with the whisky. 'She enjoys her work much more than you realise.' He patted his trousers and leered. 'I should know; I've been there often enough.' A wide grin replaced the lascivious smirk, revealing a mouth full of nicotine-stained teeth.

Mallory gripped the arms of his chair. It took all of his restraint to remain seated; he would have liked nothing more than to smash Fowler's pig-like face. But what would that achieve? Instead, he took out a Camel and lit up. It was a few minutes before he was able to calm down. Then he thought of the previous night; Madeleine certainly knew what she was doing there. So was he just another client? Surely she wouldn't ... *would she*?

Andrei furrowed his eyebrows at Mallory, signalling for him not to do anything foolish. Then he spoke. 'Mr Fowler, we are both busy men. I have no intention of taking up any more of your time than is absolutely necessary.' He glanced across at Mallory again. 'I have a proposition that I feel will suit both parties admirably.'

Fowler's eyes shifted between the barrister and the door, or rather whoever was behind the door. Then the heavy moved forward in his chair. His hand was on his lapel again.

'Yes?'

'There is obviously a difference of opinion as to what debts Miss Laurent has incurred and in what manner she is to repay them.'

'Her wages repays her debt.'

'Wages for what?'

'She's a fucking singer! And not a very good one at that.'

Andrei showed no signs of being ruffled. He took a deep breath and calmly spoke again. 'What I propose is that you release the girl from any future obligation she may have with you.'

'Impossible. She–'

'Hear me out.' The Russian's voice was cold and hard. 'You are well aware of my concerns regarding sex trafficking?'

'How dare you, I–'

'I asked you to hear me out, Mr Fowler.'

You could hear a pin drop. This is where the shit hits the fan, Mallory thought, sitting on the edge of his seat.

Fowler looked fit to burst; the veins on his forehead throbbed and he closed his eyes before draining his whisky. This was clearly not the way he was used to conducting his business negotiations. But then he was well aware of the relationship between Vadislav and Tommaso. The barrister had the upper hand and it was not to his liking. 'Forgive the interruption, Mr Vadislav,' he eventually said, in a somewhat more subdued tone.

Andrei bowed his head, satisfied that the moment of confrontation had passed. 'As I was saying, Miss Laurent no longer wishes to remain in your employment and neither of us would want to force her to do anything against her will, now would we?'

Fowler poured another shot of whisky – he was clearly having trouble controlling his frustration. 'Your proposal, Vadislav.'

'I suggest that we settle Miss Laurent's account with a cheque in your favour to the tune of one thousand pounds. This will no doubt cover your expenses until you can find a replacement singer – you did mention she wasn't up to standard, so I'm sure she won't be missed.'

'If you think a grand will cover her debt, you must be fucking crazy.'

'Am I correct in assuming you are referring to the money her boyfriend owed you, for the heroin your associates supplied to him?'

'I don't know shit about any bloody dope. The bitch is lying through her fucking teeth!'

'Well, that is by the by. What I am far more interested in today is your undertaking that you will not proceed with any further action against Miss Laurent. This includes dropping the contract that you have out on her.'

'Contract? Where are you getting this shit from?' Fowler said, feigning surprise.

'It's of no consequence.' Andrei had clearly had enough of the obnoxious sycophant. 'Look, Mr Fowler, I don't really care much for the way you run your business. And I'm certainly not interested in your past history, or how Miss Laurent incurred this debt. We both know where we stand; I wouldn't want to resort to other means of persuasion.' He removed his cheque book from the inside pocket of his suit jacket. Then, reaching over the desk for the Manila envelope, he passed a single sheet of paper across to the nightclub owner. 'Miss Laurent's letter of notice to quit. Your signature at the bottom of the page, where it is marked with a pencil cross, will note your acceptance of her resignation. If you'd be so kind.'

Fowler picked up the legal document and read it slowly. He then reread it. Mallory knew what was in the document. He suspected, however, that whatever contract Madeleine did have with the Green Door – indeed if there was even such an agreement in existence – would have been obtained under duress. Fowler's lips remained tight and the veins still throbbed in his forehead. He shifted uncomfortably in his seat, clearly hesitant about his next move. Then he picked up a pen, signed the letter and handed it back to the barrister, who finally passed it over to the heavy to witness.

After Mallory had counter-signed and witnessed, Andrei opened his cheque book. 'I hardly need to remind you that what you have just signed is a legally binding document. If anything should happen to Miss Laurent – accident or otherwise – her case history will come to the attention of Scotland Yard's Specialist Crime and

Operations department. They might also like to take a look at the other evidence I have on record.'

Fowler's eyes narrowed further. 'What *other evidence*?'

'Bodashka's witness statement. It was withheld as evidence at the trial. Shortly afterwards, his body was found in the Thames.'

The mobster shifted uncomfortably on his seat, his eyebrows screwed up in utter confusion. 'I know nothing of this shit.'

'I didn't think you would. However, I'm sure that neither you nor Mr Cavatore would like to see the case reopened?'

Mallory chuckled to himself. So that's what Andrei had been hinting at the other day.

Fowler's eyes widened and it took him a moment to regain his composure. 'You're not threatening me in front of witnesses are you, Vadislav?'

'Good Lord, no! Merely a warning from a barrister to his client. Perhaps you'll recall how difficult it was for you to find a law firm to defend you at the Old Bailey. I believe I was the only barrister in London who would even consider representing you?' His voice turned hard again. 'Don't make me regret my decision, Mr Fowler. And if I suspect that you are ever again involved in this mucky business, I will personally put in a request to Silk to prosecute.'

'You double-crossing bastard!' Fowler screamed, slamming his fist on the table.

'In my case, an act of nature. But you are a born-again *sukin syn*, sir,' Andrei said, calmly. The Russian slur for son-of-a-bitch rolled easily off his tongue. The tension was unbearable.

Fowler grasped the implication of the Russian's words and his mouth twisted into a bitter grimace. 'My signature is on your bloody legal document. And you have my verbal assurance that the matter is settled,' he said, venom in his voice. 'The whore is free to pursue her career elsewhere; we will have no further contact with her.'

Mallory didn't believe this for one minute. And there was still Tommaso to appease. Was a grand enough of a settlement? Time would tell. He looked across at Andrei. The Russian's eyes were fixed firmly on the gangster.

'One last request, Mr Fowler.' His gaze never wavered. 'As Miss Laurent is no longer in your employment, we would appreciate her passport being returned.'

Mallory winced. He was still on the edge of his seat from Andrei's last curse. This was the moment of truth, where it could get ugly. The hairs stood up on the back of his neck as he watched Fowler reach down to a drawer in the desk. His hand rested lightly on the desktop, prepared for the inevitable. Then he saw the long key and he breathed a quiet sigh of relief. Fowler walked to the wall safe behind the bookcase and twisted the dial before inserting the key. He shuffled through files and papers until he found what he was looking for. This was the final act in the charade: the return of the girl's documents, her passport to freedom. Fowler was a beaten man and he knew it.

One down, two to go. Cavatore was no doubt next on Andrei's list. Although less of a problem than Tommaso, he was nevertheless a threat. And what of the Sicilian, the newly inaugurated Head of European Affairs? Was he aware of what was going on? He certainly wouldn't take kindly to Bodashka's statement being used as blackmail. Had they played their hand too soon? Sure, the Russian had won the battle, but Mallory was convinced there was more to come.

Andrei examined the Bordeaux-red document and then tucked it into his pocket, together with his cheque book. 'Thank you for your cooperation, Mr Fowler, I'm so pleased that we were able to settle this simple matter like gentlemen. I'm sure you do not enjoy confrontation any more than I do. We'll see ourselves out,' he said, picking up the file and the envelope.

'Fuck you, Vadislav!'

Andrei ignored the obscenity. He was halfway across the room when Fowler pressed a hidden buzzer beneath the desk. The door opened and the black man's enormous frame seemed to fill the opening. He appeared ready for a showdown. Fowler shook his head. Without further ado, the Russian and the immigrant left the room.

Andrei's men stood deep in conversation across the street from the Green Door. He briefly acknowledged them as he walked by. When they reached Whitechapel Road, well out of sight of the nightclub, Andrei hailed a cab. They sat in silence for most of the journey to Soho. Something was bothering him. Then, just before the taxi dropped them off at Antonio's restaurant he handed over the passport.

'I've been in some tight situations, Andrei, but you are one real cool dude. Shit, at one point I thought the heavy was going to pull his shooter.'

'Can't say I noticed.'

'You were too busy negotiating the deal. And what a deal! I thought Fowler was going to burst a vein. You really had him by the balls in there today.'

Andrei's body language indicated otherwise. 'I'm not sure a grand will satisfy Cavatore. Or Tommaso, for that matter.' He reached into his jacket for his wallet. 'Although in the Don's case, I suspect your girl is insignificant. It's the fact that I have evidence that could shut the club down that will really annoy him.'

So that's what was worrying him. 'Do you expect trouble?'

Andrei shook his head. 'I don't know. I guess we'll have to cross that bridge when we come to it.' There was little confidence in the words.

Mallory peered out of the cab window. The Soho streets were coming to life. Across the road from Antonio's, the girls were waiting for the punters. He smiled and waved when he recognised Lillian. Then he turned to the Russian.

'Is Madeleine safe now?'

'One never knows,' Andrei said, removing a ten-pound note from his billfold and handing it to the driver. 'You have her passport so she could disappear.'

'Disappear? Where?'

'Anywhere! Go home, back to France.'

'You think that would be for the best?'

Andrei shrugged. 'I've done all I can for you now. If anything should happen to her, I'm sure the Yard would be highly delighted to read my dossier.' He opened the cab door. 'But I'm hopeful it won't come to that.'

'From the way Fowler reacted I don't think we have any worries there.'

'Don't be too sure,' the Russian said, an element of doubt thickening his voice. 'Cavatore is a completely different kettle of fish. Now, let's forget about these reprehensible creatures and have that drink.'

Chapter Twenty-One

It was midnight when Mallory caught the last train home. The first thing he noticed when he reached his street was that the lounge curtains were open and the pendant light was on. Standing in the shadows, he lit up a cigarette and thought of how the girl's face would look when he handed over the document. Then an uneasy thought crossed his mind. The passport would give her freedom. She could travel, perhaps return to Paris, as Andrei had suggested, and find another life. She was young and this infatuation surely couldn't last forever. But he found it difficult to think of another man holding her, loving her, and yet in the back of his mind the truth prevailed; this would surely happen one day.

Madeleine was sitting on the settee reading her book when she heard the door open. The welcome smile on her face said it all. She stood up and threw her arms around his neck, holding him close. Then she stepped back. '*Bonjour,* Mallory! Drink?'

He noticed the change straightaway. She was wearing a sleeveless black and white polka-dot dress. Her legs were bare and although they had not seen the sun for some time, they nevertheless contrasted vividly with the white dress. But what impressed him most was the lack of inquisition. She could have said a thousand words – all of which would have annoyed him. Suddenly he felt guilty at having had thoughts of losing her. Here they were, just the two of them, and he felt spirited and alive. There were surely prettier women than this painfully thin girl. But none that would hold him the way she could. 'I'll get it.'

'No,' she said in a firm voice.

Mallory smiled and sat down at the table. Suddenly he was pleased she had not gone to bed. She poured the drinks and passed him the neat vodka with one ice cube. 'You're getting to know all my habits – especially the bad ones.'

She giggled shyly and sat down opposite him. 'Now, tell me about your day,' she said, oblivious to his thoughts.

The smile in the corner of his mouth appeared lopsided, giving his face a pretentious look.

'Mallory,' she said, prodding him with her bare foot, 'don't you know it's rude to keep a girl waiting?'

He removed the passport from his pocket and placed it face up on the table in front of the girl. For a moment she said nothing, just gazed in disbelief at the document. The cover was emblazoned with the French coat of arms. She picked it up and opened it cautiously to the back page. It was only when she recognised her photograph that she started to scream. 'Oh my God! Mallory! Then she jumped up and threw her arms into the air. '*Mon Dieu*, here I am babbling away and you have my passport!' She looked down at the document again. 'I can't believe this is happening!'

Mallory placed his glass on the table. He studied it for a moment. The ice cube was slowly melting and changing the complexity of the vodka. He understood, perhaps more than anyone, how she felt because he did not have a passport – indeed, no means of identification to speak of. He took the girl's hand. 'You have Andrei to thank. Without him we'd never have stood a chance of getting it back. Whatever you might think of him, today he was magnificent.'

Happiness flooded her soft brown eyes. She looked quizzically at him. 'Tell me what happened,' she said, trying to catch her breath, 'I want to know everything!' He narrated the meeting, keeping

123

it simple and to the point. Madeleine remained silent until he mentioned the money. 'A thousand pounds,' she said in exasperation, 'why did they accept that?'

Mallory refilled the glasses from the vodka bottle she'd brought over to the table. Then he added tonic to the girl's glass. The ice seemed irrelevant. He had hoped to avoid going into the details, but there seemed no way out now. Nevertheless, he decided to keep it brief. 'Let's just say they have history. Fowler was not happy with the settlement, but as much as it gripes him, he has released you from your contract.'

A frown appeared on the girl's forehead. 'And the money?'

Andrei will arrange with Mitterrand to deduct it from your wages. All right?'

She shrugged and reached for the packet of Camel. 'Whatever. You have no idea what this means to me.'

He squeezed her hand in assurance. 'Let's hope this is the last you'll ever hear from either Fowler or Cavatore.'

Suddenly she appeared reticent. 'Your Mr Andrei – does he do this for you or for me?' Had the vodka given her the confidence to ask the question?

'Does it really matter?'

'Perhaps not,' she said, languidly. The indifference had lasted but a minute. 'How can I repay you for what you have done for me?' He remembered that she had asked that question before on a less significant matter. Her voice was soft and plaintive now. 'All I can do is love you.'

'It's enough, Madeleine,' he said, lighting up a cigarette.

She stood up and walked over to the bed.

His glass was nearly empty. He thought about pouring another but he wanted the girl more than he wanted the drink. But something stopped him getting up – something that Fowler had said: *You don't know this woman. She enjoys her work much more than you realise.* Was this her work? Was he just another client and this was her way of repaying him?

124

'Are you coming, Mallory, or do I have to take the bottle to bed alone?'

What the hell! This was what he really wanted. Nothing else was of any consequence right now. He took a last draw from the Camel and then stubbed it out.

'Bring the glass,' she said, turning off the light. Only the gentle explosion of a flickering street neon now crossed the room. She put the bottle down on the side table and took the glass from his hand. Her arms were wrapped around his neck and she held him where she wanted him. She was so very sure of herself. Then her fingers moved to the buttons of his shirt and she peeled it off. She was still kissing him when he felt her release the belt to his jeans. Finally, she pushed him onto the bed. Mallory lay on the sheet and watched her remove the polka-dot dress. She was standing over him and her small breasts were just visible in the half-light that dusted the room.

'You have to do what I tell you,' she said, softly.

He picked up his glass and swallowed the last of the alcohol. 'And what would you like me to do?' he asked, somewhat nervously.

She took the glass from him and threw it to the floor. 'Just love me,' she said, crushing his lips with a kiss.

There was nothing more to say.

Chapter Twenty-Two

The doorman at the French Revolution recognised Mallory from the audition and beckoned a waiter to show him to Andrei's table. He had come to see the show for the first time and was astonished to see the club filled to capacity. Tables were lively with conversation. Soft jazz music piped from the sound system floated across the room. The Russian sat alone, in a darkened corner away from the stage. Nightclubs were like offices to him, and the French Revolution was one of his favourite meeting places. 'I had almost given you up for lost,' he said, looking at the ostentatious gold watch on his wrist.

Mallory sat down, his back to the stage. 'Sorry about that. Engineering works on the District line. Have I missed much?'

'It's not started yet.'

Mallory smiled nonchalantly. It was only 10 p.m. He removed the large Manila envelope from his briefcase and placed it on the table. It detailed the harassment case against the African waitress. The brief had taken him longer than he'd expected because the disclosure was riddled with contradictions.

Andrei half filled a tumbler with vodka from the bottle of Stolichnaya and handed Mallory the glass. Then he withdrew his monogrammed black leather wallet from the inside pocket of his jacket and counted out a wad of notes. The cash was an inconvenience, but then, as Mallory was *persona non grata*, there was no other way. 'I'm surprised this is the first time you have come to see your woman sing,' he said. 'She really has been quite the sensation.'

Mallory smiled – the Russian still rarely used Madeleine's name. Sometimes it worried him, as he was well acquainted with Andrei's remarkable perception, especially of girls from nightclubs where he spent half his life. He had never married, preferring instead to pay for his pleasures – perhaps he saw Madeleine as no different to any of the other girls he'd shared his bed with over the years. 'There hasn't been much time lately for socialising.' The legal work was only partly to blame. Madeleine had moved into her new flat ten days ago. The afternoons were taken up rehearsing with Sam, and Mallory had done most of the decorating work himself. When he'd finally finished the painting, she'd added her mark with new curtains and soft furnishings. Ever since then he'd been caught up with the harass-ment case. He had missed her and was looking forward to the show.

'All work and no play…?'

He looked at the Russian, searching for some hidden meaning. But there was no hint as to his thoughts. Then he touched his glass. '*Nostrovia*, my friend.' The toast had distracted his attention and he failed to notice the jazz pianist taking his seat behind the Steinway. Sam started to play introduction chords and the floor lighting dimmed. Candles flickered on the tables and the conver-sation died. There was something wildly enchanting about it all. 'The place is packed.'

'It's all down to the girl!'

Mallory looked over at the stage. 'Perhaps this will finally give her the independence she craves.' The words were hollow, almost flippant. It was what he'd hoped for in the early days of their relationship, but now the thought was of no comfort.

The Russian smiled. 'Is that what you want?'

'Not really. But, as you yourself once said, she is not good at playing happy families.'

Andrei nodded.

A spotlight settled upon Sam as he began the introduction to 'Feeling Good'. Then the audience broke into applause as Madeleine sauntered slowly between the tables towards the stage, like a model on a catwalk. She wore a long black evening dress slit down the side. The shimmering outfit was complemented by a black, wide-brimmed fedora that all but hid her eyes. Around her neck was a string of pearls and in her hand a long ivory cigarette holder. There was an air of confidence about her which Mallory recognised from the last time they'd made love. Her eyes were on the stage and she greeted Sam with a smile. When the spotlight moved across to her the room fell silent and she took her seat at a stage table. Her face was pale in the harsh light. She was in a world of her own. The setting was that of a Parisian street café, with the Eiffel Tower as the backdrop. On the table was a vase of flowers and a glass of wine. She removed her long black opera gloves, picked up the glass and sipped the wine. It was all so enchanting, an actress playing to her audience. They waited in anticipation. Then she hit the first notes of the song and her voice was drowned out by the applause. Sam's eyes were on her the whole time, following her every note, his fingers moving deftly over the keys, complementing her seductive voice. After each number, the room erupted into a rapturous ovation. When she had completed a repertoire of eight numbers, which included her own sensual version of 'Je T'aime', she signed off with 'Non, Je Ne Regrette Rein'. It brought the house down. Smiling that secretive smile of hers, she held her hand up in the air. 'Please,' she whispered in her sultry French accent, 'you have to let me go. I will finish with "Con Te Partirò".' The announcement was greeted again with wild applause. The song was both nostalgic and sad … a time to say goodbye. Sam played out the final bars and the entire room rose to their feet, shouting for more. Then the spotlight darkened and the girl and her pianist left the stage.

'You're right, Andrei, she is wonderful,' Mallory said, watching her walk back between the tables. 'Mitterrand will have to be careful – the West End clubs will be after her.' He was about to raise his hand and call her over when she stopped to talk to a group of men not far from where they were sitting. It was obvious, from the brace of champagne bottles that they were big spenders. A tall, young man in a smart jazzy suit pulled up a chair and offered her a glass. Although she no longer peddled drinks, she was free to accept them. They were all talking to her at once but Mallory could tell that she wasn't really listening to them. Her eyes, beneath the wide-brimmed fedora, were on the room, as though she was searching for someone. But in the subdued lighting it would have been difficult to recognise anyone. Then the room was forgotten and her attention was with the men and the champagne. The laughter was loud and flirtatious. The man in the jazzy suit whispered something into her ear. She shrieked with laughter and Mallory heard her voice. 'Oh Richard, you are naughty. Not tonight!' He felt an immediate pang of jealousy. She'd certainly not hung about. So this is what she was doing while he'd been working. His lips tightened and he picked up the half full glass of vodka and downed it in one. 'Another,' he said, slamming the glass down on the table.

'Easy, my friend!'

Was it jealousy or perhaps envy? The big shot no doubt had papers and a passport to go with his substantial bank account. Mallory wasn't even allowed to work legally in England. It was a bitter pill to swallow. Madeleine had once asked him what would happen if the police ever caught him. He'd told her he'd probably face deportation back to Zimbabwe. She'd been horrified and had broken down. But Mallory knew she would move on. Perhaps this was what she was finally doing, right now, in front of him. All of a sudden he realised he could not stay here any longer. The bird had flown.

'I've got to go.'

The Russian looked at him with the understanding eyes of one who has been there before. 'In the words of the immortal bard: "All the world's a stage", my friend, '"and all men and women merely players". We have our appearances and our farewells. At any one time we play many parts but sooner or later we have to bow out. I'm sorry.'

Mallory was relieved; better Shakespeare than 'I told you so'.

Andrei picked up the bottle of Stolichnaya. 'One for the road?'

Mallory glanced across at the table where Madeleine sat. Her back was to him but he could see the champagne flute in her hand and the man's arm resting on the back of her chair.

'I've had enough.'

'I'll give you a call when I've been through your notes. Take care of yourself.'

'Don't worry about me,' Mallory said, with a forced laugh, 'illegal immigrants operate better alone. Isn't that what you've always said – head below the parapet and all that shit?'

The Russian sighed and paused to take a drink. 'Look. I know that work has been rather stressful lately. I've just been offered a big fraud case that should commence in two to three weeks.' He put his glass down gently. 'I'll need your help. In the meantime, why don't you take a break? A different environment will do you the world of good.'

Mallory wanted to laugh out loud. 'What do you suggest? You know I can't leave the bloody country.' The bitterness in his speech left a bad taste in his mouth.

'I am aware of your situation,' the Russian said, again ignoring the irony. 'That is why I am recommending my friend; he has a small boarding house on the seafront at Whitstable.'

Mallory put his hand to his forehead. 'Shit, sorry Andrei – I'm a bit uptight tonight.'

'You need to move on, my friend.'

Mallory managed a wry smile. 'So, where's Whitstable?'

'On the south coast of Kent; it has a lovely shingle beach and you can take the train or bus from Victoria. Do you like oysters?'

'I can't remember when I last ate them. Probably back in Mozambique.'

130

'Well, my friend, in Whitstable they are reputed to be the best in Britain. Rumour has it that Julius Caesar also enjoyed them! But that was a long time ago.' He laughed at his little joke. 'So, what do you say?'

'I could do with a break.'

'Good! I'll give Dominick a ring tomorrow.'

Mallory stood up and shook the Russian's hand. 'Sorry about tonight.' He looked again at the girl. She had changed, of that he was sure. Her staying away over the last week was only a small part of it. There was something deeper, a commitment to a past life of pleasure she'd once enjoyed. Oh God, hadn't he seen it in the club tonight. But then, why was he so surprised?

'Look, if you'd rather not walk past the girl and her friends, use the fire escape behind the bar – the door just past the toilets.'

Mallory peered at the table one last time. The girl had her arm around the sleazy high-roller and she was whispering something into his ear. Whatever it was, he was enjoying it.

Chapter Twenty-Three

Two weeks in another town. The small seaside resort of Whitstable was perfect. At low tide one could walk a mile out to sea along a shingle strip known as 'the street'. Just offshore, fishing boats with colourful flags bobbed about in the choppy sea while along the pavement fronting the pebble beach, flats vied with hotels and boarding houses for every inch of space. It was so quintessentially English. On days like this, Mallory would walk out beyond the town to where the beach huts lay beside the dunes in the bracing wind, their tiny windows staring out to sea, an array of colours, from poppy reds to marigold yellows. Beside the huts families sat in deckchairs, eating fish and chips while seagulls hovered overhead, lingering impatiently for the scraps.

Mallory had sat around for three days at his London flat waiting for a knock on the door. But Madeleine had not come. There was nothing, not even the ring of the telephone in the hall downstairs. What was he doing? After everything he had said to Andrei about giving the girl her independence, now here he was hankering after her. Had he not warned himself that by trying to hold onto her, he would lose her? Besides, she deserved her freedom. And the last thing in the world he wanted to do was to try and change her mind. It was too late for that. When had it all changed? He didn't really know. Yesterday she had told him she could not live without him, and now it was as if there was a barrier between them.

From the window of the boarding house he could see the bay. Autumn leaves had just started to colour the trees and there was a tinge of coolness in the air, exacerbated by the sea breeze. On the horizon, the sun was setting against a clear blue sky. It cast an orange glow across the water. Occasionally a yacht would pass by, her sail momentarily blotting out the twilight. It was almost time to go. He was about to close the curtain when he noticed the young couple sitting on the shingle beach. They were kissing, oblivious to the screams of the children playing in the surf. This simple act of love made him think of Madeleine. Then the couple were on their feet, walking back to the street. And Madeleine was forgotten. He closed the curtain on what had been a memorable day and left the room. The book at long last was finished. He would take it to his favourite bar – a short stroll from the boarding house – and over a glass of wine, he would read what he had recently written.

It was almost 6 p.m. when he arrived at The Gallery. A sign outside the bar advertised happy hour, all drinks half price. Plastic tables, each set with an ashtray and a menu, lay scattered over the timber decking that faced the sea. Mallory ordered a large glass of red. He'd been in Whitstable twelve days now, and The Gallery was his favourite place to sit and watch the sunset. He never tired of the view and at times it felt like there was nothing in the world but the little bar on the edge of the shingles. The draft was lying open on the table and he smiled to himself. There was a sense of accomplishment in having finally finished what had seemed a never-ending project, another step along the road of a journey he'd started so many years before. An elderly couple, wrapped up in coats and scarves, were loudly debating that favourite topic of the English, the weather. Mallory ignored them; his eyes were fixed on the sea and the way the sunset transformed the colours from a luminous blue to a deep gold. The change of

133

scene, living in this beach town, was refreshing and a world away from the East End of London.

He thought how simple the days were. In the early morning, when the sun had just penetrated the flimsy net curtains at the boarding house, he would wake up and fling open the old wooden casement to listen to the waves crashing on the beach. By nine o'clock the little town had come to life and combustion engines drowned out the shriek of the seagulls. The birds' familiar hungry cries in the distance were not a distraction. Rather, in a way they reminded him of the scavengers on the wild, west coast beaches of Africa. After breakfast he would work on the book. Then over a long lunch at the small street café on the seafront, he would read through what he had just written. It was all falling into place. But he was conscious that in a few days he would have to go back to the city. With that in mind, he had put in longer hours. What now lay before him was the reward for all the hard work: the finished manuscript.

The sun continued to drift lazily towards the horizon. Once it had disappeared he would move onto Blues Restaurant. Invariably, the meal consisted of fish and chips but this evening, in the form of a small celebration, it would be oysters followed by lobster. Then he would carry on the spree with a few whiskies in the hotel bar before stumbling back to the boarding house. The only downside was that he was on his own. But that didn't really bother him because he had his characters. He picked up the manuscript, written in longhand, and opened the page to where he had started the last writing session. Then, glass of red wine in hand, he started to read. Just before the sun touched the horizon he finished the manuscript. His thoughts wandered back to the bush and the fate of the leopard hunter. The old man had lived a wretched life in that remote place on the edge of Gorongoza. It made him shiver. For a moment he wondered if it was the ghosts of the past or the cool wind blowing off the sea. He heard the girl's footsteps on the wooden decking before he saw her.

'Can I get you another?' He peered up at the waitress silhouetted in the last of the sunset. She was smiling at him. 'Same again?' He nodded.

When she had disappeared with his order he looked again at the sea, at the gentle waves caressing the shingles. Without the sun, its waters were grey and cold. Then he remembered this was the very same ocean that he had crossed all those years ago – a stretch of water separating chaos from civilisation. Somewhere out there, beyond where the sun had set, was a woman he had once loved, and for a brief moment he felt a sadness for something lost.

Rhodesia – that too was lost, as were the lives of so many young men; soldiers that were once his friends. He thought, too, of the Africans, the freedom fighters that had died, by bullet or rope. Their leaders had promised them a new life in America, but they had ended up in a remote camp in Moscow or Beijing. Even an assurance of education and lessons in how to farm the land had been a lie. Instead, they had been schooled in terrorism – how to make a bomb and fire an AK-47. When the indoctrinated Africans had returned to Zambia or Mozambique, they were ferried across the borders and integrated back into the community, where they unleashed the violence and mayhem that started the uprising. These were the men that were caught with their crude bombs. And these were the men that were sentenced to hang. The same men he had once defended in puppet trials, where the conviction was always a foregone conclusion. How could he forget hunting men as one would hunt animals? And because racism had never been a part of his life, the killing fields were difficult to forget. 'We are all the same men', a guerrilla had once told him before he was due to hang. 'Why does the colour of our skin make us hate each other?' Those words had stayed with Mallory long after the African had died. The scales were always tipped against them and the last sound these young men ever heard was the clanking release of a steel trapdoor. They were even deprived the privilege of a decent burial at their kraal. Instead, their only identification in death was a number in a prison yard. He continued to stare at the sea, at an ocean that separated him from Africa. He could almost hear the screams across the water as he breathed in the salt air. Was there, somewhere in all of this, a ray of hope, a future for an indigenous people?

The waitress brought the fresh glass of wine. Her long blonde hair and youthful figure reminded him of Anna, that wisp of creation that had stumbled into his life before the war, when he was still a teenager in Rhodesia. Mallory paid her with a large note and told her to keep the change. Her eyes lit up and she mouthed her thanks. She had her whole life ahead of her, a life unblemished by hatred or death. A breeze had blown up from the sea and somewhere along its path it had picked up a hint of lavender from the cottage garden beside the tavern. Breathing in deeply of the fragrance, he looked at the girl and smiled. 'It's nothing,' he replied. Then he watched her walk away and out of his thoughts. She was as fresh as the morning daisies that clung to the side of a mountain path.

But really she was nothing at all like Anna.

Chapter Twenty-Four

The French Revolution was just how Mallory remembered it from the last time he was here. He sat beside Andrei facing the stage. Sam had just started to play the opening bars of 'I've Got You Under My Skin' when Madeleine's voice reached out across the room. Then the spotlight picked her up and for a moment he did not recognise her. She was dressed in the same low-cut, shimmering gown, which clung to every part of her body. In her hand was the black fedora. It was all a part of her new, sophisticated look. Brown hair, cut in a different style, rested gently on her shoulders. The stage lights were reflected in her eyes and there was an easy-going laughter on her lips when she started to sing. He thought his feelings had changed in the two weeks he had been away. But they clearly hadn't. He closed his eyes. He should never have come. But then what else could he have done?

Madeleine still had the spare key to his flat, but she had not been there while he was away in Whitstable. Why did he think she would? The old cigarette butt, stained with her red lipstick, in the ashtray beside the bed had reminded him of the last time they'd made love. He'd opened a bottle of beer and looked at the bed. It was just as he had left it, hastily made up, a blanket covering sheets where they'd last laid together. He could see her again in just her pants and T-shirt, teasing him with a drink, making love to him. He knew it was never going to be easy coming back but he never imagined it would be this difficult. She was so much a part of the room and it seemed empty without her. God, Whitstable was supposed to have blown away the past. Now the nightclub seemed to resurrect it all again. The Russian would've told him to get himself a woman. Anything to take his mind off the girl. Instead he'd come to the Revolution, where he knew he would see her.

Andrei pulled out a packet of Sobranie. Mallory put the gold foil filter in his mouth and inhaled deeply, blowing the smoke out towards the stage. Through the haze, he watched her act. 'She is even better than when you last saw her,' the Russian said, charging the glasses with Stolichnaya. 'Do you not think so?'

He nodded. There was sadness in the gesture. 'She has changed so much.'

'Ah, like a matryoshka.'

'A what?'

'Matryoshka – they are little wooden dolls that fit into one another? The outer layer is often a woman dressed in a *sarafan*, a colourful peasant dress. But each doll is painted differently. They can resemble almost anything, from Imperial monarchs to courtesans.'

'I don't understand what you are saying.'

The Russian stubbed out the Sobranie. 'I've been watching your face while the girl sings; God forbid, could it be obsession?'

'Nonsense, I hardly know the girl!' It was what he had once told Madeleine.

'*Hardly know her*!' He shook his head. 'You've slept with her! But far more importantly, you were the one who rescued her. Perhaps making love to you was her way of repaying you?'

Mallory was about to deny the accusation – the words were on his lips – but he didn't say them, because deep down he wondered if the Russian was right. Before he could speak, the song ended and the girl bowed to the audience. Then she started to sing 'Plasir d'Amour'. He'd last heard her hum it in the shower. How long ago did that now seem?

The Russian's eyes were still on him. 'Do you want to go?'

'No. If I go now she will forever be on my mind. But this is the last time I will ever come back here, Andrei. I have to move on or she will continue to haunt me.'

The Russian shrugged. 'It's of no importance,' he said, downing the last of the vodka. 'There are other clubs in London. La Piguella also has a very good act.' He paused for a moment, a humorous expression reaching out across his face. 'But I can always come here occasionally and keep an eye on her; update you on her lovers?' Then he laughed his booming laugh and, in spite of the fact that Mallory didn't find it funny, he couldn't help but join in.

Madeleine finished the repertoire with her signature tune, 'Con Te Partirò'. Then the lighting above the tables flashed into life. The girl stood talking to Sam, her eyes on the room. They stopped at the Russian's table and her face turned pale. She hesitated but a moment. Then, in her long strides, she crossed the dance floor, her hands clenched tightly by her sides. 'Where have you been?' she hissed, fixing her stare on Mallory and totally ignoring Andrei. He may well have not even been in the room.

The welcome smile on Mallory's face instantly disappeared. 'Whitstable.'

'Where?!' she asked, still trying to catch her breath.

'It's a small seaside town, in Kent; you'd really like–'

'Don't get clever with me, Mallory! Why am I the last to know?'

'Perhaps because you have been pretty busy yourself.'

'What is that supposed to mean?'

'I was here two weeks ago. Sitting over there.' He pointed to the corner table. 'Not that you would have noticed – you only had eyes for one table, and it wasn't mine.'

A tiny smile crept across her face. 'Are you jealous?'

'Go back to your friends, Madeleine.'

She crossed her arms in defiance, her voice raising an octave. 'They are not here tonight.'

God, at least she was candid. He sighed. 'That was why I went away.'

'You could have taken me with you!'

He reached out for her hand but she drew back from the table. Okay, so this was how she wanted to play it. 'Look, Madeleine, I don't want to make a scene. You've not been in touch since you started working here – did you really think I was going to sit around waiting for you forever?'

The girl's mouth dropped open and her whole demeanour changed. 'I've been tired,' she offered. 'It's not easy when you start a new job.'

He hadn't thought of that, the stress of a prestigious club. It must have been a huge change. He almost felt sorry for her. Then he remembered her arm around the high-roller. 'I understand,' he said, finishing his drink and reaching for his jacket. 'But I must go now.'

'Did you come here tonight just to see me,' she asked, a knowing look on her face.

'No, Madeleine – I came here to have a drink with Andrei.' He lit up a Camel and then offered them around the table. Only Madeleine accepted the cigarette. She put it in the holder. Another style icon to complement the fedora? The match, in the cup of his hands, lit up her face. There was too much make-up on her skin – she was beautiful enough without it. But he said nothing. A silence descended over the table. Mallory stood up. He'd had enough. 'I really have to go.'

She looked at him steadfastly. 'Wait here while I get my coat.'

'No, Madeleine,' he repeated again. 'I have to go alone.' He glanced at the Russian for assurance. 'I'm working on a big case tomorrow. I don't want any distractions.'

For a moment the girl said nothing. Her eyes were wet. 'That is always your excuse – another case, always another case.' Then she looked at Andrei. 'I knew it would be your fault!'

'Whoa, steady *devotchka*. All I'm—'

'I am not your *girl*,' she screamed, turning her back on the table and storming off towards her dressing room. Her departure was followed by a slow handclap from the Russian. Mallory threw up his arms in despair. Surprisingly, he found that his hands were steady.

'Bravo, my friend!' the Russian said, in a mocking tone, 'for a man from the bush, you handled the situation most admirably. Yes, even I was impressed.'

'Perhaps this has finally put an end to it all.'

Suddenly Andrei's face changed and it took on a solemn look. He handed Mallory the thick file. 'You will see her again, my friend.'

Mallory stood up slowly, sobriety in his manner. 'You sound very sure of yourself.'

'I am.' The Russian smiled. 'She has not had the last word yet.'

Chapter Twenty-Five

Mallory was woken by shuffling footsteps. Someone was in the room. Suddenly he was alert. He waited for his eyes to adjust to the dark; the four glasses of Stolichnaya he'd downed before bed weren't helping. Then the figure moved into the shaft of light cast by the nearby street lamp and he recognised the black fedora.

'My God, Madeleine! You scared the shit out of me! What time is it?'

'Three o'clock,' she replied, as if it was completely normal to turn up at such an hour.

'*Three*! What the hell are you doing here?'

'I'm sorry I woke you – I tried to be quiet. I was just going to sit here and watch you.'

The flat was cold and Mallory shivered in the dark. Madeleine was wearing a fur coat, but she was no doubt frozen, too. The temptation was there, but he was not about to offer her his bed; he'd made that mistake before. Shit, this was the last thing he needed. He made a mental note to get the key back off her. Then he turned on the bedside lamp. She looked even more beautiful in the half-light. He closed his eyes for a moment to regain his senses.

'Madeleine, I don't need this. You're going to have to go home.'

'I couldn't sleep!'

The faded moon cast her shadow across the flat, not quite reaching into the far corners of the room. He rubbed his eyes. 'Look, this is no time for games. It's the middle of the bloody night and I'm shattered – please just get a cab and go home.'

'How can I go home if I'm not happy?'

'You're not making sense.'

'You left me.'

'*I left you*?!' He sat up. 'What do you mean "I left you"? You seemed perfectly happy with the high-rollers at the Revolution.'

Her face dropped. Then she put her shock aside as she would a book and walked over to sit on the bed. She was carrying a bottle and a single glass. 'So you *are* jealous,' she said, putting the glass down on the side table.

God, she was impudent. 'No Madeleine, I'm not jealous, just … disillusioned.'

'Don't be – it's only business,' she said, self-assumingly, throwing the fedora on the chair. 'It's a part of my job to talk to the customers and keep them happy.' She continued to hug the bottle.

He couldn't quite make out the look on her face but he could imagine it. Did she really think he would fall for her lies again? The expensive dress, the make-up, the men? But the last thing he wanted now was another argument – hadn't they had enough of those already? Besides, he was exhausted with it all. 'Madeleine, I could never be cross with you.'

She put her hand on his face, the way he remembered. There was the faint suggestion of a smile. 'Just a little possessive?'

'Get away with you, woman! Stop all this silly talk and pour me a drink.'

All of a sudden her demeanour changed. 'What would you like?'

'What do you have there?'

'Cognac.'

'Cognac it is,' he said, watching her remove the cork.

She poured a glass and handed it to him.

'Are you not having one?'

143

'Don't tell me you have forgotten already? We share *everything* – it's going to be just like it was before.' She paused and then whispered softly, 'In every way.'

It had been a while since they'd last made love and he'd thought he was over her. Now this. He swirled the amber liquid around in the glass before drinking it. 'You have expensive tastes. This is as good a cognac as I've ever drunk,' he said, handing her back the glass.

'It should be; it's a very rare old Courvoisier.' She drank slowly from the glass where his lips had been and then handed him back the brandy. 'A gift from a friend.'

In spite of himself, Mallory laughed. 'Well you certainly have the gall, I'll give you that.'

Her lips tightened. 'You won't ever leave me alone again, will you, Mallory?'

He drained the glass and passed it back, grasping her hand as he did so. 'You are never alone. I saw you tonight. When you sing, you have everyone eating out of the palm of your hand.'

'But I don't care about *everyone*.'

There it was again, the suggestive smile of someone who knows how to play the game. Watching her sitting on the edge of the bed in the moonlight, he thought again how much he wanted her. And he knew there was no escape. She reached over and held the glass to his lips.

'I don't know what I'd do if you ever left me.'

The smell of her body was irresistible. That was something else that was different, too – the perfume. He didn't recognise the scent but he knew it was expensive. Perhaps another present from an admirer?

'You must be patient with me, Mallory,' she said, unaware of his thoughts.

'Of course, *mon adorable*,' he replied.

'Now it is you who is flippant!'

He ignored the remark. 'You remind me of a Russian doll.'

She smiled, presuming this to be a compliment.

'A matryoshka.'

'I know of these dolls. Each fits inside the other.'

'And each face beneath the other is different. So Andrei tells me.'
For a minute the girl was subdued. 'Why does he hate me so?'

She'd asked the same question before but he couldn't remember
when. 'How can you say that, after all he has done for you?'

She peered out of the window, between the cracks in the
curtains. The street was quiet. Even the mongrel dog that barked
at the slightest provocation was sleeping. And when she spoke,
it was as if she was talking to the night, to the lone straggler who
always slept rough on the pavement below. 'He did all of this for
you, Mallory.' There was a sadness in her voice he had never
heard before; not even on that first night. 'Can you not see that
he loves you?'

Mallory was not altogether sure what she meant and the words
came as a shock. He shrugged. 'Look, does it really matter who
he did it for? The fact still remains: if it wasn't for him, you
wouldn't have a job or a flat, let alone be free of Fowler.'

The crushed look was still on her face. 'I guess not.'

'Now stop all this silly talk and pass the glass. Let's make a toast.'

She hesitated. 'To what?'

He lifted the glass and spoke gently. 'To our reunion.'

She wanted to say something more. Her mouth was open and
the words were partly formed. But then she must have realised
that there was nothing new she could add. All of this was just talk
and she'd had enough. Unbuttoning the fur coat, she then laid it
across the foot of the bed before reaching behind her back and
unzipping the slinky cocktail dress. It dropped to the floor.

Suddenly, tomorrow seemed a long way away.

Chapter Twenty-Six

Mallory awoke to the noise of the traffic. The girl lay beside him, her arm across his chest, asleep with the remnants of the night. He noticed a small scar on her shoulder and wondered where it had come from. Gently moving her arm, he kissed the tiny imperfection. She half opened her eyes. 'Time for me to go to work,' he said, 'and for you to go home.'

'Just five minutes more.' She put her arm back on his chest. It made him smile. 'Then I'll make you a coffee and go.'

'Five minutes.'

'Mallory, did you mean what you said last night or was it the brandy talking?' Her eyes were open now and she searched his face for an answer.

'I'm sorry?'

She sat up and propped her head against a pillow. 'You told me you would never let me go,' she said, softly into the sheet. 'After we had made love.'

'I can't hold you, Madeleine – you of all people should know that. I wish I could, but I can't.'

'But why?' she cried, her head now on his chest.

He stroked her hair. 'I've done all I can. Your wings are mended and now you are able to fly.'

'Then put me back in my cage.'

'I can't do that either – you would always resent me for holding on to you. You have to go out into the world and find your happiness. I convinced myself down in Whitstable that I was over you, but I realise now I was deluding myself. It's enough that sometimes you come back.' He paused and looked down at her. 'It's not easy, but it's enough.'

'What are we doing to each other? I love you, you know that! Everything I have I owe to you. There may be other men but there will only ever be you!'

That was one hell of a consolation, he thought. But, by God, at least she continued to be honest. He knew they had something that could not last. Domestic happiness cannot be built on the wings of a dragonfly. 'I can never give you the security you have always yearned for: I am an illegal immigrant, an itinerant surviving from day to day.' He had told her that once before and she had cried. Now it was as if she had not even heard him.

'But you'll always be around to pick up the pieces, won't you?'

Was it a question or a plea, a plaintive cry for help, spoken in a voice he did not recognise? It touched his heart. 'I can't promise you that, but I'll try.'

Words, only words, but they moved the girl to tears again. 'One day it will be different, you'll see. Please try to understand that all of this is new to me; I am experimenting with life, like a child who is given a new toy. I do all of these things because I know you will always be there for me.' She sat up and ran her fingertips over his lips. The warmth rose and he buried his face in the nape of her neck. She pushed his head gently but firmly down towards her small breasts. From somewhere beneath the sheets he heard her gasp as he kissed her body. 'Oh, *mon Dieu*,' she sighed. She wanted more, so much more. And she wanted to see him. Throwing the blanket to one side, she then took him in a final act of desperation.

Sometime after, she lay beside him, her hair fanned out across the pillow. She was smiling contentedly, almost as if she had achieved her objective and made him again her bondsman. 'Madeleine, you must go home now.'

'*This* is my home,' she said, kissing him softly on the lips. 'Let me stay with you today.'

'No, woman of temptation! I'll never get any work done with you around.' He wasn't entirely sure he'd be able to concentrate after all that had happened anyway. Did she think he was a machine that could be switched on and off whenever she so wanted? She had to go.

'I'm frightened to go home alone.'

'Sweet bird of youth, you are never alone.'

'Oh Mallory, I love it when you say such words to me. No one else ever says such things.'

Yes, he could imagine that to be right, with the kind of men she was seeing. 'Please – go now before I no longer have the strength to resist you.'

'Tell me you love me once more before I go.'

'Madeleine–'

'Tell me!'

'I will always love you.'

'I know you will,' she said. 'And I know you will always be there for me.'

Then you know more than I do, he thought, watching her slip out of bed. She put the dress on over her head and zipped it up. Then she picked up the fur coat. Another present? He didn't bother to ask.

'Thank you for giving me this time – I am happy we are together again. Now, a coffee and then I will go. With cognac?' Reaching down, she kissed him gently on the lips. The smell of her love was on his face.

Mallory watched her stride across the room. She would come to him again and again and each time he would be weaker, until one day he would no longer have the inclination to ask her to leave. She did not do any of this intentionally. It was just the way she was. And as long as he was there, she would continue to play the game. He lay back on the pillow and closed his eyes. Then he heard the kettle click off and the clink of the spoon stirring the alcohol into the coffee. But the last sound he heard was the front door softly closing. He opened his eyes; the girl had disappeared as if she had never been there. Had it all been just a dream? Then he saw the mug of steaming coffee and what looked to be a note. He reached over and picked up the scrap of paper. On it were just four words. They tore him apart.

Goodbye, my love
Madeleine

Chapter Twenty-Seven

For the next ten days Mallory saw nothing of the girl. Neither
had he wanted to. He was totally immersed in the fraud case. The
only time he took a break was when there was a suitable place
in the contract to do so. And that was to go to the office to pick
up information that could not be obtained over the phone. It
was after one such excursion, over a late lunch with Andrei, that
he finally gave in to his preoccupation. In the broken sunshine,
Antonio had set up tables on the pavement out front of the
restaurant. 'How's the Revolution?' The question, when asked,
was casual, almost as if he was talking about the weather or some
other irrelevant topic.

Andrei looked up from his pasta. 'Do you not mean "How is
Madeleine"?' Mallory shrugged sheepishly. 'She's not been around
for over a week – a short break, Mitterrand says. They have a
Jamaican girl standing in for her but it's not the same.' He put his
fork down and picked up the wine glass. 'Poor old Christophe; he
looks like he's been left at the altar. What is it about this girl that
she can wind men around her little finger and have them running
after her?' Mallory knew what it was. He was just surprised the
Russian could not see it. 'And the place is as dead as a dodo. The
only consolation is that one can at least get decent service now.'

'Where has she gone?'

150

'I thought *you* might know – no one has seen her around Soho.'

Across the street a young girl in a summer dress was playing Chopin. A small crowd had gathered around her. The violin briefly reminded him of Whitstable, where he'd sat for two hours listening to this haunting instrument. It was much the same scene, just a different venue – unpretentious and unrehearsed. He closed his eyes and let the music wash over him. The Russian's voice finally brought him out of his reverie.

'So what have you done with her? Mitterrand is not a happy man.'

Mallory gave a wry smile. He didn't really give a shit about Mitterrand. 'The last time I saw her was that night at the Revolution.'

'And not since?'

'She came round to the flat in the early hours of the morning.'

A hint of a smile appeared on the Russian's face. 'I thought you never wanted to see her again?'

'It was 3 a.m.; I woke from a deep sleep and there she was, standing in the room, a bottle of cognac in hand!'

'I hope you threw her out.'

'I drank the cognac. It was a rare Courvoisier – a gift. From a friend of hers.'

Andrei burst out laughing. 'You are getting more like a Russian every day! But why was she there?'

'Because of Whitstable – she was upset that I'd gone away without telling her. Said that I made her unhappy.'

The Russian looked thoughtful and when he spoke, he appeared to choose his words carefully. 'She didn't look that upset when she was downing champagne with the clientele after her late-night session – Louis Roederer, no less! The price they charge! I have never seen Christophe so happy. She left with them when the club closed.'

Mallory clenched his hand into a fist. She must've come round to his flat straight after leaving them. He couldn't believe what he was hearing. Three in the bloody morning. And that was after he'd waited up for her. He had convinced himself that she would come that night. He had even tried reading but the words were just letters on a page. They meant nothing. Eventually he'd put the light out but he could not sleep. Finally in desperation he had attacked the vodka bottle. The Stolichnaya had given him an hour of intermittent sleep. Then just as he was falling into a deep sleep, there she was. Louis Roederer champagne! He didn't ask who the client was. It didn't matter – if it wasn't the man with the jazzy tie, it would be another. 'I thought that might happen,' he said, pausing to listen to the busker. She was playing Tchaikovsky's 'Violin concerto in D Op. 35', from the *Canzonetta (Andante)*. The tune brought back memories and his anger dissipated.

'You know, Andrei, when she does this, I hate her and never want to see her again. But then she returns to my bed and the next morning we wake as lovers – and I only see her and not the men she has been with.'

The Russian was unconvinced. He took Mallory's hand and his voice was gentle. 'You need to treat her with the same indifference with which she treats you.'

'What do you suggest?'

'Change the locks on your front door for a start. Better still, move.'

'I've thought about it, many times. But knowing I would never see her again…'

'I once had a similar experience.' Andrei looked away meditatively. 'Her name was Svetlana – Lara, as I knew her.'

'You've never mentioned this before.'

'It was some years ago.' The Russian straightened his tie and then removed his cufflinks. 'I had returned to Russia from England under a different name; the country was a mess. It was a terrible time, the Cold War. That was when I met her. She was an activist, engaged in the fight for democracy. I struggled with her, pleaded with her to stop the politics, but to no avail; the secret police came for her in the middle of the night.'

Mallory furrowed his brow. 'I'm sorry, and this does sound terrible, but what has Lara to do with Madeleine?'

'That is what I'm trying to say. Neither woman could ever be satisfied with normality.'

'But you loved her?'

'With a passion that was single-minded. But she shared her love for me with a vision of a brighter future. That was her downfall.'

'What happened?'

'The state murdered her. When the police released her body, they told her parents that she had hanged herself. But the torturers' scars told another story. Everyone knew of the hangings and the bodies thrown out of the top-floor windows of the interrogation building. What made it all so bloody sick was reading in the newspapers – state-run, of course – that the victims had jumped of their own free will.'

'And then you came to England?'

'Not right away. I joined the opposition, the same group Svetlana had belonged to. For two years I fought an unjust system. Then one day I got a tip-off that the KGB were looking for me and I knew then that my days were numbered. Not that it mattered, because there was nothing worth living for. But the opposition leaders persuaded me otherwise, said I would be more useful to the cause overseas. Against my better judgement, I escaped across the border into Poland.'

'You had a passport?'

Andrei nodded slowly. 'A British passport, no less. I missed Russia and I missed Lara, but when she died it was the end of both relationships. Had she lived it may have been a very different story.' He took a sip of his coffee.

Strange how Andrei had never spoken of this before. Had he ever truly escaped Lara's death? What other secrets were there? He had briefly touched on Tommaso before their meeting at the Green Door. But was there more? Could the Sicilian gangster be the reason why Andrei worked for the underworld? What hold did they have over him? All these damn questions without answers. One thing was certain, there was a dark side to the man – this stranger from the East. The busker was playing the final chords of Tchaikovsky's *Swan Lake*, ironic given the Russian's story. 'I'm sorry, Andrei, I didn't realise.'

'It's of no consequence – water under the bridge, I think you say. It is *your* predicament that concerns me now.'

'What predicament?'

'I told you when you first met Madeleine that it would not be easy. Without wanting to be clever, I think my prediction was accurate. Your relationship is complicated. In Russia we say that women should either be revered or forgotten. In your situation, you have to forget. So listen to me; I have a solution.'

Mallory half knew where this was going but he remained silent.

'I have a friend who has ten beautiful girls. The youngest is only nineteen. They are medicine for the soul; they can make you forget everything in your life, even a broken love affair.'

'That's where you go?'

Andrei sat back and smiled. 'Twice a week. I pay my money and there are no further complications, no hidden agendas or emotions – a straightforward business arrangement. They know what I want and they have the experience to make it happen.'

'Come on, Andrei, love is more than just a quick fuck with a prostitute!' As soon as he said it, he regretted it – it was of no concern to him what Andrei did in his spare time, and neither was there any reason to bring the dialogue down to gutter level. Yet the remark hardly seemed to bother the Russian.

'I'm not looking for love. I learnt that lesson a long time ago – the hard way.'

From the tone of his voice, that was the end of the discussion. There really was still so little Mallory knew about the man. But perhaps all of that was for another day. The waiter returned with the bill and Mallory picked it up.

Andrei snatched it from his hands. 'This is the least I can do for all your hard work.'

Mallory stopped beside the busker. She was just packing up. He dropped a ten-pound note into her violin case and she smiled in surprise. 'Thank you!' she murmured. 'That's very kind of you.'

'It's nothing. You play beautifully.'

The girl blushed. 'I'm at the Troubadour on Thursday night.'

'Singing?'

She nodded shyly. 'Dylan numbers. On my violin.'

'I'll look out for you,' he said, walking off towards the Tube station.

He had taken the long route and he knew only too well why.

Chapter Twenty-Eight

'Bitch, fucking whore!'

'Calm down, Luca,' David Fowler said, passing his partner a tumbler of neat whisky and patting his shoulder as he did so.

Luca Cavatore slapped his colleague's hand away. '*Calm down*? The *cazzo puttana* has screwed us!'

'Luca, you know the bitch has always been trouble. At least we got a grand out of her.'

'*A grand*?' Cavatore screamed again, slamming his fist on the desk. 'Are you bloody mad? She owes us twice as much! What the fucking hell have you done, David?'

'I thought you would be happy to see the back of her.'

'What the fuck are you talking about? I've already promised her services to important clients.' He picked at a scab on his arm. 'And after all we've done for the ungrateful cow. What were you thinking?'

'There was nothing I could do,' Fowler said, placing his glass on the desk and holding his hands in the air in mock surrender. 'Vadislav had me over a barrel.'

'What the fuck is that supposed to mean?'

'The bastard threatened to open the Ukraine case. He's got Bodashka's witness statement that was withheld at the trial.'

Cavatore picked up his glass. The whisky seemed to have a calming effect. He tried to think logically about what to do next.

The threat from Vadislav was a problem, especially if he had damning evidence that could put them out of business. He'd always assumed Bodashka was dead and buried. None of it made sense. The Russian was Tommaso's favourite barrister in London. So why would he risk his relationship with the Don over some nondescript whore? It was his livelihood. If the bastard was playing games or switching allegiance, he needed to be removed from the equation. His eyes were fixed firmly on Fowler. 'I told Tommaso years ago never to trust a fucking Russian!' Cavatore scratched his head. 'You know, something doesn't quite add up here – how does the bitch afford the services of a barrister? She has no money. Unless she's been screwing us!'

Fowler shrugged. 'I did hear a rumour that Rudinsky was paying her cash under the table.'

Cavatore studied the framed picture on the desk. It depicted happier times, a smiling group outside the Green Door when the club had first opened. His arm was around Fowler's shoulder and they were surrounded by four of the nightclub girls. The gala night had been one hell of a party, with celebrities and a never-ending flow of champagne. Two years later, he had started bringing in the first of the Ukrainian girls. They had only a limited command of English, but that never mattered to the punters, who were more interested in their bodies than their conversational skills. In time the girls learnt enough of the language to protest about their working conditions, and he had to constantly keep them in line. It hadn't been difficult to feed Fowler the story that they were from destitute families and wanted the work, if only to send the money back home. Then Madeleine Laurent had appeared on the scene under the mistaken illusion that she was a singer. When confronted with her new job description she'd gone berserk and told him in no uncertain terms what he could do with his club. For three weeks they'd held her in the basement, beating her daily. She'd eventually got the message and started to cooperate. Then Fowler had begun to take liberties, ignoring the old adage that you never shit on your own doorstep. Like most of the punters, he'd lusted after the girl and she'd taken full advantage of his needs, making trouble whenever she could. On more than one occasion Mo, the bouncer, had to take her back down to the basement to reinforce the message. Now here she was, up to her old tricks again. She needed to be taught a serious lesson, one she would not forget. But first they had to find her. Cavatore was still deliberating over what he would let Mo do to the girl when the thought suddenly came to him. 'Have you banked the cheque?'

'It's already cashed.'

'Pity; I would have liked nothing more that to ram it up Vadislav's arse.'

'I'm really sorry, Luca. The bastard was blackmailing me. I just didn't know what to do.'

'For fuck's sake, will you stop with the fucking apologies?' Was the arsehole trying to make amends for his monumental screw-up? Cavatore was a short man – no taller than five foot four – with a face like a ferret, but he had a big opinion of himself. He ran his thumb and forefinger over his moustache, still deep in thought. He'd managed the Green Door for years now and one measly French whore wasn't going to fuck that up for him. The London operation made good money. As such, Tommaso pretty much kept his nose out of the day-to-day running of the place, which was precisely how he had managed to extend his business operations into ... other activities. The whore had to disappear. He turned to Fowler. 'Don't worry about Miss Laurent. She is fucking history.'

'I don't understand.'

'We no longer require her services,' he said, picking up the telephone and dialling a number. It rang only once before it connected. 'Mario! Luca – *buon pomeriggio.*' The man he was talking to was Mario Falcone, Head of Operations in the East End. Otherwise known as The Liquidator, for it was his job to authorise all of Tommaso's extermination orders. Cavatore cleared his throat. 'We're having trouble with one of the girls.

158

The whore has done a runner. That's right, we need her gone. And possibly the barrister who represents her.' The response was brief. 'Vadislav, that's him.' Cavatore played with the whisky glass. 'An accident perhaps? Mmm-hmm. That's the idea. Can we get together tomorrow: say ten at the Green Door?' He knew Falcone would run it by Tommaso. Everything had to be done 'by the book', so to speak. '*Grazie, amico.*'

'Shit, Luca, what the fuck are you doing?' Fowler was pacing the floor. He reached for the whisky bottle and poured himself a stiff measure. 'Vadislav couldn't have been clearer; should anything happen to the girl, he'd drop Bodashka's statement on the Met's desk.

Cavatore ran his hand over his heavily gelled hair. His angular face was expressionless. Why the hell had he ever gone into partnership with this stupid fucker? He knew the answer. Fowler had his contacts and for some strange reason Tommaso thought them 'useful'. But a few days away in Sicily and it had all gone tits up; the man was weak and had no stomach for this business. He was finished. He made a mental note to review the situation, perhaps have a word with Mario when the problem with the girl was sorted. In the meantime, he needed his partner's cooperation. He smiled at Fowler but there was no warmth in the expression. 'We have to handle this carefully. Our first concern is the Russian – we need to know where his loyalties lie. If it's a simple misunderstanding we can leave him alone. For now. After all, we don't want to draw any more attention to the club than is absolutely necessary.'

Fowler's hand was shaking when he lifted the glass to his lips. 'It's good to have you back, Luca; I've been a nervous wreck with this blackmail threat hanging over my head.'

'When this is all over, why don't you take a few days off,' Cavatore said, softening his manner. Then he let out a disturbing laugh. 'I'm sure Mario will resolve the matter to our satisfaction.'

Chapter Twenty-Nine

A cool wind had sprung up. It caught an advertising banner outside the newsagents and fluttered its shadow across the cobblestones. Suddenly the street lamps erupted to life, like glow-worms lighting the path. In the narrow alley, opposite the fish shop that led to Madeleine's flat, a call girl stood on the pavement, hustling the revellers, her thin frame silhouetted in the early evening dusk. Mallory paused. Every sense in his body told him to walk away. But he had to know.

Against his better judgement, he entered the street. Madeleine's flat was two doors down from the Malaysian restaurant and there was a light on in the bedroom. Was she back? Or had she just left the lights on? She was always frightened of the dark. Why was he doing this? Jealously was an emotion he'd never embraced. Yet here he was, standing in the shadows yearning for the girl, watching her window and waiting for some sign to go to her. There is no fool like an old fool, he thought. He took out the packet of Camel and, turning his back to the building, lit the cigarette. The paper was dry on his mouth but the smoke tasted good. It was a cold night, accentuated by an arctic wind. His collar was pulled up tight around his neck and the cigarette was cupped in his hand. He took one last draw and flicked it into the gutter.

Then a shadow at the window made him look up.

The curtain was drawn back and the window opened. Mallory jumped back in surprise, almost tripping over the raised kerb stone. The figure of a man was just visible. He was smoking a cigar. God, that was close – what an idiot he would've looked if he'd walked in on them. Then he heard a woman's laughter – Madeleine's laughter – and he retreated further into the darkness. Just when he was wondering what to do next, a hand reached out and closed the window, obliterating the laughter. He felt the insufferable pain. It was as if a knife had been plunged into his breast. So this was what she called 'love'. *Don't leave me, darling, I can't live without you* – what a bloody fool he'd been. It was footsteps on the cobblestones that brought him to his senses. An old man with a walking stick was coming towards him, coat buttoned up against the cold. Mallory greeted the stranger. The man responded with a grunt, almost as if it was normal to see someone lurking alone in the shadows.

Mallory heard the thunder before the lightning struck. Then the rain came. It hammered the pavement like the staccato of a machine gun. He stood in the storm, raindrops splattering his face and he cared not. He was alive! What mattered next to that? Not whether he was happy or sad – in love or alone – miserable or elated. He was alive! The pouring rain had penetrated his clothes and was running down his skin. He looked up at the window through the shimmering curtain of water and shouted to the girl, 'Madeleine, it's over, you will never again have this hold over me. We're finished!' He wiped his hand over his face to clear the rain from his eyes. The only light in the room now appeared to be the soft glow of a candle. How bloody romantic. But why was he surprised? After all, wasn't this just what she'd told him the other night? She *wanted* this double life; to live with someone else and still keep him as her friend and lover. Well, it was one thing talking about it but quite another seeing it happen in the flesh. He refused to be kept around for the odd times she needed him. Neither did he want to live with the llies and deceit, nor the recriminations that he knew would surely follow.

He was alone again, yes. But he was alive.

Chapter Thirty

Mario Falcone was noted for his punctuality. At 10 a.m. sharp he was sitting across the desk from Luca Cavatore in the office at the Green Door.

'Mario! *Bello vederti*,' Cavatore said, extending his hand. 'Strega? Or perhaps an espresso?'

Falcone shook his head and removed his sunglasses. A smooth character in a lightweight cream suit, he was always dressed immaculately. His hairless baby face would almost be handsome were it not for the large, pointed nose and expressionless eyes. Neat, prematurely grey hair gave him a distinctive appearance. 'Let's get down to business.'

Cavatore nodded and handed over the photographs of the girl.

'A pretty one,' Falcone said, studying the picture intently. 'Only last month we had a similar problem with a club in Manchester. The Doctor had to attend to the girl.' He shook his head indifferently. 'Very sad, but at least it stopped her wandering.'

Cavatore shivered. 'Can he help with another patient?'

A callous smile stretched across Falcone's lips. 'It's possible. What do you have in mind?'

'An accident.' Cavatore held the Strega over his glass, a look of uncertainty on his face. 'Can he handle it?'

Falcone's eyes narrowed. 'Antonio Luciano is a professional.' The distaste was difficult to disguise.

'I apologise, Mario, this business with the whore has put me on edge.'

Falcone nodded; the brief moment of confrontation had passed. 'I spoke with Tommaso last night; he trusts your judgement on the issue with the girl. But he has one reservation–'

'The barrister?'

'Vadislav is useful to the organisation. We don't want to lose him. Neither do we want to risk drawing attention to the club.'

'I understand. But what about Bodashka?'

'If the girl "takes her own life", Vadislav won't get involved. Most of his business comes from our clubs so why would he want to rock the boat? Enrico will have a word with him about Bodashka. We assumed he was dead and buried. The boss does not take kindly to resurrections.' He ran his hand over his flabby chin. 'So I understand you know where the girl lives.'

'She sings at the French Revolution. Her flat is just down the road from there, on Peter Street.' Cavatore jotted the details down and handed them to his counterpart.

Falcone memorised the address and tore up the scrap of paper. He then put the girl's picture into the inside pocket of his jacket. 'I'm taking a break in Sicily when this is all over – a period of mourning, one might say. Perhaps it would be wise for you to do likewise.'

'I don't have the same respect for the dead,' Cavatore replied sarcastically.

Falcone gave a thin smile. 'Nevertheless, the Don would like to see you.' His voice carried a hard line. It was an order not a request.

'Of course!' Cavatore wiped his sweaty palms down his trouser legs.

Falcone stood up and straightened his jacket. 'I'll be in touch shortly.'

'The girl has her passport,' Cavatore said, a worried look on his face, 'if she gets wind of all this, she may try and do a runner. We need to–'

'How did she get her passport?'

'Vadislav.'

Falcone's lips tightened again. 'Put a shadow on her. Any unusual activity, call the office.'

Chapter Thirty-One

After what had happened on Peter Street, Mallory did not return to the French Revolution. Neither did he answer his hall telephone. He left a message with the landlady, saying he was not available to anyone other than Andrei. And then he changed the locks on his front door.

On the table was the finished manuscript; he hadn't looked at it since returning from Whitstable. He tried again to read what he had last written but it was impossible. Damn the woman – why couldn't he get her out of his bloody mind? He loathed her and revered her in equal measure and the craving was killing him. The only answer was to find a bar. The electric clock on the bookshelf told him it was almost ten – sufficient time to get to his local before closing. The manuscript could wait.

When the Jolly Sailor shouted last orders at eleven, Mallory was still stone-cold sober. Going home to an empty flat was simply not an option. In his head was an old Negro spiritual. He hummed the tune as he crossed the main street. After a twenty-minute walk he was outside the Troubadour folk club. The place was a Mecca for noisy Australian and African expats, but occasionally they hosted a singer who was half good. He hoped tonight it might be the busker he'd seen outside Antonio's restaurant. She had mentioned Thursday.

The woman on the door welcomed him with a smile that could be turned on or off like a light switch. After ordering a large whisky, he perched on a bar stool. His head was in his hands. He stared into the mirror above the scrubbed-top counter and hardly recognised the image. At least the whisky helped him to forget the shit. What a bloody life! The violin cut across his thoughts. It was the busker from Soho! She was playing an unusual rendition of 'House Of The Rising Sun'. He closed his eyes and let the tune wash over him. It resurrected so many memories. Then suddenly he heard someone shouting a name from across the bar. It was a familiar name, albeit one buried deep in the distant past. For just a moment he thought he was going crazy. He looked down at the glass. Shit! What the hell was he drinking?

'Mike? Mike Rawlings!'

A large man appeared beside him. Mallory immediately recognised the face in the mirror.

'Hey *bru*, is it really you?'

It wasn't possible. He looked down again at the glass. But then how could he ever forget the South African accent tinged with an Irish lilt? He turned on his stool and there he was, all six-foot-four of him. 'Jacob ... Jacob *bloody* Lannigan!'

'*Kunjani shamari*!' The greeting was accompanied by a smile as wide as the Zambezi.

'Jacob, you can't believe how good it is to see you again!' He really meant what he said – if there was one person in the world he'd want to run into from his past, it was this guy standing beside him – his old army buddy. 'It's been a long time!'

The ex-soldier threw his arms around Mallory's neck. '*Long time*? Shit man – it's been, what, something like nineteen, twenty years?' said the excited voice in his ear. 'Don't you remember, after we came through that *fokking* ambush in the Zambezi Valley?'

Mallory knew only too well. December '78. Apart from Lieutenant Anderson, he and Jacob were the only two soldiers to have escaped with their lives. In a semi-conscious state, Mallory

166

had listened to the young corporal calmly giving the grid reference that had saved their lives. Without Lannigan, he wouldn't be here today. 'Did I ever thank you for calling up that chopper?'

Lannigan smiled. 'The one that carried out the air-vac after you'd been shot? Don't think you did. How about buying me a drink?'

'God, I can't believe this is happening, Jacob.'

Just for a moment the faded memories came rushing back: the frantic shouts of his comrades, the view from the edge of the open chopper door and a vast plain covered in mopani trees and acacia bushes. The helicopter flew at ground level. He remembered the rondavels and the African children waving at them. And then the chopper banked away. They were over the river and he caught a glimpse of the spray in the distance – what the Africans called *Mosi-oa-Tunya*, the Smoke that Thunders. Victoria Falls. He loved the river above all others. Had he been hallucinating or did he see the fish-eagles, the proud fishermen, gliding serenely above the water? He knew it was the dry season because Zambezi had retreated like a snake in the bush and the waterfall was merely a whisper. That was how the terrorist bastards had managed to cross into Rhodesia. When the rains returned and Zambezi became angry, it wouldn't be so easy. These were the images he'd seen before passing out. Twenty hours later, he'd regained consciousness in a Salisbury hospital and there beside his bed – with that old familiar smile – was Lannigan.

'Shit, mate, you haven't changed much since I last saw you. Just as ugly as ever.'

Lannigan laughed. 'Still full of the *kak*, hey?' He ran his hand over his crew cut. Although his hair was going grey, his face was still youthful, clean-cut. It was only spoilt by a nose that had been broken on numerous occasions and a couple of missing teeth. Not that it worried the big man – vanity had never been a priority with him. 'But come on, Mike, tell me: what the hell are you doing here in Pommie-land,' he said, tightening his jaw, just like he did in the old days.

Mallory smiled broadly and patted his friend on the shoulder. 'I was about to ask you the same question!'

Lannigan stepped back from the bar. For a moment he appeared unsure of where to go next. 'Look, mate, there's no point me trying to bullshit you.'

Mallory squinted his eyes in suspicion. 'I read you like a book, Jacob; always have done.'

'Shit, don't I know it? Well I gotta tell you, Mike, it's no accident I turned up in this bar. I've been looking for you.'

The long arm of the law? Surely not Jacob? 'Oh yeah?'

'I made a number of discreet enquiries in Zimbabwe as to your whereabouts, without success. Shit, man, I thought you'd fallen off Inyangombe! Then I came across an old African contact, one we'd turned during the war. He knew you and told me to try London. This is the fifth bloody expat club I've visited in the last week! I tell you, mate, I was going to call it a day after this one.' He laughed. 'I honestly thought you'd given up drinking.'

'Why were you so desperate to find me? It's been twenty years.'

'All in good time, *boet*. Look, it's nothing sinister but before I go on, I do need to know what you're doing here.'

'Why? What are you, Jacob, the bloody CIO?'

The very mention of the notorious Criminal Investigation Organisation made Lannigan shiver. He gave a nervous cough. 'Hey, *bru*, it's not a *blerrie* interrogation. I'm just interested.'

Mallory nodded. But in spite of his affection for his ex-comrade he decided to keep things brief – Lannigan was his friend, but a man in his position could never be too careful. 'I had to leave Zim in rather a hurry.'

'*Jou bliksem*! Don't give your old mate that *bul kak*!' Lannigan said, laughing wildly. 'Have you forgotten what a small place Zim is? We both know how the bush telegraph works.'

Mallory smiled but his lips were tight. He knew exactly what the rumours would be like. He was a wanted man and his picture would have been circulated throughout the country, on every army

168

barrack noticeboard. There was no point trying to play the innocent. 'I had a bit of a dispute with G2.'

'*Jislaaik boet*, that's got to be the understatement of the year!
From what I heard, you had the security guys running around
like blue-arsed flies trying to find you!'

'It's a long story, Jacob. Beer?'

'You bet, *bru*.' He looked over at the pumps hosting an array
of English beers on draft and was clearly unimpressed. 'All the
stuff on tap is *kak*. Do they have a Castle? Or a Windhoek?'

'This is one of the few bars in London where you can still get
African beer. But it's in short supply, so they keep it hidden under
the counter.' Mallory placed the order. God, how strange was this?
And why the hell was Lannigan looking for him. He needed
answers to settle his nerves. 'So, what brings *you* to London?'

'You won't believe this.'

'Try me.'

Lannigan took a swig of the cold lager and wiped his lips before
answering. 'I work for a company called Somerset Holdings. Their
HQ is here in Pommie-land. I've come over for a meeting with
the head honcho.' He laughed. 'The bullshit boys as I like to call
them.'

Mallory closed his eyes for a moment. God, how he'd missed
the banter. 'Look, let's grab a table away from the noise, where
we can talk.' There was a vacant seat in the corner. The girl was
now singing an old Dylan number, 'A Hard Rain's A-Gonna Fall'.
He half-closed his eyes again, listening to the haunting violin and
words that were reminiscent of those long-ago days.

'So here's where I'm at,' Lannigan said, leaning forward in a
conspiratorial manner. 'Somerset Holdings, as the name suggests,
is a holding company.'

'You say it like I know what you're talking about.'

'Holding companies buy and own shares in other companies,
shares which the holding company then controls. We go one step
further,' he said, dropping his voice to a whisper, 'we buy and

control *governments* – or, to put it another way, we initiate *change* in governments. Most of our work has been in West Africa, around the oil and diamond fields. But now Head Office wants to move into Zim – the human rights issue is the perfect cover to instigate change there.'

'Why Zim? Apart from a few white farmers trying to scratch a living out of the land, there's not a hell of a lot left there.'

Lannigan hesitated for a moment. 'Human rights are just a by-product. Somerset Holdings are not in the benevolence game – they're only interested in wealth.'

'Okay ... so why Zim?'

Lannigan kept his voice down to a whisper. 'A couple of years ago, a *muntu* was walking through the bush – south of Mutare, at a place called Chiadzwa – when he came across an object that looked like a lump of dirty rock. But what attracted him to the stone was that a corner of it sparkled when the sun caught it. Well, he didn't have a bloody clue what it was but he showed it to the store-keeper at the Kwik Save in Mutare West. The Indian knew exactly what it was. He gave the *dof muntu* a trolley full of provisions in exchange for the "lump of stone" – made the *Loskop*'s day.'

Mallory shook his head and laughed. 'Good old Africa; nothing ever changes.'

Lannigan tilted his head back and half the bottle of beer disappeared in one swig. 'So, when a dealer eventually got hold of the diamond, the shit hit the fan and there were *muntus* crawling all over Chiadzwa.'

'What's the diamond field called?'

'Marange. And it's just like the old Wild West.' He shook his head grimly. '*Ag* man, you know Africa – to the *muntu* the *fokking* AK-47 is still the rule of law.'

Mallory glanced around the room. There was no one close by. 'So let me get this straight: Somerset Holdings wants a change of government? By replacing Mugabe with someone from the opposition you effectively allow the Matabele to govern the country. It would no doubt give your holding company a substantial stake in the diamond fields?'

'Clever stuff, hey?'

Mallory ran his fingers through his hair. Now he was all ears. This part of the Eastern Highlands was familiar territory, from the Bush War. And from G2. God, if the Rhodesian government had known about the diamond fields back then, it might very well have changed the outcome of the war. *Just like the Wild West*, Jacob had said. He could picture the scene: diamonds scattered amongst the acacia trees, ripe for the picking – just like it had once been on Namibia's Skeleton Coast – excited Africans descending upon the bush, riches beyond their wildest dreams. 'So who owns the rights?'

'That's the tricky bit.' Lannigan put his mouth close to Mallory's ear. 'De Beers used to hold the concession. When that expired a Pommie company known as African Consolidated Resources took up the rights. Now Bob's Zimbabwe Mining Development Corporation has nationalised the whole bloody lot.'

'If the find is as rich as you're telling me, I can see why Somerset Holdings is interested.'

'Mike, you have no idea. This is probably the biggest diamond discovery anywhere in the world in the last one hundred years. It's serious *kak*!'

That name again; how strange to hear it after all this time. 'So what's your role in all of this?'

'The company want lawyers out in Zim representing Mugabe's opposition party, the MDC – men who know the country and the justice system. I have the experience, so they've put me in charge of recruitment.'

'Justice system? That's a joke.'

'Hear me out, *bru*. We're going down the human rights road. Do you remember *Gukurahundi*?'

Of course he remembered it. Who could forget the massacre of twenty thousand Matabele men, women and children? That was where his hatred of Mugabe's Fifth Brigade had really taken

171

seed. The ethnic evil sickened even those hardened to a country where death and destruction was an everyday occurrence. His face twisted and his eyes narrowed when he thought of the true meaning of that Shona word *Gukurahundi*: the early rain that washes away the chaff before the spring rains. Only this time the chaff was the Matabele. 'I've seen the images of the victims. They never even got a decent burial. But I'm still not sure how I fit into your plans?'

Lannigan paused, clearly considering his next move. 'To be quite honest with you, this is exactly why I've been looking for you. I need a lawyer with the right experience to help me in Zim. A good man who won't buckle under pressure. And you were one of the best.'

Mallory desperately wanted another beer. He knew exactly where this was going and his face betrayed his concerns.

'Look, *bru*, I know your reputation and what you were doing in the years before the war. At the time, I must admit, I didn't altogether agree with you aiding ... terrorists,' he paused, then, 'but I admired you for it nonetheless. There is no one I would rather have by my side.'

'Cut the bullshit, Jacob, just give me the bottom line.'

'Agh man, that's more like it!' Lannigan sat back in his chair and raised his beer. 'So let's see; without bonuses the job pays a hundred and twenty grand for an initial contract of six months. That's twenty grand a month in Pommie Pounds. You could pick up where you left off before the war.'

Mallory whistled softly under his breath. Shit, that was money beyond his wildest dreams. But pick up where he'd left off? He could never do that. Too much hatred had surely destroyed any chance of him going back to those days. But then what did he have here in London? Maybe this was his chance at last to go home. 'So I'd be working for Somerset Holdings. But in what capacity?'

'Zimbabwe elections are due to be held in six months' time and we want to ensure that it is a fair reflection of the people,

172

without all the intimidation shit that accompanied the last fiasco. Our brief is to challenge Mugabe through the Supreme Court on any issues relating to the election.' He downed the last of the beer and held the bottle up in the air. 'Another?'

Mallory nodded. As he watched Lannigan push his way through the crowd to the bar, he tried to fit all the pieces together. The Supreme Court? That was a joke. Zim was a bloody one-party state. On the table in front of him stood an empty bottle of Castle and for just a moment he saw it as a symbol of what was once Rhodesia. Could he really return? Really make a difference to underprivileged lives and finish what he'd started in the courts, twenty years before? But he was under no illusion that Somerset Holdings were Zimbabwe's knights in shining armour. Their intention was to overthrow the government and reap the benefits. And where would he be standing when the game was over? Nevertheless, it was a chance worth taking for the money they were offering. The more he thought about the proposition, the more it appealed to him. Suddenly a half-smile crossed his face. By leaving town he'd also finally rid himself of the girl and her complicated life. He was still deep in thought when Lannigan appeared at the table with four bottles of Castle.

'So how about it, *vriend*?' He touched Mallory's bottle. 'It'll be just like old times, only without all the army *kak*. This is an opportunity to do something for Zimbabwe and get well paid for it. And it's a bloody sight better than fighting for a cause that was going nowhere – eight years of tribal fighting and Uncle Bob still has the country where he wants it – by the balls. Let's get out there and change it.'

It had been some years since Mallory had heard anyone speak so passionately about the cause and it came as rather a shock, knowing Lannigan's background. He'd grown up during the Apartheid regime and had been as keen as any other Rhodesian to see the country remain white. Now here he was representing Africans in court? Somehow Mallory found it difficult to believe.

173

But in spite of his misgivings, it was simply too good an opportunity to turn down. 'There is one small complication, Jacob.'

Lannigan removed a packet of Texan from the inside pocket of his jacket. He offered one to Mallory, who gazed at the cigarettes in disbelief.

'God, I haven't seen one of these in years!' Drawing out the short cigarette, he smiled to himself when he recalled the banter: *Smoke Texan and cough like a cowboy.*

'Rhodesian tobacco, *ou boet*, the best there is,' Lannigan said, lighting them up. 'So, go on, mate? You were saying there's a complication?'

Mallory drew deeply on the Texan before speaking. 'Mike Rawlings is dead. He ceased to exist twenty years ago.' If he was going to take on this contract, he had to tell Lannigan the real reason he was here. But could he trust him? He scratched his head, deep in thought. He had to – after all, Zimbabwe was no longer Rhodesia; most of the old army units had been disbanded. Hell, Mugabe would probably give him a bloody medal for what he had done all those years ago in that interrogation room.

Yes, perhaps it was time at last to tell his side of the story.

Chapter Thirty-Two

For the next ten minutes Mallory related all that had happened since that fateful day in the Zambezi Valley. He did, however, omit any mention of his escape. That was best left buried.

'So that's what all the fuss was about? I tell you what, Mike, after all these years it's good to hear it from you. Straight up, mate. I never did imagine you going that far without provocation; those G2 bastards are the most sadistic fuckers around. It's only a shame you didn't top them all. Especially that *fokking* officer.'

'What was his name?'

'Van Neikerk. The depraved bastard was transferred from Military Police to G2. We called him "the butcher".'

'If Julian hadn't stopped me, I would've killed him.'

'Well you certainly put him out of action! He had a nervous breakdown. Three months later he ended up in a mental institution. So, who was the *muntu*?'

'One of the liberation army's top guys.'

Lannigan was impressed. 'You know, *vriend*,' he said, 'I would've done the same thing myself if I'd been there. I have no time for those shits – they were a law unto themselves. I once saw an African corpse they'd been working on – the poor bastard had no nose, ears, eyes or bollocks, and they'd incinerated most of his skin with a hot iron. I don't know anyone in the forces that has a good word to say about G2.'

'Thanks, Jacob, I needed that. I've lived with what I did for too many years – it's good to finally get it off my chest.'

Lannigan shrugged. 'Agh mate, it's nothing.' He took a piece of liquorice paper from his top pocket and filled it with a pungent smelling tobacco mix.

Mallory burst out laughing. 'Shit, man, you can't smoke that in here!'

Lannigan grinned like a child. 'No worries, I'm not the only one. When I went for a slash, I could smell *dagga* in the bog.'

Mallory took the rolled up cigarette and drew in the acrid smoke. The *zol* made him shudder and then relax. It was just what he needed. 'Last time I had one of these was in the Zambezi Valley.'

'It settles the nerves. Hey look, *bru*, if you want your old identity back I can arrange it. Or maybe you would like to use the name you have now which, by the way, is…?'

'Mallory.' All the cards were now on the table.

'Up to you, *boet*. Either way it's no problem. We have operatives all over the world and most of them need passports; it's a way of life for them, working under a nom de plume.' He laughed. 'Kinda like being born again, hey?'

Mallory put the bottle of beer on the table and fixed his eyes on his old comrade. The girl had left the stage for a break and the crowd had started to disperse. He thought again about the proposition. It was almost too good to be true. With a new identity, a passport and this much money he could return to England legally. Or maybe even buy a parcel of land in the Drakensberg and start again. But there was still something bothering him. He looked at Lannigan. 'Am I still on Zim's wanted list?'

'Hell no! Mugabe wouldn't give a shit what you did all those years ago! G2 were his enemies. What did you say the *muntu*'s name was?'

'Julian … Julian Chikembe.'

'*Julian Chikembe*? Not *the* Julian Chikembe?'

Mallory's eyebrows furrowed. 'Sorry?'

'*Fok* me,' Lannigan's face registered the shock. 'Have you any idea who that *muntu* is?'

'Sure. He was a lieutenant in Mugabe's liberation army.'

'*Was* a lieutenant in the liberation army? *Ya boet*. Now he's one of the opposition's right-hand men – he changed his allegiance during the conflict, joined ZIPRA to lead the guerrillas from Zambia. I'm probably telling you something you already know.'

'Actually, I had no idea.'

'It was logical for him to move to the People's Revolutionary Army – he's Matabele, from the Sindebele tribe.'

Mallory nodded in agreement. 'Makes sense; most of ZIPRA was made up of Matabele tribesmen during the war.'

'That's right. In fact there's a rumour that Chikembe's name is being put forward for party leader of the MDC when the current *muntu* stands down.'

'The Movement of Democratic Change. Uncle Bob's opposition?'

'*Ja boetie*!' He took a long swig from the bottle of Castle. '*Fok* man, have you any idea how much this could help us with the legal contracts?'

'I can imagine.'

'*Struik*, man, I need a brandy. Don't suppose they have KWV here.'

'You must be joking! We'll drink the KWV in South Africa.'

We'll drink the KWV in South Africa. The sentence stopped Lannigan in his stride. For just a minute he looked as though he'd failed to grasp the implication of what Mallory had just said. Then it clearly hit him like a sledgehammer. 'Shit, man – does that mean you're in?'

Mallory held out his hand. 'You have a deal.'

Lannigan threw his hands up in the air and brought them down on Mallory's shoulders. 'And now we celebrate! The best brandy this establishment has – I'll buy the bloody bottle.'

When Lannigan returned to the table, he had a bottle of Remy Martin and an enormous grin. Mallory lit up two Camels and passed the cigarette to his friend. 'One last question: what happened to G2?'

'No worries there, mate,' Lannigan said, pouring a generous measure of brandy into each glass. 'ZANU disbanded them. Most of the operatives fled south with their tails between their legs. Bob would have fried them alive if he'd caught them.'

'So they're in South Africa now?'

'With their interrogation skills,' Lannigan said, 'the Apartheid government probably recruited them. There was always going to be a job for them while the ANC was chasing independence. Either that or they would have headed north to Angola, to help Jonas Savimbi sort out the Cuban rebels and the communist-backed MPLA.'

'So they worked for the South African Defence Force?'

'Ya man. The SADF also offered me a commission in Angola. Before I took on this job.' He laughed. 'Can you imagine me, a captain in the South African army?'

'Actually I can.'

Lannigan shook his head. 'I'd had enough of killing *fokking* Kaffirs.'

Mallory winced at the racist remark. Strange how Lannigan could still never quite get his head around the fact that Africa, as a continent, was changing. South Africa had already made the transition when it pulled Mandela off Robin Island and put him into Government House. He still remembered the speech Nelson made when he took office: *'Each of us is as intimately attached to the soil of this beautiful country in much the same way as are the famous jacaranda trees of Pretoria and the mimosa trees of the bushveld – a rainbow nation at peace with itself and the world. We are all one people.'* No revenge, no bitterness, just unity.

Lannigan downed his brandy. The inebriated smile said it all. '*Fok* me, Mike, what were the chances of me bumping into you

178

tonight? Of all the bars in all the world?' He was trying to impersonate Rick in *Casablanca*, rather badly, 'and you happen to walk into this one.' His words were slurred but he still had hold of his faculties. 'Why?'

'It's a long story. I was trying to forget a woman.'

'Obliterate her with alcohol?' Lannigan held up the brandy glass. 'If that's the reason you're here, I'll have to thank her one day.'

Now that would be interesting, Mallory thought. What would Lannigan make of Madeleine? 'She's no longer around.'

The silly grin on Lannigan's face disappeared for a moment and he tried to focus on the room. Then he shook his head, as if the very action of doing so would clear the fog. 'So where do I get hold of you? I mean, we can't keep hoping we'll cross paths in one of London's many African clubs. And another thing,' he slurred, scratching his head. 'What do I call you? Or have I already asked you that?'

'Mike is fine for now,' Mallory said, grinning at his drunken comrade. 'Give me your number and I'll ring you the day after tomorrow with all the details.'

'Hey, I like that – no address or contact number, no way for me to find you.' Lannigan's smile transformed itself into a worried frown and he looked sceptical. 'How do I know I will ever see you again? Shit, man, I can't afford to lose you.'

Mallory pondered the thought. Mrs Johnson mustn't know what was happening yet. 'I gave you my word. And my handshake is my bond – you of all people should know that.'

'*Ja* man, sorry for asking. Look, I'm staying at the Russell Hotel on Russell Square – give me a call there. If I'm not in, just leave a message and I'll call you back.'

Mallory helped himself to the Remy and then poured another generous measure into Lannigan's glass. 'When do you go back to Africa?'

'We leave for Harare in two weeks.'

Two weeks. The reality was hitting home. There was so much to sort out in just fourteen days. But then, maybe not. The most difficult task would be breaking the news to Andrei.

In spite of the brandy, Lannigan nevertheless noticed the look of hesitancy on Mallory's face. 'Look, *bru*, I'm sorry it's such short notice.'

'What's the rush?'

'The first hearing at the Supreme Court is in a month's time.'

Mallory took a deep breath. God, that soon. 'Okay. I'll be in touch.'

'When you contact me, I'll have the details sorted. You'll need four passport photographs.' Gripping the edge of the table, Lannigan teetered to his feet. He then handed Mallory what remained of the bottle of brandy. 'Here, take this – I need to keep a clear head for the next couple of days.'

Chapter Thirty-Three

'Your friend has called again,' said the landlady. 'I keep telling her you're away.'

'Friend?' Mallory was standing in the hall.

'She's very rude – said I was discriminating against people of "her kind". Whatever does she mean?'

Ah, so the 'friend' was Madeleine. She must have come round last night when he was out with Lannigan. Maybe she'd tried to get into his flat and discovered he'd had the locks changed. Little wonder she was furious.

'I'm very sorry, Mr Mallory, but she can't possibly think she can get away with–' The old lady's voice trailed off. Her shoulders were stooped and she kept fidgeting with her hands. 'You really must see her. I just can't go on like this. She calls at the most unsociable hours, sometimes in the middle of the night! It's got to stop!'

Mallory could understand why she was upset; he knew better than anyone how persistent Madeleine could be. 'Look, Mrs Johnson, I'm really sorry for the trouble – I'll see her tomorrow and sort it,' he said, trying to remain composed, despite his throbbing head. 'You have my word.'

'You'd better,' she said, slamming the door.

Chapter Thirty-Four

Mallory dropped the thick Manila envelope and the file on the desk. 'Sorry for the delay, it's pretty complicated stuff.'

'How so?'

'The prosecution are saying that the images of the girls were taken without their consent and then sold on illegally.'

'That's bullshit.'

'I know that. We have proof the girls were paid for the photos.'

'I thought so,' Andrei said, scanning the notes.

Mallory rubbed his bleary eyes. 'I could use a drink. Do you have a brandy?'

'My God, Mallory, you look like death warmed up,' Andrei said, retrieving the bottle of cognac. 'What has our matryoshka doll been up to now?' He poured a generous measure of Remy Martin into a cut glass tumbler. 'Not another middle of the night visitation?'

Mallory ignored the jibe and looked up at the sky. The sun was just starting to dip below the tall buildings, casting shadows across the street. It was a familiar scene, a part of London that would be forever embedded in his mind. The brandy was the hair of the dog. The fog lifted and his eyes returned to the Russian. 'My *babbelas* has nothing to do with Madeleine – well, not altogether.'

'So why the hangover?'

Mallory brushed his thighs with his hands. Unable to hold Andrei's intense stare, he looked down. 'I have to go back to Africa.'

It was the Russian's turn to be surprised. '*Africa*? Has immigration got hold of you?'

Mallory shook his head. 'No, it's nothing like that.' He paused, his brow furrowed. 'When I came back from Whitstable everything seemed different.'

'You are not making sense!'

'I know. It's difficult to explain. What was acceptable before is now depressing … the flat, the East End … my life. I've tried to forget Madeleine … it's not easy.'

The Russian nodded to indicate he understood. 'So that was what it was all about? And your solution was to hit the bottle?'

'That was my intention, but it didn't quite work out that way.' He took a deep breath. 'I met a soldier, a friend from my old regiment.'

'Your Rhodesian regiment? Where?'

'In the Troubadour. A guy called Jacob Lannigan. He saved my life in the Zambezi Valley. Do you remember me telling you about the ambush?'

The Russian shifted uneasily on his seat. 'I remember.' He picked up the glass. 'So what was he doing in the East End of London?'

Mallory's mouth felt dry. What he wouldn't give for a *zol*. Taking out the packet of Camel, he offered one to the Russian – anything to give his hands something to do. Surprisingly, Andrei accepted the cigarette. 'He was looking for me.'

'*Looking for you…*?'

'He wanted to offer me a job.'

'A job?' Andrei was conscious the conversation was sounding repetitive but he couldn't think of any other way of asking the questions.

Mallory sighed. 'The work is for an international holding company – it takes on legal contracts in conjunction with oil fields, diamond mines, anything of value in foreign countries. It just so happens that Africa is rather busy at the moment.'

Andrei scratched his nose. 'I can imagine. Am I permitted to know which African country you are referring to?'

Mallory looked down at the empty brandy glass. 'I'm going back to Zimbabwe.'

Andrei whistled softly. 'Why Zimbabwe? What do they have in that shithole that requires the services of an international law firm? Apart from the odd farmer who wants a fight with Mugabe in a Namibian court.'

'The very same thought occurred to me. But turns out they've found diamonds up in the Eastern Highlands, just outside Mutare. At a place called Marange.'

Andrei sat up in his chair, his eyes wide and his attention gripped. 'Well you don't need me to tell you how dangerous it is to go back there.' He reached up to the shelf above the sideboard and plucked out *The Times World Atlas*. Flicking through the pages, he eventually came to the map of Zimbabwe and ran his finger across the page. Then he looked up, his brow creased. 'Marange ... Marange ... ah! Now I remember. Some months ago I read an article in *The Times* about a rights dispute between De Beers and African Consolidated Resources. Unfortunately, I didn't pay much attention to it.'

'There's no reason why you should have.'

'I was under the impression that African Consolidated was a UK company?'

'Correct! Except there's now been a further development.' Mallory looked away. His mouth was dry and his head throbbed. 'Mugabe's Mining Development Corporation has recently nationalised the entire area.'

'You're not working for him, are you?'

'No! There's an election on the horizon. I'm representing the opposition, the MDC.'

'The Movement for Democratic Change.' Andrei whistled softly. 'You sure can pick them.'

'Their case for ensuring the election runs smoothly is a human rights issue. You know what happened in the last election with missing ballot boxes, intimidation and all the other shit these guys get up to. The plan is to take the case to the High Court. That's where I come in. I don't have all the details yet; I'll know more about it tomorrow when I contact Somerset Holdings.'

Andrei almost dropped his glass. 'Good God, Mallory, do you know who Somerset Holdings are?'

'They're a holding company, involved in foreign development projects.' Considering the fact that prior to meeting Lannigan he hadn't a clue what a 'holding company' even was, he managed to speak with some authority.

'That's what they want you to believe. It cloaks them in respectability.' Andrei laughed cynically. 'These guys, Mallory, are not your average "High Street holding company". They *move* governments! They have mercenary armies on tap, ousting presidents and replacing them with friendly faces. But they're not interested in the "rights" of ordinary Africans, oh no – what they want is money and power, and they invariably get it, through corruption and murder. So don't give me this horse shit about human rights – it's a cover to get their greedy hands on the diamonds.'

Mallory remained composed in the face of the onslaught. He was well aware of all of this. 'Are they any different to Mugabe?'

Whistling softly to himself again, Andrei reached for the brandy and poured another stiff measure into each glass. 'You have a point.' He sat back and contemplated his drink. 'I guess not. So – they're looking for a power switch in Zimbabwe.'

'Andrei, I know how African politics work–'

'But that's just it, Mallory – they don't work. It's the law of the gun over there.'

Mallory shifted forward in his seat. 'It remains to be seen whether the MDC will be any better than Mugabe. I have my doubts but I guess you have to at least give them a chance.'

The Russian nodded slowly. 'And what about your illegal background – your identity, passport, or rather lack thereof? Or do they propose to smuggle you in and out of the country?'

'They've promised me a new identity and a British passport.'

'That figures.' The Russian smiled but it was more of a grimace. 'So will you still be Mallory?'

Since his conversation with Lannigan last night he'd asked himself that very same question many times. Rawlings was his given name, but Mallory had worked well for him in England and had only ever brought him luck. He looked at the Russian and smiled. 'I've become rather attached to the name.'

'Good! And I take it they're paying you substantially for your services?'

'Very much so.'

The Russian laughed. 'Ah well, if it gives you a legal identity and a lot of money, who am I to persuade you otherwise? I'd have done the same in your situation.' He eyed his friend cautiously. 'This wouldn't have anything to do with the girl, would it?'

'It's a consideration, I guess.'

'A rather extreme way to end a relationship,' Andrei said, somewhat sadly.

From the tone of his voice, Mallory wondered which relationship Andrei was referring to. Was he putting on a brave face? He thought of what Madeleine had said – *Can you not see that he loves you, Mallory?* Strange how he had never even considered Andrei as part of his decision. But then they'd gone pretty hard on the drink, and he'd been swept along by the euphoria of the offer. Nevertheless, he felt bad about it; sure, the barrister would be able to find another lawyer to assist him, but it was their friendship that was irreplaceable. 'I'm sorry Andrei, it's–'

The big man waved his arms in the air magnanimously. His long blonde hair was in disarray from running his fingers through it. 'Think nothing of it, my boy! I will miss you terribly – and your assistance, which has been invaluable. But if nothing else

I'm pragmatic. And I understand that all good things come to an end sooner or later.' He turned to look out of the window. Storm clouds were gathering. The silence was onerous. Then he spoke. 'I've known from the day I first met you that this might happen. In fact, our relationship has actually lasted far longer than I thought it would. So no recriminations.' He waved his arms in the air. The gesture seemed forced, as did the smile. 'When are you going?'

'We leave for Harare in two weeks.'

'*Two weeks*!' Andrei almost dropped the glass again.

'The elections are in six months but the first hearing on voting rights is in a month's time at the Supreme Court. I need to get out there and familiarise myself with it all. Besides, the sooner I go, the better – if I have too much time to think about it, I might end up changing my mind.'

'Think carefully about what you are doing, my friend, and make sure it is for the right motives. I made much the same journey when I returned to Russia. And, as you know, it didn't end well.'

'If I can help people who have been murdered, tortured, raped and beaten, for no other reason than they come from "the wrong tribe", it will have been worth the effort.'

'Maybe.' The Russian stood up to his full height and raised his glass of brandy. '*Nostrovia*!'

Mallory had never seen him so emotional. There were tears in his eyes. 'This is not easy!'

'Rubbish! Come now, my friend – let us go out and get terribly drunk and forget about tomorrow. It is still a long way away.'

Mallory shook his head. He knew it was closer than they thought.

Chapter Thirty-Five

The Russian was familiar with all the best bars in Soho. The girls greeted him with an enthusiasm that was reserved only for the high-rollers. It was late evening when they were finally shown to their table at Antonio's restaurant. 'Tonight is on me,' Andrei said.

Mallory shrugged. After all that alcohol, he needed food, and he didn't really care who paid for it. Luigi immediately arrived to personally serve the table. It was a gesture the head waiter reserved for the owner and important customers only. Or more to the point, diners who tipped well. 'Tonight's special is Karoo lamb, Signor Andrei,' he said, handing them each a menu.

'Perfect! Now this is a significant occasion; my friend here is leaving us for the colonies – Zimbabwe, to be precise. So we need to give him something to remember us by.' He pointed to the Amarone on the wine list.

'Hang on!' Mallory raised his hand with a flourish. There was a silly grin on his face. 'Tonight I would like to … to share a South African wine with you.'

The Russian shook his head in dismay. 'Oh my God, Mallory. Well, if we must.' His eyes searched the section of Stellenbosch wines. When he recognised the Meerlust Rubicon, he smiled. It was a fifteen-year-old vintage and one of the most expensive wines on the menu. 'Can you decant a bottle of the '83 Meerlust please, Luigi?'

188

'*Si, signor.* Will there be anything else?'

Andrei looked at his guest. 'Do you want to stay on the vodka?'

Mallory shook his head. 'Just a jug of water, please.'

'*Si, signor.*' The waiter was about to leave with their order when he gasped. 'Excuse me! I almost forgot! We have an excellent old Napoleon Calvados – Antonio bought it from a cellar that has recently closed down. He said it must be offered to you before it is sold to anyone else.'

'How considerate of him.'

'Does that mean you would like the Calvados, *signor*?'

'Of course, my good man!'

Mallory shook his head in mock dismay. 'God knows how I will ever get home.'

'Let's worry about that later – the Calvados will awaken your appetite,' Andrei said as Luigi approached the table with the old encrusted bottle. The label was indiscernible, faded from the years it had lain in some dark cellar. It was almost sacrilege to bring it out into the daylight. Luigi opened it carefully, sniffed the cork and then nodded in satisfaction before pouring a small measure into Andrei's glass. 'Let my friend taste it first please, Luigi.'

'No, Andrei, you are the connoisseur.'

Andrei picked up the balloon glass. He held it up to the light. The apple brandy was golden brown in colour with just a touch of red mahogany. He breathed in the bouquet. The nose and palate were delicate and he could taste the concentration of aged apples and dried apricots balanced with butterscotch. 'This is divine. It reminds me of the fields of Normandy where apples are blessed by the sun on windswept hills.' He nodded to Luigi and the waiter poured a measure into each glass. Then Andrei touched Mallory's glass. 'This is the best you will ever taste,' he said, 'one does not drink it, one merely breathes it.' Luigi nodded his approval.

Mallory raised his glass. 'To friendship!'

'Friendship!' For a man who was seldom embarrassed, the Russian looked distinctly uncomfortable and failed to hide the emotion. To allay his discomfort, he took out a packet of Balkan Black Russian. When they had lit up, he leaned back in his chair, cigarette in one hand and brandy glass in the other. 'Is there anything I can do for you while you are away?'

'Come to think of it, there are a couple of things that need taking care of. I've decided to keep the flat. It's convenient. Not to mention the pleasant memories it has given me.'

'Of Madeleine?'

'Perhaps I'll be able to go back there one day without feeling sad. I'll learn to live with the times I shared with her and not ask for any more. Does that make sense?'

Andrei glared at Mallory and then laughed. 'Do you think we Russians have no soul? When you come back you will have forgotten the girl and then I will take you to St Petersburg and introduce you to Russian culture! Also to Russian girls – the women from Kazan are said to be the most beautiful in the world. And the best lovers.'

'That's exactly what I'll need after six months in Zim!' Mallory laughed.

'It's preferable to playing with African women.'

Mallory smiled to himself. There was nothing Andrei could tell him about that.

Luigi was standing beside the table. Pouring a small measure of the Meerlust from the decanter into Andrei's glass, he waited for his approval. The Russian took his time savouring the deep purple hue. The wine had a classic nose of ripe plum, cedar and violets with an almost intense spiciness. Like the Calvados, it was exceptional. 'Luigi, you have done us justice tonight. My compliments to Antonio and his cellar!'

'It's always a pleasure to serve one who appreciates the finer things in life, *signor*.'

Mallory swished the red wine around the glass and tried to remember the last time he was at Meerlust. The original estate, in the Western Cape of South Africa, lay on a granite outcrop in the hills above False Bay. He could still picture the long, oak tree-lined drive with the vineyards either side. At the end of the avenue was the imposing white façade of the old Cape Dutch manor house. The cool ocean breezes and damp evening mists rolling in from the Atlantic coast refreshed the vines in the long, hot summers. He touched the Russian's glass. 'To the pleasure of the seas.'

'What is this "pleasure of the seas"?'

'*Meerlust*,' Mallory said, laughing, 'that's what it means.'

The Russian smiled at the waiter. 'You see, Luigi, my friend here has taught us something new tonight! Not that you will persuade many people to buy the wine at this price.'

It wasn't just the wine. The lamb, too, reminded Mallory of South Africa, especially of the Northern Karoo, where there is an area known as Namaqualand. There the sheep graze beside the spring flowers on the side of the mountains below Kamiesberg. It was one of the most unbelievably beautiful places he'd ever seen.

'*Gracias, signor*,' Luigi said. 'Please, enjoy.'

'So tell me,' Andrei started, once they were alone again, 'what are you going to do with all this money they're paying you? I hope it's not in Zimbabwe dollars?'

Mallory almost choked on the wine. 'Bloody hell no!'

'Excellent. Now what is it that you want doing?'

'I need to make a will.'

'Going to Zimbabwe, that makes sense.'

'Can I use you as my executor?'

'It will be a pleasure.' The Russian reached into his pocket and withdrew his wallet. Taking out a business card, he passed it to Mallory. 'This chap will sort it out – I'll give him a call to let him know you'll be in touch.' Then he picked up his glass. 'Now, let's forget about these trivial matters and concentrate on more important things. To Zimbabwe! And your safe return.'

'I'll be back before you know it.'

The Russian nodded solemnly. His eyes were serious. For a barrister who was usually so eloquent, he was momentarily lost for words. 'Look, my friend,' he started, putting his hand on Mallory's arm. 'Would you consider getting together again when you come back?'

'There's nothing I would enjoy more.'

'No. I mean on a partnership basis – fifty-fifty.'

'God, that's ... but I don't have anything like your earning capacity!'

The Russian shrugged and dismissed the remark. 'Money, work – what do they matter? Who is counting? Friendship is what matters. And I am rich in your company because you are a man I trust and love. Money cannot buy these things.' He stood up and held out his hand. 'Do we have a deal?'

'God, yes,' Mallory said, taking the Russian's hand in a firm grip. 'And whatever I get from Zim can go straight into the company.'

'There you go again, talking of money. It's more important that you come back – and as a bona fide citizen of the United Kingdom, with your new passport. Not to mention the valuable experience you'll have gained working for a major corporate company.'

A citizen of the United Kingdom ... a partnership, a regular salary and most importantly, a future. Born again, as Lannigan had said. Were they just drunk and talking nonsense? Then he thought briefly of the girl and let go of the Russian's hand. 'There's one last thing. If you see Madeleine, can you spin her some cock-and-bull story about why I had to leave?'

'I'll say you have gone to Zimbabwe to find her a diamond.' The Russian belly-laughed, much to the amusement of the fellow diners.

Mallory joined in. 'Perhaps something a little less gung-ho!'

When Luigi brought the chit to the table, Andrei signed it without even looking at it and then stuffed a number of notes into the waiter's palm. 'Now, Luigi,' he said, in a loud voice that could be heard all over the restaurant, 'please have a word with Antonio. Ask him if I can buy the rest of this bottle of Calvados. It's a gift for my friend, that he may remember us on his journey.'

The waiter was about to respond when Antonio rushed over to the table. '*Signor* Andrei, I would like you to have the bottle as a present. I too will be very sorry to see *Signor* Mallory go. He has been a most entertaining dinner guest.'

The Russian stood up with his glass in the air. '*Poka my ne vstretimsya snova.*'

'You will have to teach me the language one day, Andrei.'

He smiled, sadness touching the corners of his mouth. 'It means: until we meet again.'

Chapter Thirty-Six

The sun was sinking beneath the Victorian terraces when Mallory woke up. Sheets were scattered in disarray on the floor. For a minute or two, he was totally disorientated. He blinked his eyes, unsure whether it was morning or evening. Then he looked at the digital alarm clock on the bedside table. 17.15. Afternoon. Shit! He tried to remember where he'd been fourteen hours earlier but it was all a blur. There were vague images of a nightclub where he and Andrei danced on the tables like wild Russian Cossacks, shooting round after round of vodka, much to the amusement of the crowd. The celebration went downhill when they threw their empty glasses against the wall and smashed a mirror. It had taken most of the staff to evict them from the premises after Andrei had paid for the damages. Then another nightclub, girls and more alcohol. The images kept appearing in his mind like frames from a movie that was thrown out of sequence. It was the bottle of Calvados sitting on the kitchen worktop that reminded him of the minicab driver who'd helped him out of the taxi and up to his flat. What the hell time had that been? Slumping back into the mattress, he closed his eyes and tried to ignore the hammering in his head. He was fully clothed and his mouth tasted like a wildebeest's jockstrap. From somewhere he found the energy to laugh at the thought, and he was still laughing to himself when he remembered Lannigan. Shit! He was supposed to ring him today! He jumped out of bed and staggered down the stairs stark naked. Lannigan was not available, so he left a message stating where and when to meet. Just as he was replacing the receiver Mrs Johnson appeared. She gasped in shock and quickly closed her door. Mallory smiled to himself. The smile was still on his face when he turned on the tap. For the next ten minutes he stood under the shower and let the cold water revive his body. Next it was coffee, strong and black and most definitely without the brandy. After two large cups and an enormous toasted bacon sandwich, he began to feel half human again.

He had decided to retain the lease for the immediate future. It was convenient. Nevertheless he wanted the flat cleared and all his possessions in storage boxes; it would make it easier for Andrei to move everything into safekeeping should the necessity arise. First, the books. It was while he was packing them into a cardboard box that he came across an old copy of Joseph Conrad's *Heart of Darkness*. The cover depicted the grotesque image of a man with half a face. This was Marlow's story of a journey into the heart of Africa, an expedition reminiscent of a trip he had once made himself through this forbidden land. He opened the book and began to read the first few pages. Strange that in all the time since the book had been written, at the turn of the century, little had changed: Africa was still a shit-hole, power and greed spurning the killing fields, and here he was going back to help yet another bloody tribe out of the mire. He'd just reached the part where Marlow sets off down the Congo River when he was disturbed by banging on the street door and Mrs Johnson's angry retort. It was a minute or two before he recognised the voice on the street.

'I know he's in there! The window is open and the light is on.'

'He doesn't want to see you,' Mrs Johnson said. 'Now go away and leave us alone.'

'I won't go until I see him!'

Mallory peered out of the window. Madeleine stood on the edge of the pavement with her hands on her hips. Passers-by were slowing down to watch, but she clearly didn't give a damn.

'If you don't go away *right* now, I'll call the police!'

The dilemma was getting out of hand. Mallory put his head out of the window. 'Let her in please, Mrs Johnson.'

The landlady turned around and looked up. 'I don't want any trouble or you'll both go!'

'There won't be any trouble.'

'I'm warning you! I've had enough of this bloody woman.'

Mallory smiled to himself again. It was the first time he had ever heard Mrs Johnson swear. But then it was also the first time she had ever seen him naked.

'The old bat! Who does she think she is?' Madeleine said, once she'd made it up the stairs. The tapping of her heels on the bare floorboards registered her indignation.

In spite of this, seeing her standing there in the doorway, wearing an expensive fur coat over a low-cut black dress and the now familiar fedora, Mallory realised just how much he'd missed her. 'She's the landlady, Madeleine. She owns the house.' It was all he could do to stop himself laughing; the situation had become so ridiculous.

'I don't care – I've tried on numerous occasions to get hold of you and she still has the audacity to tell me you're out!'

'In her defence, I've not been in much.'

'They are lies!' she said, completely ignoring him.

'Calm down! It's not her fault. I told her not to put your calls through! She has already notified the telephone company to have the number changed.'

'Why do you not want to take my calls?'

'I don't share my women with other men.'

Madeleine's eyes tightened and she stamped her foot again. 'What do you mean by that?'

'Let's not play games, Madeleine. You're seeing other men – not just seeing them, but also sharing your flat with them. So please don't come around here acting the righteous woman and upsetting my landlady.'

'Is that Russian friend of yours spreading rumours again?' she said removing her hat.

Mallory took her arm and pulled her into the room, closing the door behind her. The smell of the Balenciaga brought back the old familiar warmth. 'Now look, stop this nonsense at once! This has nothing to do with Andrei! If you must know, I came to your flat last week. I saw you with a man. And I heard your laughter.'

The anger dissipated immediately. It was replaced for a moment by an apprehensive frown. 'He is just a contact,' she said lamely. 'You should have come up and seen for yourself!'

The deceit again. Had they already sunk to this level? 'Your friend was shirtless, Madeleine. Please, no more lies.'

'So now you are spying on me? I would not have thought this of you.'

He wanted to put his hand over her mouth to shut her up. Andrei was right: she was smarter than one gave her credit for. 'No, Madeleine – Mitterrand said you'd been off work for a week. I wanted so much to see you. I would've come up if I'd not seen your friend.'

'He is not my *friend*! Just someone who is useful to my career.'

'So that's what you call it?'

Her shoulders slumped. 'It's not as you see it.'

'It never is.'

'From anyone else, I could understand that comment. But not from you. You are strong and always in control, and you do not need me like I need you. I hoped I could make you love me but you go back into a shell where I cannot reach you.' The blood drained from her face. 'So there is a man.'

'Your admirer. The one who buys you cognac and expensive perfume?'

197

'He does not buy me cognac!'

'Ah! So there are others?'

'No! It's not what you think! Richard has promised me a recording contract.'

A recording contract? So that's what this was all about. He eyed her suspiciously, but the anguish remained. He didn't know what to think. The jousting was spinning out of control. 'Look, I'm sorry for what I said.' Her face immediately changed. He thought again of the Russian dolls with their transparent faces, then of Zimbabwe and his imminent departure. He was tired and he realised the girl would never understand where he was coming from. 'Let's not fight any more.'

She walked across the room and put her arms around his neck. Then she kissed him. There was a smile of satisfaction on her face, like a cat watching its victim struggle before it plunges its claws into its heart. 'Remember, Mallory, when you are in love, there is nothing to forgive.'

Damn the woman! She used this word 'love', like any other word. It had no special meaning to her. It only justified what she did. He would have liked to wipe the smug look off her face but, as so many times before, he did nothing. She was standing close to him and he knew if he was not careful he would once again fall under her spell. 'Can I get you anything?' he asked, purposefully changing the subject.

She shook her head. Then, putting her wrist against his nose, she aligned her face in a look of serenity. 'Do you like it,' she said, referring to the perfume. 'Does it suit me?'

He nodded. The smile told him she knew exactly what she was doing. But had she forgotten that she was wearing the same perfume the last time she was here. A present from a lover, he'd thought then. 'It's exquisite,' he said.

'I thought you'd like it so I wore it especially for you. You see, nobody knows me like you do.' Her face was relaxed and her whole body language had changed. Like a matador about to plunge the sword into the bull's neck, she sensed victory. Soon he would be on his knees and she would be triumphant again. Then she would go back to her men, and her contracts, to anyone who could further her career. Until the next time. And by then he would be just another one-night stand, to be used whenever she so desired; to be trodden upon and cast aside in the same manner as she would do with all her other lovers. It had to end. There was only one course of action. He removed her hands from around his neck and held them gently. 'You must go now.'

Just for a moment a look of uncertainty flashed across her face. 'Why don't you believe me? I am on the point of signing a contract and then I can leave the Revolution for good. I'm doing it all for you – can you not see that?'

'It's very good of you,' he said, somewhat sarcastically.

It was almost as if the words had not been spoken. She moved closer to him. 'Then we can be together.'

So she had it all planned. She'd use those people to get what she wanted and then abandon them, just as she had done with him. 'Madeleine, sweet, darling Madeleine, whom I love so much that at times it hurts. There will never be a flat or a life together.'

'What? Why not?' The words were clearly unexpected.

'Because,' he explained patiently, 'there will always be another contract, another record producer or film director, whatever. And each time it will break me up a little more. You'll eventually kill what attracted me to you in the first place. I cannot wait around for that to happen. Please understand, my lovely – this is why you must leave.'

'But those people mean nothing to me! You are the only one I love!'

Words of desperation. He should not be having this conversation; he should never have even asked her up. 'I'm not the only one in your life and this is the way it should be. You deserve everything you have achieved because you have struggled so much to get there.'

'Then why?'

'Because I cannot be just another step on your ladder to fame. And I will not wait for you to wipe the floor with me.'

She put her arms around his neck and nestled up close to him. 'Please,' she whispered, 'let's just try, one more time.'

The oldest trick in the book. It had to stop before it became cheap and nasty. He removed her arms from his neck again. The perfume lingered. Holding her wrists, he then kissed her gently on the lips. 'Goodbye, Madeleine.'

She stepped back. There was fear in her eyes. 'So that's it? You just throw me out; after all we have been through? And then you say that you love me? How can you love me and then do this?'

'It's *because* I love you, Madeleine. Please understand I can't keep going on like this! I'm just flesh and bones, and I also have feelings, which might surprise you.'

'So I have come back to you and you treat me like some kind of slut?'

'But you haven't come back! There are other men in your life, but more than that, they are still *in* your life. Can't you understand?'

'But I want to come back!' She was crying now. 'Please, just give me time!'

He looked at the girl long and hard. She stood by the window, wiping the tears and running mascara from her cheeks. In the back of his mind was Zimbabwe. In two weeks' time, none of this would matter. And six months away would feel like a lifetime.

'All right, Madeleine.'

Suddenly her face changed. She let her bag fall to the floor and rushed into his arms.

The sun had disappeared. The only light came from the street lamps, which threw dim shadows across the room. It was just how she remembered it, that first day, when he'd rescued her from the Green Door. How long ago was that? Suddenly everything was as clear as a bell. She would sign the record contract and leave Richard. In spite of the fact that Mallory couldn't see them sharing a life together, she was confident she could change his mind. She watched him as he poured the Calvados and smiled softly when he touched her glass. 'To the future!' he said, looking deep into her eyes.

The future! Hadn't she once rejected that toast? But she could no longer remember when or where the words had been spoken. 'Mallory, I love you so much – please be there for me.'

Chapter Thirty-Seven

It was late afternoon when Mallory caught the Tube to St Pancras. He wanted time alone to think of Africa and Somerset Holdings before he met Lannigan. Around the corner from the station he found a cheap back-street hotel; he'd stay the night and meet with Jacob in the morning. A print of St Raphael on the Cote d'Azur looked distinctly out of place on the wall above the hotel bed, but it did at least brighten up the room. He picked up the Gideons Bible from the bedside table and flicked through the pages, feeling a sense of guilt. How long had it been since he'd last seen the inside of a church? He knew exactly when it was but the thought brought him no solace.

Mozambique 1976. The rebels had barred the doors, locking the congregation inside. Then they had set fire to the building. The hymns of praise had turned to screams of terror when the flames swept through the church. His platoon had arrived too late.

There were no survivors. When they had moved the bodies out of the blackened building, he had asked himself: where was their God that day? There was no answer.

He had never been back to a church.

Autumn clouds heralded the start of the evening and hunger replaced the sadness. Just across the street from the hotel was a tiny Spanish restaurant. Only one of the eight tables was occupied. Mallory sat by the window and ordered a bottle of Sauvignon Blanc and a seafood paella. The menu advertised it as a dish for two, but since business was slow, the waiter was only too happy to make an exception. A plate-glass window covered much of the front of the restaurant. It allowed Mallory to watch the people scurrying by like ants on their way to the station, trying unsuccessfully to avoid the early autumn drizzle. But his mind was elsewhere.

Madeleine had come back. The thought brought him little comfort. But wasn't it what he'd wanted all along? Deep down, he knew it was not. Something had died – the little rose bush covered with flowers that she called love had withered – beauty growing on dung that disappeared with the seasons. And yet she continued to draw him in, like a bee to the spring blossom. Did it really matter that he shared her with others? He'd never been jealous before, so why now? People were born and people died, and in between all of this was life. Somewhere in this blessed confusion the girl had stumbled into his world, coming out of the night with a cry for help. And in return she had shared her body and soul with him. For this, if nothing else, he would always love her. And it was this love that made him a slave to the entanglement.

But not this time. He was going away, and where he was going she could not follow. But would six months be enough? Would all of time be enough?

The chemist opposite the restaurant advertised passport photographs. Tucked away in the corner of the shop and hidden behind a curtain was the booth. Mallory adjusted the stool and stared impassively at the little mirror. The resignation showed plainly in his eyes as he waited patiently for the shutter to click.

The face he was looking at would become Christian Mallory.

Mike Rawlings was now dead and buried.

Chapter Thirty-Eight

The large clock over the counter at Fouquet's Bistro read ten to nine. Mallory took a stool by the window and gave his order to the waitress. Her T-shirt was emblazoned with the slogan FOUQUET'S BISTRO: SATISFYING YOUR EVERY NEED. It brought a moment of amusement. 'Black coffee – and a brandy,' he said, trying to figure out the message.

Just as the waitress reappeared with the drinks, Lannigan strode through the door with that infectious smile. '*Hoesit*, man?' He noticed the brandy on the counter. 'Bloody hell, Mike, it's nine in the morning!' He rubbed his head, which still throbbed from the last drinking session. 'No *babelaas*?'

Mallory laughed. 'I don't get hangovers. Will you join me?'

'I'll give it a miss,' Lannigan said, before placing his order with the waitress. 'Hey, I tell you, man, you can't believe how good it is to see you. To be quite honest, I wasn't sure you'd turn up until I received your phone call.'

'I gave you my word,' Mallory said simply.

'I know, I know. But we were so pissed.' Lannigan paused to find the right words. 'So look, I spoke to the company – they can't believe you know Julian Chikembe. And have experience of Zimbabwean law.'

'You mean *Rhodesian* law?'

Lannigan chuckled at the thought. 'There's very little difference: Mugabe has retained much of the old colonial legal system.'

Mallory leaned forward, his elbow on the table, his voice soft. It was the meeting he wanted to know more about. He looked at Lannigan, who was dressed in a dark grey suit and company tie; a direct contrast to his own slacks, desert boots and linen jacket. Smart casual, he'd said, not that it really mattered: he wasn't there to impress them with his attire. 'So what's the plan?'

The waitress, hovering in the background, noticed the empty mugs and came over with the bottle of brandy. Lannigan glanced down at the large Omega Chronometer on his wrist. 'Same again,' he said to the girl, 'without the brandy, please.' Then flicking a cigarette out of the packet of Texan, he offered one to Mallory. 'Look, it's just an informal chat. Alastair Brown wants to meet you. He's responsible for operations in Africa and he'll want to ask you a few questions. I'm told it's nothing too intrusive. I take it you don't have a CV?'

Mallory laughed. 'Not one your Mr Brown would want to see.'

'No problem, I've filled them in on your background and your requirement that they supply you with a new identity.'

'What about Mike Rawlings? And G2?'

'No mention of G2 – the less we tell them about your past life the better. I'll introduce you however you like – have you made a decision yet?'

Mallory nodded.

'Good! Then we're all set.'

'What, that's it?'

Lannigan smiled slyly. 'Rhodesia is history, *ou boet*. Somerset Holdings want men who know the system and the way Mugabe and his tribe operate. More importantly, they want men who aren't *kak* arsed to face the consequences should things get … nasty.'

Mallory's lips tightened and a bewildered expression crossed his face.

'Look, you know Mugabe's reputation; the bastard will run roughshod over anyone who doesn't toe the party line. Let me remind you of our friend Joshua.'

'Joshua Nkomo?'

Lannigan nodded.

The name brought back memories. 'We tried to get rid of him in Lusaka,' Mallory said. 'Unfortunately he wasn't at home when the bomb went off.'

Lannigan shivered. 'Well, after the war he was appointed to the cabinet as a minister, albeit without a portfolio. There was no love lost between him and Bob.'

'Can't blame Mugabe on that one. The guy was plotting a *coup d'état*.'

'He was stitched up.'

'So they say. But am I not right in thinking that Nkomo is Ndebele and arms were found on Matabele-owned farms?'

'You are right,' Lannigan said, 'but they were planted.'

'Whatever. It doesn't change the fact that Mugabe wanted him dead, no matter the cost. I heard the statement he made: "Nkomo is a cobra and the only way to deal effectively with a snake is to strike and destroy its head". He sure as hell destroyed the snake when he slaughtered 20,000 civilians in Nkomo's homeland.'

'It was an attempt to create a one-party state! Come on, *bru*, the Shona have always sought the extermination of the Ndebele, and vice versa. It's just another bloody tribal war.'

Another bloody tribal war! He remembered his conversation with Madeleine and a shiver ran down his back. It was as if someone had walked over his grave. 'And here we are, working for the underdogs? Your Somerset Holdings sure can pick them!' He drew deeply on the Texan and exhaled the smoke slowly. *An informal chat!* Was there any such thing? However, it did appear that Jacob had everything covered. But then he would expect nothing less: this was a struggle for survival, and he was just a pawn in a dangerous game. He looked at his comrade.

206

'I'd prefer not to reveal too much of my life here in London.'

'That's up to you.' Lannigan finished off the last of his coffee and signalled for the waitress to bring the bill. 'I've told Alastair we were employed in different law practices in Salisbury before the Bush War. When the hostilities started, we joined the Rhodesian Light Infantry and eventually ended up in the same platoon, patrolling the Zambezi Valley.'

'That's all kosher.'

Lannigan nodded. 'I also touched on the fact that you were involved in Special Ops and, as such, you had to get out of the country before Zimbabwe became independent. So you immigrated to England – it substantiates your alibi and explains why you wish to remain *persona non grata*. Furthermore, it'll give you a valid reason for wanting the new identity. I can vouch for your credentials, so there shouldn't be any further concerns.' He picked up the bill. 'Not that any of this should bother them; they want the right men and they don't usually care what skeletons are in the closets. The skills are more important than the identities.'

Too right they were – ruthless killers were what Somerset Holdings wanted.

Men with no qualms about exterminating Africans.

Was he ever that man?

Chapter Thirty-Nine

SOMERSET HOLDINGS – IMPORT – EXPORT. The words were etched into the smoke glass on the front of the modern structure. The building sat serenely beside the Thames. Its enormous expanse of glass reflected the river and a pair of swans struggling upstream. It all appeared somewhat surreal. He shuddered when he recalled Lannigan's story. Import and export – importers of blood diamonds and exporters of mercenaries? However, the smile on the reception- ist's face seemed to allay his initial fears.

'Good morning, Mr Lannigan,' she said, showing them both to a comfortable waiting area with four easy chairs and a glass-top table bearing a selection of newspapers. 'Can I get you anything? Tea, coffee?'

'Not for me thanks, Lucy,' Lannigan said, looking at Mallory, who shook his head.

'Very well – Mr Brown will be with you shortly,' she said, leaving them to peruse the papers.

'Pretty flash pad! Africa must be doing well.'

Lannigan glanced up from *The Times*. 'It's no different to the old days.'

'You mean the corruption and intimidation?'

Lannigan shook his head. 'Look, Mike, you can't go back down that road. You know the score. Brown is about to interview you and the last thing he wants to hear are your views on Colonial Africa or what he is up to. That will seriously go down like a brick.'

It was Mallory's turn to smile. 'I'm not that dumb.'

'I need you, *vriend*.' The big man looked serious. 'You can't believe how much.'

'I'll be on my best behaviour.' His eyes were on Lucy walking across the foyer.

'Mr Brown will see you now,' Lucy said, beckoning them to follow her. The receptionist used a swipe card to access the private lift. Seconds later, they exited the elevator at the top floor and Lucy led them into an open-plan, oak-panelled room. She then entered a code on a touch screen and a section of the panelling slid away. A smartly dressed woman in a stiff tweed suit, her grey hair in a tight bun, greeted them. She wore a pair of heavy-framed bifocals and carried a large diary, which she constantly referred to. Her stern expression – that of a strict convent teacher – reminded Mallory of his school days.

'Thank you, Lucy. Mr Steenburg from African Consolidated is due at eleven. Will you call me as soon as he arrives please?'

'Yes, Miss Greaves.'

Mallory was sorry to see the girl go. She was young and pretty with long blonde hair; a marked contrast to the severe personal assistant.

'Follow me please,' Miss Greaves said, in a gruff, authoritarian voice, leading them down a corridor that was adorned with signed Picasso prints from his neoclassical period. At the far end of the passageway was a frosted glass door. Tweed-suit consulted her diary again before speaking briefly into an intercom. 'Mr Lannigan, sir.' The glass door slid open and she stepped aside, allowing them to enter. Everything was as Lannigan had described it.

Three directors sat behind a vast polished mahogany desk. In front of each board member was a nameplate. The chairman, Alastair Brown, sat in the middle. He was heavy-set and looked to be in his early sixties, although the face was ageless. He could just as easily have been ten years younger were it not for the ruddy cheeks that betrayed a penchant for fine wine. He was flanked by a serious-looking man in tortoise-shell framed glasses – the financial director – and a middle-aged attractive blonde woman, the head of HR. 'Thank you, Amanda, that will be all,' said the chairman before rising to his feet.

'Jacob, good to see you again!'

'Same here, Alastair!' Lannigan said, turning to introduce Mallory. 'This is the lawyer we spoke about – Christian Mallory, an old friend and comrade.'

The chairman extended his hand. The immaculate suit, no doubt made to measure by Saville Row's finest, and the fact that the smile did not reach his eyes contributed to his conservative demeanour. And like some political leaders, what you saw was not necessarily what you got. 'Any friend of Jacob's is a friend of ours. Please, sit down.' He touched the shoulder of the woman taking notes. 'May I introduce you to Alicia, my "right-hand man", so to speak, and,' he glanced back at Tortoise-shell Glasses, 'Edward, our financial director.'

Edward stood up and took hold of Mallory's hand. 'It's a pleasure.' Alicia remained seated and acknowledged him with a half-smile and a nod of her head. He ignored her and examined the room. A constantly moving CCTV camera swept the office and on the wall behind the desk was a large two-way mirror, lending to the suggestion that maybe someone else was privy to the interview. He waited patiently while Alastair Brown idly flicked the pages of a folder. Eventually, the chairman looked up. 'So, Christian – may I call you Christian?'

Mallory nodded.

'Jacob informs me that he would like to recruit you as a member of the team working for Somerset Holdings in Zimbabwe. In your capacity as a lawyer?'

'Yes, sir.'

'Excellent. I take it you are aware of the risks?'

'Risks?'

'Zimbabwe is a dangerous place.'

'I happen to know the country, sir.' Mallory smiled at Alastair Brown.

The chairman had a slow, confident manner, giving rise to the idea that he thought carefully of what he said before opening his mouth. 'When did you leave?'

Keep it vague, Mallory. 'The year before independence.'

'I see.' Alastair Brown crossed his arms. 'Well I'm sure I don't need to tell you that the situation has changed beyond all recognition.'

'I read the papers, sir.'

The chairman smiled thinly. 'I'd be surprised if you didn't keep abreast of current affairs. Has Jacob informed you of where you'll be working and what you'll be doing?'

'He mentioned Harare and Bulawayo. I believe the initial brief was to ensure the forthcoming elections were conducted in a free and fair manner.'

'That is correct. So how do you see us achieving this goal?'

Mallory leaned back in his chair and thought about the question. 'Well, sir, Mugabe is an African liberation leader who believes in a strong and ruthless government. He won't tolerate defiance – his security forces see to that. The opposition accuses him and his ZANU-PF party of rigging the ballot boxes.' He looked across at Lannigan, who was smiling encouragingly. 'If we forget about the first election – the one immediately after independence, when a strong Shona majority elected him as president – his subsequent campaigns have been consistently marred by violence and intimidation. I believe there is a need to challenge the way elections have been conducted in the past – if possible, through the Supreme Court.'

'You realise, of course, that he has a strong suspicion of capitalism and the West in general?'

'More of a paranoia, I would say.'

The chairman smiled and turned to Alicia. After briefly conferring with her, he made notes on a desk pad. 'So how do you see us overcoming this paranoia and giving the opposition a fair crack at the whip?'

'I would press the courts for a referendum, sir. Zimbabwe needs a new constitution.'

'What about the presidential term?'

'That should be limited to five years, two terms only. Furthermore, I would like to see restrictions on all presidential powers.' He paused to consider the next statement. 'Finally, I would advocate for provincial legislation and constitutional courts.'

'And you believe you can achieve these objectives?'

Mallory's eyes narrowed. Brown's cut-glass English accent and patronising stance annoyed him. 'I wouldn't be sitting here if I had any doubts, *sir*,' he said, somewhat sarcastically.

This change in tone clearly rattled Brown, who stiffened in his chair. 'Quite, quite, my dear chap.'

Alicia tapped the chairman on the shoulder and handed him a note. Brown frowned. Then he turned to Mallory. 'So, let's see – what have you been doing since coming to the UK?'

Mallory looked at the HR director. She held his gaze. The half-smile still played around the corner of her mouth – she was enjoying baiting him. But what the hell was her game? It was not only an intrusive question but one he hadn't bargained for. She was a hard nut and neither her stance, nor Brown calling him 'my dear chap', was to his liking. He immediately went on his guard. 'I work for a barrister.'

'Yes, but doing what?' This from Alicia. Her smile widened – she obviously regarded him as an object of curiosity and was playing the mental game. Psychological assessment.

His eyes narrowed and he held her gaze. 'I defend clients accused of fraud.' It was a white lie. Nevertheless, it would cover a multitude of sins and be difficult to trace.

Alicia uncrossed her legs and smiled. The act was suggestive. 'With which company?'

'I'm self-employed.' His face was deadpan.

'We meant, who do you work for – the name of the barrister?' Alastair Brown said.

'I'd rather not divulge that information.'

The chairman made more notes on the pad and then looked up. 'You're not making it at all easy, Mr Mallory. All these secrets...'

Mallory shifted in his chair. Lannigan had assured him the interview would be a mere formality; an informal chat was what he said. This was anything but. Then he thought of Marange and fixed his stare on Alastair Brown. 'Are we really that different, sir?'

'I'm sorry?'

'We both have a past we want to protect. Call it a "hidden agenda". I don't know yours, and there is no need for you to know mine.' He didn't need this shit and pushed back his chair, ready to terminate the interview.

Alastair Brown's face turned purple and the smile disappeared from Alicia's. Lannigan flinched and was about to say something in defence of his friend when the chairman recovered himself. 'Well, Mr Mallory, you certainly call a spade a spade. I admire that in a man. But you must understand,' he said, in a somewhat more derisive manner, 'that you come to us without a CV. We have no knowledge of your qualifications or expertise.'

You sanctimonious bastard! Mallory was aware the director had backed down, as were the others in the room. And he knew why. They were running out of time and it would appear they needed him, secrets or not; his association with Chikembe was too important to them. But he also knew he would have to watch his back. 'Mr Lannigan is aware of my background and what I did in Rhodesia. He wouldn't have approached me for the position if he didn't think I was capable of doing the job, sir.'

The chairman nodded and locked his fingers together. He appeared somewhat more relaxed. 'There's one other aspect and I'm wondering whether you've taken it into consideration.'

'Which is?'

'As I have already mentioned, there is an element of danger that goes with the job. Mugabe won't take our plans lying down. Are you prepared for a long, hard fight?'

Long, hard fight? His whole bloody life had been a struggle. 'I believe it comes with the territory, sir.'

Alicia leant over and spoke softly. Alastair Brown smiled with relief. 'Good, good. Well, I must say you do come highly recommended.' He gestured to Jacob, who nodded in return. 'Nevertheless, there is a procedure we go through with all our new employees.'

'Oh?' Lannigan hadn't mentioned this either.

'After lunch you'll be taken to our assessment and training centre, what we here at Somerset Holdings fondly know as our "Enlightenment Hub".' He glanced across at Edward who adjusted his glasses and nodded imperceptibly. 'They will issue you with the appropriate paperwork on the Law Society of Zimbabwe. You will be joining our subsidiary firm, Sibanda, Hussein & Partners. They are human rights attorneys and form part of the statutory body regulating the practice of law in Zimbabwe.'

Suddenly a ghost walked across Mallory's grave. His lips tightened. 'I know the company,' he said softly, interrupting the chairman. 'I've dealt with them in the past.'

Brown was euphoric and missed the signal. 'Amicably?'

'We were on different sides of the fence.'

'I understand. So you'll know of Mohammed Hussein?' Mallory shook his head. The images in his mind told a different story. 'He's rather a firebrand. I'm surprised you don't know him. Been with us for some time. Totally supports Somerset Holdings strategic objective, which is the creation of a culture of equality in Zimbabwe. As you might not be aware, we have a strong commitment to the rule of law and independence for the legal profession. Mr Hussein shares our goals. I'm sure you will like the chap.'

What a load of bullshit. All these bastards wanted were the diamonds. Nevertheless he nodded his agreement.

'Splendid! Next we'll bring you up to speed on Zimbabwe, that is, Mugabe's government, the political structure as it stands and finally the dangers involved in your role as an opposition lawyer. Before you accept the post, we would like to ensure that you are comfortable with the terms and conditions of the contract and that you fully understand what you are undertaking. This role is non-negotiable and there's no get-out clause. All clear so far?'

A slight nod of the head again. 'Sure.' Mallory's eyes remained fixed on the chairman.

'Good. Now we are conscious that you have been out of the country for some time and that you may be somewhat rusty. But it's important you are aware of what we are trying to do in Zimbabwe society, with regards to human rights.'

All this crap about 'human rights'. Enlightenment Hub? Shit, more like Brainwashing Hub! What sort of idiot did they take him for? But did it really matter? Here was an opportunity to return to Zimbabwe and help an entire people living under oppressive rule. He was not about to turn it down. 'I look forward to working with you, sir.'

Alastair Brown smiled and for the first time since the start of the interview the gesture appeared genuine. 'Now, I understand you require a passport.'

This was said as if it was an entirely normal practice; thank God that was the last of the invasive questions.

Edward pushed his tortoise-shell glasses back up his nose and slid a form and ballpoint pen across the desk. 'Please be good enough to fill in all the relevant details on the application. I trust you have your passport photos?'

Mallory scanned the forms while Brown made small talk with Lannigan. When he came to the box asking for his address, he hesitated. It was his intention to keep his flat for the imme-diate future. And because he was retaining Mallory as his given name, the arrangement would suit Mrs Johnson. Not that she would care, as long as the rent was paid. The rest of the form was straightforward. He signed and dated it before handing it back, along with the photographs.

'Thank you, Mr Mallory,' Alastair Brown said, standing up and offering his hand. 'Amanda will show you out. After lunch, please make yourself available at reception – I would like Jacob to go with you. Then shall we meet back here later today?'

Mallory looked at his watch. 'What time?'

'Say five o'clock? I'll have the contract ready. If you're entirely happy with the terms and conditions as outlined for you at the Hub, we'll go ahead and sign the agreement.'

Mallory glanced across at Lannigan. He nodded and smiled.

'Excellent, then that's all settled.' He picked up the telephone and spoke briefly. The smoked-glass door slid open. Tweed-suit was waiting on the other side. 'Show these gentlemen to the canteen please, Amanda.'

Canteen was an understatement – top-drawer restaurant would have been a more apt description for the boutique space, with waitress service and full à la carte menu. Lannigan cast his eyes down the extensive wine list and selected a pinotage, South Africa's signature grape. He turned to Mallory for assurance.

'Not if I'm going to have my wits about me this afternoon,' he said, declining the offer.

'It's a mere formality!'

'So you keep saying. Nevertheless, I'll give it a miss.' He requested a jug of water instead. 'Perhaps we can have a beer after our meeting with your friend Brown.'

'I think that can be arranged. Hey look, Mike ... or do I call you Chris now?'

'Just call me Mallory.'

'I think you were a bit of a hit with Alicia. She couldn't take her eyes off you. *Lekker anties* hey! But watch her; she's shagged her way up to the board. We call her a posh *stukkie*. Not to her face, of course.'

'She's not part of the assessment is she?'

Lannigan burst out laughing. 'She could be!'

Mallory frowned. 'Well, if that's what I have to do to get the job, forget it.'

Lannigan smiled wryly. He then turned serious. 'I wasn't aware you knew our subsidiary firm?'

'Sibanda, Hussein & Partners? It was a long time ago.'

Mallory left it there but Lannigan was more persistent. 'Come on, *boet*, was it really amicable?'

'Are lawyers ever?' He thought about Brown's words – 'the creation of a culture of equality' – and wanted to puke. 'Sibanda, Hussein & Partners were the lawyers prosecuting the terrorists – the same prisoners I defended. After the death sentence was pronounced, the firm would hold mock executions at the Country Club, making the African waiters stand on the tables and putting a noose around their necks. Their idea of a joke!'

'But you said–'

'I know. But if I'd told Brown the truth, would he have employed me?'

'What if they recognise you?'

'I doubt they will. It was a long time ago.'

Lannigan shrugged. 'Well, I guess in the final analysis you have something they want very badly.'

'What's that?'

'Chikembe.'

'You will find him fascinating, Jacob. Did you know that the guerrilla hierarchy operating out of Mozambique were all known by card names?' A half-smile crossed his lips. 'Our friend Mugabe was the King of Diamonds. Ironic, hey, when you think of Marange?'

'What was Chikembe?'

'He was the Ace of Spades.'

'*The Ace of Spades*?'

'I'll leave you to figure that one. It was all a bloody game of cards. Unbeknownst to them at the time, we had cracked the code.'

Mallory's eyes misted up. 'Strange to think of an ex-guerrilla leader as my bargaining chip.' He thought briefly of the night they had escaped the interrogation cell. Would Julian really want to resurrect the past? Suddenly the sun broke out from behind a cloud, casting a beam through the plate-glass window. It caught Lannigan's glass of pinotage and appeared to transform the wine to blood, bringing back memories of Sibanda, Hussein & Partners … prosecuting barristers … and Silas Chipoka, a young, innocent African boy who he watched hang. Would Mohammed Hussein remember the trial?

More importantly, would he remember Mike Rawlings?

Chapter Forty

A Mercedes with blacked-out windows picked them up from the underground car park beneath the offices. The driver spoke only to say good morning and then never uttered another word. Conscious that the vehicle may very well be bugged, both passengers remained silent. Although Mallory had a sound knowledge of London, he knew nothing of the country beyond the capital. Because of this he religiously studied the street signs, committing to memory the route they were taking. The Mercedes eventually turned onto the A21 in the direction of Biggin Hill and before long they were on a narrow B road. The last village he noted was Downe, before they descended into the countryside. It was devoid of all civilisation.

After driving through a heavily forested area they eventually arrived at an army camp, encircled by a high fence of razor wire and warnings of it being electrified. These guys certainly weren't expecting visitors. Assessment centre? Just what did it assess? Apart from the safety notices, there were no other clues as to who, or what, lay beyond the grey buildings. The two guards standing inside the barrier wore army fatigues, again without insignia. They held Heckler & Koch MP5 submachine guns, the favoured assault weapon of military and law enforcement tactical units across the world. The driver spoke briefly to the sentry and a man in the bulletproof enclosure raised the impregnable electronic barrier. The Mercedes came to a stop across the road from the guard room. A tall man dressed in khaki fatigues approached the vehicle. From the way he carried himself, he appeared to be an officer. But there was no military insignia on his shirt to confirm it. What the hell was this place? He was about to voice the question when the man spoke.

'Good morning, Jacob. This your new fellow?'

'Charles ... yes, this is Christian Mallory. We were together in Rhodesia.'

Charles studied Mallory for a moment or two and then extended his arm. The handshake was firm. 'Rhodesia you say? Bit of a change from the old days with Mugabe at the helm. Rather unpredictable chap, what?' He removed his glasses. 'Had much to do with him?' Mallory shook his head. 'Not to worry. Max will bring you up to date.'

Mallory scowled. Why all the secrecy? Although the camp resembled an army barracks, it was a world away from any garrison he'd known. Apart from a couple of Land Rover Defenders, painted in desert camouflage, the place appeared abandoned. Maybe it was some kind of redundant army billet? Somerset Holdings obviously had clearance and the encampment would certainly have been sanctioned by the Ministry of Defence, perhaps even used by the Regiment.

Lannigan looked at his watch. 'What's the plan, Charles?'

'Mr Maxwell is expecting you, gentlemen,' Charles said, leading the way to a prefabricated building, which had been converted into an office. For the next three hours Mallory was given a complete run-down on Zimbabwe, from the time of independence, when the government amended the Constitution, to the present day. He was well aware that in those long-ago days seats reserved for whites in the country's parliament were abolished, as was the office of prime minister. In its place, Mugabe had created an executive presidency. Then he was shown how Zimbabwe had moved away from democratic governance. This was not brainwashing, this was fact. He turned to Maxwell. 'It's common knowledge that Mugabe abolished democratic elections and the rule of law. He runs a bloody dictatorship!'

Maxwell looked up from his notes. He appeared to be in his late fifties with a sallow complexion. This was probably due to the fact that he'd spent most of his life in a classroom. The passing years had reduced his mousy brown hair to a patch on either side of his head and by constantly running his fingers through what remained of his thinning crop, he covered his shoulders with dandruff. His face was inscrutable but when he spoke his voice carried a note of authority. 'He also disposed of the independent media, not to mention the academia and civil society. One of your first tasks when you return to Zimbabwe is to re-establish the independence of the judiciary and change the law, to create freedom from racial discrimination.'

'That's one hell of a mountain to climb,' Mallory said, 'when you consider he has every fucking judge on his side.'

'We understand, sir.' The instructor hardly batted an eyelid.

'Do you? So tell me; how the hell do we overcome the political violence and intimidation? And then there's the bloody politicisation of the military, police force and public services – the list goes on. Look at Mugabe and his so-called politicians: they routinely refer to the country as being at war, or *Chimurenga*, as the bastards call it.'

'Alastair did try to warn you,' Lannigan said, 'this won't be easy.'

'I don't think he realises just how difficult it will be, Jacob. You know the country and all the crap that goes on in the media – before we can have a free and fair election we have to restore all newspapers that are non-aligned with Mugabe. Furthermore, we have to ensure that members of the judiciary are neither threatened nor arrested, and that the opposition is neither harassed nor subjected to torture. Nor sentenced to jail.'

Maxwell nodded. 'Sibanda, Hussein & Partners have already filed for a hearing to legally challenge the repressive laws aimed

221

at preventing freedoms of speech, assembly and association. Zimbabwe's legal system has come under increasing threat lately and attempts to change it have been subject to police brutality. As you quite rightly say, old chap, no easy task.'

God, not another one using this 'old chap' talk. It was all so bloody 'British public schools' – reminiscent of the old colonial days, when foreign armies had marched over a land that had lain undisturbed for centuries. African spears were no match for their guns and canons. Under the banner of a Union Jack, British forces had conquered a continent from the Cape to Cairo. In their ignorance, they drew lines on a map, settling on borders over gin and tonics. It was arrogant and stupid. The lines were for their convenience and ran through tribal lands, separating communities and religions that had previously lived in harmony for centuries. Therein lay much of today's problems, from Africa to Arabia. Now Somerset Holdings were at it again, meddling in the affairs of Zimbabwe, disguising their greed for democracy. He put the thought out of his mind and finished reading through the paperwork. Then he studied the contract. Apart from a couple of minor issues, which he raised with Maxwell, the agreement met his approval. In just three weeks' time he was due to appear in Harare's Central Court for the first hearing of the Freedom of Speech Bill. All of a sudden, he couldn't wait to get started.

'Everything in order, sir?' Maxwell asked, when Mallory had turned over the last page of the draft contract.

Mallory nodded. 'Could I get a copy of everything we've just been through?'

'It's all here, sir,' Maxwell said, handing him the large brown envelope. 'Mr Brown has the original. Are there any further questions before you go?'

Mallory looked down at the dotted line that would carry his signature and change his life. He shook his head.

'Splendid! Then all that's left for me to say is, best of luck, sir! When you're ready, your driver will take you back to HQ.'

Best of luck. He was certainly going to need all the luck in the world after what he'd just read, and this was only the half of it. What if the plan was a failure? Did the answer lie right here, in this ex-military camp? Suddenly his suspicions were realised and he remembered Andrei's words. How could he have been so dim? Somerset Holdings *was* training an army of mercenaries. If they failed to secure Mugabe's downfall through the courts, they'd resort to other means. To make matters worse, the British government appeared to be implicated in what could eventually become a *coup d'état.* And if the overthrow also failed, Zimbabwe faced the prospect of civil war. Now he understood why the camp was shrouded in secrecy. Yes, he was just a pawn all right – a tiny pawn surrounded by kings, queens and bishops. Or in this instance, corrupt corporations and hard-arsed African soldiers, wielding AK-47s.

Chapter Forty-One

'I've had a call from Maxwell,' Alastair Brown said, when they were seated back in his office. 'He informs me that you fully understand the conditions relating to the contract?'

'Everything appears to be in order, sir.'

'Before you go ahead and sign the contract, I'd like Alicia to run through the details once more. Just to ensure you are entirely happy.'

'As you wish.' He thought of Lannigan's words: posh *stukkie* – a woman for casual encounters. Alicia hardly looked the sort. But then you couldn't always judge a book by its cover.

The HR director looked up from her notepad. The lazy half-smile was back on her face. 'The contract is for an initial period of six months. The conditions allow for it to be renegotiated and extended by either party should circumstances permit.' She briefly consulted the financial director and then made a few notes on the contract. 'The remuneration is £120,000 sterling, payable in six equal instalments. In addition to your salary there is a bonus of £200,000 pending a successful change of government.'

'By change we mean the MDC,' Alastair Brown interrupted.

Mallory smiled to himself. Two hundred grand to get their hands on the diamonds? It was a drop in the ocean!

'We'll need your account details,' Alicia said, 'number, swift code and IBAN. If anything should happen to you during the course of the contract, appropriate compensation will be paid out to your next of kin. Again, we will need those details. You can leave the information with reception. Mark it for my attention, please.'

'Appropriate compensation?'

'Fifty per cent of the contracted remuneration,' Alicia said softly.

This last clause left Mallory in no doubt about the danger of the undertaking. But then Somerset Holdings clearly didn't pay out this kind of money unless there was an element of risk. It was considerably more than 'Mad Mike' Hoare had offered him years before, to join his band of mercenaries fighting in the Congo. However the nature of the beast was the same: 'fat cats', faceless bureaucrats hiding behind glass screens, moving pieces (soldiers of fortune) across the board. He shuddered at the thought and took a fountain pen from the inside pocket of his linen jacket. 'Right, where do you want me to sign?'

Alicia slid the document across the desk. 'If you're happy to go ahead, please sign here,' she said, indicating a line marked with a pencil cross, 'and initial each page.'

Ensuring the document was the same as the one he had read at the centre, Mallory did as he was asked and then signed on the dotted line. Fait accompli! There was no going back now.

'Welcome to the club!' Alastair Brown said, adding his signature to the document before offering Mallory his hand.

Edward and Alicia did likewise. Her hand was soft but the squeeze was intentional, suggestive even. 'Good luck, Mr Mallory. We hope to see a lot more of you.'

He ignored the salacious remark and turned to Alastair Brown. 'What about my passport?'

'You can pick it up from Lucy at reception tomorrow, together with your airline tickets. Jacob will take care of all other travel expenses. Is there anything else?'

Mallory shook his head. They had all angles covered. But then he would expect nothing less. It was time to go. 'I guess I can read the brief at my leisure.'

'Of course, and if there are any other questions, again please contact Lucy.'

Mallory was about to get up when the phone rang. Alicia picked it up, spoke briefly and then nodded. 'Thank you, Mrs Greaves.' She turned to Alastair Brown.

'Excuse me one moment,' the chairman said, acknowledging his colleague. They spoke in hushed voices for a minute or two. Then Brown looked at Lannigan. 'There is a small change to the plans, Jacob. Are you able to leave the country any sooner?'

'What's the problem?'

'We have just received a message from Mohammed Hussein. It appears that they need you out there as soon as possible.'

He glanced across at Mallory and shrugged as if to apologise. 'How soon?'

'The beginning of next week? Miss Greaves has provisionally booked you on flight AZ 101 to Harare,' Alicia said. 'If it's acceptable, we'll confirm the seats. It departs Gatwick at 0700 hours on Monday. You'll stay in Harare for the night and transfer to Bulawayo for your meeting with the MDC the following day.'

God, that was bloody quick. What had happened? And why the change of plan at the eleventh hour? Not that it really mattered – there was nothing worth hanging about for here. He made a mental note to inform Andrei of the new arrangements. 'I'll be ready,' he said.

'Good. All that remains now is for me to say goodbye and wish you the best of luck.' Alastair Brown paused to study the lawyer one last time. 'You are an interesting man, Mr Mallory. It's good to have you on board. Please don't let me down.'

Was that a request or a threat?

Chapter Forty-Two

Mallory stood for a moment, gazing up at his flat. It had become a habit whenever he returned home to the East End. He knew it was because of the girl, who he was half hoping would be waiting for him. The thought was ludicrous; she had her own place now. Her own life. Then the shadow of a figure crossed the transparent curtain and all of a sudden there was the joy of expectation. His thoughts were still with the girl when he opened the door. She was sitting by the window where she always sat, reading his manuscript. 'I thought you'd have gone by now,' he said, dropping his holdall onto the floor and trying to act non-committal, even though he was touched by tenderness. The room was warm and inviting and he knew it was the girl who made it so. 'Do you not have to be at work?'

'I phoned in sick.' She rose to her feet and walked across to him in her long strides. 'Are you not pleased to see me?' she asked coquettishly, putting her arms around his neck and kissing him. 'Just a little bit pleased?' She let her tongue touch his lips.

'Madeleine, stop playing games.' He could feel the fire in his body and tried to dampen the sensation. But it was to no avail; he wanted her.

'I said I would wait. Don't you remember?'

So much had happened in the last twenty-four hours. What had he said before he'd left? Not that it really mattered now. 'You must go home,' he said half-heartedly.

'No, I've told you before, I am your responsibility!' Her arms were still around his neck.

What the hell was she talking about? 'This is ridiculous.' He tried to remove her arms but she refused to budge. 'Okay, you win,' he said at last, accepting her will and knowing that no matter what he said, she would hear only what she wanted to hear.

A wide smile spread across her face. 'You see, it doesn't take much to make me happy! Now, where have you been all this time?'

'It's a long story.'

'Well you don't have the scent of a woman.'

So that was what the kiss had been about. In spite of himself, Mallory laughed – once again he'd fallen for the oldest trick in the book.

'What's so funny?'

When he finally managed to control his laughter, he took her hand. 'Madeleine, you have to stop this silly talk; I need another woman like a hole in the head. Anyway, don't play all high and mighty when you're sleeping with another man.'

A frown appeared on her forehead. 'That's not the same. And you know it.' On the table in front of her lay the open manuscript. She pushed it to one side before continuing. 'You keep bringing up my relationships with other men as if they are something to be ashamed of. I thought you understood; I only do this for my career.' Her gesture was delicate, and her voice soft and employing, as though she was talking to a child.

He stared at her, speechless.

'I come back to you because I love you and want to be with you. Why can't you appreciate what I'm doing?' She sat looking at him, waiting for his response.

The night had come quickly and with it had descended a silence on the street. A glimmer of a street lamp brushed her shoulder.

God, she was so very alluring and because of that a sadness touched his face. You will never be with me, Madeleine; I cannot hold the wind. The words were in his head but he did not say them. Three more days and he would be gone. And then there would only be the memories. 'Let's not talk of what might have been. Let's just enjoy this night and forget the past.'

'Oh Mallory, I knew you would finally understand!' Then she was on her feet, walking to the fridge, seemingly surrounded again by that invisible air. He would never tire of watching her. When she returned there was a bottle of cold Pouilly in her hand. She put it on the table and then pressed her body close to his face, wrapping her arms around his head. 'Why do you punish me when I love you so much?'

Love. What does this creature of the night know of love? This girl with a passion for life, an exquisite butterfly grown from a moth, flitting from man to man. Her hands were in his hair and she was whispering something, but he did not hear the words. Then he pulled the girl on to the settee, burying his head in her body. How long he sat there, he did not know – he would have stayed there forever. And for the moment, even Zimbabwe was forgotten.

Chapter Forty-Three

The morning came quickly, as it does when there is autumn sunshine in the sky. Mallory heard the girl before he saw her, heard her leave the bed and walk across the room. When he opened his eyes she was standing by the window, pulling on her pants. She wore nothing else and her skin shone pale in the early morning light. God, she was beautiful. 'Where are you going?'

She looked at him in puzzlement, as if the question was somehow irrelevant. 'Home,' she said, retrieving her dress from the back of the chair and stepping into it. 'Isn't that what you want?' Her heels were on the floor next to the settee and she picked them up.

'Madeleine, look, I–'

She walked over to the bed and placed her finger softly on his lips. 'Shush, darling, let's just keep the memories. You say such beautiful things.'

Last night they had made love. He'd told her it was for the last time. But she had not heard him. She was asleep and so the words were left in the air. Somehow he couldn't imagine never walking the streets with her again ... or seeing her face over the rim of a wine glass ... or waking up next to her in the morning as he had just done. 'Look, I'm sorry it has to be this way.'

Her lips carried a melancholy smile. It almost broke his heart. 'You will never leave me, Mallory.' He'd heard the words before. Only now they were spoken with assurance.

'Never is a long time.'

'I don't know what I would do if I thought I would never see you again.'

She sat on the bed. The thin fabric of her dress touched the sheet. He put his arms around her. 'I would always stay with you if it was just the two of us.' He read the look of pain in her eyes and averted his gaze.

Suddenly the girl was up and striding towards the door. Her voice faltered. 'Mallory, *why* do I keep coming back? With all the others, I can forget them and move on. But not with you. *Why*?'

He could not look at her. There was a pigeon sitting on the window-sill and even the bird reminded him of the girl, the one whose wings he had mended. He knew exactly why she returned. It was because he had never given himself completely to her. If only she knew, if only he could tell her of the hurt and the suffering he had endured.

She was waiting for an answer to her question, but he remained silent. Then, with leaden steps, she grabbed her coat from the back of the chair and turned to go. Her skin was pale and her eyes were wet. And for the first time since the night he'd rescued her, her shoulders seemed to collapse in resignation.

The door was so far away. All he had to do was ask her to stay and he knew she would. Say the words, Mallory, just say the words! But he could not say them. He could only watch her go.

She turned around when she'd reached the door, still waiting for him to call her name. There was a look of such dejection written across her face. It was almost as if she knew what he was thinking. Then she smiled. And in this simple gesture he saw not only love, but also pity and regret. 'Goodbye, Mallory.' Then the girl disappeared, and the door closed softly behind her.

*

231

'Madeleine!' he shouted after her. 'I love you!' But the words could not be heard. At least not by the girl who had waited so patiently to hear them. He lay back on the bed. The sheet was down by his waist. It still carried the faint smell of her perfume and he cried, more than he had in years. Then he closed his eyes and tried to imagine her there again. But when he opened them, the room was empty – more so than he'd ever known it to be. Suddenly the thought that he would never see her again hit him like a blow to the stomach. Run after her, Mallory, find her before she reaches the station, and take her back. But he knew he would never do this.

It was too late.

The black fedora on the clothes hook by the front door caught his attention. Why hadn't she taken it? The hat was integral to her new image, a symbol of her freedom. Then he finally understood and with the knowledge came the chill. She was not coming back.

This was her way of saying goodbye.

Chapter Forty-Four

The lean, dishevelled man sitting across the table from Mario Falcone and Luca Cavatore was Antonio Luciano. He was a soldier of the streets, a man hardened to violence through a boyhood that saw him move rapidly up the criminal hierarchy, from delinquency to petty thievery, and finally to serious robbery and assault. Now he was a proficient contract killer, who took a morbid delight in his work. His preferred method of execution was poison and drugs. And because of his precision in applying the 'treatment', he'd earned himself the moniker 'The Doctor'.

'*Buon Pomeriggio*, Toni,' Falcone said, sliding a glass of whisky across the table. 'This is Luca, he manages the Green Door.'

Cavatore held out his hand but The Doctor ignored it.

'You have disposal.' His eyes were narrow slits of ice, his voice as cold. Falcone placed the photo of the girl on the table. For a minute The Doctor said nothing. Then he removed the bifocals from the tip of his nose. 'Which service you require?'

'Suicide,' Falcone said, 'perhaps an overdose?'

The hitman cleared his throat and spat the resultant phlegm into a dirty handkerchief. 'Where?' His eyes never strayed from the photo.

'She lives in Soho. Peter Street.' Falcone placed his shades carefully on the table. 'She sings at the French Revolution.'

'The girl is alone?'

'Some guy has moved in with her. Record producer, apparently. But according to my source, he's currently out of town on business.'

'Away how long?'

'Until the day after tomorrow.' Falcone glanced down at his watch. It was ten past seven and he had other business to attend to. 'My associate here,' he said, gesturing impatiently at Cavatore, 'is rather concerned Miss Laurent is about to flee the country.'

'How you know?'

'She handed her notice in at the club two days ago; she's purchased a ticket to Paris.'

Luciano rubbed the stubble on his chin. 'You require urgent service.' There was a vacant look on his face. 'When?'

'Tomorrow night.' Falcone held the hitman's gaze. 'It's our last chance before her boyfriend returns.'

Luciano looked down. A puzzled look had replaced the vacant expression. 'Is difficult,' he said, continuing to rub his hand down the side of his face, 'if complications…'

Cavatore sat up. 'Perhaps I can be of assistance?'

The Doctor stared at him, clearly unimpressed. He had taken an instant dislike to the nightclub manager. 'Why I need *your* help?'

'The bitch has done a runner with my money! I personally want to see her dead.'

The hitman's mouth tightened. 'I review in morning.' There was an undertone of anger in his voice. He stared morosely at Cavatore. 'I have Mario contact you.'

'We haven't talked money yet,' Cavatore said, shifting nervously in his chair.

'The fee is eight grand,' Falcone said, without hesitation.

'But that's–'

'There is no negotiation,' Falcone said, shaking his head. 'Also, as this is personal matter, you are responsible for my money. *Capire*?'

'Eight K! The girl from Slovakia cost less than four grand.'

234

'I dump her in river. Suicide is ... *complicato*,' Luciano said, looking at his watch. 'And you no forget, cash on completion of job.'

Cavatore nodded, trying in vain to control his frustration.

Falcone's eyes never left Cavatore's face. 'All we need to do now is arrange a time and place for collection.'

'If the bitch is sorted tomorrow, I'll see you at the Green Door,' Cavatore muttered angrily through clenched lips, 'seven-thirty on Saturday.'

Falcone smiled. His thin lips hardly parted. 'Perfect!'

The Doctor stood up. Madeleine's photo was tucked away safely in his coat pocket. He put his gloved hand on Cavatore's shoulder. It was not meant as a gesture of good will. The strong smell of body odour was nauseating and the nightclub manager struggled to stop his hand from moving to his nose.

'A warning, *amico*. No fuck-ups.' He squeezed Cavatore's shoulder. 'You work with me, you control anger, you do as I say. *Capire*?'

Cavatore nodded. Looking into the killer's eyes was like looking into the eyes of the devil. He shivered, a coward at heart. 'I hear you, Toni,' he said, attempting to put on a brave face. There was no other option but to cooperate if he was to see this through.

Antonio Luciano ignored the gesture. He held out his hand to Falcone.

'*Grazie per l'aiuto*, Toni.'

'*Niente, il mio amico.*'

Then, without another word, The Doctor buttoned up his black raincoat and disappeared into the murky darkness of the East End.

Chapter Forty-Five

Richard Parker cut a dapper figure in his multi-coloured shirt. The flamboyant pattern complemented his mop of ginger hair, permanent red face and enormous pink glasses. He'd formed Retro Red Recordings, or Triple R as it became affectionately known, in the wake of the late sixties music boom, his company going on to gain a significant foothold in the industry as a major inter-mediary between artist and record label. A rough diamond rather than a smooth operator, Parker was known for breaking the rules, and had made and lost a fortune. But along the way he had devel-oped a passion for fast cars and jazz music. And that was how he came to be at the French Revolution on that miserable evening in October.

The night that Parker first heard Madeleine Laurent sing, he'd been, like so many others, mesmerised. But it was only when he was introduced to her that he'd fallen totally under her spell. Initially their relationship had been purely platonic, but it had soon developed into something more and, as such, it seemed logical to move in with her. The Soho bedsit was a perfect base when he was down in London. But the girl was flighty and he'd soon realised he needed something more to keep her. That was when he'd dangled the carrot, hinted at a record contract. Violent rows dispersed the good times and he didn't trust the girl. But if the only way to sustain the affair was to resort to deviousness, then he would do exactly that.

Now here he was in Liverpool. Auditions had been arranged over three days and they could not be avoided. He missed Madeleine, but she'd assured him the break would do them both the world of good. He didn't see it that way. Each night, after her performance at the club, he would call her, relating his day and enquiring about hers. To keep the bed warm, so to speak, he intimated her recording contract was almost in place. It just had to be approved by Justin, his business partner. Two days later he'd had enough of sitting through third-rate cover bands and decided to return to London. It was early in the evening when he put the call through. Madeleine was getting ready for work.

'Hello?' There was a cautious note to her voice.

'Madeleine, darling!'

'Richard! Where are you?'

'Still in Liverpool, unfortunately. Look, I've had enough of this auditioning crap – I'm coming back to London later on tonight. I have something special for you.'

'Really? What is it?'

'You'll have to wait up for me to find out. I have one more band to audition this evening and then I'll be on my way. Should have it all tied up by eleven.'

'Richard, you're so cruel! Give me a hint. *Please*!'

'Patience, baby!' He chuckled with glee. 'All I'll say is it's something you've always wanted and it's going to make you very, very happy. Something that will need your signature.'

'Oh Richard!' she cried excitedly. 'Hurry back. I'll wait up for you!'

He laughed. It was so easy. 'See you around two, baby,' he said, replacing the receiver. Perhaps he shouldn't have hinted at the contract. But when he thought of how she would show her appreciation, he knew the decision was the right one.

Chapter Forty-Six

At 8.30 p.m. sharp, Cavatore was seated in Benvenuto's. The name translated as 'welcome', an over-rated description for a low-life dive. Unwashed beer glasses and cigarette butts lay scattered on the filthy tables. What a dump, Cavatore said to himself, knocking back the whisky. There had been a brief message from Falcone to say that the operation would go ahead. He looked around the shabby café. It was deserted but for himself and the bottle of booze. Angelo, the proprietor, had locked the door and hung up the CLOSED sign. The only suggestion of life was a single table lamp that shone brightly on the counter. The gangster's eyes searched the street. Suddenly a limping shadow moved across the plate-glass window. There was a rap on the door and Cavatore opened it.

The Doctor was wearing the same raincoat. Water dripped from his shoulders.

'Is everything in order?' Cavatore asked, pulling down the blinds.

The Doctor nodded and patted the small suitcase he was carrying. 'The patient?'

Cavatore shook his head. All this shit about doctors and patients. It was a bloody joke. Like some sort of child's play. 'I checked – she's due on stage at 10.30. Her show finishes an hour later.' He poured himself a shot of whisky. 'Drink?'

The look on Luciano's face spoke of his revulsion. 'I no drink when operate. The boyfriend is away?'

'Like I said, he isn't due back till tomorrow.' The whisky had bolstered Cavatore's confidence; his voice was thick with sarcasm.

The Doctor took a seat at the table. 'I been this morning Peter Street. You know Malaysian restaurant, Saluki?'

Cavatore nodded and then burped. The stench of whisky was overpowering.

Luciano looked at the cheap digital watch on his wrist. 'I meet with you, 9.50. Across road is backyard entry. You wait there.' He coughed without putting his hand over his mouth. 'You see me open street door – you follow. Close door, *capire*?'

Cavatore nodded nonchalantly and downed the whisky. He poured another.

The Doctor stood up. He looked at the glass in disgust. Then before Cavatore could blink an eye, a SIG semi-automatic pistol was pointing at him and the whisky bottle lay smashed on the floor. 'I tell you – *no* fuck-ups! I no like working with drunks.' The light from the table lamp accentuated the craters on his pockmarked face. '9.50, Peter Street. You arrive late, operation *finito* ... *capire*?'

The door closed silently. Suddenly Luca Cavatore was alone in the room. He prided himself on being a hard man but this psychopath was something else. He wasn't human. The man was a ghost. He picked up the whisky glass and then remembered the threat. And suddenly his desire for the drink disappeared. He walked over to the counter and pressed the bell. A door behind the bar opened and the proprietor appeared.

'A taxi, Angelo.'

'*Si signor*,' the proprietor said, quickly dialling the number. His hands were shaking.

Cavatore listened to the conversation and nodded when he heard Angelo say five minutes. 'What do I owe you?'

'It is no bother, *signor*. Please, it is a pleasure to serve such important customers.'

Chapter Forty-Seven

Madeleine arrived home just before midnight. The clear night was ablaze with stars that formed a sparkling ceiling over the ancient buildings. They seemed brighter tonight, or perhaps she was imagining it? Suddenly the moon showed itself from behind a solitary cloud. It shone with a brilliant silver light, reflecting off everything it touched. The buildings, the cobblestones, the glistening pavements were all enshrined with a luminosity that transformed the street. How wonderful to be alive, she thought, a newfound anticipation in her step. She was about to put her key in the door when a stranger walked by and she found herself enthusiastically greeting him. And she knew the reason why. Richard had negotiated the record deal. It had come in the nick of time. A couple of nights ago she'd had an argument with Christophe and told him she was tired of entertaining clients late into the night. He'd reluctantly accepted her resignation. Now, at last, she was free.

She opened the door and reached for the light switch. Nothing! Damn, not the fuse again. The same thing had happened just last week when a table lamp had blown and knocked off the power. Fortunately Richard had shown her how to flick the circuit breaker back on. Stumbling across the room, her eyes unaccustomed to the dark, she had just reached the kitchen wall unit that housed the electricity fuse board when a hand clamped over her mouth, stifling the scream that was already in her throat. Then another pair of hands tied what felt like a scarf over her eyes. She struggled wildly but felt her feet leave the floor, and then she was being carried across the room and laid on the bed. The hand was replaced by a rag stuffed in her mouth and she heard for the first time a voice that sent a chill down her spine.

'Miss Laurent, no struggle or scream or you be hurt.'

She lay absolutely still.

'I need cooperation,' the voice was soft and suave, 'if I no hurt you. *Capire*?'

She nodded.

'*Bene*! *Bene*!' He rubbed his hand gently down the side of her face. 'I call you Madeleine – is okay?'

The voice was unreal and she cringed with revulsion.

'You write now, a note, for Signor Cavatore. *Scusa*! He no like you right now. He so upset.'

Madeleine shivered and it had nothing to do with the cold. Severe exhaustion had reduced her to a physical wreck. She had no idea what was happening but if that was all they wanted…? She nodded again to indicate she understood.

'*Vedi*,' said the voice. 'See? Is easy you cooperate.'

She was then dragged up on the edge of the bed and a ballpoint pen was placed in her hand.

'Now, you write what I tell,' the voice said, removing the blindfold.

She tried looking around but the room was too dark to make out her assailants' faces. 'I … I can't see,' she spluttered through the gag.

'Shush Madeleine, is no *problema*,' said the soft voice. '*Pronto*.'

Before she could respond the stark light of a pencil torch lit up the notepad and she began to write the words the voice dictated.

No sooner had she written those three words than the pen was removed from her hand.

'*Perfetto*, Madeleine. *Per favore*, drink. We forget bad things, *si?*' He continued to stroke her face. 'You like whisky.'

The words had a strange chill. She shook her head vehemently, a smothered cry on her lips.

'No like this drink?' Luciano said, in a condescending manner. '*Per favore*, we *amici*, *si?*'

There was no way she was going to accept anything from these evil bastards. She tried to move her head to one side to make it difficult for them to reach her mouth.

'Awkward little bitch, aren't you,' said Cavatore, gripping her hair tightly and violently forcing her face away from the pillow.

She recognised the voice immediately and froze in terror. This was the abomination that brought back all the horror of her confinement in the basement of the Green Door. The Doctor's sharp voice cut across her torment.

'Now, I take away cloth,' he said, one gloved hand on her forehead and the other over her mouth. 'You make noise and I hurt you. *Capire?*'

Madeleine's eyes darted around the room. The Doctor grabbed her shoulders and shook her.

'You understand?'

She nodded her agreement, tears now streaming down her face. She didn't want to die. But neither would she make it easy for them. She lay still, pretending to cooperate.

Then The Doctor removed the rag.

'Help! Hel–,' she screamed with all her might, resuming her struggle against her captors. It took the strength of both men to hold her down. A rubber mask was hurriedly thrust over her mouth. The cotton lining would leave her face unscathed. Then her hands were bound together in front of her body and her head was driven into the pillow.

'You no help, Madeleine,' The Doctor sneered through clenched teeth, as he ran his fingers through her hair, 'I want so much be your *amici*.'

The first taste of the whisky, poured down a tube attached to the mask, made her heave. The air-tight contraption had been designed in such a way that she could not avoid swallowing the substance; the man held a pad over her nose so that she had to breathe through her mouth. She coughed and spluttered but with every breath the regurgitated liquid ran back down her throat. She could feel herself drifting away and the energy of her struggle diminishing.

'There, there, *dolse* Madeleine, all over now,' The Doctor said, removing the mask. '*Dormi bene, per favore*. Sleep well.' Then a pillow was placed over her face.

Madeleine's last vision, before she blacked out, was Paris in the spring, walking with Philippe beneath the cherry trees on the Champs-Élysées. They were in blossom and flowers covered the pavements beside the Seine with a pink carpet.

She was going home.

When the body ceased to twitch, The Doctor felt for a pulse. There was no sign of life. He placed the rubber mask, the bottle of contaminated whisky and the funnel into the suitcase. After they had untied the girl, he removed the pillow he'd used to suffocate her and stuffed the evidence into an empty pillowcase, together with the towel, the blindfold and the rag. They then manoeuvred her into a natural position on the bed and he half-filled a glass with the cocktail mixture of whisky and drugs. This was placed on the bedside table, next to the note, packets of drugs and a bottle of clean whisky.

Cavatore walked to the fuse board and switched on the electricity. The girl appeared to be asleep. But he knew the whore was dead. It would be difficult for the police to deduce that it was anything other than suicide. Analgesic overdoses are common.

Any fool could obtain those substances over the counter. He was happy with the outcome, so much so that he resorted to the language Luciano loved. 'An excellent operation, Doctor. And you're sure the post-mortem won't show any foul play?'

The Doctor wiped Madeleine's face and nodded. 'Is no *problema*,' he said, holding up his gloved hands. 'See, no fingerprints ... *nessuna prova*.' He bent over to examine the body lying on the bed. Then, satisfied that everything was as it should be, he gently ran his gloved fingers over her face to close her eyes. What a shame, he thought. She was so very beautiful.

Chapter Forty-Eight

Richard Parker stepped out of the limousine. As he handed over the money for the fare, two men pushed past him on the street. 'Steady on, fellas!' he shouted, but they never turned round. He looked at his watch. Almost one; he was earlier than expected. All he could think of as he climbed the stairs was the expression on Madeleine's face when he handed her the contract. It had taken all his charm to convince his partner that she was a sound proposition. Jazz wasn't exactly a big earner, but the girl had an unusual voice, which was also suited to both folk and blues. He hoped the deal might finally persuade her to leave the club and move up to Liverpool. The thought was still on his mind when he opened the door and turned on the light.

Excitement soon turned to disappointment. Madeleine was stretched out on the bed, fast asleep. He reached over to wake her. The smell of the whisky made him shudder. Why was she drinking that foul stuff again? He gently touched her face and was surprised to find it was not as warm as he remembered. Her eyes remained closed. Then he saw the drugs and the notepad lying next to the bottle of whisky and suddenly he was overcome with nausea. He rushed for the toilet and for the next five minutes he retched into the bowl until there was nothing left but a foul taste of bile in his mouth. The face in the mirror was as white as a sheet. He splashed it with cold water and then nervously edged his way back to the bedroom.

'My God, Madeleine, my God, my God! What have you done?'

He shook her body. Then he felt her pulse – nothing. Oh God, holy shit, what should he do? Call the hospital? No, it was too late for that. What about the police? But wait, would he be a suspect? His fingerprints were everywhere. The investigation … the mess … the intrusion into his life … where would it all end? But this was a suicide, right? She'd mentioned her depression once or twice before; the fact that she was stressed at work and wanted out. At times she'd also confessed to feeling lost and insecure. But she had always managed to snap out of it. He never imagined she would take her own life! She had so much to live for.

But hang on! Perhaps he was barking up the wrong tree. Maybe she'd struggled to nod off and had taken a few pills with a whisky, and then something had gone horribly wrong? But what about the phone call? She'd seemed far from desperate to get an early night. And what of the note? He tried to look at her, lying on the bed as if she were sleeping, but he had to avert his eyes. Then he recalled reading somewhere that taking an overdose was the favoured method of suicide for females and the panic once again set in. Trying desperately to collect his thoughts, he suddenly remembered the conversation they'd had a couple of days before he'd left for Liverpool. She'd drunk far too much champagne and had started ranting on about her old job, something about a nightmare boss, overdue debts and God knows what else. When she'd mentioned her life was in danger, he'd accused her of being a drama queen. They'd had a furious argument. Had he got it all wrong – was it bad enough to have driven her to suicide? Depression was an illness and drugs were the easy way out. But it could not be! She'd been in such high spirits over the phone.

He paced about, stumbling in a daze from one room to another, his hands continually rubbing his eyes. Sweet Jesus, what now? He could barely bring himself to look at her, let alone anything else. *Think, Parker, think.* His heart was in his throat and he was about to lose the contents of his stomach again. A glass of water would help. Standing by the sink, his wild, darting eyes settled on the cork noticeboard hanging by the fridge, and the scrap of paper pinned to it. And then he remembered: wasn't that the number he was to ring if there was any trouble? Mallory someone? God, maybe the threat from the Green Door was actually real? Shit – what the hell had Madeleine got herself into? One thing was for sure, he didn't want anything to do with it. Perhaps this Mallory guy could fix it for him. Madeleine sure as hell thought he could. Richard Parker dialled the number.

There was no answer, so he continued to let it ring.

Chapter Forty-Nine

A loud knock shattered the stillness of the night. Mallory sat bolt upright. For a moment he thought it was the Spaniards. Then it came again – the pounding! He threw on his dressing gown and opened the door to see a bedraggled Mrs Johnson.

'Look at the time, Mr Mallory! How dare your friends call you at this time of the morning? I've told you before; I've had enough of this nonsense!'

Mallory rubbed his eyes and tried to summon the energy to respond. 'I'm sorry, Mrs Johnson; I can't imagine who it would be.'

'I'm not putting up with any more of these calls,' she said, before storming off. 'This is your very last warning!'

Mallory sheepishly followed the landlady down the stairs. He picked up the receiver that was dangling by the side of the call box. It had to be Madeleine. The bloody woman had no consideration whatsoever. Where was the telephone company? It had been over a week since they said they were coming to change the number. He made a mental note to have Mrs Johnson chase them first thing in the morning; Madeleine's behaviour was beyond a joke. 'Hello?' he said bluntly, running his fingers through his mop of unruly hair.

'Mallory?'

'Who's this?' he shouted, taken aback by the man's voice on the line.

'It's Richard – Richard Parker!' There was no mistaking the desperation.

Who the bloody hell was Richard Parker and what the fuck was he doing ringing at this godforsaken hour of the morning? 'Yes?' He realised he was shouting and tried to get control of the situation.

'There's been a terrible accident. It's Madeleine–'

Mallory felt the blade of a cold knife pierce his heart. He closed his eyes and whispered a silent prayer before asking the only question that really mattered. 'What's happened?'

The voice on the other end of the line struggled to keep control. 'It's bad, she's not moving, I just arrived, I–'

'Don't touch anything. I'm on my way.'

Fate was on Mallory's side. The taxi approaching the High Street was returning home when he'd noticed the man standing in the middle of the road, waving his arms in the air. He pulled over. 'Sorry, mate! I'm off hire.'

Mallory could hardly get his words out. 'It's … it's an emergency.'

The driver smiled warily. 'That's what they–'

'My girlfriend. I think she might be dead.'

'Which hospital?'

'Her flat – Soho, Peter Street.'

'Jump in, pal,' the driver said, hitting the accelerator and speeding straight through the first red light. After what seemed like a never-ending journey through deserted streets lit only by sodium lamps, the taxi pulled up outside Madeleine's flat. Stuffing notes into the driver's hand, Mallory then reached for the door handle and was already out of the car when he heard the cabby shout. 'Do you want me to wait?'

'I don't know – thanks, I'll…' he offered, already inside the building. Climbing the stairs two at a time, Mallory forced himself to calm down before banging on the door. Suddenly a strange thought went through his mind. The last time he was here he'd been decorating the flat. He hadn't been back since, never shared all those moments that Madeleine had promised. Instead someone else had taken his place, and that was the bastard he was about to confront. He banged again, this time louder. The door opened.

'Richard Parker,' the stranger said, holding out his hand. 'Thanks for–'

Mallory didn't recognise the man and he ignored the hand – the last thing he needed now was an introduction. Was this the creep responsible for her death? If so, he wasn't sure he'd be able to hold himself back. He shouldered his way into the room.

Madeleine lay on the bed, fully clothed. Her hair was spread across the pillow and her eyes were closed. There must be some mistake – she *was* asleep. How many times had he woken up next to her and seen her just like this? Any moment now she would open her eyes and say, 'Oh Mallory, how wonderful, you have come at last!' Like a dying man drowning, the images of his time with Madeleine flashed through his mind. He picked up her lifeless hand. And he knew, before he even felt for her pulse that she was gone.

What the hell had she done? This wasn't how he wanted to remember her. The sheet lay by her feet and he slowly pulled the cover over her body, up to her neck. Then bending down, he kissed her lips. The stench was overpowering and it was then that the first hint of suspicion entered his mind: she'd been off the stuff since starting the job at the Revolution. It was giving her headaches. So why now? He looked at the bottle on the bedside table and the empty packets of pills beside it, and it all became clear: the whisky helped to dissolve the drugs. It would've made it easier for her to stomach them. He picked up the notepad. And all of a sudden he knew that Madeleine had not taken her own life. The illegible scrawl could never pass for her handwriting! Neither would the misspelt sentence. He was about to comment when he noticed the gold cufflink glinting on the floor. One of her admirers? Or perhaps lost in a scuffle? He turned to look at Richard Parker. The man was at the sink, pouring himself a glass of water. Mallory bent down and picked up the cufflink. And it was in doing so that he saw the initials engraved into the gold: LC.

He looked at the face that was once so full of love, a face that had brought him so much life and tried desperately to contain his anger. Her lipstick, always so carefully applied, was smudged. Another giveaway: she would never sleep in her make-up. Then he kissed the cold lips one last time. 'Goodbye, my darling,' he whispered softly, so only she would hear, 'you gave me everything and now there is nothing left.'

Some five minutes later he realised he was still holding her hand as he had that last time, when they'd fallen asleep after making love. For a moment he could not see for the tears in his eyes. He blinked. Then he rubbed his free hand across his face. It made little difference. Not that it mattered; he couldn't look at her any longer. Pulling the thin cotton sheet over her head, he half turned towards the boyfriend. This guy was no killer, he could see that now. No, this was a professional job. It had to be the bastards from the Green Door. But who the hell was LC? Certainly not Fowler. Then he remembered the name. *Cavatore*. Andrei had mentioned him after their meeting at the club. And Madeleine had said he was evil. What was the son of a bitch's first name? He screwed his eyes tight and gritted his teeth. How long he stood that way he did not know. Time no longer meant anything. Eventually he opened his eyes. A sheet covering a corpse was all he saw through the tears. 'Madeleine, my darling Madeleine, I only ever loved you,' he whispered, 'you are now free to fly.' Then the anger returned and he wiped his face again with the back of his hand. 'Rest assured I will find the bastards responsible.'

They were the last words he would ever say to her, but she would never hear them.

Richard Parker stood helpless by the sink. 'I don't understand. I wasn't due back until tomorrow.'

'What made you change your mind?'

'I'd had enough of listening to second-rate bands. I phoned Madeleine and told her I was coming home tonight with a contract for her to sign. She was so excited – she said she would wait up for me. And then this. Why?'

A contract, her dream of a new life, what she had always wanted. If only this sad bastard knew that once she had the golden egg, she would kill the goose. Like all the others, he was just another two-bit player on her stage, fulfilling her ambitions while he waited in the wings. Suddenly Mallory felt sorry for him. 'Look, there's nothing we can do here now,' he said, as kindly as he could, walking over to the crestfallen man. 'It's best left to the authorities. You need to call the police.'

Richard Parked gasped in shock. 'The police? I'd really rather not, I mean–'

'You found the girl and you're living with her. They'll want to question you.' Then he gently placed a hand on the man's shoulder and ushered him over to the phone. The scrap of paper with his name and number was lying on the worktop beside the receiver. It was the only evidence that linked him to Madeleine. He screwed it up and shoved it into his pocket. 'And please, do not mention you contacted me. For obvious reasons, I'd rather not be involved.'

'But–'

'Please – do this for her.'

For her! What did that mean? Who was this man, Mallory – was he just a friend? Richard Parker let out a resigned sigh and nodded. He was still clearly in shock. 'There's something I must tell you,' then he hesitated, 'it's probably nothing.'

'Go on?'

The record producer was standing beside the telephone, his hands cradling his head. 'I saw two men – they ran past me when I arrived tonight. I can't be totally sure, but now I think back on it, they seemed to be leaving this block of flats.'

252

Mallory shook his head. 'There are other residents in the building next door. I can't see a connection. It's pretty obvious from the note that Madeleine took her own life.' This was what he wanted Richard Parker to believe; it would give him breathing space. Whoever had carried out the hit had done a bloody good job. It was the mark of a true professional and would certainly fool the police into believing this had been a straightforward suicide. There was no incriminating evidence – in fact, nothing to suggest foul play. Apart from the cufflink. And that was safe in his pocket.

'Yes, perhaps you're right. I'm probably just imagining things; this whole night has got me completely spooked. But why would she do this?' And then he started to sob.

God, this was all he needed, her bloody lover crying over her! He placed his hand on the man's shoulder. 'What little I know of Madeleine, she was prone to bouts of depression.'

Parker nodded. 'She once mentioned there were problems with some club she used to work at.' He sniffed and blew his nose on a clean white handkerchief. 'Something about money she owed them.'

If he only knew the half of it. How easily this poor sop had been deceived. But then Madeleine was a dab hand at the game. It was all so bloody farcical he wanted to laugh. 'I must go now,' he said, looking one last time at the bed. 'When the police have been and the body has been removed, take a tablet and get some sleep. You will find everything looks different in the morning.'

Richard Parker cautiously offered his trembling hand. 'Thank you – Mr Mallory – for taking the trouble to come over. I don't know what I would have done without your help.'

Mallory closed the door. The taxi had disappeared. Neon lights lit up the sky in the distance. There was the scream of a police siren. But where he stood beneath the redundant street lamp, all was still. Only the light from a single window touched the dark street. Madeleine's window. He inhaled the cool night air. And then suddenly he recalled the last time he had stood here. It was across the road, there in the shadows. He had looked up at her flat and heard her laughter. Why the hell did everything look the same? He realised then that he would never be free of the girl. The memories of their brief time together would always bind him to her. 'You will never leave me, Mallory,' she had once said. In the past he would have plied himself with drink to numb the pain. But he had no taste for that now. There was business to take care of and, in his anger, he did not want to see anyone.

Except perhaps one man.

And that man was just a few blocks away, above the strip joints of Soho.

Chapter Fifty

The light was still on in the Russian's office. Strange, Mallory thought, but then the barrister did keep odd hours. He pressed the intercom. It was a minute or two before it was answered. 'Who's that?' The voice was gruff, irritable.

'Andrei, it's me.'

'*Mallory*? What the hell time do you call this?'

'I need to see you.'

'Just a minute,' said the voice, rather reluctantly.

When Mallory entered the room, the Russian was sitting in his shirtsleeves at his desk. Papers had been hurriedly cleared away and he looked anything but composed. 'What brings you here at this godforsaken hour of the morning?'

'Madeleine.'

'*Madeleine*!' The voice was high-pitched, nervy. 'What the hell has–?'

'She's dead.'

'Oh! My God, Mallory. What happened?'

'A drug overdose.'

'When?'

'About two hours ago. Her boyfriend found her and called me.'

'Why not the police?'

255

Because she knew I'd come running, he thought. 'My number was on her noticeboard.'

The Russian straightened up in his chair. 'Obviously you have seen her.'

Mallory nodded.

'But I don't understand – why would she–'

'She was murdered, Andrei.' He scrutinised the Russian's face as he spoke the words.

'*Murdered*? No!' Andrei's hands started to shake and he poured himself a brandy. Mallory noticed the action. It was the first time ever the Russian had not offered him one. Something wasn't right. 'I don't understand.'

'There was a bottle of whisky and a packet of drugs by her bed.' Mallory spoke slowly, almost as if he was talking to a child. 'It all looks very convincing and will no doubt fool most people, including, I suspect, even the police.'

'So what makes you suspicious?'

'Madeleine didn't drink whisky. It gives her headaches.'

The Russian laughed nervously. 'If she wanted to take her own life then this is one of the simplest ways to do it! Drugs dissolve easily in spirits, especially whisky – the headache is not even a consideration.' The voice was poised and had taken on authority. 'God, Mallory, think straight; what she was doing would *kill* her, not give her a headache!'

'And then there's the note,' Mallory said, ignoring the interruption.

'Note?' Andrei gripped the tumbler.

'Three words written in a misspelt scrawl, which was certainly not Madeleine's.'

A shadow crossed the Russian's grave and he felt the cold sensation. Nevertheless, he hurriedly composed himself. 'How can you be sure?'

'I know Madeleine's handwriting. And her English is good.'

'Dear God, you must be paranoid. The poor girl would not have been thinking straight.' He laughed half-heartedly. 'Come now, try to think like a lawyer and don't jump to conclusions. We both know what she's like, how unpredictable she can be. I mean, take–'

'*Jump to conclusions*? Then what's this?' Mallory removed the cufflink from his pocket and dropped it onto the desk. It landed with the initials facing the Russian. He looked the barrister straight in the eye. 'Now what do you suppose LC stands for?' It was a question he had been asking himself ever since he had left her flat. He already half-knew the answer.

'I've no idea!' Andrei spluttered, draining the brandy.

'Come, Andrei, think! Don't you recall telling me about Fowler's partner – what's his name? Cavatore, isn't it?'

Andrei's face was as white as a sheet. He rose and then started pacing the floor like he was back in court, facing a jury and a difficult judge. 'It's not possible.'

'What was his first name?'

'He's a nightclub manager, not a hitman. It's just too preposterous.'

'His name, Andrei.'

There was nowhere to hide.

'Luca. His name is Luca Cavatore.'

Mallory nodded slowly.

The Russian was unable to speak.

'Look, Andrei, no secrets or lies. We've been friends long enough to be straight with each other. I know Madeleine better than anyone and I can assure you she would not want to take her own life. Why would she when her boyfriend had arranged to meet her this very night with a record deal?'

'Record deal? What record deal?'

'He'd rushed back from Liverpool, had the papers for her to sign. She was looking forward to finally accomplishing her dreams. When the bastards hit her, they had no idea he was on his way.'

Andrei settled back down in the office chair, trying to collect himself. Then he reached for the bottle of brandy. 'A drink?'

Mallory shook his finger. He needed a clear head. 'No, this can only be the work of Fowler and his partner in crime – Luca Cavatore.'

For a moment the Russian said nothing. Putting both hands on the desk, he closed his bloodshot eyes. 'Supposing you are right, what do you intend to do about it?'

'You're the only man in the world I can confide in. My first thought was to come to you.' The next question was one he had considered very carefully. 'I need a gun, Andrei.'

'A *what*?'

'You have a Heckler!' Mallory's gaze was unwavering. It was almost as if he was asking for a cigarette. Only his eyes were different. They were cold and hard and the Russian could never ever remember seeing them like that. All he saw, in their reflection, was a wasteland.

He slumped back in his chair and downed the half glass of brandy, a broken man. 'I have a confession.' The voice took on an expression of sadness. Mallory said nothing. All along he had suspected that something was not as it should be. 'Many years ago, I had an affair. It's not something I'm particularly proud of.' Mallory waited. 'It was a boy. Cavatore knows about the liaison. It was a set-up but ever since then the threat of blackmail has hung over my head!' He looked away, unable to meet Mallory's eyes. Finally when he spoke, his voice was a whisper. 'You could be right about Madeleine. Tommaso said they wanted to see her.'

'Why didn't you tell me?'

'I was threatened and told to keep my mouth shut. I had no idea they would kill her.'

So it was blackmail! These bastards were experts at the game. Mallory felt sick in his guts. He certainly hadn't expected the Russian to be a part of the conspiracy. But then who was he, with his past, to judge his friend? He had involved Andrei and asked for his help. Now this thing with the boy was out in the open, he didn't want to hear the sordid details. God, how he wished he could turn back the clock! 'I'm sorry, Andrei.' There did not seem much else to say.

Andrei merely nodded slowly. Then he moved his hand to a catch beneath the desk. A false drawer opened and behind it was a hidden compartment. He laid the gun on the table in front of Mallory. The 9mm Heckler & Koch tactical weapon was a universal self-loading pistol with a magazine holding twelve rounds, what the Russian had always called 'his last line of defence'. Perhaps, in this case, it was. The identification serial numbers had been filed off the barrel. Andrei took no chances. But then he was a pro. 'Do you need the silencer?' His voice was drained of all authority. Sadness had crept into the room.

'We don't want to disturb the neighbours now, do we?' Mallory said, taking the pistol. He removed the magazine, which was fully loaded, and then checked the mechanism. Twelve rounds should be enough for what he had in mind. This had been easy, too easy. And now he knew why. 'You don't need to worry any more about Cavatore.'

Andrei was unable to lift his head. 'When you have finished with the gun please dispose of it in the river.' Then he handed Mallory a sealed envelope he had removed from the safe. 'Cavatore is expecting this.'

'What is it?'

'Something I owe them. It will get you past the front door.'

'Rest assured, Andrei, I will put this right.'

'I know, my friend, I know.' There was a deep melancholy in his voice. 'Fowler and sometimes Cavatore are at the club in the evenings before it opens, usually between seven and eight. The first punters don't appear until after nine. And the girls are on from ten till two.' He eased himself back into his chair and stared morosely out of the window. 'You do realise there is no going back from a homicide?'

Mallory stood up and slipped the gun into the waistband behind his back. 'I've killed soldiers in the bush that I did not know. I have sleepless nights over that. When I think of Madeleine and what they did to her, blowing away these bastards will not even prick my conscience.'

'I understand,' the Russian said, nodding his head, 'I understand.'

Out on the pavement the wind had picked up – an icy chill that invaded the air. They parted and said their last goodbyes outside Antonio's. It seemed appropriate after all the good times they had shared there. An old woman, wearing too much make-up, staggered along the pavement, hanging onto the arm of a young man. The lingering smell of cheap perfume followed in their wake.

'You'll be hard pressed to find a taxi at this time,' the Russian said, seeing a solitary black cab disappearing into the distance.

'There's bound to be one on Shaftesbury Avenue. If not, I'll walk.'

The Russian shrugged. Then he draped his enormous arms around Mallory's shoulders, holding him in a bear hug. 'Look after yourself. And watch your back,' he said, finally able to meet Mallory's eyes again. 'You know where I am if you ever need me.'

'I know.' Mallory stepped back and contemplated the man who had changed his life.

'And don't take any chances.'

Don't take any chances. He knew exactly what Andrei meant. A gust of wind swept through the alley, swirling the papers and packets that lay discarded in the gutter. The front page of a newspaper was trapped against a lamp post beside the Russian's feet. The headline caught Mallory's attention: MUGABE'S FIFTH BRIGADE MASSACRES CIVILIANS. He crouched down to get a closer look. Below the bold black print was a picture taken somewhere in Matabeleland. For the second time in as many days, he felt footsteps on his grave. God, was this a warning? What was he going back to? He stood up and hugged Andrei again. And then he kissed him on each cheek. The man was like a father to him and he loved him above all others. 'I'm sorry it had to be this way.' Up until that moment the atmosphere had been tense. Suddenly

Mallory relaxed and for perhaps a minute or so they stood together on the damp pavement, entwined in each other's arms. Everything they had shared for the last twenty years was about to disappear. He finally broke free of the bear-like embrace and noticed the tears in the Russian's eyes. Swallowing hard, he turned and walked away. Before he reached the corner, he looked back.

Andrei was standing in the same spot with his arm in the air, as if frozen in time.

Chapter Fifty-One

The bird had perished. With her freedom had come her death. He thought for a moment of what she had once said: 'When you love me completely...' It was what she had wanted above all else. Love! The word didn't even begin to encompass what he felt for her now. It was a drop in the ocean, a grain of sand on a beach. God, why couldn't they have just gone away, escaped the depravity of the East End? But where would they have gone? Even when she lived with another, she had at least come back to him. Now it would never happen again. The bastards from the Green Door had made sure of that. All that was left now was to avenge her death.

Lingering patiently in the shadows, Mallory thought of the last time he had stood like this, behind a tree in a valley, waiting for the enemy. Suddenly a clap of thunder struck the air like the detonation of a mortar bomb. Instinctively he ducked his head. Then the rains came, short and hard, hitting the pavement like the rattle of a machine gun, washing the dirt and grime into the sewers of London. The analogy of sewers and rats and what he was about to do was not lost on him. He felt alive and on edge. Back in the war zone. As quick as the rain had started it abated, leaving the air fresh and the street clean. He so much wanted a cigarette but this was neither the time nor the place. A lit match ... a sniper's bullet ... your position compromised.

The darkened back alley ran between two deserted shops, next to the former ironmongers. From here Mallory continued to watch the Green Door. The passage afforded him a good view of the club and gave him some degree of protection from the cold night. Now all he had to do was wait – a trait he had learned well in the Zambezi Valley. Suddenly a pair of full-beam headlights lit up the street. For a moment he thought his luck was in. But it was not to be; the Green Door remained in darkness.

He'd had the whole day to ensure his plan would work but in spite of this, there was still a nagging doubt. Improbable factors. That was what his old CO, Lieutenant Anderson, had called them. How to deal with it? Anderson had taught them to confront the problem and then to isolate it. He'd no sooner thought of this than the questions came. What if one or the other of the partners didn't turn up? What if they were late and arrived after the club was open to the public? And then what if the doorman – what was the black bastard's name? – Mo, that's it. What if this Mo shit recognised him? That was the one thing he did have covered. Andrei's envelope – his entrance ticket!

Then, as if by fate, the black man appeared out of nowhere. He unlocked the metal grill and the heavy front door. Minutes later, lights appeared in the downstairs windows of the club.

The luminous dial of Mallory's watch shone like a glow-worm in the dark and he was careful to conceal it. His hands were clenched together and to give himself something to do, he checked the pistol for the umpteenth time. The magazine was in place, the silencer screwed onto the barrel, the safety catch on. Come on, you bastards – where the hell are you? He forced himself to relax, breathing deeply. Then he saw a figure coming down the street towards him and he hurriedly retreated towards the rear of the alley, his black clothes blending in with their surroundings. But he had nothing to worry about – the stranger walked by without so much as a glance in his direction. He checked his watch again. 7.15. They should be here by now.

And then, as though he'd willed them into being, headlights appeared again at the entrance to the street and a taxi pulled up outside the nightclub. There was no mistaking the elephantine proportions of the man. Fowler! But he wanted them both. Especially Cavatore. So the wait continued. His hands were in his pockets to keep them warm and to occupy the time he went through the plan for the umpteenth time. The only factor he was unsure of was his escape. Mo would have to be put out of the equation. But did he do this before the hit or after?

He was still churning the problem over in his mind when a silver Mercedes pulled up outside the club. The driver opened the boot. This had to be Cavatore. Then he heard the black man's loud voice saying, 'Okay boss!' as he lifted a crate out of the car. At last. When the sidelights of the car flashed once, indicating the vehicle was locked, Mallory moved the pistol to the right-hand side of his waistband. Last check of the watch. 8.10. Less than an hour to opening time. It was now or never. Then, in spite of his beliefs, or lack of them, Mallory whispered a little prayer: 'Please God, let Cavatore be in the office with Fowler.' He was about to make his move when he suddenly spotted a man limping towards the club. Mo opened the door and greeted him warmly before the two of them disappeared inside. Who the hell was this? No matter, it was too late to change course. He'd have to improvise.

'We're shut!' The shout was in response to the knock on the door.

Mallory held up the envelope in his left hand to the spy hole. 'My boss asked me to give this to Mr Fowler.' He heard the door click open.

The doorman examined him under the glare of the street lamp. 'Ah, I know you. You were here with Vadislav last month.' He held out his hand. 'Give me the envelope.'

Mallory whipped it back into his pocket. 'It's a cash payment. If I don't hand it to Mr Fowler in person and get a receipt, I'm dead.'

264

The doorman was aware of such arrangements. After all, he too worked for unscrupulous bastards. He eyed Mallory up and down. Then he moved out of the way and gestured for him to step inside. 'They're in the office. You follow me,' he said, leading the way down the dark steps.

Thank you, God, Mallory thought, bringing the gun out of his waistband. His fingers automatically checked the safety. It was on. For just a moment he was back in the bush and the black man was again the enemy. It was all so familiar. When Mo reached the bottom step, Mallory was nine inches above him. He swung the gun with all his force in a low arc, catching the unsuspecting doorman just above the ear. The blow would have killed a lesser man, but Mo was no ordinary man. Nevertheless, he dropped like a sack of potatoes onto the stone floor. Mallory stepped over him and searched the dark corridor. The office beyond the circular room was still embedded in his mind. Low, red lighting, where the girls danced, illuminated the route past the long bar. The door was slightly ajar when he came upon it. He could hear voices and strained laughter. Then he heard Madeleine's name. With the Heckler in his right hand and the safety catch off, he stepped into the room. The conversation ceased immediately. Cavatore was the first to regain his composure. He'd been amongst gangsters for too long not to know the procedure; attack was the best form of defence. 'What the fuck is this all about?' he screamed. 'Who the hell do you think you are, storming in here like this?'

'It's Vadislav's assistant,' said Fowler. 'I remember him from our meeting.'

'Back from the desk! All of you! Face the wall and keep your hands above your heads!' Mallory's voice was menacing and there was no mistaking the threat. The gangsters did as they were told. There was an edge of fear in Fowler's voice. 'Please, Mr Mallory, I–'

'Now turn around – *slowly*! Keep your hands above your heads.' He wanted them to know exactly why they were about to die. And he wanted to see their faces. 'Look at me, you bastards.' His voice was calm and collected. 'Which one of you scum murdered Madeleine Laurent?'

'Wait, it wasn't–'

The shot hit Fowler in the centre of his forehead and he went down hard. Then the stranger with the limp went for his gun and Mallory shot him twice in the chest.

It was Cavatore's turn. 'Please, please! Fowler gave the order!' He was trying to point to the stranger on the floor. 'That ... that is the man who killed Miss Laurent!'

'Name. *What's* his name?'

'The Doctor! Luciano! Toni ... I mean Antonio Luciano! He is the one! Please, I–' He was wetting himself with fear. The urine stained the front of his beige chinos. 'Please sir, plea–'

'You left your calling card, Cavatore,' Mallory said, dropping the cufflink on the table.

The gangster's face was as white as a sheet. He collapsed to his knees and folded his hands in prayer. 'Please sir! Money, I have mon–'

'You're a lying, cold-hearted, murdering son of a bitch. Your killing days are over. You had a partner in crime – now join him in hell,' Mallory said, shooting Luca Cavatore twice in the chest. Then he walked over to the bodies lying like broken dolls on the floor and put another carefully placed shot into each of the gangsters' heads. Luciano stopped twitching. It was then he noticed the money lying on the table. They must have been counting it out for the hitman. Well, he wouldn't need it where he was going. Without another moment's thought, Mallory pocketed the cash. But it was small pickings compared with what he found in the open depository. Stacks of used fifty-pound notes, bundled together, filled the top shelf of the safe. There was no point in leaving that either. He looked around the room one last time. I guess that about takes care of this lot, he said to himself, before finally closing the office door.

The doorman was still unconscious. What to do with him? A shot to the back of the head would put him out of his misery. But although the man was no saint in Mallory's eyes, he had no bone to chew with him. Killing in cold blood wasn't his forte. He looked at his watch. 8.21. It had taken just eleven minutes to avenge Madeleine's death.

Once out of the club, Mallory breathed deeply of the cold evening air. Then he locked the door and placed the CLUB CLOSED sign on the metal grill. The Heckler was burning a hole in his pocket. Nevertheless he remained calm and walked slowly down the High Street before catching a taxi to the deserted Wapping docks. Standing alone on the side of a pier that had seen the departure of many a ship to distant lands, he threw the gun and the nightclub keys into the dark waters of the Thames. An evil had been exterminated.

It was not until Mallory was walking back along Highway Road that he thought of Madeleine. After the Bush War, he'd told himself that he would never again advocate revenge. But this was different. He'd made a promise to Madeleine on her deathbed. Besides, there was no place in a decent world for the likes of Fowler and Cavatore. He suspected that even the police would be delighted with the outcome. After all, Scotland Yard had had their suspicions about the Green Door and their involvement in human trafficking. When he was satisfied that he was far enough away from the vicinity of the docks, he hailed a taxi and gave the driver Andrei's address in Soho. Returning the envelope was the last job he would do before leaving the country. But why did the Russian owe them money? Actually, he did not want to know – about the money, or the boy. He had always taken Andrei as he found him – they were friends. And in friendship there had to be forgiveness. On the brink of his return to Africa, he wanted no hidden agendas. Taking a pen from his pocket, he then wrote a short message on the outside of the envelope.

The rats are exterminated. Your money returned.

The taxi waited while Mallory posted the envelope. Antonio's restaurant was in full swing, but no one saw him. Then he gave the driver an address of a nondescript establishment in the East End, a safe-house used by illegal immigrants. A place to hide before his flight. As the car pulled away from the pavement, Mallory screwed up his eyes to constrain the tears. How the mighty had fallen. All the promises of a future, a shared partnership built on friendship, lay in the gutter, amongst the dregs of beer and cigarette butts. And the last image of Soho he saw, in the rear-view mirror of the taxi, was Andrei's empire slowly disappearing into the dark.

It was a cold night. Even Lillian was nowhere to be seen.

Chapter Fifty-Two

When Mo regained consciousness he felt like he'd been kicked by a mule. But it was nothing compared to the shock of finding his employers murdered and the safe empty. The clock above the desk showed it was 9.20 and yet there was no one at the club. What the hell was happening? Suddenly he was terrified. Mo's sheer size had earned him the nickname 'The Brown Bomber', and he was used to raining terror down on overzealous revellers who dared to face up to him. But now he was on the receiving end of the tremor. Somewhere out there was a Mr Big who controlled this gangland empire of drugs and prostitution from abroad. He had once overheard the name spoken with fear and respect. Enrico Tommaso. And what had he done? Only gone and let an assassin into the very club he was paid to protect. Without even frisking him. But then didn't Mr Vadislav's assistant have money for Mr Fowler? He had seen the envelope with his own eyes. Nevertheless the thought persisted: 'secure your house'. The number one rule in the underworld, and he had broken it. How could he vindicate himself? There was only one way. In large letters on the desk pad, he wrote the words:

Vaddyslaf assistant - killer.

Was it enough? Or would they still hang him out to dry? In his ignorance, there was only one way out. And that was to run.

It was Mario Falcone who discovered the bodies of Fowler, Cavatore and Luciano. He had opened the club late Sunday with a skeleton key, after an associate had reported the place curiously closed. The gangsters' corpses had already started to putrefy in the heated office and a stench of death and defecation hung in the air. On the desk was a note and a cufflink. Then he checked the safe and a cold dread came over him. The money was missing. Shit! He read the note. So, Vadislav was responsible for the bloody mess. The fucking traitor. What the hell was he going to tell Tommaso? Somebody's head was going to roll and he hoped it would not be his. His hands were still shaking when he dialled the funeral director in Sicily.

The little chapel of rest outside Palermo stood on the side of the hill and overlooked the bay of Naples. The Omertà used the crematorium behind the building to dispose of its victims. It was here that Falcone had recently attended the funeral of Adrianna Conaglio, the Mafia widow gunned down in Palermo by a rival mob. After the service he had stood amongst the tombstones, gazing across the bay. A curl of smoke from Mount Etna in the distance had touched the sky. It had been many years since the volcano had last erupted but that explosion would have been nothing compared to Tommaso's temper when he heard about the executions.

Falcone waited patiently for his call to be connected. Eventually an answer machine cut the ringing tone and Falcone left the coded message – 'three bodies for cremation – contact The Singer'. Then, just before leaving the nightclub, he placed two calls: an anonymous 999 call to the Met and a brief message to Luciano's assistant.

The bouncer was on borrowed time.

*

When the police arrived, the front door was open, the safe empty and the place deserted. After the killings, the Met shut down the Green Door for good and the murder of Messrs Fowler, Cavatore and Luciano appeared on the police records as an unsolved crime.

They found Mo's body a week later, floating in the Thames near Limehouse Reach. There was a single gunshot wound to the back of his head.

No one ever came forward to claim the body.

Chapter Fifty-Three

'Andrei? You are well?' This was a call the Russian had half expected. He had tried to contact Mallory after he'd found the envelope with his money returned, but it was too late: according to his landlady, her tenant had already departed.

'*Buonasera*, Enrico,' he said, opening his eyes. He had taken to sleeping on the couch in the office since Mallory had left and the call had woken him up. 'Good to hear from you.'

'The pleasure, as always, is mine. First of all, my apologies for calling you at this unsociable hour. Especially after the weekend. It is extremely rude of me.'

'What can I do for you, Rico?' He could barely stop his hands from shaking.

'Ah! My friend, we are in so many ways like blood brothers that I feel I have to speak with you on a matter that grieves me sorely.'

The Russian remained silent. He was aware of what was coming.

There was a short pause, then the voice again, chillingly soft. 'The problem is one of our London clubs.'

'What's happened?'

'I'm surprised you have not heard.'

'Sorry, Enrico, you are talking in riddles.'

Another moment of silence. 'It appears my good friend and associate Luca, has come to an untimely end. Mario found him

272

with Fowler *and* Luciano last night – so much blood…' a pause, 'but what grieves me most, Andrei, is that Antonio was there to pick up his money. Only it seems to have disappeared, along with fifty grand from the safe. So now we have three bodies and no money, which you will surely agree is a rather sad state of affairs.' Then Andrei heard a wry laugh that turned his stomach. 'You wouldn't be able to throw any light on this nasty business would you?'

'Good God, Rico! You know that's not my game.'

'Of course, of course.' The sigh was audible. 'My apologies for asking the question.' He wavered, choosing his words carefully. 'In the light of what has happened, I have just reread the report of your meeting with Mr Fowler. Mario informs me that your assistant – a Mr Mallory is it? – was responsible for Miss Laurent's disappearance? Why is he involved?'

Andrei loosened off his tie. 'She's a friend.'

'A friend? And now look what has happened.'

'You are talking in riddles again, Rico.'

'Miss Laurent is dead. *Suicidio*, I believe.' He coughed and apologised.

Andrei knew they were looking for the girl. He had even informed the Sicilian *mudak* of her movements. She was a thorn in his relationship with Mallory and he felt no remorse for her death. If Cavatore had not screwed it up by leaving evidence at the murder scene, none of this shit would be happening. Then he thought about his last conversation with Mallory. 'Was it really suicide, Rico?'

'I can't think what you are implying. Miss Laurent was difficult. But none of us would have wanted this to have happened. We all had a vested interest in her – including you, Andrei.'

'If you are referring to what it cost me to release the girl from her contract at the Green Door, then, yes, I'm a grand out of pocket. She was, to say the least, an inconvenience. But Mallory wanted to help her. That was my reason for becoming involved.'

273

'It was most generous of you.' This said with sarcasm.

Andrei ignored the jibe. 'She was in the process of paying me back. But I'm really not sure what you are implying. What happened at the Green Door has nothing to do with me.'

'*Nothing*?' The sardonic laugh reverberated down the receiver. 'Here I go again, always jumping ahead of myself without giving you the facts. I would not make a very good barrister now, would I?'

Andrei's heart was beating out of his chest. What the hell had Mallory done? He remained silent and waited for Tommaso to continue.

'Evidence, facts – is that not what you are always telling me and there I go, forgetting your advice. Please, forgive me.' Suddenly the Sicilian's voice hardened. 'Mario found a note that our doorman left in the club before he did a runner. Unfortunately Luciano's assistant does not have the professional flair of The Doctor, bless his soul, and he forgot to question Mo before he despatched him.' He paused to allow the words the impact they deserved. 'Nevertheless, I am sure you would be interested in the contents of the note.'

Shit, why the hell didn't Mallory get rid of the black *svoloch*? But then he realised that this wasn't really his line of work. 'I'm sure you will tell me, Rico,' he said, trying to maintain some degree of composure.

'I will read it out for you, Andrei. Word for word.' Tommaso was taking his time, clearly enjoying the baiting. 'It says: Vadislav assistant – killer. The note is very brief, but then doormen aren't employed for their command of the English language nor, for that matter, their intelligence.'

You could hear a pin drop in the Russian's office. For a moment he was unable to speak; unable to even breathe. He was desperate for a drink, anything to help calm his shattered nerves. It was not easy when the silence prevailed. Then Tommaso was speaking again, in his smooth voice. 'I thought it would surprise you, Andrei, but what on earth does it mean?'

You know bloody well what it means, Andrei thought. He stared hopelessly at the empty glass trying desperately to maintain some degree of composure. 'It's a question you will need to ask Mr Mallory, Rico.'

'Have you seen him since this unfortunate affair?'

'No. He phoned me yesterday morning and said he wanted a few days off. He sounded very upset but wouldn't elaborate. I'm afraid that's all I know.'

'A few days off? You wouldn't happen to know where he was last night?'

'No idea, Enrico. As I said, you will have to ask him that question yourself.'

'I would love to but unfortunately Mr Mallory is proving a difficult man to find. He appears to have disappeared off the face of the earth! However, his landlady was most cooperative. She mentioned that he was going back to Zimbabwe for a while and that she would be keeping his flat for him. Perhaps you might care to enlighten me?'

'You know I would help you if I could.'

'I know! But please, Andrei, no more hidden truths. We have worked together successfully for a number of years. I need not remind you that most of your lucrative work comes from our association. We would certainly not want to jeopardise that now, would we? Nor would we want your *friendship* with the boy to become public knowledge.'

The silence was chilling. The bastards had set him up and now they were pulling the strings. The Russian's eloquent wordplay, so often spoken in courtrooms across the city, was nowhere to be heard. His body was shaking so violently he was unable to speak. Tommaso maintained the tension before speaking again. 'I realise you would of had nothing to do with this mess, Andrei. Especially after kindly informing us of the girl's whereabouts. However, Mario does not share my views – he maintains that you were involved. It has taken all my persuasion to convince him otherwise. Can you believe, he was about to award a second contract to our new man? Dear me, we don't want that now, do we? What would I do without the services of my most trusted barrister in London? But I really would like to speak with Mr Mallory.' The voice was soft yet it held an undertone of menace. 'Without your help, Andrei, I'm going to have a hard time keeping Mario off your back.'

There was no way out. He loved Mallory but the man had taken things too far. Was he out of the country? If so the Sicilian son of a bitch would never find him. He collapsed in his chair, his head in his hands, and wracked his brains for the flight time. Then he was being pushed again.

This time the voice was fearsome. 'No more games, Vadislav. *Where* is he?'

'He told me he was going back to Zimbabwe.' Andrei's voice quivered.

'Don't fuck around with me. That I already know. Who is he *working* for?'

'I don't–'

'No more shit, Andrei, I'm giving you five seconds to give me a name or I swear to God I will personally see to it that you join the doorman in the river – after I have pulled out your fucking fingernails and teeth. The *name!*'

There was a sinking feeling in the pit of Andrei's stomach. A cold sweat spread across his forehead. He gripped the receiver. 'He's been employed as a lawyer for a company called Somerset Holdings. It's a six-month contract in Zimbabwe. I swear that's all I know, Rico.'

'There you go. That wasn't so difficult now, was it?'

'Please Rico, he loved the girl! Please let him go,' Andrei pleaded. 'I'll repay all the money!' Even as he begged for Mallory's life he knew it was futile. There would be no mercy shown.

'You will certainly do that, Andrei, *with* interest. The business with Mr Mallory is another matter; shall we say, more a question of honour. I will tell you a story and then perhaps you will understand.'

276

Now that he had the information he wanted he was back to his old charming self.

Andrei's head was on the desk, the receiver glued to his ear. He was a beaten man. What the hell had he done? Just sold out his best friend.

Then the voice again, calm, deadly. There was no escape. 'When I was a little boy, my father told me that there is a price to pay for everything in life. I have never forgotten those words of wisdom, bless his soul. So let me ask you, Andrei, what sort of recompense do you think I would get for losing one of our most important London clubs and all of my money? Not to mention a good friend and my most reliable exterminator?'

'We can come to some arrangement, Rico.'

'No, I didn't think so. It's not just the killings, is it, Andrei?'

'I don't understand.'

'You don't understand. For a smart barrister you are not coming up with many answers. Allow me to explain. I learnt last night that Scotland Yard have had enough of what they call "gangland crime". They are now determined to clean up the East End. Where will it all end, Andrei? We could lose our whole London operation! You do understand that someone has to be accountable for the mess, someone has to pay the price.'

Andrei felt a deep dread. 'There must be some other way, Rico.'

'There *is* no other way. The Omertà never forgets,' Tommaso sneered, 'it just gets even! Remember that, the next time you have an inclination to resurrect our old friend Bodashka.' He paused and Andrei could hear the blood pounding in his head. 'I believe you have in your possession his witness statement. If you would kindly let me have it when I pick up my money. And, Andrei – *no copies*.'

The Russian had played his final card. His hand was empty. It seemed a lifetime before Tommaso next spoke.

'I am so pleased that we have this small problem out of the way. I value our association. We have enjoyed so much success

277

together. All that remains is for me to convince Mario that you are clean – you know how hot-headed he can be.'

So he was to be spared? Not that the reprieve was of any consolation – he had played the Judas card. When he next spoke his voice was unconvincing. 'I appreciate that, Rico.'

'*Ciao*, my friend, keep safe.'

The phone went dead in the Russian's hand. His first thought was to get a message to Mallory. He looked at his watch. 7.15. *Dermo*! Was it too late? He straightened up from the desk and, still holding the phone, he dialled 100.

'Operator. Which service please?'

'Gatwick Airport. Zimbabwe Airways. It's an emergency. Please hurry!'

'Hold the line please, sir.'

The phone rang. And rang. Come on, come on. A girl's voice finally came on the line.

'Zimbabwe Reservations. Can I help?'

'May I speak to a Mr Mallory, please? He's on flight AZ 101 to Harare.'

'I'm sorry, sir, the flight to Zimbabwe left ten minutes ago.'

'Was Mr Mallory on the flight?'

'I'm afraid we are unable to divulge the passenger manifest, sir.' There was brief pause. 'But I can tell you that we didn't have any no-shows.'

Andrei breathed a sigh of relief. So Mallory was out of the way. Or was he? The Omertà had long arms. If the Sicilian learned he was trying to tip Mallory off, he was a dead man. But he had already gone past the point of no return. He poured himself a large brandy and collapsed into a chair, staring out of the window. And then he remembered Lara.

Why did it have to end this way?

It didn't.

At 9 a.m. sharp Andrei picked up the phone and dialled Somerset Holdings. Nobody had heard of an Alastair Brown, but he was able to leave a message with a girl called Lucy at reception. He requested the telegram be marked urgent: Please forward to Christian Mallory. TOMASSO IS LOOKING FOR YOU: STOP: DISAPPEAR: STOP: ANDREI. He then phoned his contact at Scotland Yard and asked him to come over in two hours' time. The street door would be unlocked. The game was not yet over.

The thought was still on Andrei's mind when he removed the thick file, entitled TOMMASO, from the safe. He opened it to the appropriate page. The dossier detailed every single activity that the Sicilian had been involved in during his reign of terror in the East End of London – murder, extortion, corruption, prostitution – evidence that had been fastidiously collected over the years as an insurance policy against exactly what was happening now. So incriminating were the depositions, the Mob boss would never see daylight again and, like a pack of dominoes teetering when pushed, many of his associates would also fall. Including that *svoloch* Mario Falcone. It was the beginning of the end of their reign of corruption and crime across the city.

The penultimate card in the epic of his existence was his will. He removed it from the safe and altered it with a codicil before calling Antonio up from the restaurant to witness his signature. Mallory was the principle benefactor.

There was just one last thing to do.

Lara.

Since he had been in London, her picture had remained hidden, shut away in a drawer, too painful to look at. He placed the frame on the desk and smiled. She looked so happy, standing in front of the Kremlin. The sun was shining and pigeons played by her feet. He reached for the fresh bottle of brandy. It was the last one. There would be no call for another.

Remy Martin and an old black and white photograph. The Russian continued to stare at the picture. When he finally closed his eyes, he was back in Moscow, back with Lara in the days before her death. They were strolling along the river and he had stopped to pick a flower. She had put it in her hair. The sun was shining, lighting up the golden dome of the Cathedral of the Archangel, and he thought that nothing in the world could be as beautiful as lovers walking hand in hand through this wonderland. But what he failed to comprehend in his nostalgic reminiscing was that he was seeing it all through the haze of a brandy glass.

Ten minutes before Scotland Yard were due to appear, the Russian was still drinking. The bottle was now almost empty. In those two hours he had relived his entire life, from the days of the ethical movement with Lara to his association with Tommaso and the filth of the East End. And then along that road had come Mallory and for a brief period there was an element of sanity to his life. So where the hell had it all gone wrong? He was still asking himself the question when he put the barrel of the shotgun in his mouth and pulled the trigger.

Chapter Fifty-Four

Bheka was born of an Ethiopian father and a Zimbabwean mother, so making his features part Arabic, part African. The name translated as 'he who takes care of'. And that's what he was good at – taking care of people who strayed off the beaten track. But the one thing he never did was get his hands dirty. There were enough willing operatives to handle that part of the business.

However, this was one job he would make an exception for. There was too much money in it for anything to go wrong. When the call came through to the run-down office in the slums of Harare it was manna from heaven. The job was a straight hit with a one-off fee of ten thousand US dollars – twenty per cent transferred to his Harare account and the balance on completion. Non-negotiable. Bheka smiled to himself. Why on earth would he want to orchestrate any other deal? It was more money than he'd ever seen in his entire life! There was but one proviso: *no mistakes*.

Ten minutes later the call was followed by the whirr of the fax machine. A grainy CCTV picture accompanied a detailed description of the subject. The grin spread across Bheka's face. He ran his fingers through his hair, a mass of black curls that he loved to grow long, and started daydreaming about what he would do with the money. It would give him his freedom. But first he needed the rabbit. He closed his eyes and there it was, hopping towards the headlights … on the evening flight from London.

'Ah, Mistah Christian Mallory, I is so lookin' forward to meetin' yous!'

It was Bheka's business to know all of the airport chauffeur drivers. He picked up the phone and dialled Harare Airport Taxis. The receptionist put the call through to Patrick Chenzira. Fifty greenbacks persuaded the Sibanda driver to work overtime. Would Patrick mind dropping off his clients at Ruby's bar? It was a favourite haunt of the former Rhodesians. He was not to worry about the downtown bars being off limits to *wazungus* – these were personal friends of Mr Hussein, and important clients; Bheka himself would be there to look after them and ensure they were safe.

After all, there was nothing like a bit of African hospitality.

Chapter Fifty-Five

Flight AZ 101 departed Gatwick at 0700 hours. Somerset Holdings had secured Mallory and Lannigan business-class seats on the 767-200, and in spite of the early start, Mallory was already on his second gin and tonic. It was difficult coming to terms with all that had happened in the last twenty-four hours and he needed that drink. The only two people in the world that mattered to him were now history: one was dead and the other he might never see again. He was well aware the Russian was not as pure as the driven snow, but he nevertheless loved his friend.

The safe-house had given him two days to reflect on all that had happened. He felt no regret for the killings but there was sadness and pain when he thought of Madeleine. Under cover of darkness, he had retrieved his luggage from Alderney Street. Mrs Johnson was asleep and there was no sign that the place was being watched. Then he had taken a cab straight to Heathrow, where he had met Lannigan.

Now that they were on their way, Mallory felt a sense of relief. The aircraft door was shut and London soon became a distant memory, disappearing into the dawn beneath the clouds. He looked down. Ten thousand feet below him a container vessel bobbed about in the rough seas on the south coast of England. It reminded him of the old Yemeni freighter that had brought him to the UK all those years ago. How different the return journey. Now he was Christian Mallory, defence lawyer for the newly formed Movement of Democratic Change party. He nudged his companion, who was watching a movie on the over-head television set.

Lannigan removed his headphones.

'To Zimbabwe,' Mallory said, touching Lannigan's drink with his, 'and to three hundred grand!'

The big man smiled. 'Why else would we go back to this godforsaken country?' The stewardess was making her way down the aisle and Lannigan acknowledged her with a wink. 'A *lekker* chick, hey.'

Mallory ignored the sexist remark and gazed out of the window. Then he thought of his new employers. Human rights and diamonds: the two linked by corruption. Of course he knew how it all worked in Africa, but he couldn't help thinking that there must be more to this underhand practice than met the eye. They were in the rear of the business-class section and the seats around them were vacant. Nevertheless, he lowered his voice. 'So come on, Jacob, tell me a little more about Marange; I'd never heard of the place till you mentioned it.'

Lannigan didn't answer for a moment, clearly gathering his thoughts. 'I think I told you, this is perhaps the world's richest diamond find in more than a century. And it's big – 66,000 hectares under the jurisdiction of a headman, Chiadzwa, and the Marange Chieftainship.'

'I tried to find it on an old Rhodesian map but it doesn't appear. I gather it lies somewhere in the south? Do you have anything more up to date?'

'The fields are 90 kilometres south-west of Mutare. Just off the road to Masvingo.'

Mallory noticed the stewardess coming down the aisle. He finished the last of the G&T and raised himself out of his seat to catch her attention.

'Same again, sir?'

He smiled and mouthed a thank you. 'So, Mugabe now controls the operation,' he said, when the stewardess had disappeared.

'Yup! That's about the size of it. When the *muntu* came across the stone, it opened the floodgates and there was a global scramble. Can you imagine – every Kaffir in creation searching the area and setting up claims? Not good news for Uncle Bob.'

Mallory suppressed a grimace. Although Lannigan still referred to the locals in his glowing vernacular, it was meant without prejudice. He already knew how they'd found the diamonds. But what was Mugabe's involvement and, come to that, Somerset Holdings' interest. 'A bit of a rag-tag affair, then.'

'That's right!' The stewardess appeared with the drinks and Lannigan waited for her to leave before continuing. 'There were artisanal miners mixing with Lebanese buyers, and thugs every-where. It's an alluvial field, which basically means you can pick diamonds up off the deck.'

'Easy pickings, if you'll excuse the pun.'

'Ya man. When Mugabe heard that they were flogging the stones on the black market, he fenced off the area and put his Fifth Brigade chums there to protect it. The problem is that these bastards are more corrupt than the tsotsis. And totally ruthless.'

Suddenly Mallory remembered the newspaper headline in the street. 'And now Marange belongs to the government.'

'All 300 square miles of it. Anyone found stealing diamonds, or even in the area, is hung up by his balls as an example to those wanting to chance their luck. But it's causing a few legal issues right now. That's why the government is in the process of nation-alising the whole show.' He picked up the lager. 'And as the government *is* Mugabe, all the proceeds go to him.'

'What about the miners and their claims?'

Lannigan's eyes were again on the young flight attendant serving another passenger. She noticed him looking at her and smiled. He took some time answering the question and appeared to choose his words carefully. 'They were slaughtered. The information we have from civilians who bore witness to the massacre states that the miners were encircled and then fired upon with AK-47s. They uncovered a mass grave at Damgamvura on the outskirts of Mutare. You must know it, or at least have heard about it?'

'I've heard of it. I just can't imagine…?'

'The idea was to clear the bush of freelance diggers and allow the military to assume control of the diamond fields. The whole area is now mined and patrolled by armoured vehicles.'

Mallory was quiet for a moment. There were still unanswered questions. 'So how do they sell these … blood diamonds? On the world market?'

Lannigan gave a cynical smile. 'Ya man, you could call them that. But the Indians and the Chinese want the stones, and they don't give a shit where they come from.'

'Just like rhino horn and ivory, hey? But surely the stones are illegal?'

'They were until the Kimberly Process paved the way for them to be sold.'

'I thought the Kimberly Process was a legit organisation?'

'I'll leave you to figure out how that happened. The big worry, of course, is that the market will be flooded. If that happens, the price of diamonds will hit an all-time low.'

'So who's mining the area now?'

Lannigan stiffened in his seat. 'I'm not sure.'

The hesitant reply was Lannigan's way of trying to shut the conversation down. But why was he reluctant to talk in depth about what was happening at Marange?' Then Mallory remembered the article that had appeared in *The Times*. It was about six months ago but he'd paid scant regard to it back then – Africa as a continent held little interest for him these days. Think Mallory, *think for God's sake* – it was something to do with slave labour. *That was it*! Mugabe was using Matabele tribesmen to dig the fields. There were even rumours of torture camps, though at the time he'd thought this was just another African atrocity. Were

Somerset Holdings involved? No doubt he would find out soon enough. Perhaps the entire issue could yet become part of another court action. Alastair Brown had hinted as much. He picked up his G&T and gave his friend a stern look. 'Is that it, Jacob?'

'All I know is that a government concession is in the process of handling the stones.'

Mallory was starting to get the picture. And he didn't like what he was seeing. Sensitive information being withheld, intelligence he'd not been made aware of at the meeting in the wilds of Kent. But it was of little relevance 35,000 feet over Africa: he was past the point of no return. The initial brief was the reform of voting rights. What happened after that was pure conjecture.

The stewardess arrived with lunch and cleared away the empty glasses.

'Do you trust the MDC?' Mallory asked, in between mouthfuls of asparagus soup.

'It's not my concern. Knowing Alastair Brown, I don't think he has any illusions of maintaining "binding contracts" with Africans. Somerset Holdings insists on all payments in advance because they realise such transactions aren't worth the paper they're written on. But I guess only time will tell.'

Mallory started to laugh.

'What's the joke?'

'I was just thinking of the last time I was in Zim, fighting Mugabe and his ZANU-PF cowboys in the bush. Now I'm returning to fight him in the Supreme Court.' He paused while the stewardess served the main course and declined the offer of another G&T, settling instead for the pinotage. 'It sure is a strange world,' he said, glancing across at his companion.

'*Yoh, boet*, but you just wait – the fun is about to start.' Lannigan's face was alight with scorn. 'No gain without pain, *ou laaitie*!'

Mallory turned to look out the window. They were over North Africa now – the Sahara Desert. The midday heat shimmered off the yellow sand. It seemed to stretch across the horizon as far as the eye could see, occasionally blotted by little settlements of pure white houses that resembled a child's crude painting. And on this harsh landscape, only camel trains left their haphazard trails as they journeyed between oases. Suddenly the fact that he was going home hit him. He glanced back at his friend and thought of his remark. 'So what's "no gain without pain" supposed to mean, Jacob?'

The derision on Lannigan's face was replaced by a serious expression. 'Somerset Holdings apportion the rate of pay according to the risk factor. Zimbabwe is Red 5, the most dangerous level. The guy you're replacing was killed – six weeks ago, by a *muntu* supposedly after his money. He was a competent lawyer and gave Mugabe a lot of shit in court. I often wonder if the robbery was the real cause of his death, but we'll probably never know.'

Mallory pushed the button on the side of his seat and it reclined. 'Well, I guess I'm going to have to watch my wallet then!'

'*Blerrie hell boet,*' Lannigan said, smiling, 'keep it like your *krimpie* – well hidden!'

But the smile was more of a grimace.

Chapter Fifty-Six

Harare, formally known as Salisbury, was once one of the most beautiful conurbations in colonial Africa. Now the sunshine city was a sewage farm and a cesspit of corruption, its citizens existing in a state of ruination, thanks to war, ignorance and hyperinflation.

Mallory closed his eyes as the Boeing 767-200 started its descent. He thought of the jacaranda trees on Montague Avenue, where he had once walked with Anna in those long-ago days before the Bush War; Anna who had left him for another man because she could not live with his 'baggage'. All she had ever wanted was an ordinary man, with an ordinary nine-to-five job. To come home to an ordinary brick, corrugated-roof house in an ordinary suburb of Salisbury – somewhere like Borrowdale. And to have ordinary children and friends, who talked about ordinary things. Then the war came and there was no longer anything ordinary about life. But by then Anna knew Mallory would never be ordinary. He was the public enemy. The lawyer everyone hated. The man who defended the Africans that were destroying all the ordinary things that meant so much to her. Yes, she had it all planned, until the freedom fighters decided they wanted their country back. How dare they. Anna could never get her head around the fact that they aspired to something more than servitude to her cosy, middle-class, white family. They wanted a piece of the action, to live amongst the *wazungus*. She had once asked Mallory why he defended *terrorists* and risked the wrath of protestors. Did the chants of 'Kaffir *lover*' not bother him when he turned up at court? These were questions coming from a girl who attended the local Baptist church every Sunday. His answer was simple: every man deserved a fair trial. He loved the country as he loved a woman. But this *inkozikazi*, Africa, was difficult. She was beautiful but also cold and cruel. Many of the terrorists he defended were hard-arsed bastards. But some were also humble tribesmen who'd been brainwashed by smart tsotsis – scoundrels in new suits. He had tried in vain to impress this simple fact on the judges. The Africans and their families had nothing. They were poor and hungry. And it was for their freedom that they fought. But to Anna, the 'blacks', as she called them, were the white man's servants. They cooked your meals, washed your clothes, tended your garden and even rocked the baby to sleep. She was unable to understand how they could be a nanny or a gardener one day and then cut your throat the next day. And after all you'd done for them – fed them, housed them in a shack in the garden and even given them some money. These facts were imprinted in the minds of white settlers from the days of colonisation and passed down to each subsequent generation.

Anna – beautiful, unspoilt girl in a crisp white dress, going to the movies on a Saturday night, stealing a kiss in the back row, then on to church on a sunny Sunday morning. Innocent child of white Africa – what did she really know about it all? She had never been anywhere near a jail – never heard the clang of a heavy iron door, or the stamping of feet, or the shouts from the prisoners. Their screams were still in his head: '*Murderers! One day you will all hang when the indunas from across the seas come to free our country*!' The indunas, or warriors, did come. They were the men who had been trained and re-educated in Russia and China. When they returned to Zambia and Mozambique, they were met by Party officials. Then they were given arms and explosives and ferried across the border into Rhodesia to blow up installations and murder innocent women and children. Yes, they had come back to liberate the country, some of their own free will, others reluctantly. But by the time the country was free, the white perpetrators had fled south across the border to South Africa.

Anna, who once sang in the choir of the Baptist church – would she have understood the priest giving the condemned man, kneeling in the cell, his last rites? Early in the morning, the door would open and the prisoner would be taken out to a holding cell. Could she picture this? Many were the times they could not even walk and the guards would drag them up the steel steps to the scaffold. And all the time in the background were the frenzied shouts from the other inmates on death row, 'Mazungu *murderers*! *We will get you*!' Africans were not allowed to say these words in the streets below – they were not even allowed to protest in the townships. But in the cells they could say whatever they wanted. After all, their threats meant nothing where they were going. So Anna would never have heard their cries for help. And then the final minutes. The executioner would have carried out his checks the day before in the gallows chamber … made sure the trapdoor held firm and then hung the rope from the oak beam and attached to it the cardboard label with the condemned man's name written on it – the same man Mallory had tried to save. Perhaps Anna would have understood all of this had she witnessed an execution. But he could never have subjected her to such brutality, even if it were permitted.

In fact, he had only ever witnessed one hanging himself. He had watched Silas Chipoka being dragged from his cell; Silas, who had been sentenced to death for allegedly torching his employers' house. And yet he had been nowhere near the house. The all-white jury refused to believe his wife's testimony, said under oath, that she was with him all night at his kraal. Further witnesses supported her statement, but their evidence was worthless. Because they were black. After all, how can you believe the word of a Kaffir? In fact, no one had been in the house on the night it was set alight. Yet here was Silas, facing the gallows. Not because he'd been at the house, nor knew anyone who had. But because he'd been seen hanging around the beer halls with the political boys. What other country would hang a man on such insubstantial evidence? The night before the execution, Silas had broken down and screamed his innocence. The warders had dragged him to a padded cell next to the holding cell. When they came for him the next morning, he was unable to walk. So they strapped him to a board, gagged him and carried him to the gallows. The Sheriff of the High Court read out the sentence of death and then he was moved to the trapdoor. Mallory was amongst the witnesses standing in the gallery below. He watched as the hangman placed the rope around Silas's neck and then he closed his eyes. But what he could not shut out was the crash of the trapdoor being released. No, not Anna, not anyone, should have to witness such inhumanity.

That was the only time Mallory attended an execution. People who were once his friends then derided him in the bars and cafés of Salisbury. The final insult came when they daubed his bungalow for the second time in white paint: KAFFIR LOVER. FUCK OFF. THE BLACK BASTARDS DESERVE TO HANG. It was the night after Silas Chipoka had died.

Anna could no longer stand the taunts. It was over.

She never wanted to see Mallory again.

That was the day he had walked away from the Bar and handed in his notice to the law firm. Five days later his call-up papers had arrived and he'd reported to the recruitment office.

But it made no difference to Anna. She was not coming back.

Anna, sweet child of youth, first love. Where have all the memories gone? Would he find them when he returned to Zimbabwe? Would he see again the Chimanimani Mountains where he had once spent some of the happiest days of his life? The noble peaks dominated the skyline above the plains of Gorongoza. Bare thorn trees lay scattered like crooked old men. In the dry season the land was burnt and reminded him of African pottery. Then when the rains came the plains would be transformed into a lighter shade of green and the eagles would leave their nests and hover in the thermals, searching for the dassies in the windswept grass. High above this land, wandering, ever-changing, snow white clouds moved slowly across the pale blue sky resting for a while against the distant hills. To the north of the Chimanimani was Nyanga, where the rivers ran clear, straight off the mountains of Mozambique, where he'd lain beside the girl in the thatched cottage next to the trout stream. She had told him of her fear of monkeys and he had laughed and put his arm around her shoulders. Her cheeks were crimson from the fresh forest air. In the evenings they lit a fire and cooked the trout he had caught, washing the fish down with cold Lion lager. In those long-ago days there were no tomorrows. They walked through villages to the beat of an African drum and stopped to listen to the girls singing. Their voices were like no others he had heard before. When they eventually came down from the mountains in the old Ford bakkie, they were oblivious to the fact that it would never be this way again. The war had changed all of that. The mountains would always be there, but a way of life was gone forever.

The final call for the cabin staff to take their seats for landing interrupted Mallory's thoughts. Lannigan was already buckled up and fast asleep. The little window framed a sight that was so familiar to him: the city of Harare. Except that when Mallory fled Africa, Harare was still Salisbury and Zimbabwe was Rhodesia. Would the roads also have new names? There they were below him, the Salisbury streets where he used to ride his old Norton motorcycle. From the air they looked no different. He even recognised some of the taller buildings. The excitement was tangible, an intense mixture of tenderness and fear, a feeling akin to that of approaching a leopard in the bush. Then he heard the rear thrust

293

of the giant Rolls-Royce engines. The undercarriage came down and the Boeing skimmed the tops of the trees onto one of the longest runways in Africa. After twenty years in exile in a concrete jungle, he was at last returning to Salisbury where the adventure had once begun. He'd been twenty-two years old then. It felt good to daydream. But only for a moment. Because there, on the other side of the tarmac runway, stood four soldiers. They were slouched against the arrivals door, their AK-47s held at ease but no less menacing. From this distance he couldn't see their eyes but he knew they would show no remorse when they pulled the trigger.

Chapter Fifty-Seven

Meikles Hotel was as Mallory remembered it. But the street names had indeed changed. Harare's most famous hotel now stood on Jason Moyo Avenue. Who the hell was Jason Moyo?

'Perfect, Chenzira,' Lannigan said to their chauffeur as he opened the doors for them in front of the grand old historic hotel. The late afternoon was warm with just a light wind blowing.

'Please, call me Patrick, sir. Good to have you back, bwana,' the chauffeur said, his face beaming at the crisp new US dollars. The Central Business District had deteriorated at an alarming rate but the hotel, much to Mallory's surprise, still retained its elegant colonial charm, an oasis in a desert. The illustrious pair of lions gazed out over Africa Unity Square towards the north wing, and he smiled to himself when he recalled the legend that the lions roared whenever a virgin walked by. He had never heard them roar but then he had never known a virgin in Zimbabwe.

'How about lunch at the Explorer's bar?' Lannigan ventured, after they had checked in. 'Everything goes on the company tab – we'll sign for it in the morning.'

'Give me five to wash and change.' Mallory watched the porter place his luggage on the rack: a small suitcase, a rucksack, a laptop and his old, worn camel satchel, which held his precious manuscript. This was his life for the next six months. Before leaving the hotel room, he checked his passport and currency. The money was in large denominations, which made the seventy grand that much easier to carry. The safe was in the wardrobe. He punched in four random numbers, but it refused to lock. He tried again with no success. The only alternative was to keep the documents and cash with him. Probably the safest bet anyway. Tucking the wallet back into the specially concealed pockets of his denims, he took in the details of the elegant suite. It was a step back in time and not at all what he had expected in the new Zimbabwe.

Thankfully, neither had the Explorer bar changed; it still retained the feel of an old gentlemen's club, forgotten nostalgia straight out of Karen Blixen's Africa. Black and white photographs of Livingstone and Stanley lined the walls. Alongside them were sepia images of hunting expeditions and big game trophies.

Mallory smiled as he watched Lannigan place the order. For the first time since he had fled Africa he felt he was home again. Only now it was wonderful not to see the signs WHITES ONLY. The steak was another good memory, as much a part of Rhodesian culture as Lion lager. But he was well aware that this was a refinement shared by few. Tomorrow they would be on a plane to Bulawayo and to another world. Back to the law courts and all the ghosts of the past. Would he be able to cope with the memories that even to this day still haunted him? It would not be easy. Anna briefly occupied his thoughts again. He tried to recall where her parents had lived in Borrowdale, even contemplated trying to find the house. But what would that achieve? It was highly unlikely they would even be there; most white Rhodesians had fled south, starting new lives in South Africa. He was staring out of the window, watching the predominately black shoppers walk the streets, when he realised Lannigan was speaking.

'Wake up, *vriend*! I was just saying, is there anything you want to do before we leave town? Bioscope or bar? Chenzira has offered to work overtime. He tells me there's something happening at Ruby's later. How do you fancy that?'

296

Beyond the tall buildings of Jason Moyo Avenue, there rose a pall of dense black smoke. In the old Rhodesia you would have heard the scream of police and fire engine sirens. Now nobody even raised an eyebrow. It was almost as if fire was an everyday occurrence. Mallory turned his attention back to Lannigan. 'Sorry, I was miles away.'

'A bit of fun before we leave town, hey? It's our last opportunity. I've just had a message from Jill at the Harare office; they want us back at the airport at 10.30 sharp tomorrow morning. I've booked a taxi for 9, which should give us time for breakfast before we leave.'

'There's not much else to do here except get pissed.'

'Great! So how about O'Leary's Irish pub for starters? I'll call Chenzira.'

Mallory couldn't care less where they started. There were too many ghosts in this town and there was only one way to obliterate them.

O'Leary's was in a rougher part of the city. Like most of Harare, it was not frequented at night by white people. Not that it worried Mallory. The interior of the pub was dark and narrow. The long bar stretched from one end of the room to the other. It was as far removed from an Irish pub as one could imagine. A couple of Africans sat on stools at the far end of the bar, drinking what appeared to be a cloudy beer, which was certainly not Guinness. Was this just another aspect of the new Zimbabwe, *tshwala*, African beer, being served in an Irish pub? Mallory ordered vodka. The barman put the bottle on the counter. It brought a smile to his face when he tasted it. Shit, it was rough! He thought of Andrei – the Russian would have had no hesitation in pouring the bottle down the drain. He topped up the glass with local tonic water, which seemed to take the edge off the spirit, and declined the offer of ice. Then suddenly he remembered the last time he had drunk vodka with tonic and he thought of Madeleine. God, how long ago was that? He had lost count, but already it felt like a lifetime.

Lannigan paid for the drinks with US dollars, which brought a huge smile to the face of the barman and he tipped the bottle over their glasses again.

'Hey man, next round on da bar. Harare special mix! Gimme shout when yous ready.'

Harare special mix! What the hell was that? He laughed out loud. 'The *muntu* must just love the greenbacks!'

'The Holy Grail in Zim, now that the local currency is in the shit.'

'You ain't seen anything yet,' Lannigan said. 'When they've finished decimating the white farms and have totally screwed up the economy, there won't even *be* a currency.'

Three US dollars for two drinks. Mallory laughed when he thought of what they would have cost in Zim dollars. But what would it be like in a few years' time? A punter walking in with a suitcase stuffed full of notes to pay the equivalent?

Lannigan refilled the glasses from the vodka bottle and placed a five-dollar bill on the counter, which soon disappeared. 'Look, let's grab a seat away from the *muntu*. The last time some of these guys saw soap and water was when they were in kindergarten.'

The bar was starting to get busy and they had to push their way through a line of Africans before they eventually found themselves a table in the corner of the room. The talk was all about the old days before the war: the call-up, the recruit training and finally going their separate ways. 'Did you never consider joining the Selous Scouts?'

The rough vodka was taking its toll and Mallory laughed. 'Not a chance! Working with those scruffy individuals? God, you could smell them a mile off in the bush.'

'Bit like the Kaffirs at the bar. That was the general idea – to smell like the locals. And by covering their faces with "Black is Beautiful", they also looked like them!'

Mallory laughed again at the memory. 'Yeah, but old Mike Stammer turned them into quite a legendary outfit. Wonder where he is now?'

'Last I heard he was training South African soldiers fighting in the Angolan civil war.'

Mallory downed his drink and the fire rose up in his belly. Talking about the past felt good. In England, he had tried to forget Rhodesia and the war, but out here somehow it all seemed different. He glanced up at the other punters, to ensure there were no prying ears. 'Can you remember when Stammer was our regimental sergeant major in the infantry? What a bastard. He had me doing jankers every other weekend. The bloody guardhouse at Cranbourne Barracks was like my second home!'

Lannigan lit a couple of cigarettes and passed one to his friend. 'But without his discipline, we might not have made it through the war.' He turned the Scouts into what was probably the toughest killing machine in Africa, unconventional but efficient. They spent so much time hunting and turning guerrillas in the bush, they pretty well *became* them.'

'And the PR guys loved them.'

'Were we any different?' Lannigan asked, stubbing out his cigarette. 'All the units at the time were unorthodox and lacking in parade ground discipline. Even the infantry.'

Mallory was about to reply when a buxom African lady in a short, colourful dress appeared at his side. God, now he knew where the saying 'mutton dressed as lamb' came from. The woman stank of body odour. She put her arm around his neck and whispered in his ear, 'Want a little jig-jig, *mazungu*? Some fun, white man?'

Lannigan burst out laughing. 'Shit, Mallory, you've pulled! Shall I make myself scarce?'

'Try my friend here, lady – he hasn't had sex for six months and he doesn't give a shit where he gets it,' Mallory said, removing the woman's arm. 'Look at him, he's gasping for it.'

Lannigan put his tongue out and started panting like a dog on heat. The prostitute was not amused. Shouting abuse at them in Shona, she scurried off to find an easier target.

The Africans around them were falling off their seats laughing. 'Hey *mazungu* man,' one of them shouted, 'the mama not good enough for you?'

When he finally caught his breath, Lannigan turned to Mallory and grabbed his hand. 'You know, Mike, this is just like the old days – the wine and the women.'

'Not quite, mate,' Mallory said, holding up the empty glass, 'nowadays most of the women are loaded up with the clap – you'll get more than you bargained for here. Another vodka?'

'A beer, mate – this vodka is *kak*. I'm starting to feel rough.'

Mallory smiled. Lannigan's problem was more likely down to the complimentary shots the barman had brought over. Harare special mix! God knows what was in the yellow snake juice. There was no way he was going to drink the shit. But by God, Lannigan was certainly up for it. 'Come on mate, just like old times,' he had shouted. When Mallory had refused, Lannigan had called him a woofter and then proceeded to knock back all four glasses in quick succession. He was still smiling to himself as he stood at the counter and waited while the barman served a customer. 'Two lagers, *shamari* – Lion, please.'

'*Howzit boet*, where you guys from?'

Mallory turned to face the middle-aged stranger, greeting him in Afrikaans. He wore a pair of dusty old khaki shorts, an open-neck, short-sleeve flannel shirt and *veldskoens*. Below the beaten-up bush hat was a wide smile. 'We're with a law firm, in Bulawayo.'

The Afrikaner nodded. 'That figures – you been overseas for a while?' He had apparently picked up a trace of Mallory's accent.

'Too long.'

'Well at least you haven't forgotten that not all chocolate tastes good!'

'From what I hear most of it's contaminated now.'

The Afrikaner nodded in agreement. 'It doesn't matter to the *Rooineks*. They go crazy for the darkies. Some are real *goffels*. But they don't seem to mind if they are ugly. Or have the clap.'

Mallory regarded the Afrikaner with amusement. Suddenly he realised he could catch up on some of the last twenty years with the friendly face. 'Look pal, how about joining us for a beer?'

'*Goeie Dankie*,' the man said, offering him his hand, 'Frik.'

'Mallory. And the lightweight over there is Jacob.'

For the next hour they shared stories, jokes and beers. Frik was a farmer from Lake McIlwaine. His land ran down to the dam, which held Harare's main water supply. 'The writing's on the wall,' he said, banging his glass down on the table.

'What will you do?' Mallory asked. He was still having difficulty coming to terms with the new Zimbabwe. God, it had changed out of all context, and he said as much

'Agh man, what can I do? You are right. Everything changes daily. Even the name of my bloody lake. The black bastards call it Lake Chivero now,' he said, lowering his voice. 'Where the hell do they get Chivero from? Old Robert Mac would turn over in his grave if he could see what the Kaffirs are doing to this country.'

'It's … it's a beautiful lake,' Lannigan said, slurring his words. In spite of his condition he was nevertheless trying to follow the conversation and, at the same time keep his eye on Chenzira, who was sitting by the door.

'Best black bream and tiger fish this side of the Zambezi.' Frik looked down at his beer. Suddenly there was anger in his voice. 'It's all over. I tell you, man, this country is *fokked*. I've had the bastards crawling all over my land in their big black Mercedes as if they already own the farm. One fat government shit even had the audacity to measure where he was going to put the extension on the side of my house! He shifted his ass pronto when I showed him the shotgun.'

In spite of himself, Mallory laughed when he pictured the scene. 'But where will you go?'

'I bought a small farm down in the Transvaal as soon as things started going tits up here. I keep moving my machinery and house contents down there, just a bit at a time so the *munts* don't realise what I'm doing. I plan to clear out as much as I can before the bastards slap an eviction notice on my door.' Then he belly-laughed. 'And before I go *ou vriend*, I'm going to spray the land with a bloody weedkiller that will poison the soil – the black bastards won't be able to grow a bean on it for years. Then I'll put a match to the house. I only just wish I could be there to see Mr Baboon's *fokking* face when he comes back.'

Mallory could understand the resentment. So many farmers had lost their land. But what was worse, the farms that had been reclaimed – that had been worked for decades – were now dust bowls, devastated and useless. He stood up and held out his hand to the farmer. 'Good talking to you, Frik. We're heading off to Ruby's bar – want to join us?'

'*Ruby's*? Are you guy's *fokken* crazy? It's full of *dronkies*! You want to stay clear of the place.' He leaned forward, his voice serious. 'Last time I was in the dump I nearly got knifed.'

'Come on, for old time's sake – sure we can't tempt you?'

'Not a chance – I'm on my way home in another hour or so.'

'Back to Lake Mac?'

'No, to the Transvaal. I prefer travelling at night – can't see the farmland the Kaffirs have *fokked* up.' A big smile appeared beneath the bushy moustache. 'I'll give you a blast on the air horn when I pass Ruby's; it's on my way. And if you're ever up at Mac, pop in and I'll take you tiger fishing. *Tot siens*!'

'*Tot siens*!' Mallory replied. How strange it was to be talking in Afrikaans again.

'Wha … what do … d'you reckon to old Frik then,' Lannigan said, staggering towards the door, 'no … not exactly wha'you'd call "Africa friendly" – bit of a down … downer on everything.'

Mallory eyed his friend. 'Can't blame him – I reckon he has good reason to be bitter. His livelihood is shot.'

'Yeah, maybe … maybe so.' Lannigan rubbed his eyes to clear his vision. 'God, they … the old *muntu* must be dist … distilling the vodka in the Kaffir lo … cations these days.'

'Put it down to the shots, mate. You were on a mission!'

'Shit. I … I'm going to have one serious *babelaas* in the morning.'

Mallory laughed. 'That'll teach you, taking freebies in African bars.' He glanced back at the pub and waved to Frik. O'Leary's was starting to fill up. Outside the sun had disappeared below the trees and soon it would be totally dark. In the fading light he could just make out the old enamel sign hanging above the dilapidated car showroom across the road: Mark Farrell and Son – Motor Traders. It had been used for target practice. The bullet holes, highlighted in the last of the sunshine, obliterated the S and O. The smile on Mallory's lips disappeared and he shivered. Shit, S and O … son … another bloody ghost from the past. Mark was the guy who had sold him the Norton. His son was killed in the war. He took a deep breath and turned back to Lannigan, just in time to stop him knocking over a table full of beer. He grabbed his arm. 'Let's get the hell out of here.'

'Anyway, what's the old *bossie* got against Ru … Ruby's bar?' Lannigan shouted, trying, but failing, to maintain some form of decorum. 'We … *I* had a great night when we … *I* was last in Harare. D'ye … d'y'remember Ruby?'

Mallory thought of her. Tall and almost anorexic, she was nevertheless a force to be reckoned with. He had only ever seen her once without her long, black wig. Her own short peppercorn hair gave her the look of a Sudanese Nubian girl, a figure not unlike the models Leni Riefenstahl, the photographer, once shot in monochrome. But that was twenty years ago. 'Don't tell me she's still around?!' he said to Lannigan, when they were outside.

Chenzira was waiting by the car door.

For a brief moment a shadow of sadness, or perhaps regret, crossed Lannigan's face and somewhat sobered him up. 'She died … of AIDS.' He closed his eyes. 'Eight years ago.'

'*AIDS*?' It wasn't possible. 'I thought she was always careful?'

Lannigan tried to open his eyes. 'She … she was.' He would have left the question there but Mallory pursued it. He paused for a moment to try and gather his thoughts. 'When Mugabe … old Bob's fuck … *fokking* Fifth Brigade arrived – moved into Harare – he … *they* closed all the Rhodesian troops' bars and … threw the owners into Chik … Chikurubi. Ruby got five years,' he said, keeping his voice low. 'Y'know what that hell-hole's like. After the black bastards were finished with her, they turned her … Ruby … over to the inmates.'

'The fucking animals!' Mallory closed his eyes. He could still picture Ruby dancing on the table to the music of Bob Marley, and everyone in the room wanting a piece of the action.

'Hey, hey, look … look man. She had a … a goo … d life while it lasted. She wouldn've wanted this, all this shit now. They at le … least kept her bloody name over the bar.'

'Some bloody consolation.' Mallory looked at Chenzira. 'Come on then, let's go and see what the place looks like now.'

Lannigan teetered off the post where he was leaning and almost fell over. His face was as white as a sheet. 'Actuall … y, d'you mind if I … I'm going to take a check … rain check? I don't feel too good,' he said, moving into the light.

'Bloody hell, Jacob, you look like death warmed up!' Those shots must have been lethal. Or had they been spiked? But why the hell would they do that? He brushed it off as paranoia. It was probably just the jetlag.

'I nee … d my bed,' he said, staggering to the open car door.

'I'll come back with you, mate.'

'No, no! Don't … drop you … you off. Don't wanna spoil the fun! You'veto say goodbye … *Sara Zvakanaka* to … to Ruby before you leave town.' He put his hand on the car to steady himself. 'Jus … tbe careful: dangerous place, Harare.'

'Come on, mate, let's get you to bed,' Mallory said, helping Lannigan into the car.

304

Chapter Fifty-Eight

Chenzira couldn't believe his good fortune. It was only 7 p.m. and they were already on their way to Ruby's. All he had to do now was to drop Bwana Mallory at the bar and then take Bwana Lannigan back to the hotel. Fifty bucks and an early night. With this much money it would be a *lekker* night. A *goeie lekker* night. Everybody is a gonna be happy – Bwana Mallory would have a good time with Mr Bheka, Bwana Lannigan would have his bed, and Old Chenzira would have his lady of the night. 'Ah Dorothy, I am impatient for you!' he said, under his breath. The few street lamps that remained in the Indian quarter had been vandalised and Chinamano Avenue was shrouded in darkness. Chenzira turned on his headlamps. All was quiet in the back of the car. Bwana Lannigan appeared to have fallen asleep and Bwana Mallory was staring out of the window. Probably reminiscing about the old days, when the shops were open and the streets were busy. That had all gone now. Never mind – Mr Bheka would ensure he had a good night. What a nice, considerate man Mr Bheka was.

The only problem that he could see was that Mr Bheka had said he would get Bwana Mallory home. Now here was Bwana Lannigan saying for him to go back and fetch his friend. Ag man, who should he listen to? He removed his hand from the gear lever and scratched his head. Mr Bheka was paying him the money,

money to ensure Bwana Mallory had a good time. Surely, it was him he should listen to. But then Bwana Lannigan was *nkozi*, very important man.

The picture of Dorothy taped to the dashboard finally swayed the decision and his thoughts returned to the township. And that was how he nearly hit the car. It came out of a side street at high speed, travelling without lights. In the nick of time Chenzira managed to hit the brakes and swerved to avoid a collision. '*Yoh mai poepoi*!' he screamed, his concentration back on the road.

'What the *fok*!' Mallory shouted. 'Doesn't anyone in this town drive with bloody lights?'

'Sorry, bwana! *Loskop* drivers – probably on da *dagga*.' He looked in the rear-view mirror. Bwana Lannigan was still asleep. That was lucky. The jolt could have made him very sick. Ah so, *kozi, kozi*, that would not be good – it had taken him two hours to clean the vehicle the last time a *mazungu* went drinking in African bars. Dorothy would not be a happy lady.

'It's not your fault, Patrick, but keep your eyes on the bloody road.'

'Sure thing, Bwana.' Chenzira thought again of the plan. Yes, that is what he would do: leave Bwana Mallory at Ruby's bar, just as Bheka had asked him to. He knew from past experience that when the *wazungus* had a drink and perhaps a little jig-jig, they became very generous. He was sure that Bwana Mallory would show his appreciation in the morning.

Chapter Fifty-Nine

Mallory's eyes were on the streets he had once walked during the days of the Federation. Winding the window down, the cool night breeze rapidly sobered him up. But it seemed to be having the opposite effect on Lannigan, who had his head against the pseudo leather seat and his eyes closed. Jeez, how could he sleep through Chenzira's erratic driving? The snake juice must have been potent. This wasn't like Lannigan; the guy was known to hold his liquor.

The Indian quarter of Harare held a fascination for Mallory. It was from here that he'd bought most of his clothes in the old days. But that was before the Indians had fled the country, before Mugabe's thugs had started their 'ethnic cleansing'. All that remained in the red-light district was one empty shop after another. The slums seemed to have swept across the city like a virus, enveloping it in a wave of filth and crime, which, like an epidemic, was unstoppable.

Under the dim street lamp, Ruby's bar appeared no different to how he remembered it. But the same could not be said for the other businesses. Most of their windows were now boarded up, and those that remained were smashed. Through one such broken window he noticed four men sitting around an open fire in what was once a thriving department store. The sign was still above the door: R H ABDUL AND SONS PTY. So the squatters had inhabited the abandoned buildings. It wasn't surprising taking into account the abject poverty. On the pavement tables outside Ruby's, hookers sat nursing drinks and waiting for punters. The bar stood alone in this sad scene, a beacon amongst the lost. Back in the old days, Ruby would have kicked all this lot into touch. But this was the new Zimbabwe, and these were desperate times. People had to earn a dollar any way they could. The car pulled up in front of the bar and Lannigan opened his eyes. Then he shook his head. 'Where the hell are we?'

'Ruby's. Sure you won't join me?'

'No … no … no way *vriend*, I wan'my bed; should … should've stuck with the Castle!' He tried to remain coherent. 'See'you'in the morn … morning, mate. Don't forget the time.'

'Just one for Ruby,' Mallory said, shuffling out of the car. 'Take care, mate. Send Chenzira straight back. I'll be ready to hit the sack in an hour.'

Chapter Sixty

The bar was out of sight when suddenly Lannigan started to gather himself. Shit, what had he done, leaving Mallory on his own? The man could look after himself, no question of that, but Ruby's looked to have gone seriously downhill since the last time he was there. That was well over two years ago now. The more he thought about the situation and Frik's warning, the more it worried him. He was about to order the chauffeur to turn around when suddenly he felt an uncontrollable urge for the toilet. They were in sight of Meikles Hotel so the deliberation was pointless. He leaned forward and spoke in a voice that carried, for the first time, a degree of authority. 'Patrick, you go … go straight back now and fetch Bwana Mallory. *Kuelewa*! You understand?'

'But boss, I–'

'*Now*, Chenzira.'

'Sure boss – I be quick,' Chenzira said, waiting for his passenger to get out of the car. Then he executed a perfect U-turn and headed off in the direction of the red-light district. At the first set of traffic lights he took a right. Dorothy was less than a mile away.

Ruby's bar and Bwana Mallory were forgotten.

Lannigan staggered up the hotel steps and ran straight to the toilet. He spent the next five minutes with his head in the pan. Even the thought of who might have sat there last didn't deter him. When there was finally nothing left in his stomach, he doused his face in cold water and drank copiously of the bracken liquid. Feeling half-human again, he made his way to the reception desk.

'Telegram for you, sir!' the receptionist said, handing him the envelope together with his key. His mind was befuddled and he wanted to be sick. Who the hell was sending him telegrams? He opened it apprehensively. It was from Lucy Mortimer at Somerset Holdings.

The message was brief and to the point. Please forward to Mr Mallory.

TOMMASO IS LOOKING FOR YOU: STOP: DISAPPEAR: STOP: ANDREI:

Then he noticed the time it had been sent from London: 09.20. Why had it taken so long for the message to get through? Bloody bush telegraph. Does nothing work in this goddamn country? Under the influence of the drink, none of this made any sense. Hell, it wouldn't have made any sense without the drink. *Tommaso is looking for you* ... who the hell was Tommaso? *Disappear*? What was Mallory involved in? And why had the message come from Lucy at the London office? He was rapidly sobering up. And then the penny dropped. The bar *was* a set-up. He rubbed his forehead. Think, man, *think*! Chenzira? Was he the key? He'd been acting rather strange. Hassling them to get to Ruby's. And the shorts – that yellow shit must have been spiked. The drinks were obviously meant for Mallory. But why? The bastards! Somebody was waiting for them there. But who? Come on Lannigan, for God's sake, work it out! But no matter how hard he tried, he couldn't come up with an explanation. All he could think of, through his alcoholic stupor, was that he had to get the message to Mallory. He turned to the receptionist. 'Call Ruby's bar – please, as quickly as you can! *Haraka, haraka*, hurry please!'

Chapter Sixty-One

When the car had disappeared, Mallory turned and walked the gauntlet of catcalls and offers of one-night stands. The bar was much busier than O'Leary's and he waited patiently behind a long line of customers. Eventually he was served a Lion lager and paid again in US dollars. 'Hey *nkozi*, you wanna da complimentary … Harare special mix … da welcome drink!'

There it was again. What the hell were these guy's up to? '*Hukuna shukrani. No thanks.*'

'Dat sure da wise ting. When you wanna da drink you come see me *shamari*. No queue!'

Mallory smiled his appreciation. Behind the bar was a faded monochrome picture of Ruby in her younger days. She was dancing on the tables. It was how he remembered her and those long ago times. He raised the bottle to his mouth and silently toasted her. Then he heard the shout from across the crowded room.

'Hey Mr Mallory! Howsit? So glad yous could make it.'

He turned around in time to see a light-skinned African approaching him. His features boarded on Ethiopian but it was his hair that set him apart. It was long and frizzy, like that of a Rastafarian. He wore a smart colourful jacket and the hand he held out in greeting was as smooth as a girl's. 'I'm sorry, do I know you?'

'Bheka – Patrick Chenzira is friend of mine; we both work for da law firm.' He laughed. 'Not lawyer's course. I am what you might call a "Mr Fix-it", da general handyman.'

Mallory took his hand. The Rasta was friendly. Nevertheless he remained suspicious. It was this reaction to total strangers that had kept him alive. 'Can I help you?'

''Tis me who do da help. Da office like to ensure you have da welcome to Harare.' Bheka stepped away from the bar. 'S'pose we find somewhere to squat away from da prozzies.'

Mallory followed him across the room. Was he being over cautious? The rules out here were different to the East End – or were they? In spite of a foggy mind, he remained alert. Tables were in short supply but Bheka somehow managed to find a couple of seats on a bench with a mixed party. They were in high spirits and hell-bent on having a good time. A pock-faced, young African turned to him.

'Hey *shamari*, what you doin in dis part of da town? Vely, vely bad for *wazungus*.' The smile on his lips did not extend to his eyes. '*Minge* trouble.'

'I've come to have a drink with Ruby. For old times' sake,' Mallory said, taking a seat on the wooden bench beside a black girl.

'Dis sad – vely sad, what da done to da *inkozikazi*,' Bheka said, 'she good lady.'

The girl beside Mallory was well inebriated. She rested her head on his shoulder. Then her fingers moved along the inside of his leg. Maybe she wasn't that drunk. Checking his pocket to ensure nothing was missing, Mallory removed her hand and eased himself away. The suspicions returned. All the smiles, the complimentary shots that had downed Lannigan – something didn't quite add up. But he couldn't figure out what it was. Perhaps it was all his imagination. These last few days hadn't been easy. And then the long flight and the booze. It was clouding his judgement. Shit, he'd been coiled up like a spring for too long. It was time to relax and go with the flow. 'Anybody for a beer?'

The strangers at the table all nodded their heads.

'Let me get dem drinks,' Bheka offered.

'Not a chance, pal, it's my round,' Mallory said, getting up and striding towards the crowded bar. He was about to pay for the beers when the phone rang. The barman moved away to answer it. Then he turned around and faced Mallory.

'You da Mr Mallory?' You could hardly miss the only white man in the room. Mallory nodded. 'Call for you, *shamari*,' the barman said, handing him the phone.

A call? In the red-light district of Harare? What was that all about? 'Hello?'

'Mallory, it's Lannigan.'

'Jacob, you all right?'

'Got rid of that yellow shit down the bog but I'm still feeling rough.' He rubbed his forehead.

'Why the call? Thought you'd be in bed.'

'I've just picked up a telegram at reception. It's from Lucy in London. Can't make head nor tail of it but you might know what it's all about. Do you know someone called Tommaso?'

Mallory waited in silence, apprehension written in lines across his face.

'He's trying to track you down, mate. The message goes on to say "disappear"?'

'Who wrote the telegram?'

'It's signed Andrei? Not much else to tell you, but it's giving me the creeps. Chenzira is on his way – get out of there quick.'

The bar was hot and sweaty. In spite of that, Mallory shivered. He knew exactly what the message meant. What he didn't know was how they had found him so quickly. But then he vaguely remembered the Russian telling him about the Omertà. Wasn't Tommaso the head of the syndicate? The brains and bankroll behind all the shit in the East End? The same mobster who had blackmailed Andrei? Suddenly he recalled Madeleine's frightened words, that first night: *They will find me; they have people everywhere.* But

313

surely not here? And then he saw it all. It was as if the fog had suddenly cleared. It *was* a set-up! Why else would this random guy approach him out of the blue, like he was some kind of friend? The spiked drinks were supposed to have softened him up. Bheka must have been enormously surprised when he hadn't staggered into the bar, pissed out of his mind. His hands started to shake and he gulped the thick, warm air. Act normal, Mallory, go along with the ruse and buy yourself time. 'Thanks for the call, Jacob, I'm on my way.' He handed the receiver back to the barman, paid the bill and carried the drinks over to the table.

'Hey man, didn't know you had da office here!' Bheka said, gesturing to the barman.

'A change in the flight times and the bloody hotel starts panicking. Why can't they wait till I get back to reception? All this hassle.' He managed to keep his voice steady.

Bheka let out a wild laugh. 'Dat's da new Zimbabwe for you, *shamari*! Everybody worried for da job. Dey donna tink straight no more.'

Mallory smiled inwardly. He didn't share the humour. Now he was alive to the danger, he knew that Bheka had not chosen the seats at random. The people sitting around the table were no strangers. They were his accomplices. It was time to get the hell out of here. 'I'm going for a leak,' he said, handing out the beers. 'Where's the bog?'

Bheka stood up. 'Yous wanna I come with you?' The leer on his thick, contemptuous lips did not go unnoticed by Mallory. 'Not very safe in da dark.'

'Hey Mr Bheka,' the girl said, through a giggle, 'you gonna hold it for him?' The Africans sitting around the table all laughed.

'Perhaps he not finds it in da dark,' said another drunk African. He spat on the floor in disgust. '*Wazungus* not gifted like da black man!'

Mallory noticed the furious look in Bheka's eyes. The woman had accidentally thrown him a lifeline – now Bheka would *have*

314

to back off. No doubt he would deal with the dozy cow later. 'I think I can manage a piss on my own, thanks.' He cleared his throat with a nervous laugh. 'Back in a mo – look after my beer!'

'Sure thing, man,' an African with a shaved head said. 'Just a letting you know, dem toilets donna work. And da smell! Wow man, you donna wanna go dere; take da slash around da back in da bush. And watch out for da puff adders.'

Watch out for the puff adders! That was a joke; all the bloody snakes were at the table. Mallory laughed again and slapped Shaved Head on the back. 'Thanks, pal!'

'No worries, *shamari*! Just donna do da *jabu pule*.'

Jabu pule. Mallory knew exactly what the Kasi township slang meant. And a disappearing act was just what he intended to do. Once he was out of the back door he turned left and ran for his life, towards the city. There were no taxis in the blacked out street. In fact, there were no vehicles of any description. Not that it surprised him. But where the bloody hell was Chenzira? The guy should have been here by now. Then he thought of the threat. How long did it take to have a slash? Two, maybe three minutes? Any longer and they would be out searching for him. After fifty yards the adrenalin kicked in. Run Mallory, for God's sake run. At a hundred yards he was gasping for breath. He had to stop. But it was not an option. By now the predators would surely be on his tail, baying for his blood. Keep running, Mallory. One block from the bar, in an area that resembled Beirut on a bad day, he saw the full-beam lights of an approaching vehicle. It had to be Chenzira. The locals didn't use lights. Please God, let it be Chenzira. He had to take a chance and stop the vehicle – there was no other option. In desperation, he flagged the car down.

Chapter Sixty-Two

Frik noticed the white man in the middle of the road. '*What the fok*!' He slammed on the brakes and the Land Rover screeched to a halt. Then he recognised Mallory. 'What the *fokking* hell are you doing?' he shouted through the open window. 'Get in, quick! Where is your–?'

Mallory didn't need a second invitation. He was in the front seat of the cab before the Afrikaner had time to finish the sentence.

Frik banged the gear lever into first and the old Land Rover surged forward. Almost immediately the headlights picked up the angry mob running towards them with pickaxe handles, knobkerries and machetes. It seemed like everyone in the bar was now on the street. Fired up with *tshwala*, the antagonists were waving their fists in the air, screaming obscenities. Mallory watched in terror as the African with the shaved head threw the rock. It bounced off the bonnet. Then another stone hit the windscreen and it shattered. Suddenly there were rocks everywhere. Frik was breathing hard. The road was blocked and in the centre of the crowd was Bheka. There was a gun in his hand. Then Mallory saw him raise the weapon. Sweat poured off his forehead. His body was as tense as an impala's when the scent of a lion touches the wind. He closed his eyes. In that moment, his former life in Salisbury flashed before him. Sitting beside Anna at a diner café, he could see the street again as it once was, with the Indian traders hustling for business. Jacarandas lined the pavements and he could hear the birdsong in the trees. There were people everywhere and the shops were open. All of this he saw in slow motion before Bheka pulled the trigger. But the vision, this mythical way of life that existed only in a dream, was not what he wanted to see and he dived for the floor as the bullet hit the windscreen. Then all he heard was Frik screaming.

'You *fokking, fokking* black bastards!' He spat out of the window and slammed his foot on the accelerator, ploughing the Land Rover straight at the crowd. The Africans scattered. Not so Bheka. He stood his ground, feet apart, gun raised for a second shot. It never came. The bull bar on the heavy vehicle caught him midriff and threw him into the gutter. The gun rolled harmlessly away.

Bheka watched the vehicle disappear down the road. He tried to lift himself out of the gutter. But it was to no avail. His eyes started to close, and the last thought on his mind, before his whole world disappeared into oblivion, was his ten thousand dollars.

Mallory picked himself up from the floor. 'Shit, that was close!'

Frik ignored him. His wild eyes were fixed on the rear-view mirror. '*Fok* you lot!' he bellowed again, thrusting his middle finger into the air.

In spite of himself, Mallory laughed. 'Jeez, Frik, talk about the bloody cavalry arriving in the nick of time!'

'There's a monkey wrench in the side compartment. Knock out the windscreen. It's about as much use as tits on a bull.'

The warm night air flooded the cab. Then the Afrikaner let out a loud laugh. '*Fok* man! You must be some sort of mad Pommie *loskop*? What the hell were you doing out there?'

'Running for my bloody life!'

'I did warn you that the place was a dump.' Frik was laughing harder now. 'The only people who drink at Ruby's nowadays are drug dealers and pimps. Who was the bastard with the shooter?'

'Bheka – said he worked for our company.' Mallory wiped the sweat from his brow. He then let his head fall into his hands. 'I was sharing a table with that crowd in the bar. I can't believe it; the bastards seemed friendly enough.'

'Those *hoender naaiers* don't do sharing. At least not in the way you imagine.'

'So I found out,' Mallory said. He was laughing again. They really were chicken fuckers. How stupid had he been? *Loskop*, Frik had called him. He certainly was a lost head.

'Why were they after you? Not messing around with their women, were you?'

'I don't do chocolate, Frik.' He thought of Tommaso. There was no need to enlighten the Afrikaner about his past. 'Maybe it was because I'm white and spending US bucks.'

The look on Frik's face told Mallory he didn't really believe him. 'They hate whites, that much is true. They must have wanted your money real bad. One more block and the black bastards would've got you – just another *fokking* statistic in Mugabe's city of sin.' He checked his watch. 'You sure had a goddamn lucky escape.'

Mallory cursed himself silently. A couple of inches to the left and his brains would have been splattered all over the cab. Frik was certainly right – it was a goddamn lucky escape.

Chapter Sixty-Three

The Land Rover drove on through the night, the warm wind blowing in their faces. Only tyres skidding on the tarmac disturbed the cicadas. Frik eventually drew up at the side of the road on the outskirts of Harare and knocked out the last of the windscreen. 'Look at my *fokking* Land Rover!' There was broken glass everywhere. A machete was embedded in the canvas hood. Frik tossed it into the long grass at the side of the road. 'The old gal was never very pretty but now she looks like she's been dragged through the bush backwards.' He scowled. '*Fok*! I wish I still had my bloody SLR. I'd have shown those black bastards a thing or two.'

Mallory pulled out a packet of Texan and offered one to the Afrikaner.

'*Baie danke*, *vriend*, I gave up. But right now I could do with a *skyf*.' He noticed Mallory's hand shaking as he lit the cigarette. 'Where do you want dropping off?' Then he was laughing again. 'Not Ruby's I take it?'

Since leaving Harare's red-light district, Mallory had turned that very same question over and over in his mind. There was no way he could go back to the hotel or to Somerset Holdings for that matter – Tommaso wanted him dead. They wouldn't make the same mistake again. 'How about South Africa?'

'Are you *serious*?'

319

'I should never have come back to Zim.'

Frik shook his head resolutely. 'I told you the place is *fokked*. Look, I've lived long enough in this godforsaken country to understand one should keep one's nose out of where it doesn't belong. I don't know why that *bliksem* was coming for you with a shooter. And I don't really want to know. But what about your luggage? And your passport? There's still a border to cross at Beitbridge. Or do you plan to swim?'

Mallory thought of the crocs in the Limpopo River. No way was he joining them in the water. 'I have my passport with me,' he said, patting his hip. Then he remembered the safe. Thank God it hadn't worked. 'I don't trust hotels, especially out here.'

Frik nodded. 'I can understand that. But you must be bloody soft in the head to go drinking at Ruby's bar with your passport. That's what living in Pommie-land twenty years does to you.' There was nothing malicious about the remark; it was just the Afrikaner's way. 'However,' he said, smiling in the dark, 'on this occasion, you made the right decision.' He jumped into the cab and took his place behind the wheel. 'It might have been difficult, going back to town.'

Mallory looked back at the road they had just travelled down. In the distance he could see the shimmering lights of Harare lighting up the skyline. And there, dotted somewhere amongst the neons, was the Meikles Hotel and his luggage. Not that it really mattered; he had everything he needed right here. It was only the satchel with the manuscript that was important. Perhaps he could get Lannigan to forward it on to a nondescript address. He closed the cab door.

Frik glanced over in his direction. 'Do you have money to tide you over?' He shuffled in his seat, seemingly embarrassed. 'I ain't got much, but I can help with a few rand.'

Mallory put his hand on the farmer's shoulder. 'I can manage thanks.' If Frik only knew how much money he was carrying he'd certainly be right in thinking he was 'out of his *fokking* mind'.

320

And maybe he was, but at least he didn't have to go back to Meikles – God only knew who would be waiting for him there. He made a mental note to call Lannigan from South Africa and hand in his notice. He would miss him. They were good together. Then he wondered what the implications would be with Somerset Holdings. Alastair Brown wasn't going to be a happy man, but right now he didn't really give a shit.

The Afrikaner started the old diesel engine. 'Ready?'

'There's nothing to hang about here for, Frik.'

'Too right! Let's go. We have an all night drive with no windscreen. *Fokking* Kaffirs!'

Chapter Sixty-Four

It was early morning when they crossed the great grey-green Limpopo River at Beitbridge. Behind them lay the land of Monomotapa and in front, the Rainbow Nation. The sun was just climbing out from behind the distant mountains when the border post became a blur in the rear-view mirror. Early morning mist covered the acacia trees like a blanket and through this mist rode the natives on their bicycles, going to work in the fields – an African scene that made Mallory sad, because he knew he was leaving it all behind. He watched the sun slowly lift the mist and expose the glistening tarmac running straight as a die all the way to Johannesburg. Beyond the gold mines, much further south, was the city of Cape Town.

'What are your plans?' Frik asked, perhaps aware that Mallory had no luggage.

Plans? He hadn't really thought of any plans. All he knew was that he wanted to get off this bloody continent. But where to, he didn't really know. 'I guess I'll head for the Cape.'

The Afrikaner hesitated, seemingly unsure of how to ask the next question. 'You're welcome to come and stay with us on the farm. I could use a bit of help. My house is right on the Crocodile River near Thabazimbi. It's not much, but Hanna calls it "God's little acre".'

Mallory drummed his fingers nervously on the seat, not wanting to offend the farmer. Somehow he couldn't quite see himself as a sod-buster, although there must be something to this simple life. 'Thanks for the offer, Frik, but I think I'll just keep heading south.' That was it! Go south, Mallory, and when you get to the Cape, keep going. Get off this godforsaken continent once and for all. It's all going to shit. He thought of this but he did not say it.

'If you're sure that's what you want to do, I'll drive you down to the railway station at Pretoria. It's not far out of my way. There's daily trains to Joburg and then onto Cape Town.'

'That's good of you, mate,' Mallory said, closing his eyes to the warm wind. The new life he had envisaged in Africa was already at an end. Gone was the law contract, the diamond fields, the chance for some kind of retribution. Gone also was ... he paused in his thoughts and looked out of the window at a ragged landscape. A single hawk-eagle hung low in the sky over the wheat fields. Yes, gone also was the East End and a girl called Madeleine. All of a sudden he missed her; missed her more than he ever had since the day she walked out of his life for the last time. She had half turned to look at him, to plead with him to call her back. And he had let her go. But what else could he have done? He loved the girl with all his heart but he would never, ever possess her. You cannot catch the wind and neither can you hold it. Had he not told her that or had he just thought it. And ironically, what you can't have, you want all the more. When would he ever comprehend this simple fact? Then he thought of that autumn morning, when the first light had come through the curtains in Alderney Road. Madeleine was lying next to him, fast asleep. The sun had touched her skin and turned it golden brown. He had a yearning for her that he felt again now. And before the morning had totally obliterated the night, he saw again her face at the door, the face of a girl wanting to be loved; a face that had never been committed to canvas and yet was more beautiful than any painting he had ever seen. It changed like the seasons and held so many different emotions that would be forever framed in his mind. And again he asked himself the question: why was he the only one who could see it? Suddenly they came over the brow of a small *kopje* and a patch of yellow daisies growing wild at the side of the road caught his eye. Just for a moment they reminded him of the daffodils on the streets of London. He breathed deeply to suppress the pain. Why did everything remind him of Madeleine and their brief time together? And then finally he understood and with the knowledge came sadness. The autumn in the East End would remain in his mind forever as the autumn he had loved … and lost again.

They stopped for a break at the little town of Potgietersrus. All around them were the wheat fields where the once mighty Ndebele had walked. How different they were from the slums of Harare. Just south of the town, the *bushveld* was covered in aloes and acacia trees, broken occasionally by the tobacco crops. This was how Zimbabwe used to be when it was once Rhodesia. And he had to ask himself what these fields would look like when the white man left. Then they were driving again, across the vast plain towards Pretoria. Only the odd sign, displaying a warthog or a buck, reminded him that once upon a time only animals inhabited this land. When they started their descent from the hills he saw in the distance the high-rise buildings. They dominated the skyline like a mountain range and he knew he was back in civilisation. Pretoria. The Jacaranda City. Driving to the station over the purple carpet of fallen flowers reminded him again of Salisbury and Anna. But he didn't want to think of those times, because all of that was behind him now.

The two men parted outside the old colonial railway building. A promise was made to meet again, though each of them knew this would never come to pass. They were travellers on roads stretching in different directions. Mallory was well aware that he owed his life to this rough diamond of a farmer and he hoped above all else that he would be able to live his life out on the land he loved before another Zimbabwe happened. '*Tot siens*, Frik, go well.'

'For a *soutie*, you're all right.'

A *soutie*, the slang for one foot in England and one in South Africa. Was that really how Frik saw him? The thought of it made him smile.

'Remember, you're welcome at Thabazimbi anytime you're passing by,' Frik said, gunning the engine. Then he eased the old Land Rover back onto the road. In no time at all it was swallowed up by the stream of rush-hour traffic. And then finally the old Rover disappeared altogether.

Mallory stood for some time, watching the road ... people scurrying here and there like ants, in and out of the shops, bumping into each other ... rushing ... rushing ... rushing. The last time he had watched such a scene was in a café around the corner from Kings Cross. That was the night before he'd met Lannigan. The night before Madeleine died. It was only weeks and yet it seemed like years. He looked out at the street again ... at the traffic forcing its way through the arteries of the city ... raging motor horns ... the smell of diesel fumes. Then, turning his back on the conurbation, he walked into the railway station and purchased a one-way ticket to Cape Town. Twenty-six hours later, after crossing the arid Karoo and traversing the Hex River Pass, Mallory saw again the vineyards of Stellenbosch that nestled under the vast mountain ranges. All around him was scenery as breathtaking as you would find anywhere in the world. He tried to recall when he had last been here. It was before the Bush War and long before the East End of London. Then the picture in the train window changed yet again and he saw the shanty towns on the outskirts of Cape Town, the dusty roads filled with the potholes of poverty and prejudice. They reminded him of the realities of an Africa of have-nots.

And he no longer felt the urge to stay.

Chapter Sixty-Five

It was a Friday like any other. Standing on a stretch of beach on the edge of Blouberg, Mallory saw the apparition of a girl walking towards him, her feet leaving tiny footprints in the sand. He could not see her face but he recognised the way she walked. Madeleine. In spite of the warm sunshine a shiver ran down his back. She stopped by the edge of a boulder and looked in his direction. Now he could see her clearly. She was smiling, though it was not a smile he had ever seen before. Matryoshka dolls. Changing faces. Why had he never seen this smile before? Then all of a sudden he knew why. It was not Madeleine at all; just another stranger on the beach. God, would it always be this way? Would every young woman he saw remind him of her? He walked towards the water. The freezing Atlantic lapped at his bare feet. Out there beyond the ocean was a whole new world. To the west was America and to the east Australia.

He breathed deeply and pulled the coin from his pocket. Heads west; tails east.

The one rand piece turned in the air and eventually landed in the sand at his feet. He bent down to look at it.

And for the first time, in a long time, Mallory knew where he was going.

Acknowledgements

The original draft to this book was written in longhand in just nine months. It then took three years of re-writing and editing before we arrived at the end of the road. Much of what has happened in the meanwhile is down to two people: my editor, Lucy Beevor, and my wife, Angie. Lucy has once again been the guiding light in showing me the way forward. Thank you for your patience and inspiration. It is much appreciated.

If Lucy was my motivation, Angie was my encouragement. Always there for me through the difficult times, backing me, helping me and picking me up when I'd fallen down. You read the book time and time again and your critical comments shaped ideas. Without you the task would have been so much more difficult. Thank you, Dusha. Thanks also to Jane Leedham for Madeleine's portrait. You have captured her wonderfully. And to Mark at Mecob for transforming the canvas into a striking cover. Thanks also to my proofreader, Helen Baggott, who misses nothing, and Rebecca Souster at Clays for leading me through the labyrinth of publishing.

Finally, I wish to express my deep gratitude to my family. Their support has been invaluable.

About the author

Michael Anthony grew up in Salisbury, Rhodesia, and was educated in Grahamstown, South Africa. He left school when he was sixteen with no qualifications and, after a period as a wild child, enlisted in the Rhodesian Light Infantry. Six months later he applied to join the SAS. He was one of only three recruits, out of sixty candidates, to pass selection into the Regiment. Michael has an abiding concern for the children of Africa and is closely involved with the Orphanage in Bindura, Zimbabwe. The people of this wonderful SOS Children's Village provide long-term family care and education to abandoned, orphaned and HIV children. All proceeds from Michael Anthony's books go towards helping them in their remarkable work.

Michael now lives with his wife in Melbourne, Derbyshire, in an 18th-century barn.

www.africahousepublishing.com

ALSO BY MICHAEL ANTHONY

The Winds That Blow Before The Rains

It is the summer of 1972 and Zimbabwe is at war. Amid the violence, Sengamo is framed for the rape of a white girl. He is forced to flee his village kraal for the killing fields of Mozambique, where an enemy soldier spares his life in a chance encounter that has far-reaching consequences.

Isabella lives a quiet life, alone on a remote farm in the hills of Nyanga. But her peaceful world is threatened when Mugabe's henchmen set up camp in the valley below, waiting for their chance to strike and reclaim the land. Despite the danger, she refuses to abandon the home she loves and the ghosts that inhabit it. One day a stranger arrives at the farm. It is the start of a love affair that will change Isabella's world forever and bring Sengamo closer to his destiny.

Out of the brutality of Zimbabwe emerges a hauntingly beautiful love story; an unforgettable tale of a tragic country, where extraordinary allegiances triumph over segregation.